Two Thousand Years Later...

A Novel by
Peter Longley

The Hovenden Press, Inc.
Minneapolis, Minnesota, U.S.A.

Edited by Dave Marcmann
Cover and book design by Morris Lundin, Mori Studio.
Cover Photograph by Courtney Milne.
Manufacture and production by Burgess International Group, Inc.

Published by The Hovenden Press, Inc.
P.O. Box 1426, Minnetonka, Minnesota 55345 U.S.A.

Distributed by Burgess International Group, Inc.
7110 Ohms Lane, Edina, Minnesota 55349, U.S.A.
Tel: (612) 831 1344
Fax: (612) 831 3167

ISBN: 0-8087-7550-2
Library of Congress Catalog Number:

Library of Congress Cataloging-in-Publication Data
Longley, Peter
Two thousand years later/Peter Longley - 1st Hovenden Press ed.
p.   cm.
ISBN 0-8087-7550-2
1. Title.

First The Hovenden Press, Inc. Edition 1996

Printed in the United States of America

9   8   7   6   5   4   3   2   1

This is a work of fiction and any likeness to any living
characters is unintentional on the part of the author.
With the exception of the ocean liner *Queen Elizabeth 2,* the
cruise ships mentioned in this story are also fictitious.
Places and venues around the world are to the best of the
author's knowledge recorded with accuracy, but within the bounds
of fictitious license.

Dedicated to
"The Clown"

my beloved father who is a
seeker.

Acknowledgments

I wish to thank my literary agent, Ron Szymanski of LeighCo, for his patience and invaluable advice throughout this project, and my editor, Dave Marcmann, for his insights, encouragement and help. I also would like to thank Norleen Parish in the U.S.A. June Applebee from Great Britain and my good friends Ken and Aileen Bridgewater in Hong Kong.

The magnificent photograph on the front cover, *Gilded Snow,* is the work of world-renowned photographer Courtney Milne and depicts snow crystals illuminated by the light of the rising sun. The significance of this image is revealed within the mystery of this book.

Most of all I would like to thank my wife, Bettine Clemen, for her patient endurance throughout the writing, proofing and manufacture of this work. She has never ceased to support me in my endeavor and has been my constant inspiration to get this message out to the world.

There are many others who have lent invaluable support to this project in their frank discussion and their own writings. My heartfelt thanks to you all in the hope that our small contribution may play its part in raising the consciousness of our planet.

TWO THOUSAND YEARS LATER . . .

is a mystery adventure set in the 1990's
with scenes from all corners of our world.
It is about three people,
the Chief Purser of a luxury cruise ship,
a gifted Concert Pianist
and an Architect with a keen interest in Archeology.
It is about human relationships.
It is a growing love story.
But its essential message
is found in the involuntary quest
that its three, central characters
find themselves seeking.

• • •

TWO THOUSAND YEARS LATER . . .

Glossary of Names

Twentieth Century Characters that have First Century counterparts

Twentieth Century	*First Century*	*Popular Name*
David Peterson *Chief Purser on* *the 'Prince Regent'*	Linus Flavian	Fictitious
Fiona MacAllister *Nurse on* *the 'Prince Regent'*	Joanna *Wife of Joshua*	Fictitious
Clarissa Peterson *Concert Pianist*	Maria of Magdala	Mary Magdalene
Jeremy Dyson *Architect* *and Archaeologist*	Remus Augustus *Roman Centurion*	Fictitious
	Joshua of Nazareth	Jesus 'Christ'
	Ravi (19th Cent.) *Indian peasant boy*	Fictitious
Margaret Corrington *Mother of Clarissa*	Miriam	'Virgin' Mary
Simon Bishop *Nephew of David*	Marcus	St. Mark
Dr. John Bishop *Brother-in-law of David*	Antonias	Fictitious
Babis Demetris *Bridge Officer on* *the 'Ulysses'*	Judas Iscariot	Judas Iscariot
Gloria Ainsworth *Hong Kong Radio* *Talk Show Host*	Naomi *Daughter of Azariah,* *a friend of Joseph* *of Arimathea*	Fictitious

Characters only found in the Twentieth Century

Dr. Malcolm Cameron   *Ship's Doctor on the 'Prince Regent'*

Richard Johnson   *Minneapolis Realtor,*
patron of the Minneapolis Symphony

Anna Johnson	*Wife of Richard Johnson*
Mr. Shaunessy	*Solicitor in Ireland, the Corrington family lawyer*
Mr. and Mrs. Peterson	*Parents of David Peterson*
Dee Peterson	*Sister of David Peterson*
Sarah Bishop	*Sister of David Peterson*
Peter Bishop	*Son of Sarah Bishop*
Michael Creighton	*Relief Purser on the 'Prince Regent'*
Samantha Dubose	*Writer and Novelist, friend of Clarissa Peterson*
Jimmy Wan	*Proprietor of 'The Two Pandas' Chinese Restaurant in Ridgedale*
Francesco Lovello	*Conductor on the 'Ulysses'*
Elsa, Ursula and Kurt	*Glass harpists on the 'Ulysses'*
Frank and Jesse	*Passengers on the 'Ulysses'*
Jim Barton	*Passenger on the 'Ulysses'*
Harry Hoven	*Cruise Director on the 'QE2'*
Patrick Ainsworth	*Husband of Gloria Ainsworth*
Martin	*Radio Officer on the 'Prince Regent', friend of David Peterson*
Mr. and Mrs. Achenbloom	*Regular World Cruise passengers on the 'Prince Regent'*
Dorothy and Michelle Connolly	*Passengers on the 'Prince Regent'*
John Pierro	*Maitre d' on the 'Prince Regent'*
James Jobson	*English photographer on Safari, acquaintance of Clarissa Peterson's late father Major 'Jack' Corrington*
Sam	*Texan tourist on Safari*
Maestro Goldstein	*Conductor in Jerusalem*
Malcolm Streeter	*New World Cruise passenger on the ' Prince Regent'*
Doreen	*Social Directress on the 'Prince Regent'*
Jim Bodsworth	*Psychiatrist (Regression Therapist)*

First Century name	Popular name in History
Claudius _Roman Emperor_	Claudius _Roman Emperor_
Suetonius _Roman historian_	Suetonius _Roman historian_
Mary and Martha _Admirers of Joshua_	Mary and Martha _Sisters of Lazarus_
Pontius Pilatus _Prefect of Judea_	Pontius Pilate _Procurator of Judea_
Flavius Septimus _Father of Linus Flavian_	Fictitious
Cephas	St. Peter
Obadiah _Maria's accuser_	Fictitious
Bartimaeus	_Blind_ Bartimaeus
Delilah _Maria's lover and friend_	Fictitious
James _Joshua's brother_	James _Jesus' brother_
Rachel _James' wife_	Fictitious
Joseph of Arimathea _Friend of Maria of Magdala_	Joseph of Arimathea
Catrina _Jewish midwife in Massilia_	Fictitious
Ben Joshua _Son of Joshua and Maria_	Fictitious
Joachim _Miriam's father_	Joachim
Saul _Joshua's accuser_	St. Paul _The Apostle_
Herod Agrippa _King of Judea_	Herod Agrippa _King of Judea_
Nero _Roman Emperor_	Nero _Roman Emperor_

Further information on the theological background of this novel can be gleaned in the author's note found on pages 301-308.

Two Thousand
Years Later...

The moon peeked through rushing clouds as the Chief Purser lent against the rail of the 'Prince Regent'. She was passing the dark coastline of Corsica and the breeze was stiffening. It had turned much cooler. 'The Mistral,' David Peterson concluded with his officer's instinct, 'in an hour or two it will probably get rough.'

Back in the warmth of the Pavilion Lounge, David watched the evening cabaret. The ship's doctor, Malcolm Cameron, stood beside him with a gin and tonic in hand. The ship lurched. The adagio dancer grimaced as he held up his partner, but he could not sustain his balance. He slipped. She fell. There was a gasp from the audience. Chairs moved. The Cruise Director rushed out on stage to offer his assistance.

"I'd better get back there," Dr. Cameron said as he handed his glass to David.

David put the doctor's glass down. "I'll come with you. That girl's taken quite a fall."

The ship righted itself before she began to roll the other way. Some members of the dance troupe, dressed in their diaphanous costumes, joined the Cruise Director to assist their team mate. A well-meaning passenger in the medical profession stepped forward to offer his advice. A steward ran up with ice in a towel.

"Leave her where she is," Dr. Cameron said in his crusty, Scottish burr. "David, call Nurse MacAllister and get them to bring up a stretcher."

David dialed the hospital from the backstage phone.

"Fiona!" he shouted, when his ex-girlfriend's voice answered. "There's been an accident with one of the dancers. I'm with Dr. Cameron. Can you send up an orderly with a stretcher? Actually, if I were you, send up both orderlies with a wheelchair and a stretcher - some of the passengers might also be shaken. That was a big one!"

"Tell me about it!" Fiona replied. "The dispensary's a mess!"

"The 'Mistral'," David explained. "October's a time of the year to expect a bout with that wind!"

It was no time before the orderlies arrived. Dr. Cameron, with the help of one of them, eased the young girl onto the stretcher and covered her almost naked body with a blanket.

The ship lurched again. In the distance David could hear the crash of glass from the bar. Dr. Cameron left with his patient. The other doctor directed the second assistant to an elderly lady in the lounge who had fallen back in her chair and hit her head against one of the pillars. She was more frightened than hurt, but as a precaution she was wheeled down to the hospital.

The Cruise Director took the center stage again. After assuring the passengers that he did not think the dancer was seriously hurt and that she was in good hands, he proceeded to go into his routine of 'one-liners'. Passengers began to titter nervously.

David made his way down to the Purser's Office. His staff had started on the clean up.

"Where did this spring from?" the Berthing Officer asked. "We had no warning."

"The 'Mistral'," David replied. "I had a hunch it was on its way, but there was no official notice from the Bridge. I knew I should have come back here first. We could have taken some precautions."

He turned to one of his receptionists. "Be prepared for a lot of calls," he warned. "I know the 'Mistral' - from here to Barcelona we can expect it to be really rough. There might be some serious problems, apart from the usual calls for seasickness. Make sure we have plenty of 'Dramamine' at the counter."

The calls began in earnest as the ship went into a corkscrew motion, pitching and rolling alternately. David telephoned the hospital again. Fiona answered.

"How's the young dancer?" he asked.

"She's fractured her collar bone. Dr. Cameron's made her comfortable. Her legs seem fine."

"Thank God!" David exclaimed with concerned relief.

"A friend of yours?" the nurse enquired with more than a hint of jealous sarcasm.

"Fiona!" David chastised her. "For God's sake! I was with the Doctor when she fell! I don't even know her name!"

"I thought as the Chief Purser you knew everybody's name," Fiona needled. "Her name's Priscilla - Priscilla Notley."

"Well, I hope she'll be alright," the Chief Purser muttered, feeling the bitterness in the lithe nurse's response. His recent marriage to Clarissa Corrington, a concert pianist whom he had met on board, had obviously hurt Fiona more deeply than David had realized.

The ship jerked as its bow slapped down into another trough. Several items fell in the Purser's Office.

"We'll probably have some more casualties for you if it stays like this," David continued. "We'll be in touch. You do a great job down there."

"Flattery won't change things," Fiona answered. "You hurt me more than you'll ever know."

"I'm sorry," David replied. "Things change. That's life."

"Okay, David. We're busy. Buy me a drink some time. It's hard when you avoid me like the plague."

"I'll try to remember."

"I hope you do!" Fiona stated, determined to have the last word.

David hung up. The switchboard was busy. He secured the drawers in his large desk and made safe his computer and printer. When he finally retired and managed to fall asleep, he dreamed of Fiona. She was in Clarissa's Minnesota home. In the dream his old girlfriend appeared to be his wife. She was even wearing one of Clarissa's satin nightshirts, yet when they had been lovers she had always slept naked.

David awoke in a cold sweat as the ship crashed down in another trough. He felt guilty. 'Why am I dreaming about Fiona? I've only been married to Clara four months!' It frightened him to sense Fiona taking Clarissa's space. "Damn you, Fiona!" he cried out, "I love Clara!"

It was some time before he could get back to sleep. This time he saw Clarissa in his dreams. But she was not with him. She was kissing Jeremy Dyson, that damned architect that had so mysteriously entered their lives and who had these crazy notions that he had known Clarissa in some past life when he had been a Roman soldier.

David awoke. He felt lonely, disoriented and slightly seasick. He was confused or was it a pang of jealousy? He looked at his watch. It was nearly seven in the morning. He reached for his phone.

His friend Martin, the Australian radio officer, answered.

"Can you call my wife?" David asked. "That's the Minnesota number."

"You lucky bugger! You've got leave coming up in Barcelona!" Martin replied. "I'll call you back. What a bloody awful night!"

About half a minute later Martin was back on the line. "There's no reply," he reported. "You can leave a message on her answering machine, but remember its a minimum of thirty three of your American greenbacks."

"It's a rip off," David answered.

"Well ... just warning you. I know how long you talk sweet nothings to her. Blimey man! You need your vacation!"

"I'll try again later," David said before he hung up.

He lay back. 'That's strange,' he thought as he looked at the clock beside his bed. 'Clarissa should be home. It's past midnight in Minnesota.'

•••••••••

Clarissa was out at the airport well ahead of arrival time. She wanted to be sure that she would be at the gate waiting for David when he flew in. She had sensed that possessive love that shares every moment, even in absence. David had asked her so intently where she'd been. He'd almost accused her of being somewhere she shouldn't have been. She'd only been out to dinner with her friend Samantha Dubose. They'd got talking about their dreams and began sharing experiences from their journals. Time had got away on them. It was nearly two in the morning when she'd arrived home. It was the first occasion she hadn't been there for David when he'd called from Europe. She had been surprised by his reaction when he'd reached her from New York after his 'Iberia' flight from Madrid landed there earlier in the afternoon. She didn't want to disappoint him further. He'd been in good time to make his connection. She could expect him on the 'Northwest' flight. The arrivals board said 6:40pm.

Clarissa kept looking at her watch. It was 6:30pm, then 6:33pm. She so hoped the plane wouldn't be late. She had set the table for a cozy, romantic dinner at home. She was wearing a long, blue 'Poncho' coat David had given her. It was really too warm in the airport to wear, but she knew he would be pleased to see it. She went into the rest room one more time and combed her golden hair. After putting on fresh lipstick, she pursed her lips in the mirror. She looked good. She felt good and she had made sure that she was wearing the lingerie that he liked the most.

It was 6:50pm and there still seemed no sign of activity at Gate 36. Then, she heard the aircraft approach and its engines whine before they shut down. The gate opened. There was a bustle as the passengers started to come off. And then, there he was - her David was home.

David ran towards her. He put his briefcase on the ground and took her in his arms. "I've missed you," he whispered. "I love you, Clara."

Clarissa squeezed him and shed tears of joy. "Welcome home, my love," she said. "I've missed you too!"

They stood there embracing each other as David's fellow passengers passed by.

"I guess we'd better go down to Baggage Claim," David said at length. "I've two heavy bags."

When they got home David noticed some late fall flowers Clarissa had arranged on the round table in their dining alcove. He knew he could have arranged them better, but he loved her for her effort.

"I wish you could have arrived here in daylight," Clarissa commented. "The colors are beautiful now. But, you'll see them tomorrow. Maybe we can go for a walk in Carver Park?"

After soup and salad, Clarissa and David found time for their passions in front of the glowing log fire in the living room. David boldly unzipped Clarissa's dress, meeting no resistance. She saw how it aroused her husband when she stepped out of the garment and stood before him in her satin briefs and bra. Her blonde hair contrasted with the shimmering blue of her lace-trimmed lingerie. She knelt before him on the sheepskin that lay before the fire place. There, he allowed her to bring him to nakedness. They rolled together on the rug in rising passion. She stroked him, teased him and kissed him tenderly. He fondled her nipples through the silky softness of her bra. He gently touched her as she arched her back and lay back to await her pleasure. He slipped off her under-things. Slowly he eased himself back, so that he lay on top of her and could kiss her gently on the lips. He nibbled at her ears, gyrated his flesh against the smoothness of her thighs. They held each other tight for a while before reaching fulfillment.

"I love you, David," was all Clarissa could say as she returned to the reality of their living room floor. "Oh, how I've missed you!"

"Me, too," David admitted, but as he said so in the burgeoning reality of their fading ecstasy, he thought of Fiona. He saw her as she had been in his nightmare, clad in Clarissa's satin nightshirt. She had been in this house. And in the horror of his confusion he saw his beloved Clarissa kissing that whiskered architect, Jeremy Dyson, that damned Roman soldier!

"A penny for your thoughts?" Clarissa asked observing David's faraway look.

"Nothing, darling," he said. "I love you, Clara." He kissed her again and they snuggled up to each other.

• • • • • • • •

When David woke up in their bedroom, the sun was shining brightly through the big 'A' frame windows that looked out over the lake. Just as Clarissa had said, the trees were showing their best, fall colors. Reds and rusts mingled with the vivid yellows and oranges of the mid-western maples. Clarissa was sitting up in the bed beside him, her hair falling about her shoulders. She was writing feverishly in her dream journal. David smiled. "So, you're recording your dreams again?" he noted sleepily.

"Yes," she replied. "It's very important. If you don't write them down immediately, you're inclined to forget them."

"That's because they're only in our sub-conscious mind and we don't retain them," David suggested. "It's nature's way of telling us that they're not important. I hardly ever remember my dreams," but as he said it he couldn't help but reflect on his recent nightmare.

"But, you would if you wrote them down," Clarissa insisted.

"Why would I want to recall them?" he said uneasily. "They're only reflections on whatever I might have been thinking about when I went to sleep."

"That's not true," Clarissa said emphatically. "Dreams can reveal our innermost thoughts, things that our waking minds suppress - often for no good reason. They can reveal things that are deep in our past. Dreams can take us back into our previous lives or they can give us glimpses into our future. They can be a window into the consciousness of our soul."

David chuckled. "You really believe all that stuff don't you? The only dreams I seem to remember are nightmares and they're totally bizarre."

"One day you'll understand. Somebody with a soul like yours has to respond to that spirit within."

"I love you anyway," was all David replied as he put his hands up behind his neck to prop himself up on the pillows. He changed the subject as he looked out at the trees around the lake. "It is beautiful here."

"This is the prettiest time of the year," Clarissa agreed. "Maybe in a couple of days we should drive up to Lake Superior. The country will be a riot of color this week."

"Let's just enjoy two quiet days here first," David suggested. "I need to unwind."

"I agree, but don't forget we have to go out tonight. We have the Johnsons' party."

David sat up. "I can't believe it!" he exclaimed. "It's my first day back on vacation and we have to go off to some boring party where I won't know anybody. Couldn't you have turned this one down, Clara? You said you didn't know them very well."

"I don't," Clarissa admitted, looking at David with her sparkling, blue-green eyes, "but they're big with the Symphony here, so it's best if we go. It's hard enough to get work with orchestras these days. I do better with my solo performances. But I can't ignore the Symphony. It's good public relations. It gets me radio and T.V. interviews and that helps to get my music out."

"What does this Johnson guy do?" David enquired. "I only met him very briefly at our engagement party."

"He's in real estate here and handles up-market homes. He likes to think he's important."

"Oh, yes. Somewhat of a social climber if I remember and his wife Anna's even worse. I have to mix with those types all the time on board ship," David continued in his disgruntled manner, "they can be a real bore."

He looked at Clarissa. He couldn't help smiling, even though he didn't feel like going to this party. There was something about the little breaks of separation in their lifestyles that made their reunions so very special and he really just wanted to share his time with her. He picked up her dream journal. "Well, what did you dream about last night?" he asked.

"I was playing in a concert hall in Japan. The piano was a 'Yamaha'."

"Appropriate," David noted. "Isn't Japan part of your Asian tour next winter?"

"Yes, but that's not really what my dream was about. I don't know what I was playing. This was one of those silent dreams. You know, sometimes we record whole conversations and at other times our dreams are quite mute. I couldn't hear the music, but above the piano I could look out of a window onto this beautiful scene."

"What did you see?" David asked, becoming more interested.

"A temple pagoda," Clarissa replied. "It was in the snow surrounded by trees at the edge of a small lake. The pagoda glinted with gold as it was caught in a shaft of light from the afternoon sun. The snow sparkled from the curving roofs. The sky around the sunlight bore streaks of pink, green and yellow. As I stared at the golden temple so it seemed to pulsate before my eyes, shimmering in its winter setting."

"Sounds like the Golden Temple at Kyoto," David stated with his extraordinary knowledge of the world. "It's the only golden pagoda that I can recall."

"I want to go to Kyoto when I'm in Japan," Clarissa said. "Is it really as beautiful as they say?"

"When you're there it will be in the middle of the winter. The spring is the pretty time in Kyoto when all the cherry blossoms are in bloom. However, if you were to see Kyoto in the snow, I'm sure it could look something like the scene that you've just described."

Clarissa gave a knowing smile. "Maybe that's exactly what I saw in my dream!" she stated excitedly. "Perhaps this was a glimpse into the future!"

"Enough of that!" David exclaimed, as he rolled over and took Clarissa in his arms, seeking his own reassurance of the reality of the present.

• • • • • • • •

David looked in the mirror of their 'Chevy' station wagon and straightened his tie. He had to admit that he didn't look bad for his forty three years. There was only the slightest hint of gray, giving him distinguished tips to the side of his hair and he still carried the bronzed look of his recent travels.

He reversed the car out into the drive. A sloping lawn ran down from the house to the edge of a lake. David had cut the grass that very afternoon. Aspens around the rim of the lawn had taken on their look of straw. Despite the rich carpet of yellow, red, orange and brown that lay beneath the gray limbs of the maple woods on either side, the grass was still a verdant green. A flock of Canada geese had alighted to rest before migrating south. David laughed as he put the station wagon into drive. "I suppose they'll leave their poop all over the grass," he said as he leaned over to kiss Clarissa before he accelerated the vehicle out into the street. "I'm not in a very good mood this evening, am I?"

"Apparently not," Clarissa replied. "Maybe it'll do you good to go to this party."

David stroked Clarissa's ringlets. In her simple, blue dress with its big, white cuffs and collar, she looked as if she had walked from the salon of some nineteenth century soiree. "Alright, which way do we go?" he asked.

"Just take the road to Wayzata. I'll direct you from there."

Some of the maples had shed their leaves, but other trees were only coming into their foliage height, glorying in the golden light as the setting sun hung low over the lakes. The beauty of the fall landscape at sunset soon improved David's disposition. Minnesota was magnificent at this time of the year.

"Tell me more about our host and hostess, then?" David asked, once they were on the highway.

"They're typically 'yuppie' if you know what I mean," Clarissa explained. "They're into organic gardening, but only because it's the fashion. The chances are that everything will be brought in by caterers at the party. I guess they're pretty normal really, although I don't care for the 'yuppie' set much. But be warned of one thing, Richard's terribly religious. He's a Jesus freak."

"In what way?"

"He's always talking about Jesus, as if this guy was still around. Jesus died two thousand years ago!"

"So he's a Bible thumper," David noted. "Sometimes it makes me laugh. I wonder what Jesus would think if he came back today? Do you think he would recognize the Christian Church?"

"Be careful," Clarissa warned. "Richard and Anna assume that all their friends are as devoted to the Church as they are, so we mustn't offend them."

"I won't. I'm not a complete heathen as you know. My goodness, it was my recognition of that deep spirituality that emanates from you and your music that brought us together."

"And that's what I saw in you, too," Clarissa said as she sat closer to him and started to lightly caress the back of his neck.

"It's just that we both find it hard to sense that spirituality in conventional Christianity." David tried to ignore Clarissa's caresses so he could concentrate on his driving. "Now, which way at the traffic lights?"

"Straight across, through Wayzata, then turn right and follow the lake."

Lake Minnetonka was much larger than their small one in Ridgedale. So were the surrounding houses. They passed several, veritable mansions set among glorious trees beside the water. Stone entranceways to these estates, bearing names like 'Maple Grove', 'Pine Acres' and 'Hollowdale', were lit by wrought iron lamps.

"The Johnson's home should be coming up soon on the right," Clarissa instructed.

As they drove over the brow of a hill in the winding, leafy road, they could see parked cars ahead. It looked like it was going to be quite a big party.

• • • • • • • •

Anna Johnson was at the front door welcoming her guests. Richard was inside playing the host. It was one of those smart, casual affairs, with lots of people in their forties who were either very successful in their business enterprises or were desperate to give that impression.

Clarissa spotted Jeremy Dyson first. "Jeremy's here!" she exclaimed.

David did a double-take as he sensed the enthusiasm in her voice. "The architect," he said coolly, "that damned Roman soldier!"

"Yes. I think he's so fascinating. I'll bet he did know me in that past life when he was a Roman soldier."

Thoughts of Clarissa and Jeremy danced before David as he reflected on his recent nightmare. "Do you really believe that?" he asked.

Clarissa didn't answer. She was already leading him over to where Jeremy stood.

Jeremy seemed a little out of place amongst the 'yuppies'. He was ruggedly good-looking, with a well-tanned face that was framed by his sandy hair and natural beard giving him somewhat of a bohemian look. He wore a flamboyant, red, paisley cravat, billowing out over a white, silk shirt beneath a corduroy jacket. His trousers were khaki twill. He carried a glass of whiskey, having turned down the habitual champagne. He was talking to Richard Johnson as they approached.

"Oh, Jeremy, I'd like you to meet two of our local celebrities," Richard said in a rather patronizing way. "David here is the Captain of the 'Love Boat'."

David gave a weak grin. "Well, not exactly Captain," he corrected his host. "I'm the Chief Purser on the 'Prince Regent'. But, we've met Jeremy before."

'Why do people always have to crack this same, sick joke about the 'Love Boat'?' David thought. 'If they only knew what it was really like behind the Purser's desk on a luxury cruise ship. My God, that 'Love Boat' crew wouldn't last a day in my job!'

"Well, whatever," Richard continued. "You're the lucky man who's always in the sunshine."

He looked at Jeremy. "Like you, David hasn't experienced our midwestern winter yet?"

"No, that's right," David replied. "I'm usually traveling around the world in the winter. Clarissa will travel with me part of this coming season."

"That'll be nice," he said, putting his head on one side as he looked at Clarissa. "Jeremy, do you know Clarissa's a concert pianist? She plays all over the world. She's one of our real local celebrities."

"I know," Jeremy replied as he looked at her.

Anna Johnson joined her husband.

David couldn't help feeling that Clarissa's simple dress looked far more stunning than Anna's over-priced pants suit.

"Aren't you scheduled to play with the Minneapolis Orchestra next month?" Anna asked.

"Yes. I believe the date's right after Thanksgiving."

"I hope you'll play for us later?" Anna suggested, batting her extended eyelashes.

David knew how much Clarissa hated these impromptu invitations to play at people's houses on status symbol pianos that were nearly always badly out of tune.

"I'd be delighted," Clarissa replied, cringing at the thought, "but it will have to be very informal."

"After supper, then? Oh that will be a treat," Anna said delighted that her mission had been accomplished. "Nice to see you again, David. One day maybe we'll be lucky enough to cruise on that ship of yours. We took a cruise last year on a Mediterranean yacht, so of course, we're spoiled!"

The Johnsons passed on to mingle with other guests.

"How is life on that cruise ship?" Jeremy asked as he sipped on his whiskey.

"It's nice to have a break," David replied.

"I've been invited from time to time to lecture on board ships," Jeremy informed him, "particularly in the Greek Isles."

"On Architecture or Archeology?" David asked.

"Archeology. I've been involved in several projects in Greece and Asia Minor as well as Israel."

"Where in Greece and Asia Minor?"

"Delos and Ephesus," Jeremy answered eagerly. "I uncovered a whole new mosaic on Delos in August. It was so complete, one of the best floors I've ever seen. Do you know Delos?"

"My ship's cruised by there. I can't say I've been on Delos 'though I've seen the island, but I know Ephesus well. We used to dock in Kusadasi regularly. Let me see ... that was three years ago."

"Tours used to come in from the cruise ships when we were there," Jeremy noted. "If you don't mind me saying, Mr. Peterson, the passengers hardly ever knew what they were looking at. Ephesus is so magnificent. It's the First Century complete."

"I agree. It is magnificent," David acknowledged.

"I've sat in the Great Theater at Ephesus and I'll swear I've heard St. Paul speak. It's magic," Jeremy continued excitedly. "You can walk those streets and see the clientele sheepishly come out of the brothel, or learned men gather outside the great library. You can hear the sounds of citizens climbing up the steps of the narrow street that flanks the hill. It's all so real."

"My mother loved Ephesus," Clarissa joined in. "She used to work on digs in the ancient world too. Samos was one of her favorite spots. That's near Ephesus, isn't it?"

"Yes, as a matter of fact it is. Samos is off shore from the great harbor at Ephesus, although the coastal landscape has changed quite a bit since the First Century. The sea's receded several miles."

"So Ephesus is now a port trapped inland," Clarissa observed.

"That's right."

"Do you think you see history so vividly because you might actually be recalling personal past experiences?" Clarissa asked.

David cautioned Clarissa, looking her straight in the eye. He was always a little nervous when his wife started in on these past life beliefs.

"Actually it's funny you say that," the archaeologist answered. "I've always felt so."

Clarissa looked at David with a triumphant expression. "Remember, Jeremy believes in reincarnation," she said. "He thought he knew me when he was that Roman soldier."

"Well, I'm not positive about that," Jeremy qualified, "but when you work closely with these things in the old world you do become transported back in time. I've definitely had that sensation of feeling that I was there before. I have felt that I was around in Roman times."

"Just association," David said, sipping on his soda, "that damned Roman soldier again!"

"Why are you so obstinate, David?" Clarissa chastised him. "Many people remember their past lives. I remember some of mine. I was a prostitute love-slave in India. Another time I was a monk. I can remember keeping the bees at a monastery in England."

"Perhaps, but to me that's a cliche," David suggested. "You know monks kept bees in medieval monasteries. That's why you believe that. As for India, all you reincarnation freaks believe that at some time you lived in India. You all have this thing about India. I've been there. I go to India on my ship almost every year. Rest assured, India's not all it's cracked up to be. It's dirty, it's poor and it stinks. The port officials are corrupt and most of our passengers can't wait to leave. It's a hopeless country. There really isn't anything very spiritual about India today."

Jeremy was smiling. "That's funny," he said. "I'm scheduled to go to India in February. It'll be my first trip out there. I've been asked in as a consultant on a hotel project in New Delhi. Actually, I'm looking forward to it."

David laughed. "Well, don't take me too seriously. There are many interesting things about India. From Delhi you must go to Agra and see the Taj Mahal. As an architect you'll find that fascinating. When there, don't miss the ghost city of Fatepur Sikri. Most tourists never go there, but it's amazing. It's close to Agra and there's this whole city that was laid out by one of India's rulers. It was his attempt to unite Hindu and Moslem architecture as an expression of national unity."

"It must have been Akbar," Jeremy observed.

"Well I wouldn't know that," David admitted, before returning to the subject. "Unfortunately the water course feeding the wells dried up after the city was completed and the place was abandoned. India does have fascinating architecture and lots of color, but just be prepared for that initial shock. It is dirty, it is poor and it does stink."

Clarissa was anxious to turn the conversation back to her favorite topic. "You've been in Israel?" she asked Jeremy.

"Yes. I worked on the digs at Sepphoris and on some of the Roman aspects of Jerusalem."

"I've only been to Israel once," Clarissa stated. "That was four years ago when I played a concert in Tel Aviv. I just flew in for the performance. Sometimes that's how it is on the road. The glamor of travel is from one hotel room and concert hall to the next. I never got to Jerusalem, but I'm due to play there next April. I'm really excited about it. This time I hope to see something. The place must have an awesome sense of history."

"First Century Palestine is fascinating," Jeremy agreed. "Sepphoris was the Roman capital of Galilee at the time of Christ. It was only about six miles from Nazareth."

"Really!" Clarissa exclaimed.

"Yes. Jesus almost certainly knew the city, even though it's never mentioned in the Bible. It's interesting actually. Many aspects of Roman Palestine are ignored in the Gospels. There was a great hatred of the Romans. I suppose the early Christian writers wanted to play down their presence. There are occasional mentions of Roman centurions in the healing miracles and of course the crucifixion was carried out by Romans under the Prefecture of Pontius Pilate, but in reality it would have been very hard not to have known that Palestine was part of the Empire at the time of Christ."

"Did you have the same feelings in Palestine that you had in Greece and Turkey - that sense that you might have been there in a past life?" Clarissa asked.

"As I go from one dig to another I get this extraordinary feeling that I am retracing my own steps. People moved about in the Graeco-Roman world much more than in later civilizations. I think if I did live then, I saw quite a bit of the old world."

"Who do you think you might have been?" Clarissa asked.

"Well, like I told you before - probably an officer of some sort in the Roman army, maybe a centurion," Jeremy answered. "I don't really know. I just have this sense that I was a soldier in the First Century."

Richard Johnson came back with a tray of drinks, mostly bubbling glasses of champagne, but there were a couple of whiskeys, some ginger-ales and a few sodas included. Jeremy helped himself to another whiskey. David and Clarissa took the soft drinks.

"On the wagon?" Richard asked rather condescendingly.

"No," David replied. "Unfortunately I can't drink champagne."

"I suppose you 'sea captains' get champagne every day," Richard replied with a wink. "Are you sure we can't get you something stronger?"

"No, a refreshing soda will do fine," David replied. "We're having a discussion here about the Roman Empire. Jeremy thinks he lived in Ephesus two thousand years ago!"

Clarissa frowned. She sensed David's sarcasm. There was so much she loved about her husband, but she didn't like it when he reacted with cynical sarcasm to her belief in reincarnation.

But Richard took the subject of Ephesus up differently. "Ephesus, the Virgin Mother's home," he said with delight. "We visited there on our yacht cruise. To visit Mary's house had to be one of the greatest thrills of my life."

Jeremy tried to look interested, but Clarissa could see that the archaeologist was not impressed. When Richard moved on, the truth eecked out.

"Mary's House can't be older than the Tenth Century if that," Jeremy said with a smile. "There's probably a first century well there, but that's about all."

"How can anyone know the Virgin Mary lived in Ephesus?" Clarissa asked skeptically.

"Well, there is a strong tradition to that effect," Jeremy admitted. "It's based on that passage in the gospels where Jesus asks John to take care of Miriam and for Miriam to consider John as her son. We pretty much know that John went to live in Ephesus so from that we can deduce that maybe Miriam did too."

"You called Mary, Miriam," Clarissa said slowly as she took a sip of her ginger-ale.

"Did I?" Jeremy replied. "Well, force of habit I guess. That was her real name. In Aramaic, Mary is Miriam."

"Somehow I knew that," Clarissa replied. "I don't know why, but I just knew it."

"Maybe you were once a Jewess of that name," Jeremy suggested with a grin. "That may be how I knew you. You're now living in America, but you say you had past lives in England and India, so why not in Israel as well?"

"Possibly," Clarissa agreed. "I also know I lived in China once, but that's another story. Look, we'd love you to come and join us for dinner one night next week so that we can explore these things. I think we share a lot in common."

'Too much!' David thought to himself.

"I'd love to," Jeremy replied. "Perhaps we can continue our discussion then in quieter surroundings. It's always a bit difficult in the artificial atmosphere of these wing dings."

"Can we give you a call then?" Clarissa asked. "What's your number?"

"I'm not in the book yet," Jeremy explained. He scribbled his telephone number on a back page of his diary, tore it out and handed it to Clarissa.

"We'll call you in the next two days," Clarissa assured him. "It's been great seeing you again."

David smiled at Jeremy politely, but Clarissa realized something was wrong.

"Don't you like him?" she asked, after he had moved away. "I think he's fascinating."

"That's just what's wrong," David muttered. "He is fascinating, but he's got his eye on you. I'll bet he's a real ladies' man. He looked at you like a Greek officer."

Clarissa laughed. "You have a thing about Greek officers," she said. "Has it never occurred to you that some people think of you in your starched, white uniform like that. You know, when we got engaged, I can't tell you how many passengers, also some of your staff, cornered me to tell me how lucky I was and that I had better treat you right. Then, what about that nurse? She was goofy about you!"

David felt a pang in his stomach. Fiona's image haunted him again. "Fiona was a fellow officer," he said. "Anyway, this conversation's stupid. Let's enjoy the party. I love you, Clara. Remember last night?"

"I'm sorry," she agreed as she realized she had touched on a sensitive topic. "But, don't worry about Jeremy, David. I can take care of myself."

They moved into the dining room.

"So, Jeremy really thinks he was this Roman soldier?" David noted, reviving the topic in hand.

"That's right. It's strange, but the feeling's mutual. I just know I've met him before. It's almost as if I share some karma with him."

"Watch it with the karma," David said as he squeezed her waist. "You know I don't believe in karma."

They looked at the buffet table. The spread was very inviting. They might not have considered themselves to have much in common with Richard and Anna, but they had to acknowledge that they shared their taste in salads and vegetables. The food was not catered and it was wonderful.

"What shall I play after supper?" Clarissa asked David. "The Chopin's always good."

"I'd give them Listz," David suggested. "It sounds more virtuoso. You know how these people are. They'll be more impressed and they'll never pick up on a wrong note."

• • • • • • • •

True to her word, Clarissa called Jeremy Dyson two days after Richard and Anna's party to ask him to the house. He was at his drawing board when the phone rang.

"I'd be delighted," he accepted politely. "I found our common interest in past lives fascinating. I'd really like to pursue our discussion further."

During the two days prior to his visit, Jeremy thought a lot about Clarissa. She seemed so familiar. He felt sure that they had met before, but he couldn't place where or when. The fixation became such that at night he tossed and turned, refusing to let his mind rest. When eventually sleep overcame him he still could not escape - Clarissa seemed to appear to him in a dream .....

He saw her at Marseilles in the First Century. Jeremy knew that at that time Marseilles was 'Massilia'. He had worked on the harbor excavations there. In his dream he was a Roman soldier. He assumed that he was about twenty years old. Being a Roman citizen he had a position of some authority over his fellow soldiers. He had been detailed to lead a small unit of men to the synagogue to close the Rabbinical school. Apparently there had been some serious problems in Rome with the Jews, so until further notice an Imperial edict, signed by Emperor Claudius, demanded closure of these schools deeming them hotbeds of revolution aimed at overthrowing Imperial authority in the name of some Rabbi known as Chrestus.

In the dream, Jeremy's men burst into the school.

"You are forbidden to teach here," Jeremy said confronting the Rabbi. "Instruction in your ways must stop immediately. This building is closed. Get these people out of here right away - I mean now - Move! I, Remus Augustus, command this in the name of the Emperor Claudius!"

The Rabbi looked stunned. He replied in perfect Latin, "For what reason?"

"You are Jews!" Jeremy answered in the personality of Remus Augustus. "Jewish schools are forbidden. You may worship your god, but not teach."

"But why?" the Rabbi insisted.

Remus Augustus smiled. "Haven't you heard of Chrestus?" he asked, pulling the Rabbi's forelocks.

"No," the Rabbi stammered. "Who is Chrestus? We don't know anyone named Chrestus."

"A rabble rouser," Remus replied. "The man whose rebellion in Rome has caused your misfortune. Send your pupils home!"

The Rabbi obeyed.

As Remus Augustus, Jeremy Dyson followed one of the young men. The youth lived in an insula close to the harbor where many of the Jews lived. It was there that Jeremy sensed Clarissa's presence.

She appeared to be the young man's mother. But the woman didn't look like Clarissa. Her face was different. She was dark-skinned whereas Clarissa was fair. Her hair was brown and tumbled down her back. Clarissa was a golden blonde.

Jeremy awoke. He just knew it was Clarissa. He had this sixth sense that he had tapped not only into one of his past lives as a Roman soldier, but that he truly had encountered Clarissa in some first century life.

• • • • • • •

C larissa liked entertaining at home. When she asked people in she cooked a simple meal, but David always made the setting romantic. There were lots of candles in the house along with an abundance of fresh flowers. Roses were Clarissa's particular favorite and David presented her with two dozen, salmon-pink blooms to honor Jeremy Dyson's visit.

Their little, wrought-iron, glass-topped table looked very pretty. Green-blue china of no great value was displayed to its best advantage, sitting on attractive place mats flanked by brilliant, blue glasses. Green, linen napkins were cleverly pulled through brass rings that each carried a small corsage of pink roses mixed with gypsophila, which David insisted on calling 'baby's breath'. Simple, clear, glass candlesticks supported three, slender tapers that matched the pink roses. The setting looked like it was ready for the cover page of 'House and Garden', but in reality had been produced with items all readily available at the nearest supermarket.

"You have such a way of making something beautiful out of the simplest things," Clarissa said as she admired David's handiwork.

"It only reflects the happiness of our home," he replied. "Now, are we going to offer him wine?"

"Yes, if you want to, but I won't have any."

"Me neither," David agreed, "but I expect Jeremy would like wine. He has that sort of a face."

"Why don't we serve him that bottle of Chardonnay in the refrigerator," Clarissa suggested as she went to change.

David got out the wine. He turned the bottle round to read the label. 'It's probably a good thing if we use this up!' he noted. 'It's been sitting in the refrigerator for some time.'

"Why don't you pour the wine into the decanter that your sister Dee gave us?" Clarissa shouted from the bedroom as she frantically pulled up the zipper of a flower-print dress.

David had already changed. He was wearing a green, silk shirt and gray, flannel trousers.

As Clarissa was fixing her hair, the doorbell rang.

"I'll get it Clara!" David shouted as he crossed the living room to go down the three steps to the door.

It was Jeremy. He looked every bit the successful architect that he was, wearing a tweed jacket and an open-neck shirt.

"Hi. Come on in," David said. He ushered Jeremy into the living room. "We're so glad you could come."

Clarissa appeared. She looked lovely. "Welcome to our house," she added. "I'm glad you were able to find it. It's a bit difficult to explain how to get here. People always think that we're on Lake Minnetonka, but actually our lake isn't joined to Minnetonka at all. It's much smaller, but we find it just as beautiful and there are a lot less noisy boats out here in the summer!"

"I suppose you get the ice fishers in the winter though," Jeremy noted.

Clarissa laughed. "Some. That's a kind of club up here. I think they just want to escape from their wives and families. They sit in those little huts all day watching T.V. and drinking beer. I don't think they ever catch any fish. Talking of fish, I hope you like salmon. I've got salmon for us tonight. If you'll excuse me for a minute I need to check it out in the kitchen."

"What can I get you?" David asked, offering Jeremy a drink.

"Have you a scotch and water?"

"Yes, let me see what brand?" David looked in their rarely-opened, cocktail cabinet. "Will 'Teachers' be alright?"

"Anything," Jeremy replied as he sat down on the comfortable living room sofa.

David fixed Jeremy's drink and poured himself a sherry, leaving another small glass for Clarissa. "So what brought you to the 'Twin Cities'?"

"The University, mostly," Jeremy answered. "They've asked me to design some new laboratories. When I came up to look at the site I stayed at a little inn outside Wayzata. I just loved the area so thought I'd see if I could find a place 'round here. Then, Richard Johnson showed me a house right on the lake. I couldn't resist it so I bought it."

"How's the University project going?"

"Well, but it'll take some time. Meanwhile I'm setting myself up in Wayzata. I've found a good studio and office. Seeing Minnesota in the fall has inspired me to paint again apart from the architect bit."

"You paint too?" David asked.

"Yes."

Clarissa joined them. "We can have supper anytime," she announced.

David handed her the sherry.

They both raised their glasses to Jeremy. "Welcome to our home," Clarissa repeated.

"Jeremy was just telling me he paints," David informed her. "We're quite an artist's community around the lake now."

"Yes, David used to paint," Clarissa commented, looking proudly at her husband. "He really should go back to it."

"I will," David acknowledged.

When they were seated at the table, they enjoyed one of Clarissa's excellent, heavily basil-laden soups while Jeremy revived their previous discussion at Richard and Anna's party. "Have you also been in the Holy Land?" he asked David.

"Jerusalem and Nazareth," David replied.

"Last year I worked on two digs that have only recently attracted attention," Jeremy continued. "One was Sepphoris as I mentioned. I was invited to spend some time there by the Hebrew University where I had done some architectural work."

David recalled their conversation at the Johnsons' party. "You said Sepphoris was near Nazareth?"

"About six miles to the northwest. In Biblical times Nazareth was really the nearest village of any size to the Roman capital."

"Sepphoris was strictly Roman, then?"

"It was the principal garrison town of Galilee. Actually there are a lot of Roman artifacts there. Although the buildings were pretty much destroyed by the Arabs, many Roman items became buried at the site. We've been able to reconstruct a lot about first century Palestine there."

"That's very interesting," David observed. "I'd never heard of Sepphoris before we met you."

"Maybe that's because it's not mentioned in the Bible - a lot of important places aren't mentioned in the Bible. For instance, another place I find fascinating is Tiberias. It seems at first to be a lakeside resort for wealthy Jews with particularly expensive seafood restaurants. But when you get out to the dig, just south of present day Tiberias, an amazing Roman city becomes evident. It wasn't wealthy Jews who lived here in abundance at the time of Jesus, but wealthy Romans from all over Syria. This was a fashionable place. King Herod Antipas actually moved his Royal Palace from Sepphoris to Tiberias. They say it was there that he had John the Baptist imprisoned and beheaded. You might remember the story of how Herod had the Baptist's head served up on a silver salver."

Clarissa winced.

"But surely the King was a Jew?" David asked.

"Only in name," Jeremy replied. "The Herodians were more Roman than Jewish. Of course there were Herodian Jews who came to live in Tiberias after the royal move, but for the most part it was a retirement center for wealthy Romans. Actually Romans loved the whole west side of the sea of Galilee. I think it reminded them of Italy. The landscape was more lush in those days. There were prosperous vineyards on the hillsides, sweeping down to the shores of the lake. Citrus groves and olives abounded. It was in many ways the garden of Galilee. Places like Magdala, or Tracchea as it was more correctly known, although they were Jewish fishing villages, were surrounded by Roman villas. Every so often a modern plough unearths a mosaic floor or atrium pool, revealing the whereabouts of those once gracious homes."

"You describe the country as if you actually knew it," Clarissa remarked. "How do you really know what the countryside looked like?"

Jeremy read her mind. He grinned. "I knew you would pick up on that sooner or later," he said. "You think I was there, don't you?"

"Well, you did say you thought you were a Roman at that time. It's very likely. If one believes in reincarnation - we all had to be somewhere in the First Century."

"And in return those souls who lived in the First Century are probably all around now. Have you thought of this one? There must be someone around today who has the same soul as Jesus Christ back then."

"Utter balls!" David chimed in, uncomfortable with this return to past life discussion. "According to Christian tradition Jesus rose from the dead and ascended into heaven. He was a reincarnation of God - not of humanity. Anyway, I'm not into this whole reincarnation thing like Clara. We have fierce discussions about this. Personally I have no recollection of any past lives."

"That doesn't mean that you haven't lived them," Jeremy stated. "You just haven't found the means to access them."

"Well, how do you say one accesses them?" David asked.

Jeremy looked at Clarissa for support. "Many different ways," he replied. "One way is the imaginative technique! Sometimes it's just a sense of belonging that's very prevalent in my archeological experience. History comes alive in your hands and you just know you were there."

"That's just association," David countered as he poured the wine.

"Not entirely, although assuredly that's a part of it. It's hard to explain. The more you handle the past the more it seems to trigger off memories somewhere in the back of your brain."

"What about dreams? Clara's always going on about her dreams," David asked.

"Dreams are a means of access for many people," Jeremy agreed, "but can I be very frank and bold?"

"Say whatever you like," David acknowledged. "You're not likely to convince me."

"Well, you know I've had this strange feeling ever since we met that I knew Clarissa once before?"

"Yes, you have mentioned it several times," David muttered nervously.

"And I've felt the same!" Clarissa exclaimed excitedly.

"Yes. I believe you were around in the first century Roman world," Jeremy confirmed.

"Why?" Clarissa asked. "Please forgive David, but he's very cynical about past lives."

She kicked her husband gently under the table and caught his eye. David frowned.

"I couldn't think where we had met before," Jeremy continued. "Then, I had this dream. I met you in Marseilles."

"Marseilles!"

"Yes, but it wasn't known as Marseilles in those days. This was Massilia, the great port of Gaul in the Roman Empire. I worked on the Roman harbor excavations there a number of years ago."

David shook his head and grinned politely. "Association of ideas again," he said.

"Possibly, but this is what I dreamed. I was a young soldier. I couldn't have been more than twenty. I was given the task of closing down the synagogue school in Massilia at the time that the Emperor Claudius clamped down on the Jews. Actually we weren't very hard on the Jews there. The port was far from Rome. After closing the Rabbinical school I followed one of the pupils - a young man about my own age. I saw his mother. She was a Jewess in her middle years - a good-looking woman, quite voluptuous and with a beguiling smile. There was something radiant about her," Jeremy looked intently at Clarissa. "When I woke up I just knew that the woman in my dream was you. She didn't look like you, but I feel sure she was you. I think you were a Jewess living in Massilia in the First Century."

David laughed. "Well, you'd better add that to the bee keeper," he kidded his wife.

"Dreams can be caused or interpreted by mental association," Jeremy admitted. "But it's not so much who you seemed to be in my dream that is important. The thing that fascinates me is why, when I woke up, I knew the woman was you. It was almost as if time became irrelevant. The energy that I see in you, that radiant inner light that seems to emanate from you, I felt to have been the same as that of this woman in my dream."

"Who do you think I was?" Clarissa asked.

"I've no idea," Jeremy replied honestly. "You must have been Jewish and you had a son about the same age as me if I was that soldier two thousand years ago."

"Do you think you met me again in that life?"

"That hasn't been revealed to me, but there seems to be some very strong energy flowing here that makes me believe I did."

David stared at them. He couldn't really believe what he was hearing, but at the same time he had become curious. He'd always sensed the spirituality in Clarissa's music and even felt it in their love-making; it was just that he didn't believe in all these weird things she liked to embrace. "If you really think you were both around in the First Century, do you think either of you might have met Jesus?" he suddenly asked. "That might account for the high energy as you call it, that you associate with these revelations."

"I doubt it if we were in Gaul," Jeremy replied, "also if my dream actually reveals truth, it would have been a scene after Jesus' death. In a well-known quote from Suetonius about the Claudian persecution of the Jews, it states clearly that the rebellion of the Jews in Rome, that caused this repression, was at the instigation of one named Chrestus. That was about forty nine A.D. - twenty years after the probable date of the crucifixion."

"Who was Chrestus?" David asked.

"It sounds very much like Chrestus was Christ," Jeremy replied. "That's the common belief. The Romans saw the early Christians as a Jewish sect."

"But if Jesus was dead at the time of this rebellion he could hardly have instigated it?" David reasoned.

"Joshua of Nazareth was dead, but 'Jesus Christ' was becoming born. 'Christos' is merely the Greek for the Hebrew 'Messiah' or anointed one. Jesus didn't call himself 'Christ'. His followers called him 'Christ' after they believed he rose from the dead."

"You called him 'Joshua'?" Clarissa noted.

"Yes, because that was his real name. Jesus is the Latin version of the Greek 'Yesous' which in turn was a translation of the original Aramaic or Hebrew name, 'Yeshua' or 'Joshua'. It's difficult to really know the correct pronunciation as there are no written vowels in ancient Hebrew. Jesus would probably have been known to his followers in his lifetime as 'Yeshua' or 'Joshua'."

"Now, that's a lot more interesting," David commented. He turned to Clarissa. "Do you think Jeremy would like to see your mother's letter?"

"Yes. Show him the letter," she agreed.

David left the table and went back to the living room.

"My mother died rather suddenly in Ireland shortly after our wedding," Clarissa explained to Jeremy. "We were married in a little church close to my family's home in the old country. Just before we left to go on our honeymoon, my mother gave David a note. It's quite moving. That's what he's gone to get."

David came back with a silver, picture frame. Inside the frame was a piece of white paper flattened against a dark, blue background. On it in pencil, was scrawled in a not too legible hand the following message - 'I am so very glad and thankful to have seen you in this world before I go into the higher world and to know how good it is for Clarissa to have found you and will be connected with you in the light of Christos.' It was signed 'For David' and carried the initials M.C. standing for Margaret Corrington.

"Clara's mother gave this to me as we got ready to leave on our honeymoon," David explained. "I didn't read it until we'd left the house and driven away."

Jeremy peered at the note. "She knew she was going to die," he said slowly. "She knew she wouldn't see you again."

"It was the last time either of us saw her," Clarissa admitted. "We'd only been home about a week when we received the news of Mother's death. It seems as if Mother had just lost her will to live. She missed my father terribly. She hated living alone in that great, big house in Tipperary. But, until I was married she felt it was her duty to stay. She often used to talk to me about death. She had little pieces of paper all over her room, poems she had written about death. She wasn't unhappy. She just wanted to be released."

"But she wanted to see you married first," Jeremy observed.

"Yes. She was very happy about my marriage to David. She really accepted him." Clarissa took hold of David's hand. "Actually, David felt her presence at the old house the day after the funeral."

"Yes, much though it goes against my reason, I really did feel the old lady's presence," David admitted. "Are you sure you want to hear about this?"

"Of course!" Jeremy exclaimed.

"Well, I don't really know if what I felt or saw is true," David pleaded. "I mean that house lent itself to this kind of thing. It was damp and musky. There were cobwebs on the chandeliers and large areas of mildew on some of the walls. Nothing had really changed since Clara's mother went there as a bride. The furniture was old. The silver was tarnished. The paintings were surrounded by crumbling, gilt frames. Many of them had darkened through years of exposure to smoke from the burning peat and wood in the great fireplaces that heated almost every room. We were all gathered in the dining room for Mr. Shaunessy's reading of the old lady's will. He's Clara's family lawyer except they call them solicitors over there. Since Margaret Corrington's possessions were not relevant to me, my mind wandered. But I really thought I saw her face up in the ceiling above. It's one of those plaster, tray ceilings that had once boasted beautiful frescoes or paintings, but they've long since faded and peeled. It was as if a medallion in the ceiling had revived. Margaret Corrington was looking down at us. She was smiling. She looked younger and she seemed happy and content. Actually, I felt a strange oneness with her as the lawyer droned on passing out notes for legal signatures. It was almost as if she was sending me a message. I knew that she was asking me to be sure to take care of Clara. All the other things were just not important."

Clarissa tried to wipe away an emotional tear. "She loved you, David," was all she could say.

David reached for Clarissa's hand. He knew how difficult her mother's death had been for her. "I know it's hard, but it's also inevitable," he said comfortingly. "Your mother just lost her will to live after your father passed away. We don't live forever."

"Soul lives forever," Clarissa replied softly. "Our bodies are not us. We are soul. We are the light of God."

"Soul drives our bodies, Clara, but we are flesh and blood," David retorted. "Unfortunately there is no escape. We grow old - we die."

"No. That's where you're wrong, David," Clarissa said as she let go of his hand. "I am soul. Soul doesn't die. Soul strives to become an expression of God. Soul lives many lifetimes to achieve its goals."

"If you say so," David said, "but that doesn't stop our physical death. I will say this though. When I saw your mother above us in the dining room at Ballyporeen she looked radiant. She looked like she was in that light to which you refer."

"The light of God," Clarissa repeated.

"Or the light of Christos as your mother so aptly put it," Jeremy reminded them.

While Clarissa served them salmon with vegetables, David asked Jeremy a poignant question. "As you can tell I'm very skeptical about this whole past life business," he said, "but you know what you said about Jesus earlier?"

"What was that?"

"That somebody is probably around today who was Jesus Christ two thousand years ago."

"Well, yes. It's possible," Jeremy agreed. "If reincarnation is true, the energy that was in Jesus has probably passed through many lives since the crucifixion - maybe four thousand or more."

"Maybe four thousand, or maybe just four or five famous persons - possibly none at all," David added.

"Who knows?" Jeremy agreed. "But that doesn't mean that all those souls recognized that they had lived in the Christ. Not all lives of great men will lead to reincarnation in the form of another great man. Greatness is a human term of reference, not a divine one. The spirit that was in Jesus Christ might well have lived on over the centuries in simpler, but no less spiritual persons, who had never understood that they had once lived as soul in the body of Christ."

David leaned on his elbow, looking penetratingly at Jeremy. "Perhaps the Church is wrong," he said. "What if Jesus did not rise from the dead and ascend into heaven, but generations of people simply saw the Christ energy in those who were his reincarnations?"

"Some probably have," Jeremy agreed. "If the circumstances were right maybe we would recognize Jesus' spiritual greatness in others who carry his energy."

Clarissa beamed as she listened to David. "So you're joining us reincarnation freaks!" she said with glee.

"What David's suggesting is no different than I thinking I was that young Roman soldier Remus Augustus at Massilia," Jeremy said.

David grinned. "That damned Roman soldier again!"

"Just because Jesus Christ is a more famous personality doesn't make the experience less likely to be true," Jeremy quipped.

"Remus Augustus? That was your name as the young Roman then?" Clarissa asked.

"Yes, Maria," Jeremy answered with a grin.

Clarissa looked at Jeremy quizzically. "Why did you call me 'Maria'?"

"I don't know. It just came out that way. It just seemed natural. Has anyone ever called you 'Maria' before?"

"No. It's not my name, at least not unless it was my name in some past life."

"The name of a Jewess in Massilia in the First Century, perhaps," Jeremy said as he patted Clarissa on the back.

"This is getting a little bit too much even for me," Clarissa pleaded. She changed the subject. "How's the salmon?"

"It's very good," Jeremy agreed, as David poured him another glass of wine.

Clarissa then returned to the subject in hand. "Isn't there a legend that Mary Magdalene went to Gaul after she disappeared from the pages of the Bible?"

"Yes," Jeremy confirmed. "The legend says that she went to Gaul with Joseph of Arimathea."

"Well, with my Irish background I certainly know that Maria is the same name as Mary." She paused ... "Is that why you called me 'Maria'?"

Jeremy looked surprised. He really hadn't thought about why he had called her 'Maria'. "Wow!" he exclaimed. "I wonder. Maybe you've hit on an amazing truth."

"Well, let's just pretend for a moment that I was Mary Magdalene in a past life. Who would the boy have been in your dream?"

"Ah, your son," Jeremy said slowly stroking his sandy beard. "Well, he could have been Joseph of Arimathea's child."

"Yes, but that's not what I'm thinking," Clarissa continued.

"No. I realize that. You're thinking about the legend that Mary Magdalene was Jesus' lover," Jeremy said seriously.

There was a pregnant silence as they all looked at each other.

Clarissa was the first to speak. "Well, even if we were to pretend I was Mary Magdalene, who says that Jesus and I were actually lovers?" she stated. "I don't think the Church ever said that, and certainly most Christians I know would be shocked by the suggestion. They have this hang up in Christianity about sex. To my knowledge Jesus is always portrayed as an ascetic."

"Who says the Church is right?" Jeremy suggested. "The Church might be wrong about a lot of things."

"True," David mused. He didn't want to reveal that as a teenager he had actually wanted to be a priest. But, he had to admit that it was because he had found so many of those doctrines and dogmas to be illogical that he had given up on his ambitions.

Jeremy reached out for Clarissa's hand. "I'm sure you were part of my first century life," he said. "Perhaps you were part of Joshua's life too?"

"Joshua?" Clarissa said gasping, now even a little incredulous.

"Yes, Joshua," Jeremy continued. "Remember, it's Jesus' Aramaic name." He paused to see what response she would make.

David's fears returned. He saw that image of Clarissa in Jeremy's arms once more and winced. He looked down at the table shaking his head.

"Now, here comes the sixty four thousand dollar question," Jeremy said playfully. "Was this young man I saw, Joseph's or Joshua's child?" He caught David's expression and noted David's fears. He could see that he had taken his thoughts just a little too far. "Forgive me," he continued, "but as you can see this whole business is becoming more and more intriguing."

"It is fascinating," Clarissa admitted, "but it's also frightening. Can you imagine what other people would think if they were ever to find out what we are talking about?"

"Yes, you could be burned at the stake!" David jested. "Not only have you suggested that Jesus might have had a lover in Mary Magdalene, but Jeremy, you've just suggested that they might have had a child!"

"Well, let's take things step by step," Jeremy countered. "Obviously we don't want to shock people who believe in history as it's been presented to them. Who knows, they may be right and we may be wrong. But, we have discovered a great deal about each other this evening and regardless of my last comments, although we have not fully agreed that our paths crossed in the First Century, at least that possibility exists for us to explore."

"It does seem that way," Clarissa agreed.

"Well, I don't know about past lives," David added, "but I do have to admit that some of these ideas are interesting."

"They are, David," Jeremy continued. "There are a lot of interesting thoughts here. We don't have to believe everything we've discussed, but there's no smoke without fire. I believe that we're onto something quite remarkable, but as you say, for now we had better keep this to ourselves."

After a thoughtful silence, Clarissa got up from the table. "I only have ice cream for dessert," she announced. "Would you like it with coffee in the living room?"

"Yes, let's go next door," David answered.

They moved into the living room while Clarissa scooped out the ice cream.

"Would you like another whiskey?" David asked Jeremy.

"Well, if you're pouring," the architect replied.

• • • • • • • •

The brilliant fall ended overnight. A warm, Indian summer's day was followed by a cold, gray one with a rawness that heralded winter. Within two weeks the first snow fell - a light sprinkling, but a taste of what was to come during the next five months. The geese migrated south.

Soon, it was Thanksgiving week. It was time for Clarissa and David to visit his family in New England. It was not a holiday that meant much to Clarissa, but David liked the Yankee celebration. Thanksgiving was his only real chance to be with his family, stressful though that sometimes was. It was very rare that he was ever home for Christmas. The 'Prince Regent' always seemed to want him over that holiday.

After their flight from the 'Twin Cities' to Boston, their drive up to Laconia was pleasant enough. Skies were blue and the young, winter landscape of New England had not yet taken on its blanket of snow. It was crisp and clear. Nearer Laconia, the arms of Lake Winnepesake reflected the sky's lovely, deep tones. The white clapboard of the village churches with their inspiring steeples, assured David that he was nearing his childhood home.

"It's still pretty here," he said as he had one hand on the wheel of their rented 'Buick' and the other clasped in Clarissa's. "It'll be good to see all the family again. We haven't seen them since the wedding."

They passed the familiar, rustic, red barns and silos before skirting the lake into the rural edges of Laconia. There, with views over the farmland, stood the old, white, clapboard house. Passing a large mail-box mounted with the family name in wrought iron, 'The Petersons', the car crunched the driveway gravel and told David's waiting parents that they had arrived.

David's mother opened the front door as he was reaching to ring the bell. Her hair was gray, rolled in a curly style that hadn't changed in fifty years. Dressed in a woolen skirt with a matching sweater, she was carrying a large, teddy bear under one arm. It was a tradition for family members to be greeted by 'Bruno'. Clarissa took the bear, hugged it and passed 'Bruno' to David. Mrs. Peterson then embraced her daughter-in-law. "You must be tired, sweetie," she said. "Come on in, there's coffee and cookies in the kitchen."

"Oh, I'm alright," Clarissa assured her. "David did all the driving."

David's father appeared from the dark shadows of the hall. "Did you have a good run?" he asked.

"Yes, traffic was very light considering the holidays, but we took the turnpike instead of the interstate," David answered.

His father, with a distinguished mop of white hair, and dressed in a slightly crumpled, tweed suit, kissed Clarissa before they all went in to enjoy the coffee in the kitchen. The smell of cooking turkey pervaded the house.

"The girls will be coming in this afternoon," David's mother informed them. "Sarah's bringing the boys and John will join us early tomorrow. He's working at the hospital tonight."

"It'll be so nice to see them all," Clarissa said enthusiastically.

Deep down David knew that Clarissa would rather have been alone with him for the holiday. After all, on December the first he would be sailing from Fort Lauderdale and they wouldn't be together again until half-way through David's upcoming World Cruise. Even that wasn't certain. The Cruise Office still hadn't confirmed that Clarissa was to play on board from Hong Kong to Singapore. They always seemed to leave artists hanging in the air until the last minute. David and Clarissa had long since learned never to take anything for granted in the cruise business. The gulf between Head Office administration and on board management seemed to be an ever-widening chasm.

"How's life on the high seas?" Mr. Peterson asked.

Somehow neither of David's parents had ever really taken his sea-going career seriously. David remembered their discussions in the past. 'When are you going to get yourself a proper job?' his father used to ask, and so often they had upheld Sarah's husband's successful medical career as an example. Sarah lived comfortably as her husband, John, furthered his career. Her boys went to the best schools and they took expensive holidays. Doctor John was an oral surgeon at the Laconia Medical Center. John was everything a hard-working, Yankee son-in-law should be. But he, David, had gone to sea on the 'Love Boat'. His parents were mildly impressed that David had traveled the world, but with his head for figures they would have been far more impressed if his purpose had been business conventions and seminars rather than as the Chief Purser on a cruise ship. David felt that they secretly hoped that after his marriage to Clarissa he would settle down to something a little more permanent. After all, he would now have to support a bohemian artiste, albeit a fairly successful one. The arts lacked permanence to the practical Petersons.

"We had some rough weather in the Mediterranean just before I left," David answered. "But I'm sure they're getting along alright without me, Dad. I'll really be quite sorry to have to go back next week. My vacation's gone by too fast. The fall was wonderful in Minnesota. It's almost more spectacular than here. The view from our house was stunning and it was so warm. The Indian summer held right through October."

"It sure changed in a hurry," Clarissa added with a chuckle.

"Yes. We've had our first snow," David admitted.

"They've had snow up in the White Mountains," Mr. Peterson informed them. "Perhaps if you're not gadding around the world next winter you can come up for skiing with John and the boys."

"Clarissa might like that," David deflected, looking at his wife as he felt the domestic tension beginning to rise. "Clarissa's a better skier than I am."

"There's not too much downhill in the Minneapolis area, but we have wonderful cross-country," Clarissa confirmed.

"Who'd like another cup of coffee?" David's mother announced.

"Oh, yes please," Clarissa accepted, "one more." She pushed her empty cup across the table.

They all filled their cups again before going back out to the car to bring in the bags.

"You're up in the attic room," Mrs. Peterson informed them. "That way you won't be disturbed by all the comings and goings on the second floor. You know what it's like when Simon and Peter are here, and I don't have to remind you about your sister, Dee."

Like an ageing porter at a country inn, Mr. Peterson asked his son if he could help with the suitcases.

"That's alright Dad, we'll manage," David replied. "Thanks anyway."

David and Clarissa hauled the bags past furniture reeking of lemon pledge, up the creaking staircase to the top of the house.

The attic room had its own private bathroom and that counted for a lot when the house was full. It was a cozy room with a magnificent view that looked out across farmland towards the rising, White

Mountains. The rolling hills caught both the sunrise and the sunset. David and Clarissa were glad to be staying away from the crowd.

The bed was a double divan. The furniture was simple. There were throw rugs of native Indian designs covering necessary parts of the wide, pine boards. Two bookcases gave an informal touch. David's old, beaten up, teddy bear from his childhood sat in a small rocker. His mother had arranged two, beautiful, vases of twigs, rose hips and chrysanthemums, adding a touch of color. A small, brass chandelier and two wall sconces with real candles, gave them light.

David held Clarissa in his arms. The room breathed romance.

"That wasn't too bad," he whispered. "They mean well."

"They're lovely," Clarissa acknowledged, looking up at David. "They just live in a different world. We'll have them come out to Minnesota in the summer."

"They would like that," David agreed. "With us away as much as we are, we really should be grateful that we have Sarah, Dee and John to take care of them. We'll do what we can for them."

Clarissa held David in silence for a moment. "I wish I could have been there for Mother," she said at length. "I was never able to say goodbye to her. It never occurred to me that when we left on our honeymoon to drive up to Donegal, it would be the last time I'd see her."

Moist tears glistened in the corner of her eyes.

David patted her back as he held her in his arms. "You can't keep worrying about that, Clara. None of us ever know when our parents are going to die. You know how much she loved you. Remember the note she wrote me. It was as much a note expressing her love for you as it was expressing her approval of me."

Clarissa smiled. "She recognized something special about you," she said. "I wish she would come to me like she visited you."

David blushed. "She will, Clara, but we'd better not talk about those things too much 'round here. I don't think any of the Petersons would understand."

"What do you think they'd make of Jeremy Dyson?" she asked, bursting into laughter.

"I fear they'd recommend he should be locked away. Now promise me, Clara, remember what I've just said. Don't talk about those things here. We Petersons are pretty conventional New England folk."

They started to unpack their things. There was a beautiful smell of old cedar in the wardrobe.

• • • • • • •

D ee was the first to arrive. She brought the usual bag of goodies with her, all sorts of extras for the table which nobody would eat, but which were traditional.

By the time Sarah and the boys arrived, the kitchen had become a hive of activity. Dee seemed to have ten pots cooking at the same time much to her mother's concern.

"We don't need all that!" Mrs. Peterson kept repeating, but she knew that her plea was in vain. Dee always did this and in the end it made a magnificent feast for them, even if it was far too much. David's father kept checking the turkey, basting it in the oven. Steam gave a warm, vaporous feeling to the room.

Clarissa tried to make herself useful helping Dee, but she really didn't know much about New England, kitchen traditions. They giggled a lot until David disturbed them with a shout from the hall.

"They've arrived! Sarah's here!" he announced.

David opened the front door and shouted a greeting from the porch where his father had hung no less than four corn shucks. His mother busied herself lighting candles in all the windows to welcome Sarah and the boys.

"You're already here, David!" Sarah shouted up from the car.

David's nephews jumped out from the back seat.

Peter and Simon were wearing dark, blue parkas and baseball caps. 'That's one good reason not to have children,' David thought to himself as he looked at their caps. If there was one thing that really irritated him, it was the universal practice of children to wear these caps back to front.

"Hi, Uncle David!" Peter squealed as he ran up the path.

"Is Dee here?" Sarah asked. "I don't see her car."

"Hers is in the garage," David explained. "The 'Buick's' our rental."

Peter and Simon ran into the house. Sarah hugged her brother before carrying in a couple of bags. "The boys were so excited you were coming," she said. "Where's Clarissa?"

"She's in the kitchen with Dee."

"Uncle David!" Simon said enthusiastically when they had closed the front door, "I'm in the Junior league!"

"Good, you'll have to tell me all about it," David replied, not having the slightest interest in the Junior league or the world of the sixth grade. School days to him were a dim memory of cold dorm-rooms, games outside in wintry conditions and freezing showers.

His parents came out and hugged their grandchildren. For a moment peace returned as they were all ushered upstairs to their appointed rooms on the second floor. David went back to the kitchen to kiss his bride and chat with Dee.

It was not long before Sarah and the boys came bouncing in and the family chaos began again as Peter and Simon started to sample their Aunt Dee's concoctions. Sarah kissed her sister-in-law. "Hi, Clara, welcome to your first, family Thanksgiving."

"It's great to be here," Clarissa acknowledged. "My goodness, Simon's grown even since the wedding."

Simon grinned sheepishly. He hated these endless comments from relatives about how much he had grown. He changed the subject. "What's it like in Minnesota now? Is it snowy and fun yet?"

"We had some snow, but I think it's all melted now. You like snow?"

"Dad takes us to the mountains to ski," Simon explained.

"You're already skiing?"

"Of course, Aunt Clara. Maybe this winter you'll come with us. Dad says you ski."

Clarissa was trying to help Dee with the vegetables.

"Yes. I know how to ski, but I really prefer to ride horses. I was brought up with horses in Ireland."

"We're getting a pony next summer!" Peter shouted excitedly.

"That's wonderful!" Clarissa exclaimed. "I wish I had a pony in Minnesota."

David's mother came whirling through the kitchen. "I've got to get the dinner ready," she shouted. "Why don't you all go into the den? We must be ready by seven."

"Alright, Mom," Sarah agreed. "Come on! Upstairs again you two! You've got to clean up for dinner."

After Sarah left with the boys, Clarissa looked at David. "I think I'll go up and change too," she said.

David followed her up to the attic room after checking the fires in the living room and den. It had always been his teenage chore and he loved the smell of the burning logs.

Meanwhile his mother had the chance to see that everything was set for the family meal from the candles to the little Thanksgiving gifts that she wanted to place at each setting.

His father poked at the turkey one more time.

David lit the candles in the sconces on either side of their bed and then turned down the light. As Clarissa changed, he saw the naked flesh of her back in the glow of the candles. He felt a warmth in the room and a delight that his family really accepted her, even if their philosophies of life were somewhat different. He was also glad that these visits didn't have to last too long.

As Clarissa slipped into her white dress and shook her hair back over the collar, he walked up to her. "You look lovely, darling," he said as he kissed her.

She felt the roughness of his five o'clock shadow, the result of an early start in Minneapolis in order to catch the seven-thirty morning flight to Boston. She stroked his chin. "You had better shave, my love," she said with an impish grin. "The candlelight exaggerates the growth on your beard."

David shaved and dressed in gray pants and a brown and orange sweater.

"Why are we all having the turkey dinner tonight?" Clarissa asked.

"That's a family tradition. We'll all go out to the Hunt Luncheon at the Country Club tomorrow. They'll expect us to go to church first. Doctor John will probably join us at the church."

"You all go to church on Thanksgiving Day?" Clarissa asked.

"I always forget that this is not really your tradition," David continued. "In New England, which is really where this whole Thanksgiving business started, almost everyone goes to church. It's not a long service. It's a thanksgiving for the harvest. After the pilgrim fathers had survived their first difficult year here they celebrated the harvest and in order to survive they shared their bounty with the Indians in a gesture of peace and goodwill. That's what this is all about."

"Well, I'd better do everything right," Clarissa responded. "If we have to go to church we have to go to church."

"Very good, now if you're ready shall we go down and join the others? Mother likes everything right on time. They're very punctual in this house, at least all except Dee - she's probably still in the shower!"

Clarissa hugged David. "I love you," she said.

They made their way down the creaking staircase to the hall and joined the others now assembled around the television set in the den. The boys were playing video games. David was right. Dee was still missing.

David's mother lit the gold candles in the dining room. The table looked spectacular as it always did. The candelabra were polished. The bon-bon dishes were filled with various nuts and candies. Waxed leaves from the fall foliage trailed down the centerpiece, weaving between dishes and cruets. A little gift, wrapped in paper striped in gold, silver and black bands, was on every sideplate. Three crystal glasses stood as sentinels to the right of each place setting. Large, china service plates, designed in colors that matched the falling leaves, held dainty porringers in which the pumpkin soup would be poured. Gleaming flatware was arranged neatly on either side of them and a lace napkin in a crystal ring gave old-fashioned elegance. All was set upon a starched, white, double-damask tablecloth that David's mother had bought in Ireland when they had gone over for the wedding. It was perfection. "Dinner's ready," Mrs. Peterson shouted to those assembled in the den.

"Dee's not down yet!" Mr. Peterson called back.

"That girl's never ready on time!" her mother exclaimed. "We can't wait more than five minutes! The soup'll get cold!"

"You know Dee's never ready. Now, come on in, relax and have a glass of white wine," Mr. Peterson suggested.

Somewhat agitated, David's mother gave in and joined them.

A few minutes later Dee made her entrance. Her dress was stunning. It was very low-cut and showed her cleavage. It emphasized every curve of her body.

"Wow!" Clarissa whispered in David's ear.

The boys didn't look up. They were still engrossed in their latest 'Nintendo' game.

"Good, you're ready," David's mother said practically, as if she hadn't noticed the sensual beauty of her unmarried daughter. "Now let's go in."

They left their half-finished glasses in the den and followed 'Grandmother' Peterson into the dining room.

"Oh, Mom!" Sarah exclaimed. "You've done it again!"

"It looks even better than last year!" Dee echoed.

"Happy Turkey Day!" they all shouted at once.

The pumpkin soup was ladled out. Roast turkey with all the trimmings followed. Wine flowed, but Clarissa chose to join Simon and Peter with fruit punch. Home-made cheesecake, rich and gooey and loaded with cream, apple pie a la mode or chocolate mousse, completed the fare. There was laughter, merriment, argument and discussion. Most important of all it was a gathering of family. Grandma and Grandpa sat either end of the table proud of their children. Sarah sat next to David and Clarissa. Dee was flanked by her two nephews. Three generations of Petersons were gathered to celebrate another year.

One advantage of the evening feast was the rapid exhaustion that overcame them all. Once the table was cleared and the dishes stashed away in the washer, it was time for bed in order to be ready for more feasting and more strengthening of family ties the next day. David and Clarissa were happy to reach the private world of their attic haven.

"I don't think I want to see turkey again," Clarissa said as she lay down fully-clothed on the bed.

"Well, you had better be prepared," David warned her. "Remember, it's Hunt Luncheon tomorrow."

David lit the candles again and put out the light. A Thanksgiving moon had risen in the night sky and showed the trees in silhouette against the open landscape.

"It's very cozy here," Clarissa admitted.

"I never realized how romantic this old room was," David agreed.

It was not long before they were in each others arms celebrating their own Thanksgiving.

· · · · · · · ·

That night Clarissa's mother came to her. Clarissa really didn't know whether it was in a dream, a trance or in fact. All she knew was that her mother came to her. It was nearly four months since Margaret Corrington had been buried. Clarissa had longed for the time when her mother might visit her. In the romantic setting of the attic room of her Father-in-law's home, it happened.

The room was dark, the candles cold. From the bed Clarissa could clearly see the pale face of the moon outside.

At first Clarissa only heard what sounded like her mother's voice. "You see the moon up above us there?" it seemed to say.

Clarissa stared at the moon. The air began to feel muggy, like a warm night in Minnesota when the mosquitos start to nip. The room faded until it seemed that Clarissa was herself outside. She heard the summer sounds of bullfrogs and crickets. Foreign aromas seemed to fill the air. She had the strangest feeling that she was no longer in New England or even in America.

The sound of her mother's voice drifted back. "Look at the face of the man in the moon. He's smiling at us."

Clarissa felt sure she could see a face in the moon as she stared at the great, white orb and its indented shadows.

The presence continued - "Every day he's there to look after us. Whatever we do and wherever we go, the moon still looks down on us. Can you imagine God's face there in the moon?"

"Yes, Mother!" Clarissa exclaimed.

Then, to her surprise, she heard the voice of a young boy. It didn't sound unlike that of Simon or Peter, but she knew they were not in the attic room.

"I can see a face in the shadows," the child said. "The moon really does have a face. He looks like Joseph when I fall in the mud at the brick kilns. That always makes him laugh." The boy seemed to giggle. "The man in the moon is laughing," he said. "Does that mean God is laughing?"

"Maybe, Joshua," Margaret Corrington's voice answered. "The more you look at it the more real that face becomes. If you shut your eyes and pray you might hear the voice of God calling to you from the moon."

"I'm praying, Mother!" the child's voice exclaimed.

Instinctively Clarissa screwed up her eyes as if in prayer. "I'm praying too!" she shouted, almost waking David who turned towards her, grunted and then fell back into slumber.

"So am I," the stranger with Margaret Corrington's voice said encouragingly. "Once when I was praying in the moonlight at the House of the Virgins, the trees caused the moonlight to flicker. Shafts of light fell all around me and I felt like I could touch the moon. Then I heard him, Joshua. I heard Gabriel, my messenger from God. He spoke to me."

"What did Gabriel say?" the boy asked.

"What did he say?" Clarissa echoed.

"That's when he told me I'd have a baby and that you would be my child. Trembling in the moonlight I felt this strange power. I heard someone crying out to me. It was Gabriel. He told me I would have a child who would be a son of God. You are that child, Joshua. He told me you'd be a Prince of Peace and that you'd be a mighty ruler."

"Mother!" Clarissa shouted, becoming quite frightened by the mysterious voice.

David awoke. "What is it Clara?"

"It's Mother!" Clarissa screamed.

David reached for her. She was warm and sweating, although the attic room was cold with the chill of the night. Clarissa had kicked off the bed covers from her side and was sitting up naked.

"You're so warm," David said with concern as he laid her gently down and pulled the covers up around her again.

"It is warm, David. Can't you hear the bullfrogs and the crickets?" she said, dazed.

David was puzzled. "No, of course not! It's much too cold for the summer, night sounds - besides, the window's closed. It's double-glazed!"

"Where are we?" Clarissa asked as she calmed down.

"At Mother and Father's place. We're in Laconia, Clara. It's Thanksgiving!"

"I wasn't in Laconia," she said. "I was somewhere completely different. It was hot and muggy and the stars and the moon were extra bright. I don't know where I was, David. All I know for certain is mother was there. She was talking to me."

"To me as well?"

"No, David. You weren't there. She was talking to me and a boy named 'Joshua'."

"Who was Joshua?" David asked. "Didn't Jeremy say that was Jesus' real name?" He chuckled before she could reply. "I suspect that you've just had a bad dream. But if you insist that you heard your mother, remember how she wrote that she would be with us in the light of Christos."

"I think she was, David, but somehow I was there too. Mother was telling Joshua how God was up in the moon and how if you prayed and believed in God's presence you could hear his messages coming from the moon. Then she said something very curious to us both."

"You and me or you and Joshua?" David interjected.

"Joshua and me," Clarissa explained. "She said this man Gabriel told her she was going to have a baby and that her child would be a son of God, a Prince of Peace and a mighty ruler."

"That sounds like Jesus to me," David said skeptically. "I think you've been dreaming about that old Bible story of the Virgin Mary and the angel Gabriel."

"It wasn't exactly Mother's voice, David. Yet, from hearing it, I know it was Mother. Perhaps it was the Virgin Mary. Perhaps Mother's soul was once incarnated in Jesus' mother."

"You mustn't keep harping on about your mother, Clara. Remember it's very rare for any of us to experience communication with our loved ones after they've gone. It was exceptional if I saw her spirit in Ireland. These things don't happen often."

"But I did hear her. I know it was her, even though she sounded different," Clarissa insisted.

"It doesn't really matter," David said trying to soothe her and at the same time wanting to get back to sleep and not become involved in a deep, philosophical discussion. "Your mother prepared herself for death. She was ready to die. She told you so. She died knowing that you were happy and she saw how happy we are together. Her life's task was complete. She was ready to go to her other worlds. That's where she is."

Clarissa snuggled up to David. She felt cold now. The balm in which she had thought she had heard her mother's voice seemed to have vanished and she realized that she was very much in the attic room.

David kissed her. "I love you Clara. Don't worry, it was just a dream. Let's get some sleep."

David hadn't slept long when he too felt Margaret Corrington's presence. Like Clarissa, at first he heard her voice, then on waking, thought he saw her standing by the window, her face illumined by the light of the moon.

"I am so very, very happy," the apparition-like figure said, "to have known you and to know that Clarissa has found you. I am very happy for you both. I will not be in this world much longer as I am ready to go into the other worlds, but I now know that I shall do so in the knowledge that you and Clarissa will be together in the light of Christos."

The words echoed the note that Clarissa's mother had given to him when they had said goodbye the last time he had seen her. This time they were not written, but mystically felt.

David stared at the ethereal figure. His mother-in-law's face was quite clear now, younger than he remembered her, but the rest of her body was like a fluorescent pillar in the moonlight. Then he looked at Clarissa. Shaking, he nudged her. He pointed at the window.

Clarissa rubbed the sleep from her eyes.

"Can you see your mother?" David whispered.

"Where?"

"Over by the window. Standing in the moonlight."

"No. What do you mean?" Clarissa asked sleepily. The open, lace curtain hanging below the valance, looked pale-blue in the moonlight - like the Virgin's robe. "There's nobody there," she said a little frightened.

"Your mother was there," David insisted. "She spoke to me. She told me exactly what she wrote in that note. I heard her voice. She spoke to me in that lilting, Irish accent of hers."

"You really thought Mother was here?" Clarissa asked.

"Yes, Clara. I swear I heard your mother's voice and in the moonlight I swear that I saw her face. Maybe her face was my imagination, but the voice was not."

"Oh, my God!"

They held each other in fearful silence.

"Do you think these things are happening just because we are in an old house," Clarissa said at length. "You saw mother at the house in Tipperary. And now, here we are in your parents' nineteenth century home. Maybe that's why we don't experience these things in Minnesota. Our house isn't old enough." She stared at the window and the pallid drapes in the moonlight. "Maybe it's all an illusion. Let's face it, those drapes do look like the Virgin Mary's robe."

"What about Jeremy?" David reminded her. "I don't think we are dealing with a ghost story here. There is some strange interconnecting bond between us all that seems to move from the present back two thousand years to a first century past."

"You really are beginning to believe in past lives, aren't you?" Clarissa said with surprise.

"Maybe there's something to it, but it's not something that I can explain," David answered.

Eventually they were both lulled back into sleep. It was light when they awoke. They could hear the others on the floor below. The boys seemed to be running around. The sun was just rising to illuminate another, crisp, late-fall day. The White Mountains looked sharp and clear.

"We had better go down for breakfast," Clarissa suggested. "You know how they are about meal times."

"We can go down in our robes," David advised her. "Give me five minutes to shave."

At the breakfast table they revealed nothing of their disturbed night when David's mother asked how they had slept.

"Very well," Clarissa replied. "Like a log. It's so peaceful here."

• • • • • • • •

D r. John Bishop climbed out of his new 'BMW' and joined them in front of the church as they had anticipated. David took a good look at his brother-in-law who was considered to be such a very model of success. He wore an expensive suit and his hair looked like it had been permed in little, crinkly waves. His hands were the expressive hands of a surgeon. He greeted everyone formally. Even the boys who had been complaining bitterly about having to wear jackets and ties to go to church, were silenced in his presence. The family moved into the fashionable Episcopal church of St. George in downtown Laconia and took their place in their customary pew.

The Rector's wife walked out from the vestry and seeing the assembled Petersons stepped over in their direction.

"Good Morning!" she said rather artificially. "Happy Thanksgiving!"

"Happy Turkey Day!" Simon blurted out to the chagrin of his father and grandparents.

"This must be Clarissa," the Rector's wife concluded, as she stretched forth a gloved hand.

"Nice to meet you," Clarissa replied.

"I was so sorry to hear about your mother."

"Thank you - it was a deep shock," Clarissa acknowledged, wondering whether all Laconia knew of her mother's death.

The Rector's wife then moved on to smile politely at others before taking her place in the front pew on the right hand side.

At length a bell rang and the choir, dressed in elaborate robes, came in from the back of the church, singing, "We ploughed the fields and scattered the good seed on the land." Everyone stood, and choir and clergy processed to the sanctuary to start the Thanksgiving Day service.

Clarissa hadn't been to church since her mother's funeral and rarely had attended before that since she had gone to live in America. But in her childhood, church attendance had been a regular feature of Anglo-Irish life. In those days there had been a blind continuity to the Church of Ireland largely supported by the Irish landed gentry in antithesis to the Roman Catholic majority. Church-going had been more a social obligation than a spiritual exercise. But certain Bible stories had stuck with Clarissa, including those about Mary Magdalene. In more recent years Clarissa had strayed from conventional Christian thought. She had been attracted to various spiritual paths along her musical journey and, like David, now found the rigid doctrines of Christianity somewhat illogical in the face of the late twentieth century world. Mary Magdalene was a sort of legendary heroine, who had appeared as a symbol of the female goddess in several of these paths.

It had been the attraction of the robes of the choir and clergy that had drawn David, as a child, to the thought of becoming a priest. Nowadays, David rarely attended church. He never went to the shipboard services on the 'Prince Regent'. These annual, family get-togethers were about as close as he came to his early Episcopal dreams. Intellect had overcome his emotions. But he knew the American hymn tunes far better than Clarissa, who was quite lost.

During the service they found that as the ritual droned on they looked around just as much as Simon and Peter, who were totally bored by the whole affair. In fact, at times Clarissa caught Simon's eye and the boy began to giggle and pull faces, knowing that neither his mother nor grandmother were watching. But, during the reading of the scripture from a great, brass eagle whose wings supported the Holy Bible, something caught Clarissa's attention.

"There, they made him a supper," the Rector read, "and Martha served, but Lazarus was one of those who sat at the table with him."

Clarissa caught the words 'and Martha served'. She nudged David. "Martha Healey was the name of Mother's maid at Ballyporeen," she whispered in his ear.

The priest read on. "Then Mary took a pound of very costly oil of spikenard, anointed the feet of Jesus, and wiped his feet with her hair. And the house was filled with the fragrance of the oil. But one of his disciples, Judas Iscariot, who would betray him, said, 'Why was this fragrant oil not sold for three hundred denarii and given to the poor?'"

After that Clarissa lost track of what the priest was saying. She thought about Mary Magdalene and her special friendship with Jesus.

When the Rector went up into the pulpit to preach, he picked up on the scriptural reading. This momentarily attracted Clarissa's attention again.

"Thanksgiving is a time for traditional feasting," the white-haired clergyman stated. "We will no doubt all enjoy a turkey dinner today." A ripple of laughter went through the congregation. "We must remember, however, that it is not the feast that counts. Martha, who busied herself too much in preparation for the feast, was rebuked by Jesus for caring too much about unnecessary details, whereas her sister Mary, who did little to contribute to the household needs, but rather sat in the parlor listening to the Lord and acknowledged him by anointing him with precious oil, was praised. What are we really thankful for?" The Rector paused and looked down from the pulpit through his half-glasses as if demanding attention from his parishioners.

"We are thankful that we have acknowledged our Lord and that in his grace we are brought to salvation. We share in feasting to celebrate this truth, that Jesus is Lord. It is more important that we recognize that Jesus is our savior than that we should celebrate the reality of our everyday necessities. Jesus rebuked Judas because Iscariot criticized Mary for anointing the Lord with precious oil, saying it could have been sold to raise money for the poor. It was no doubt worth a lot of money - three hundred denarii we are told. As one denarius was considered to be a full day's wage for a working man in Jesus' time, this ointment constituted three hundred working days of wealth. Yet despite this seeming waste, our Lord said to Judas' objection, 'the poor you will always have with you, but you will not always have me, your savior, your Lord.' O, how true, my friends. For all of us who live well on the shores of Lake Winnepesake here in our beautiful State of New Hampshire, there will always be turkey, venison, sweet potato pie and roasted chestnuts, but will there always be Jesus in our lives as our savior and Lord?"

At this point in the sermon, Clarissa tuned out. Her imagination became caught up not in the Rector's words, but in the stained-glass windows, and in particular to one in the transept to her right. It depicted Jesus in an old, brown smock, somewhat similar to that worn by poor farmers in the time of the pilgrim fathers. On his head, surrounded by the glow of his halo, was a peasant's hat. In his hand he held a gardener's spade. Kneeling in front of this unusual rendering of the Christ, was a saintly-looking, young woman, her halo adjusted to the tilt of her adoring face. The caption below read in Victorian Gothic script, 'Mary Magdalene sees Jesus in the Garden.'

Clarissa stared at the window, fascinated by its image. She saw in the kindly face of the gardener a serenity that was more real than the usual saintly image that the Church portrayed. Mary Magdalene looked typical enough, bearing no resemblance to the sinner that she had once been, but this face of Christ was different, more human, altogether one of us. She nudged David again and got him to look at the window as the monotonous voice of the Rector droned on from the pulpit. "Look what it says," she whispered.

"Mary Magdalene?"

"Yes, David, that's 'Maria'."

David gave her one of his looks.

The sermon concluded and they were all asked to stand and sing another hymn. David sang especially heartily and slightly off key. He knew this would attract Clarissa's attention and hoped it would take her mind off this 'Maria' obsession.

When the service ended the festive aspect of Thanksgiving Day began. There were shouts of surprise as teenagers and college kids saw their friends home for the break. Children ran around shouting "Happy Turkey Day!" Parents proudly presented their families to one another, while grandparents beamed with pride. Everyone was dressed in their best and many of them were heading in the same direction, the Hunt Luncheon at the Country Club.

It was a splendid feast. The Rector's words were quickly lost as the Grand Buffet was admired. The members were greeted with a bowl of punch and a caldron of steaming, pumpkin soup. There were butter sculptures, ice-carvings, decorated turkeys and New England hams, whole salmon that revealed succulent, pink flesh, chaffing dishes of venison, vegetables and sweet potato pie. Assorted breads tumbled down from a cornucopia amid sheaths of wheat and a filigree of fall foliage. Then, there were the desserts. There was apple pie, pumpkin pie, New York cheesecake. There were assorted ice creams, sherberts and mousses amidst chocolate cookies, chocolate cakes and chocolate sauce. Marzipan figures dodged between the dishes like gnomes, and plates, between folded napkins, rose up like pagodas.

"They've excelled themselves this year. It's better than ever," Mrs. Peterson observed.

"I'll bet you don't often see buffets like this on your ship?" Doctor John sniped at his brother-in-law.

"Well, almost," David replied. "It's one of the features of cruise ships, but I can't say I get to them too often. It's more likely to be sandwiches in the Purser's Office."

"Watching your waistline, eh?" John Bishop chuckled. "How's Clarissa's cooking? Lots of potatoes and Irish stew I suspect - wonderful, unwholesome, hearty food. It goes well with the skiing. You should come up to the lodge with us later this winter. I hear Clarissa's an excellent skier."

"Mostly cross-country these days," Clarissa replied, realizing that she needed to rescue David from his overbearing relative. "We don't have much downhill in Minnesota!"

"I guess not," Doctor John acknowledged. "That Indian country's flat as a pancake."

Simon grabbed Clarissa's hand. "I want to sit next to you!" he shouted.

"Me too!" Peter echoed.

"The boys have taken quite a fancy to you Clarissa," John Bishop said with approval. He nodded towards the center of the room. "We always have that big table in the middle."

Doctor John joined Sarah as they set out on the journey down the buffet table, piling up their plates. The boys joined Clarissa, picking out their favorite items. Dee used the time to chat alone with her brother.

"We really love Clarissa," she said, "but we were so sorry to hear about her mother. That was terrible - so soon after the wedding! Clarissa's mom looked so healthy and happy when we were in Ireland."

"It was a shock to us both," David agreed. "I guess Clara's mother just wanted to go. Apparently she went out to the stables before she died. The last thing she did was talk to her horses. Clara's convinced that her mother knew she was going to die. She loved those horses and she couldn't go without telling them goodbye. She came in, sat in a chair in the kitchen and passed on."

"What a way to go, but still it must have been a shock to poor Clarissa."

"It was, but in many ways it cemented our marriage. Her family were really pleased that I was able to get away from the 'Prince Regent' in time for the funeral. If my schedule had been different I couldn't have made it, but we were coming into Nassau and the timing was perfect. I'm glad I was able to be there. Clara had argued with her mother just the day before it happened and she has this terrible fear that she caused her to go. I've done my best to reassure her that wasn't the case, but it haunts her."

"Of course not," Dee said reassuringly. "Clarissa's being far too sensitive."

"Actually, Mrs. Corrington was very happy about our marriage," David explained. "She gave me the strangest note when we left you all in Tipperary to drive up to Donegal. She wrote how pleased she was that Clara had found me and that she would soon be passing on into the 'other worlds' as she called it. She concluded by saying she was going to pass on knowing that Clara and I were in the light of Christos."

"You mean the light of Christ? Oh, David! How moving!" Dee exclaimed.

"Well, yes. She knew, Dee. She knew that she was going to die. Once Clara and I were married, she was ready to go."

At this point the others returned to the table with their plates piled high.

"Yum, that turkey looks good," Dee said to her nephew.

"Yeah!" Simon replied, "but I need to save room for the chocolate!"

Clarissa and Peter were busy discussing important things like monsters from outer space. Dee and David collected plates so they could help themselves to the buffet.

• • • • • • • •

L ater in the afternoon, when the family had assembled in front of the television set to watch the game, David and Clarissa took a walk in the fields.

"The boys are quite sweet when you talk to them individually," Clarissa noted. "It's just when they get into this sports hero bit that I find it hard. Why do they have to wear those stupid, baseball caps back to front?"

David laughed. "I have to agree with you," he said. "I can't stand those baseball caps!"

They held each other in the weak afternoon sun, before continuing their walk, skirting the residue of a harvested corn field and out into a meadow. When they looked back, they could see the sparkling waters of the lake and the white, clapboard house on the edge of town peering through the trees of the garden. The window of the attic room caught the rays of the lowering sun.

"You know something, David," Clarissa said, "I had the strangest feeling in church today. It seemed that everything was about Mary Magdalene. They read about Mary. The priest preached about Mary and then I saw Mary Magdalene in that stained-glass window."

David resented this interference in their harmonious mood. Just when he felt really close to Clarissa she returned to this past life nonsense. "That's not true," he replied triumphantly. "The reading was about Martha's sister Mary - it wasn't about Mary Magdalene."

"But what about the precious oil?" Clarissa insisted.

David sighed. "What about it?"

"I always thought it was Mary Magdalene who anointed Jesus with the precious oil and wiped his feet with her hair."

"That's not what they read in church today," David repeated. "You may be right, but it was not that passage."

"But it's one of those Bible stories you learn about as a child. Somehow it's always stuck in my memory," Clarissa continued. "Mary Magdalene was a sinner, whatever that means. They tried to stone her.

Jesus stopped them. He rescued her, which led to Mary Magdalene pouring precious oil over his head in grateful thanks before washing his feet with her tears. It makes a good story. It sounds like a fairy tale."

David stopped walking and let go of Clarissa's hand. "You're really serious about this Mary Magdalene thing, aren't you? All because that 'damned Roman soldier' thought you were Maria."

"Well it is rather strange that everything in church today was about Mary Magdalene. I suppose you'd say that was just a coincidence."

"Alright, let's see where that story comes in the Bible," David suggested begrudgingly. "We'll look it up."

"There was more to the fairy tale if I remember rightly," Clarissa continued. "Mary Magdalene went to the cemetery early on Easter Sunday and found Jesus' tomb empty. She saw a gardener and asked the man where they had taken Jesus' body. Then, she realized that the gardener was Jesus risen from the dead. That was the story in the stained-glass window."

"Yes, you're right. It's a dramatic story. It would make a good children's book, and that's all!" David asserted.

"But what if it's true?" Clarissa asked, looking up at David nervously, knowing how much her obsession had upset him. "What if I was Mary Magdalene in a past life? Then this would be my story."

David shook his head. "You're so gullible, Clara." They stared at the fading sun. At length he took her hand. He changed the subject. "Sarah, Dee and I used to play in these fields when we were growing up. We used to fly kites here and hide in the corn."

"I'm so glad you like the simplicity and wonder of nature," Clarissa said, warmly hoping to bridge the emotional strain between them. "It's one of the things I love about you most. I'm so glad that we have our garden in Minnesota. It's such a joy to see you working in the garden."

David grinned. "It can't be all bad to work in a garden," he said, "at least not if the Christ really was the gardener at the tomb. I'm sorry, I shouldn't have got so upset."

They laughed, then kissed.

"We'd better go back in to the others," Clarissa whispered. "I suppose we'll have to eat cold turkey tonight. This feasting really is too much for me."

"Mother loves it," David said as they turned to walk back. "Now, no mention of 'Maria' at the house."

"Agreed," Clarissa confirmed.

• • • • • • • •

D inner was casual, but it was cold turkey. It was right after dinner as they were washing up in the kitchen that David asked if there was a Bible in the house.

"Of course," his father said, although it took the old man a little while to find it.

When Mr. Peterson returned from the den with a 'King James' version that looked like it had been in the family for generations, he expressed his curiosity. "What do you want with the Bible?" he asked.

"I want to check on the passage of scripture that the Rector read this morning," David replied. "There seems to be some confusion between the story of Mary and Martha and that of Mary Magdalene."

"I don't recall Mary Magdalene coming in today's reading," David's mother chimed in.

"No Mother, that's exactly what I want to check out. I think there are two stories about a woman pouring precious oil over Jesus. Do you remember which gospel the Rector read from today?"

"Since when have you become so interested in scripture?" his mother continued. "Is this Clarissa's influence?"

Dee laughed when she heard them discuss the scripture in this way. "Have you forgotten, Mom? When David was a boy he wanted to be a priest."

"Yes, but that soon passed," Mrs. Peterson answered cynically. "I think it was St. John. If you really want to know, let me get the service sheet."

David's mother went out into the hall and found the sheet in her coat pocket. "St. John chapter twelve, verses one to eight," she said as she returned.

"I noticed a beautiful window in your church today that was dedicated to Mary Magdalene. That's what made me curious," Clarissa explained.

"Well, the Bible should be able to reveal the truth," Mrs. Peterson agreed confidently. "Let us know what you find out. Right now, I suggest we all go back into the den for coffee."

David looked at Clarissa. Dutifully they obeyed.

It was not until they were alone in the attic room that they could begin their research. Fortunately, the Bible David's father had found was one of those with extensive margin notes. It was easy to make cross-references.

"Mother said this morning's reading was from St. John didn't she?" David asked as he thumbed through the pages while Clara was in the bathroom. "It might take me a while to find it because I can't remember what chapter she said."

"Twelve!" Clara shouted back through the steam.

David looked it up. "Jesus! You're right! What a memory!" he replied, when he found the passage.

Clarissa stood dripping in the doorway with a towel around her pink body. "I remember pouring that sweet-smelling oil from a jar," she said mysteriously. "David, I know I poured it over Jesus' head. It was the oil that a blind man gave me because I helped him get to Jesus to be cured."

David was startled by this sudden revelation. "Now ... wait a minute," he stammered. "When did you dream about that?"

"I didn't. It's just something I know. I don't think I knew it until today, but I swear to you I know it now."

"It sounds nonsense to me," David suggested.

"No David. It's the truth. I was given a jar of precious ointment in this bazaar by a blind man who Jesus tried to cure. I helped the blind man, so he asked me to select a gift from this old merchant in gratitude. My boy selected the jar because he liked the smell."

"Your boy?"

"Yes, my child. The young man Jeremy Dyson dreamed about. He looked like Simon," Clarissa revealed. "He had the same, fun-filled eyes and was curious about everything. He was with me all the time I was with Joshua."

David could not deny that the revelations were interesting. He began to feel that he was part of some strange, clairvoyant scene. "Joshua ... Clara?" he noted. "You've never called Jesus 'Joshua' before. Isn't that the name Jeremy Dyson always gives to Jesus?" He hesitated. "Maybe you are onto something. Can you remember the name of the blind man?"

"Bartholomew," Clarissa answered. "I don't think that's right, but it was something like that."

"Bartholomew was one of the apostles."

"No, this man wasn't one of Joshua's regular followers. He was only with us a few days until he could see again. Maybe the name will come to me. It was similar to Bartholomew."

Clarissa leaned against the bathroom door frame, but her eyes looked far away as if she really had gone into some sort of a trance.

"What was the boy's name?" David asked, beginning to feel like a psychiatrist exploring her mind.

"Marcus. My son Marcus," Clarissa said clearly.

David put the Bible down and walked over to Clarissa. He believed her, but he couldn't deny that he was scared. This whole, past life revelation was becoming too real to be just academic discussion. "Clara darling, are you alright?" he asked as he took her in his arms."

Clarissa shook as if woken from a dream.

"What ... ?" she stammered. "David, you startled me."

He felt her warm body, still moist from the bath. Clarissa was real. "I love you," he said, kissing her gently. "You frightened me, Clara. You were in some sort of a trance."

"I was?"

"Yes, you told me about your son, Marcus, and this blind man who gave you the precious oil which you used to anoint Jesus."

"Yes, it's true, David. I did pour oil over Jesus' head."

"Alright, 'Maria', I believe you," David said. "Dry yourself off and let's talk about this." He picked the Bible up again. "Let's see if we can pinpoint your identity."

After Clarissa had dried and put on her satin nightshirt, they sat up in the bed. Candles burned in the two sconces. The bright, full moon was again looking in through the attic window.

"St. John chapter twelve," David said. "Here it is."

He glanced at the passage that the Rector had read to them. "It doesn't say anything about Mary Magdalene here," he admitted. "Just as I said, this is a story about Mary, Martha's sister. But let me see if there's a cross-reference to the story about the precious oil."

There was a reference - St. Luke, chapter seven, verses thirty seven and thirty eight. David looked them up.

"Here it is!" he announced with glee, proud of his new-found ability to find his way around the Bible. " 'And, behold, a woman in the city, which was a sinner, when she knew that Jesus sat to eat in the Pharisee's house, brought an alabaster box of ointment, and stood at his feet behind him weeping, and began to wash his feet with tears, and did wipe them with the hairs of her head, and kissed his feet, and anointed them with the ointment.' "

"That's it!" Clarissa agreed.

"It might be, but it doesn't say that this sinner was Mary Magdalene and you keep saying you anointed Jesus' head, not his feet."

"I know it was!" Clarissa insisted.

As David glanced further down the same page the name of Mary Magdalene jumped out at him. It was in the next chapter. "Wait a minute, Clara, you may be right!" he said with surprise. "Right after this story about the sinner and the ointment, it says this. 'And it came to pass afterward, that he went throughout every city and village, preaching and showing glad tidings of the kingdom of God: and the twelve were with him, and certain women, which had been healed of evil spirits and infirmities, Mary called Magdalene, out of whom went seven devils, and Joanna the wife of Chuza, Herod's steward, and Susanna and many others, which ministered unto him of their substance.'"

David closed the Bible and put it on the bedside table. In the candlelight he cuddled Clarissa under the covers. "It might have been you as 'Maria'," he acknowledged. "There are two stories in the Bible about precious oil being used to anoint Jesus. If you could only be certain of this blind man's name and tell me something about your son Marcus, maybe I could find out more. Perhaps Mother's right after all. The Bible will reveal the truth."

After they had lain together for a while, David blew out the candles and they slept.

• • • • • • • •

David and Clarissa had to leave on Friday because Clarissa was to play a concert in Minneapolis on Saturday evening. Doctor John, Sarah, the boys and Dee were all staying through the weekend. They were going to drive up to the mountains.

Clarissa hugged Simon and Peter as they gathered in the hall to say farewell. She had a natural affinity with children even if she was not over-anxious to start her own family. David and Clarissa had discussed this many times and had expressed the opinion to each other that it is easier to borrow other peoples' kids.

"When will you come again?" Simon asked, looking up at his Aunt Clara through wide, innocent eyes.

"Probably in the spring," she answered, mesmerized by the child. Clarissa hadn't realized until she had been alone with David the day before, that something deep within her drew her towards his nephew in a very, intimate way. 'Are you Marcus?' she thought. "Next time we'll go to the mountains with you and maybe we can ski together."

"We'll race you!" Simon shouted. "Dad's going to take us on the big mountain this winter."

"That's right," Doctor John confirmed as he came to politely see them off. "It's been wonderful having you with us for the family Thanksgiving. I hope you'll come back east more often. It must get a little isolated out in your Indian territory."

"It's beautiful in the 'Land o' Lakes'," Clarissa reminded him. "Maybe Simon and Peter would like to visit us out there some time in the summer."

Doctor John looked thoughtful. "That could be great fun," he acknowledged without committal. "Maybe we can fit it in."

"I'll come!" Simon shrieked.

David's mother had Bruno the bear under one arm. "Have a good concert tomorrow," she said as she and the bear hugged her daughter-in-law. "I only wish we could hear you, but it's so far away."

Clarissa hugged Bruno. "Be a good bear," she said before joining David in their car. As they drove off, they could see the family standing at the driveway entrance, Mrs. Peterson waving Bruno's arm to say goodbye.

"They love you, Clara," David said triumphantly, once they were out of sight. "You've passed the test."

"My mother and brothers loved you too," Clarissa responded. "They couldn't believe that you came over to Ireland for Mother's funeral. That was so special."

"Our lives and goals are very different to theirs," David admitted, "but we owe them a great deal. I know it was tight with your concert tomorrow, but thanks so much for coming with me for this annual Thanksgiving fiasco. It meant so much to them."

"It was wonderful," Clarissa replied. "You don't have to thank me. I found it all fascinating. I got to know them so much better, especially Simon. We just ate too much."

They drove in silence for a while as David made his way out from Laconia towards the interstate down to Concord and Boston. It was another, crisp, sunny day.

"You know something," Clarissa said at length. "I really think we were meant to be there. We had such extraordinary experiences over the past three days."

"True," David agreed. "I wonder what Jeremy will make of them!"

"Those experiences with my mother were so real. It gives me new hope. There is some tangible relationship with our loved ones after death."

"Maybe it's more than that, Clara. Your mother appears to be very much a part of these strange experiences we are going through. You all seemed to know each other in the time of Jesus!"

"Yes," Clarissa agreed, "including Simon. I just know that Simon was my child in those days. I know he was Marcus."

"Despite his baseball cap?" David asked, looking at Clarissa in the car with an impish grin.

"That bothers you even more than it bothers me. You've got to admit that there is something special about that boy when he looks up at you from those great, blue, saucer-like eyes."

"Yes, you begin to worry what he's got up his sleeve to taunt you with next," David suggested.

They laughed.

Three hours later they were back on a 'Northwest Airlines' flight home to Minnesota.

"I wish I could remember the name of that blind man," Clarissa said, as David began to doze.

"What blind man?" he grunted, not really wishing to be disturbed.

"The one who gave Mary Magdalene the oil."

"It'll come to you; now, let's take a nap."

Clarissa made herself as comfortable as possible. She closed her eyes. Then, in a flash it did come to her. She sat up. "Bartimaeus!" she exclaimed.

"What!" David said, as her sudden movement disturbed him again.

"Bartimaeus! I knew it would come to me!" Clarissa continued excitedly. "The blind man's name was Bartimaeus!"

• • • • • • • •

Gray skies and a cold wind welcomed Clarissa and David back to the Midwest. Winter was definitely settling in.

"Maybe it's not such a bad thing that we'll be away much of the coming months," David admitted as he struggled with the suitcases.

Although the house was nice and warm inside, David lit a fire in the big, stone fireplace of their living room. Soon logs were cheerfully blazing.

"What shall I get us?" Clarissa asked as she looked in the refrigerator. "We have a few tomatoes. I could heat up a can of soup and add them with some basil. You usually like that."

"Sounds fine!" David shouted from the living room. "Let's have it in front of the fire."

When the soup was ready, Clarissa carried it through in two, steaming bowls. It tasted good.

"Do you think we should share our recent discoveries with Jeremy before you go back to the ship?" Clarissa asked. "You only have a week."

"Yes, I think we should. I imagine he'll be most interested. I have to leave Thursday, so early in the week would be best."

"I'll give him a call and set something up," Clarissa agreed. "And then after that, David, I must practice. I haven't touched a piano in five days and I have to play tomorrow night."

David chuckled. "I don't know how you get away with it, Clara. You hardly ever practice."

"I know. I've simply got to. You must make sure I do."

Clarissa went over to the phone. She shuffled through a bunch of papers and found Jeremy Dyson's number, dialed it and waited.

A voice answered.

"Jeremy! This is Clara. We've just got back. Did you have a good Thanksgiving?"

There was a brief pause as Jeremy explained how he had spent his 'Turkey Day'.

"Sounds great!" Clarissa replied. "We had a good time at David's parents. We ate too much and it was a lot of traveling. But it was very revealing. Both of us had some strange experiences there. We thought we could share them with you over dinner. What do you like, Chinese, Indian, Thai, or ... ?"

Jeremy went for the Chinese.

"Do you know the 'Two Pandas' out at Ridgedale?" Clarissa asked. He did.

"Good. We'll meet you there on Monday at seven-thirty. I'm going to have to run now and practice for this tedious concert tomorrow. We'll see you Monday. It should be interesting."

Clarissa finished her farewell and hung up.

"I'll wash up!" David shouted. "You start practicing."

Soon the strains of Chopin's 'Etudes', intermingled with selections of Rachmaninoff and Listz, wafted through the house. David picked up Ludwig's 'Napoleon' which he had started reading before Thanksgiving, and settled down in a comfortable armchair by the fireplace. He hadn't read more than a page before he nodded off.

• • • • • • • •

The concert went well and the matrons among the patrons of the Minneapolis Orchestra were all over Clarissa.

"I wish you would play here more often. It's so hard to get artists of your quality," a well-dressed woman from Stillwater said as she waylaid Clarissa outside her dressing room.

'Why don't you invite me more often?' Clarissa thought, but smiling politely, answered her positively. "It was such a pleasure to play with the orchestra again. They are the best."

"You and your husband are going to join the committee for supper now, aren't you?" the woman insisted.

"That would be lovely," Clarissa agreed. "It's so kind of you all. Usually after concerts we have to search for 'McDonalds' or 'Truckstops of America'. They are the only places still open, but the food is just not what you want after a concert."

The ladies of the Committee had gone to a lot of trouble. A magnificent spread had been prepared at a house in a fashionable, old part of town not too far from the Concert Hall. It looked like Thanksgiving all over again.

"I think they've all pooled their turkey leftovers," David whispered in Clarissa's ear as they took plates and started to attack the buffet.

They had just about taken their fill when Richard and Anna sought them out.

"Clarissa! You were magnificent!" Anna praised.

Richard was smiling magnanimously. "Good evening, David. You're still home?"

"Yes, until Thursday."

"Clarissa gave a tremendous performance," Richard continued echoing his wife's accolade. "It's so wonderful to have artists of her stature here in Minneapolis."

"She is exceptional," David agreed, noting that Clarissa was now surrounded by a knot of admirers whom Anna seemed to be trying to impress with her intimate knowledge of the musical scores Clarissa had recently performed.

"I ran into Jeremy Dyson over Thanksgiving," Richard continued. "He told me he'd been over at your place. I'm glad you like him. I think he adds a lot to our community. He's a great architect."

"He's interesting," David replied cautiously.

Others joined them and Clarissa and David tried to balance plates and eat while politely answering a barrage of inane questions.

Then, the ultimate moment came. The Chairman of the Orchestra Committee asked Clarissa to play.

Exhausted, Clarissa obliged.

There were shouts of 'Bravo!' after a rendering of Debussy's 'Clair de Lune'. Then, the guests started to leave and finally Clarissa and David could return home.

• • • • • • •

David and Clarissa arrived early at the 'Two Pandas' restaurant. They wanted to be sure that they would be there ahead of Jeremy Dyson. The place was almost empty. Jimmy Wan, the proprietor, showed them to a nice table just below a large tank of tropical fish.

"You wan to wait for your flend come," Mr. Wan said.

"That would be nice," Clarissa agreed.

"Meantime, I bling you tea?"

"Wonderful."

In a moment a Vietnamese waitress came over with a pot of green tea.

About five minutes later Jeremy arrived.

David stood up. "We're over here!" he shouted.

Jeremy joined them. "We're so glad you could make it," Clarissa said. "We have so many things we want to discuss with you. But first things first. Can we get you a drink?"

"It looks like you have green tea there," Jeremy noted.

"Yes. Would you like one?"

"I'd rather have a scotch on the rocks," he answered honestly.

The Vietnamese waitress came back, took the order for Jeremy's scotch and handed them all menus.

For a moment the three of them thumbed through the several pages of Chinese dishes.

When the girl returned with Jeremy's scotch, she took their order. As she collected up the menus, Clarissa asked her if she could bring them her favorite sauce. The waitress smiled. "I know - special sauce."

"Well, what's this exciting revelation you have for me?" Jeremy asked, leaning back expansively in his chair and watching the tropical fish.

Clarissa looked at David as if to ask who should start the discussion.

"Clara thinks she had some more past life experiences when we were in New Hampshire," David said, taking the initiative.

"Actually, we both did," Clarissa continued.

"More first century experiences?"

"Yes, Jeremy. It all started when I saw my mother."

Jeremy turned his attention from the fish tank to Clarissa. "You saw your mother in the astral?" he asked.

"Well, not exactly, Jeremy. I heard her voice and in my dream I saw her as a much younger person whom I took to be Miriam."

"Joshua's mother?"

"Probably. She was talking to Joshua. It was a cold, frosty night in New Hampshire, but the moon was full. In my dream I saw the same moon, but it felt hot and muggy and I could hear the night sounds of crickets and bullfrogs and smell the aromas of the Middle East. I felt like my mother was sitting with Joshua. They were looking at the moon. My mother said the moon reflected the face of God and that if you look at the moon long enough, you can receive God's messages." Clarissa looked directly at Jeremy as if in a trance. "My mother was the Virgin Mary, I swear it. She talked to Joshua about messages she heard telling of his birth."

"The voice was always that of your mother?" Jeremy asked.

"Yes and no. I'm sure the words were my mother's, but the voice was different."

"Then perhaps your mother was the Virgin Mary. If you were Maria of Magdala in the First Century you would have known your mother then as Miriam," Jeremy said calmly.

"I saw Clara's mother that night too," David interjected. "I saw her standing by the window in our room. She was bathed in the moonlight."

"Did she speak to you as well?" Jeremy asked.

"Yes. I heard her voice clearly. She spoke the words that she wrote me in that letter she gave me."

"The one you have framed at the house?"

"Yes."

The waitress returned with Pot Stickers and Egg Rolls. She smiled at Clarissa as she put a dish down in front of her. "Special sauce coming," she said putting her head daintily on one side.

"Wonderful!" Clarissa exclaimed.

The waitress went off to fetch the sauce.

David tried to cut a spring roll in half with his chopstick and picked up a crumbling morsel. "I'm not too good at this," he said apologetically.

Jeremy did rather better with his Pot Sticker. "Plenty of experience in Vietnam," he said.

"Thank God I missed that," David affirmed. "I missed it by a couple of years."

"You were lucky. It was hell." Jeremy turned to Clarissa. "Was your mother very religious?" he asked.

"Not in a conventional way," Clarissa admitted. "She believed in the Christ-consciousness as she called it. For Ireland, she was quite a rebel. She always said that she believed that we are all divine, somehow inter-connected with the same spirit that was in the Christ."

The waitress returned with the special sauce.

"You should try this with the Pot Stickers," Clarissa suggested to Jeremy.

But Jeremy wouldn't drop the subject in hand. "Your mother's energy seems to be acting as some sort of a channel here. These past life experiences seem to be revealed through her presence."

"Not always," Clarissa insisted. "there have been other revelations that didn't involve my mother."

"There will probably be many, but it seems to be your mother who has initially opened the window for you both."

"What about you?" Clarissa continued. "You never knew my mother, but you have this idea that you knew me in the First Century. Who was it you thought you were - Remus Augustus?"

"Yes, I do feel I knew you when I was Remus," Jeremy admitted. "I knew you as 'Maria'."

"That's really what we want to talk to you about today," Clarissa said looking at David for support.

David took up where Clarissa had left off. "Clara had some other visions and premonitions when we were away," he explained. "She remembered an incident that seems to confirm her association with Mary Magdalene."

Jeremy lent forward, "Go on," he said with a keen interest.

"Clarissa remembered pouring precious oil over Jesus' head, or Joshua as you say," David started to explain, but at that moment both Jimmy Wan and the waitress reappeared with several, steaming platters.

"Phoenix Dlagon," the proprietor proudly announced, "a speciality of the House." He placed it in front of David. "Velly hot. Be careful of plate."

The waitress set down the other dishes including Clara's separate order of Buddha's Delight.

"You wan flied lice or why lice?" Jimmy Wan asked. "I bling both."

Jeremy opted for fried rice, but Clarissa and David requested the plain, white rice. Once they were served, they returned to their deep discussion.

"As I was saying," David continued, "Clara remembered anointing Jesus with precious oil. We heard a version of this story read in church when we were staying with my family over the holiday. But the story we heard was not about Mary Magdalene, it was about Mary and Martha."

"Ah, yes," Jeremy grunted, raising a finger, "but there are two stories in the Gospels about Jesus being anointed with precious oil."

"That's what we found out!" David exclaimed, surprised by Jeremy's knowledge. "One is about Mary, Martha's sister and the other is about a sinner who bursts in on Jesus when he is having supper with some Pharisee."

"But neither of those stories specifically report that it was Mary Magdalene who did the anointing," Jeremy added.

"It's a very strong tradition, though," Clarissa reminded them. "When I was a girl in Ireland the story of Mary Magdalene was one of my favorites. It was almost like a fairy tale, but because Mary Magdalene was an ordinary person who sinned like the rest of us, it somehow meant more to me than all the Roman Catholic stories about the Blessed Virgin that abounded there. Mary Magdalene was rescued from being stoned to death by the gallant Jesus. In grateful thanks she poured precious oil over his head and washed his feet with her tears and hair. Finally, after Jesus is crucified, Mary's the first person to whom he appears. At first she thinks he's a gardener, but when he speaks she recognizes him as Jesus. All that's left out is that they lived happily together ever after."

"There have been a few weirdos who have suggested just that," Jeremy chimed in. "Of course the churches don't accept such suggestions, but there are some who think Jesus might have been married to Maria of Magdala. Others have even suggested that Jesus didn't die on the cross, but that he was rescued from death at the last minute and went on to live a happy life with Maria."

"What about that film a few years back, 'The Last Temptation of Christ'?" Clarissa asked. "Wasn't that what all the fuss was about then? There were terrible riots over that movie because it suggested that Jesus married Mary Magdalene."

"Well, that's not entirely true," Jeremy corrected her. "The scenes depicting Mary Magdalene and Jesus living together were in a dream sequence while Jesus was on the cross. In the film Jesus was tempted to escape death on the cross in this final dream, but he didn't succumb to the temptation so it never really happened. He woke up from his dream to die on the cross as the Church says. Actually, the story really follows the Church's teaching. Outside the dream sequence it's very conservative. Anyway, all of this is a little removed from your recent revelation. Tell me what you experienced."

"I wasn't dreaming," Clarissa continued. "What I experienced was more like a flashback memory. I just knew I'd done this thing to Joshua as Maria. Hearing the story about Mary and Martha that morning in church somehow triggered this off in my mind. Actually, I thought the Mary in the gospel story was Mary Magdalene. It was David who put me right on that. I never read the Bible much, Jeremy. That's why I'm really fascinated by these particular, past life revelations, especially these deep-rooted memories, because I'm not conditioned by reading about them."

"So what did you remember?" Jeremy repeated.

"I just knew that it was me who had poured the precious oil over Joshua's head," she repeated. "Marcus my son, back in the First Century of course, probably the young man you saw when you dreamt about being a Roman centurion in Gaul, selected the ointment in the bazaar. We were taken there by this blind man whom Joshua had helped to heal. His name was Bartimaeus."

David interrupted them. "It's interesting, Jeremy, Clara couldn't remember Bartimaeus' name at first. She called him Bartholomew in her trance, but the name 'Bartimaeus' came to her later - actually in the middle of our flight home last Friday."

"Some facts and names aren't always accurate at first in these experiences," Jeremy pointed out. "That only makes me more interested, especially as the name came to Clarissa later. Carry on Clarissa."

"Marcus picked out the jar because he liked the smell and Bartimaeus, whose sense of smell was also well-developed due to his years of blindness, bought it for us. That's how we came to have it and that's why I was able to use it later to anoint Joshua's head."

"You know, I believe you for a reason that at first may seem strange to you both," Jeremy stated. "The Bible doesn't say either Martha's sister or the sinner in the Pharisee's house, anointed Jesus by pouring precious oil over his head. The scripture says the women anointed his feet with ointment. Also, there is a story about a blind man named Bartimaeus who was cured by Jesus. You have the right names and events, but not exactly as they are recorded in scripture. Maybe that is because you were there."

"I was there," Clarissa insisted. "There was something else too, but perhaps we should eat a little of this good food first. We don't want it to get cold."

They liberally helped themselves to each other's dishes, sharing the total Chinese combination.

"We love this restaurant," Clarissa said. "One of the first things David suggested when we came back to the States after our honeymoon was 'Let's go to the Two Pandas'."

After they had made a start on their meal, Jeremy returned them to the topic in hand. "Now, what were you saying - there was something else?"

"It was another strange link between our past lives in the First Century and today," Clarissa answered. "I met David's nephews last week. They are seven and nine years old. Simon, the younger boy, feels just like Marcus to me."

"Your First Century son?"

"Yes. Simon and I were drawn to each other. It seemed to work both ways. There was a certain understanding between us. When David asked me about the anointing of Joshua and the incident with the jar of precious oil, I felt certain that Simon was Marcus."

There was something about the name 'Marcus' that bothered Jeremy. He didn't know if this was really the time to bring it up, but he felt compelled to ask. "Who was Marcus' father?"

"I don't know," Clarissa replied. "That hasn't really been revealed to me. I just know that Marcus was with me and that he was my child."

David caught on. He could see Jeremy's concern. "You think Marcus may have been Jesus' son, don't you?" he said, trying to keep calm. "We are talking about the First Century and not the present after all."

Jeremy looked down at the debris of his meal. "It might be possible," he said slowly. "But the young man in my dream was only about twenty at the time of the Claudian persecution. As I said before, that was forty nine A.D. I don't think your Marcus could be the same son. It seems that your Marcus was a boy of eight or nine years during Jesus' lifetime. He could have been Jesus' son and the young man in my dream might have been Joseph of Arimathea's child as I first indicated."

"So you think Mary Magdalene had two sons?" Clarissa noted.

Jeremy smiled and his eyes twinkled like Santa Claus. "What do you think, Maria?" he asked.

"I've no idea," she replied, putting her hand to her forehead. "I just know that Marcus was with me when I got the ointment."

Jeremy opened up his hands in a nonchalant gesture. "I believe you," he said as he looked down his nose as if he was wearing a monocle. "But there's one thing that bothers me. Why would you and Jesus have given your child a Roman name? 'Marcus' is definitely Roman. Actually it was quite a common name in the First Century."

"What are you trying to say?" Clarissa said with concern. "Are you implying I had yet another lover?"

Jeremy couldn't help chuckling. "Forgive me, Clarissa, but history does rather support that this could be the case. Weren't you a prostitute?"

Clarissa blushed. "That was in India," she said indignantly.

"Yes, but what about the Biblical tradition that Mary Magdalene was a prostitute?"

David came to his wife's defense. "Does the Bible actually say Mary Magdalene was a prostitute? I think it only says she was a sinner and Jesus cast seven devils out of her. It's Church tradition that has labeled Mary Magdalene as a prostitute."

"It's a very strong tradition, though," Jeremy asserted. "Anyway, Marcus didn't have to be an accident of the brothel. He simply had to have a Roman father, or possibly a Jewish father who was a Roman sympathizer."

The waitress returned to clear away their plates. "Any dessert?" she asked.

"Have you tried the Green Tea Ice Cream?" Clarissa said to Jeremy.

"No," he replied.

"Well, do. It's very refreshing."

Jeremy nodded at the Vietnamese girl. "Alright."

"Count me in too," David agreed.

"Make it three," Clarissa ordered.

Jeremy reached over and took hold of Clarissa's hand. "I'm sorry if I shocked you," he said, "but this is all so goddam fascinating. We are in the middle of a first century, mystery story and the results of our detective work could change the world, or at least change the way the Western world has looked at itself for two thousand years. This is heady stuff. I don't think I've ever become involved in anything this important. We can't give up now. We've got to see this through. Once the energy has gotten this high there'll be other revelations, believe you me."

The girl came back again with the ice cream and six fortune cookies.

"These could be interesting today," David observed. "Let's see what they say."

He shuffled them up and proffered the dish, first to Clarissa and then to Jeremy. "Take two each," he instructed.

Pulling the hard cookie crusts apart David read his fortunes. 'Lucky in Love shows a road to a happy marriage' was the first and 'Secrets shared will reveal hidden truths.' "I don't believe these!" he snorted, sharing the contents with Clarissa and Jeremy. "They could have been written just for us!"

"You want to hear mine?" Jeremy asked.

"Of course," David replied.

Jeremy broke open the first cookie. "A happy man is always making new friends," he read out loud. Then, cracking open the second, he continued, "A business venture may fail." He shook his head incredulously. "That's very strange. I lost a bid in California last week."

"Not a big one, I hope," David sympathized.

"No, nothing serious, but it is uncanny how you can always read something into these damn fortunes."

They both looked at Clarissa.

"What about yours?" Jeremy asked.

Clarissa broke open her cookies. "Beware of overbearing strangers," she read, "and here, if I turn it around - Travel will broaden your horizons." She laughed. "Nobody can say I don't travel. I'll be away on ships for most of January, February and March!"

"Will you be sailing with David?" Jeremy asked.

"Not to begin with. Actually we'll be separated for nearly three months starting next Thursday. David will be on the 'Prince Regent'. I'll be here until the New Year. After that I'll be giving concerts on two or three different ships as well as a tour in Japan and Hong Kong. After that I hope to join David on the 'Prince Regent'. I expect to be able to sail with him from Hong Kong to Haifa which will take me to that engagement in Jerusalem."

"Yes. We have quite a busy winter coming up," David concurred.

"I can see why it was a good thing for us to get together tonight," Jeremy noted. "The new revelations only convince me the more that we all knew each other in the past. Don't worry about those variances with the traditional Bible stories. If we were there we are the better witnesses. You must remember that most of what is written in the gospels was second-hand material dictated well after Jesus' death. They were entitled to make some mistakes. It's very important that we all keep in touch. I think we're only beginning to find out some incredible things, not only about ourselves, but about one of the most important periods in human history."

They got up to leave as David settled the bill.

Outside the restaurant they went their separate ways.

"It becomes more likely every day that you really were Mary Magdalene," David repeated incredulously.

"I know," Clarissa agreed.

• • • • • • •

December brings some of the best weather of the year to the 'Bay' area. San Francisco was bathed in sunshine as the 'United Airlines' jet circled above, carrying David back to his ship. David could see the 'Prince Regent' at her berth. Opposite the docks lay the little, fortress island of Alcatraz and beyond was the Golden Gate Bridge. Marin County stretched to the north. As the plane wheeled, the beaches that were usually blanketed by rolling fog were visible along the peninsula to the south. It was clear from Half Moon Bay right down to Santa Cruz. On the far side of the bay, Oakland, Berkeley and Walnut Creek sparkled like jewels. The great bridges that linked the peninsula with mainland California looked like sharp lines drawn across the blue water. One more circle and the plane came in to land, dropping in from the south to run in along the west shore.

"Welcome to San Francisco and the Bay area," the parrot voice of the stewardess announced after the plane touched down. She then went into her standard patter before their arrival at the gate. Few were listening and the usual body of anxious passengers disobeyed her instructions and tried to get up to gather their possessions. At length, the plane came to its complete halt at the terminal.

David gave a sigh of relief when he was in his taxi. The hustle and bustle of the airport chaos, as harassed travelers desperately tried to beat the clock, reminded him too much of shipboard disembarkation. Passengers who had been the model of gentility and refinement throughout a voyage often became monsters on that last morning. 'They go back into subway gear,' he mused. 'The stress of petty officialdom seems to bring out the worst in people.'

David gathered his thoughts as he sat back in the cab. It was strange to be returning to the ship after his first real spell at home as a married man. Now would begin his long separation from Clarissa. He knew he would miss her terribly, but that was the nature of their careers. He wondered how long he would be able to sustain his life at sea. 'Perhaps the time has come to think about a land-based job,' he mused, 'but it would mean foregoing the pension.'

The cab took him along the highway past Candlestick Stadium and on into the downtown area. The familiar landmarks of San Francisco loomed before him - the triangular building to defy all earthquakes, the towers of Embarcadero, the silhouettes of the great hotels like cairns on their respective hills. Then all of a sudden the taxi was there, right in the labyrinth of overpasses, underpasses and the shadowed heights of the business district, before opening up to the waterfront and the piers of commerce. The 'Prince Regent' was docked at pier 'Thirty Five', the only remaining passenger ship terminal.

David reflected on the old days of the 'Matson' liners taking celebrities and happy travelers to the enchanted islands of Hawaii. 'It's ironic,' he thought, 'that today there are no American ships on that once famous run. Now it's impossible to take passengers to Hawaii without boarding them in Mexico in order to circumnavigate the 'Jones Act'. It's strange that this law, which was introduced to protect American shipping, is now the very cause that disallows direct access to Hawaii by sea. There simply are no American passenger ships.'

He could see the funnel of the 'Prince Regent' riding high above the shed - black with three gold rings. Part of the white superstructure also showed. David was proud of her. 'She's still a ship,' he thought. 'She has classic lines and tradition. So many of the new cruise ships are nothing more than floating 'Hyatts'. They are super de luxe, but they lack the most important ingredient of all - the nostalgic ethos of travel on the high seas.'

The taxi turned in through the pier gate. David flashed his crew pass at the security check. Ahead was a hive of activity as stevedores moved endless pallets of provisions required for the Christmas Cruise. One could easily wonder where it was all going to be stored, but David knew his colleagues in the Hotel Department had all that well in hand. He paid off the taxi and was greeted by the on-board, security officer.

"Welcome back, sir. Did you have a good vacation?"

"Wonderful, Jack," David replied.

"I'll get one of the utility boys to bring in your bags," the security officer suggested.

David walked up the gangway beside a conveyor belt moving boxes of California strawberries. In the Provision Master's Square there was that pre-cruise smell of a greengrocer's stall as debris of loaded lettuces, cauliflowers and the outer skins of onions littered the steel deck. He made his way up the central, crew stairway to Main Deck where he could leave the inner workings of the ship and find the plush carpets and laminated wood of a more civilized world. He reached his domain at Purser's Square.

When he walked in to his office, Minnesota seemed far away. The copy machine was in pieces as the 'Canon' representative attempted service, while the switchboard telephone never stopped ringing. The girls were busy sorting out mail. His relief, Michael Creighton, was shuffling papers in preparation for his handover. Everyone was talking at once.

"Welcome back to the mad house, David," Michael said. "No major changes, all the usual problems, and the Christmas calamity ahead. Thank God it's not mine."

"So nothing strange," David chuckled.

"One death two days ago. It's all in hand now. The Doctor's standing by. The ambulance should be here in about thirty minutes. The widow is already with her son. They'll go with the ambulance to the hospital. Should be a straightforward, coroner's report after the autopsy. The poor bugger just died in his sleep."

"Routine," David agreed.

They sat over a cup of coffee, chatting in general before getting down to business. It was always a little bit of a culture shock to step back on board after a couple of months in the outside world. David needed the coffee.

The Purser's direct line rang.

"I'll get it," Michael said.

He listened for about half a minute interrupting the conversation with periodic grunts and a repeat of the word 'Good'.

"That was the hospital, David. The body's gone. Everything's cleared," he announced on hanging up.

"If you don't mind, Michael, I'll just go to the cabin and get into uniform," David suggested. "When are you leaving?"

"My flight's not until five."

"Good, let's convene in about half an hour. We might even have time for a sandwich in the officers' mess. In the meantime I can sign on and get my passport down to the crew office."

David made his way to the cabin with its lonely, double bed. There, he filled in his papers. For the most part it was a familiar routine, so much so that he started to write down his father's name and address for next of kin. He crossed it out and smiled to himself. 'Damn it! I nearly forgot, Clarissa's now my next of kin!' After writing her name and their Minnesota address, David completed the form. He was now officially back in his job.

● ● ● ● ● ● ● ●

E ach day became more gray. It was assuredly going to be a white Christmas in Minnesota. Sure enough, three days before the holiday, down it came. Clarissa watched through the large, picture windows of the living room. The gentle snowflakes mesmerized her. She missed David tremendously and wished he could be there to see their beauty as each flake slowly drifted to the ground. She knew such things were his spiritual, power house. Clarissa didn't want to go out, although there was shopping to do. David would be in Hawaii - she expected him to call.

The phone rang. It was too early to be David.

Clarissa picked it up. "Yes. Hello."

"Clarissa Peterson?" a deep voice asked from the other end.

"Yes, this is she."

"This is Jeremy - Jeremy Dyson."

"Oh my goodness!" Clarissa exclaimed apologetically. "I didn't recognize your voice."

"Guess what?" Jeremy said. "I got to thinking about our travels after Christmas. I have to be in Delhi on February tenth. It will take about three weeks to take care of everything there, but it crossed my mind that rather than fly back to Minneapolis for a month before going out to Israel, maybe I could travel with you all on David's ship. I'd love to have the opportunity to carry on with our research."

Clarissa felt a strange excitement as Jeremy made this suggestion. "What a great idea!"

"Well, I went along to see some travel agent in Wayzata and it looks like it's all going to work out. I've booked passage on the 'Prince Regent' from Bombay to Haifa. I've no idea what sort of a cabin I've got. She said it's an 'EE' grade whatever that means. Anyway it looks like I'll be on board."

"That's wonderful!" Clarissa said excitedly. "I'm expecting David to call me from Hawaii today. I'll tell him what you've arranged. He'll know exactly what an 'EE' grade means. If it's not up to par I'm sure he can get you something better on board. He's not just a bean counter, amongst other things he's in charge of cabins!"

"I'm not really that concerned about my cabin," Jeremy stated. "The great thing is we'll all be together."

Clarissa was anxious to discuss her latest revelation with Jeremy. "Have you a moment?" she asked.

"Of course," Jeremy replied.

"I've had another dream. This time I saw David's nephew again, you know, the surgeon's son, the one I told you about after we came back from Thanksgiving with David's family."

"Yes, the boy who you thought had a Roman name."

"Well it was you who said he had a Roman name," Clarissa corrected him. "His name was 'Marcus'."

"That's right," Jeremy remembered. "So what did you dream this time?"

"I saw him with his father, his real father, Dr. John Bishop, David's brother-in-law."

"Yes," Jeremy noted, wondering what was strange about that rather obvious revelation.

"I think they were together in Roman times. Doctor John was a Roman. He was Simon's father back then too! He looked completely different, but I instinctively knew who he was - sort of like if you hear a piece of music played by two different instruments. The music doesn't sound the same, but it carries the same message. It just seems the same! His voice was different, but spoken by the same soul."

There was a pause for a moment as Jeremy collected his thoughts. "That's not impossible," he replied at length. "A close relationship today could actually be reflecting the energy associations of a past life. I think it's very probable that close, family ties follow through in this way." He gave a cynical chuckle. "Unfortunately, for many of us our family ties are not that happy - lots of karma! Anyway, what was your dream about?"

"I saw Simon as my son Marcus. He was with his father on this pebbly beach. Doctor John seemed to be a very good father. This was different. I can say this without David being around, but I really don't care for his brother-in-law. Anyway, in my dream Doctor John seemed to be a Roman named something like 'Anthony'."

" 'Antonius'," Jeremy suggested. "Quite a common Roman name just like 'Marcus'. Well, Clarissa it looks like you've found a father for your two, first century children. Your older child, Marcus, appears to be the son of this Roman, Antonius and your younger son, I assume was the child of Joseph of Arimathea."

Clarissa felt a little disappointed. Although it was awesome, she had somehow hoped that if she had really been Jesus' lover back then, that she should have borne him a child, but apparently Jeremy didn't think this was so. "So it doesn't look like Mary Magdalene and Jesus were lovers after all," she suggested.

"Hold on, Clarissa. I never said that. I'm just suggesting that Jesus was not the father of either of Maria's sons."

"Maybe that's just as well," Clarissa replied as the reality of such a suggestion dawned.

There were a couple of loud clicks on the phone line.

"Oh, Jeremy! I have another call! Can you hold on!" Clarissa cried. "It might be David."

She pressed the release button.

"Is this Mrs. David Peterson?" a voice asked.

"Yes," Clarissa replied.

"My name is Tony Muller and I represent 'Double Heat'. Are you satisfied with your winter protection? We are specialists in double-glazing in the Ridgedale area and we are conducting a survey of Lake View Road. We thought you might like us to come out and check your windows."

"I'm sorry," Clarissa replied. "We're quite happy with our windows as they are."

"Alright, I'm sorry to take up your time. Have a nice day," the salesman concluded.

Clarissa pressed the release button again.

"Are you still there, Jeremy?"

"Yes. Was it David?"

"No, just some double-glazing salesman."

"Well, look, I have to leave now. Please feel free to call any time," Jeremy continued.

"Before you go, have you had any more revelations?"

"No, not since we last met. I'll be in touch if I sense any further developments. Meanwhile send my regards to David and tell him I'll look forward to seeing him on that ship of his."

"I will. Merry Christmas, by the way."

"Oh yes. Merry Christmas to you too," Jeremy acknowledged. "I'd almost forgotten. I wonder if Joshua's birth was really anything like they say?"

"Who knows? All the best, Jeremy."

After she put the phone down Clarissa looked at the big picture windows. 'Nothing wrong with them,' she thought before settling down at the 'Steinway' for her morning practice.

David telephoned at about three-thirty in the afternoon. It was still snowing and by now had accumulated about eight inches on the ground. Clarissa's heart pounded as it had in the days of their engagement.

"David, is that you!" she excitedly called out before she had even heard his voice.

"Yes, Clara. I'm calling you from beautiful Honolulu. It's already eighty degrees and just gorgeous."

"Ten below and snowing hard here," Clarissa answered. "But it's so pretty David, I just wish you could see it."

"One day I will, darling. I can't tell you how much I miss you. Is everything alright?"

"Just fine, but guess what? Jeremy called today. He's booked passage on the 'Prince Regent' from Bombay to Haifa!"

"What?"

"He has these engagements in India and Israel and the dates just happened to fit in. He says he has an 'EE' grade cabin. What's that like?"

"Pretty awful," David acknowledged, "but we can probably upgrade him on board. Leave it with me. Any other startling news?"

"I had another dream two nights ago."

"A dream?"

"Yes, another first century dream."

"Oh, have you time to share it?"

"I dreamed about Marcus."

"Maria's son?"

"Yes. We were with Simon's father, or at least what felt like a slightly younger version of Doctor John. Once again I was transposed back in time to the First Century. We were beside a lake. Simon's father was dressed in Roman clothes. He was much nicer then, than your brother-in-law as he is today. He played with Marcus like an adoring father. There was nothing artificial about him. He had crinkly hair very like Doctor John, but his voice was different and he wasn't at all proud and haughty. As a Roman he was very sweet and rather shy. He obviously liked me and I must say I was really very taken by him, mostly because of the tender way he treated me and my son."

"Maybe he was Simon's father back then," David interjected.

"That's what Jeremy Dyson thinks."

"Do you think you were married to this Roman then?" David asked.

"I don't know about that. I'm not sure he was my husband, but he seemed to be courting me."

"You seemed to have a thing about these Roman men," David noted. "I'd better not take you to Italy in this lifetime!"

"Be serious, David. I'm sure this Roman was Simon's father. I think his name was 'Antonius' or something like that."

"Are you writing all this down in your dream journal?" David asked. "It's going to be difficult to share our experiences over the next two and a half months. Write everything down, including anything that

Jeremy might share with you. I'm going to have to go soon, I just snuck out for a moment. Maybe I'll have a chance to call you later. I love you, Clara."

"Me too," Clarissa replied.

They blew each other kisses down the phone.

"Bye for now!" David shouted. "I've got to go! They're paging me."

"Bye my love," Clarissa said softly.

It was one of those days when the phone never stopped ringing. No sooner had Clarissa hung up and David's mother called from Laconia. She had made a point of telephoning every few days since Thanksgiving. Clarissa felt flattered. It was a sign she had been accepted.

"Simon's always asking when Aunt Clara will come back," Mrs. Peterson said. "You were quite a hit with my grandson."

"Tell him I dreamed about him the other night," Clarissa chuckled.

"We had better be careful," David's mother cautioned. "He really has quite a crush on you. By the way, when you speak to David wish him a merry Christmas from us all. We never hear from him."

She promised she would and they went on to talk about the weather and other mundane things.

A few hours later David called again.

Clarissa had done her shopping in between. "I've just got back," she explained. "I bought a new journal just as you suggested. I'll start writing up all our experiences pertaining to first century past lives. I'll include Jeremy's thoughts and dreams as well as mine."

"Great idea, Clara - I'll do the same if anything comes up. But you know how it is on board, I doubt I'll have time to think about these weird, first century experiences."

"Your mother called earlier," Clarissa reported. "She telephones about every five days now."

"You see what a hit you were."

"She wanted to wish you a Merry Christmas from them all."

"When you next speak, tell them I got their card today in Honolulu. Oh, and send a card from us both to 'Bruno' the bear. I forgot. Mother likes that. If you post it today it should get there for Christmas. There's still three days to go."

"How's the ship?" Clarissa asked.

"Full from tonight - the extra Christmas passengers who flew into Hawaii are boarding now. Most of them get off in Papeete and another package comes on for the New Year. It's all go here, Clara."

"I know, darling, I'm thinking of you."

"I won't be able to call you until after Christmas now," David noted. "I guess I'd better wish you a merry Christmas. I should catch you again before the New Year. Remember New Year's Eve I'll be out on deck at midnight blowing you a kiss."

"Just as you did last year when we were engaged," Clarissa reminisced. "I love you, David. What time will it be here when you celebrate the New Year?"

"I'll let you know for certain from Papeete, but I think we'll be seven hours apart."

"So it'll be seven in the morning. I'll be awake in our own bed, David. I'll be waiting for your kiss."

"Bye, darling!"

"Bye!"

"I love you. Merry Christmas, sweetheart!"

"Merry Christmas to you too! Bye!"

The line went dead.

Clarissa shed a solitary tear. Two and a half months seemed such a long time.

•••••••

Clarissa spent Christmas with her best friend, Samantha Dubose. She had thought of flying to Laconia, but once again she was needed in St. Paul for a concert right after the holiday. It was a Christmas, charity concert to which she had committed herself months before. Why, if she hadn't accepted, she could have gone from San Francisco to Papeete with David on the 'Prince Regent.' Sometimes a long-standing, solo date could really mess up other plans and engagements, but Clarissa knew the uncertainties in the life of a concert performer.

Samantha was an author. She had written a couple of novels that had sold fairly well, but for the most part acted as an editor and columnist for a midwestern magazine. She was bubbly, petite and blonde. She cooked them guinea hens for Christmas - the type that come all prepared and only have to be heated in the oven. But she did make fresh, carrot juice and prepared a wok of stir-fried vegetables. Clarissa felt quite at home.

"Do you still keep your dream journal?" Clarissa asked.

"Of course," Samantha replied rather surprised.

"I've started to keep one too," Clarissa admitted. "I've had so many, past life dreams lately. I can see now why you always said write them down. It becomes quite complex as aspects of past lives start coming through. Do you still have the journal where you recorded my marriage to David?"

"Yes. Do you want to see it?"

"If you have it here."

Samantha got up and rummaged through some drawers in a big desk on one side of her living room. She lived in a condominium complex that looked out over an area of Minnesota swamp. The view was stunning in the snow, but Clarissa knew only too well how the area bred mosquitoes in the months of high summer.

"Nineteen eighty eight, I think this is the one," Samantha said at length. "It might take some time to find it. Can you remember roughly what time of the year it was?"

"Let me see. It was in the summer," Clarissa said confidently. "It was shortly before I went over to Ireland on the visit before my father died. Try around late June or early July."

"Make some coffee while I'm looking," Samantha suggested.

Clarissa put the pot on the stove.

As the aroma of the coffee began to rise, Samantha shouted triumphantly, "Here it is! July third nineteen eighty eight. We had lunch together on July fourth. I must have told you my dream then because it would still have been fresh."

"What did you write?" Clarissa asked as she started to fill two mugs with the coffee.

"It says here, 'I dreamed of Clarissa. I was at her wedding. It was a beautiful day and there were magnificent flowers everywhere. Her husband was dark-haired and handsome. His name was David Peterson.'" Samantha read.

"Not quite right," Clarissa corrected her. "It was not a beautiful day - it poured with rain. But I have to agree he is dark and handsome and his name certainly is David Peterson. It's quite remarkable. It was another three years before I met him."

"Why does that surprise you?" Samantha asked. "We're all so hung up on this time track. Time really is irrelevant in the greater order of things. After all, the stars we see in the sky probably don't exist in the present, having burned up long before their light reaches us. We're so conditioned by the idea of time, that we tune out that part of our brain that can access a world beyond time. But we can access it - many of us do."

"You can look into the future, then?" Clarissa asked.

"Sometimes, such as in this case, yes," Samantha replied cautiously, "but it's more likely that our revelations out of the time track will be in the past."

"Why?"

"I suppose because it's hard for our brain to pick up on the future, since it can't be conditioned by future knowledge as it can be with that of the past. Time flows like a river. The future is fluid and the past is solid. There's no container for providing a shape to the future, like a glass can give shape to water. But, if we predict the container shape, we can estimate the future. We know from the river-bed how the water usually flows."

"True, but what if there are excessive rains at the source and the river rages, bursting its predictable banks along the way? The flow changes."

"Prophetic predictions of the future can only be based on observation of the river as it is in this moment. This can change," Samantha agreed.

"So you would say that is why we remember past lives, but rarely perceive our future?"

"There certainly seems to be a far greater affinity with our past than with future lives," Samantha admitted. "Maybe if we're prophetic we can see the solidity of a future cycle, but only as a tentative reality."

"What do you think causes us to relate to our past lives, then?"

"Perhaps the karmic needs of soul to resolve its balance; to purify, in order to enter the gates of Heaven as a 'Worthy One' - that, and strongly bound relationships. As one unfolds spiritually, one's increase in vibratory rate, or soul attunement, permits a sort of natural access to the time track and subsequent insight into one's past lives if necessary. Magnetic forces, energy fields - I really don't know and I don't know that anybody else does, either," Samantha admitted. "It's recognition by the soul that is within us of its past energy bodies, but more than likely some energy affecting our present lives is required to start it off."

Clarissa looked bemused. "I may be losing you, Samantha," she continued as she presented her friend with one of the mugs of steaming coffee.

"In more scientific terms call it magnetic forces," Samantha explained. "We all give off energy fields or electronic forces that relate to everything around us. Our energy fields, which really are the vibration that I referred to, can effect what is around us and can be effected by the greater, magnetic forces of the universe."

Clarissa was still not sure that she really understood what Samantha was saying, but she was anxious to share her recent experiences. "I have to tell you about these strange, past life revelations that David and I have had recently."

"Really, Clarissa! The product of your energy fields! How exciting!"

"Now, I'm trusting you not to tell anyone about this," Clarissa cautioned. "But knowing of your interest in past lives and the extraordinary way in which you predicted my marriage, I would like your feedback."

"Go ahead! Mum's the word!" Samantha assured her.

"David and I started having strange visions, or near visionary experiences, right after my mother died. Some have been straightforward dreams, some daydreams and sometimes the facts have just come to us as a sort of premonition. The more we seem to become involved in these insights into our past, the more frequent the access has become. Quite a lot has just developed out of discussion as we have started putting together a kind of jig saw puzzle on our past lives."

"Tell me about your mother's involvement?" Samantha suggested.

"Well, strangely enough it was David who first had an experience with my mother. He felt her presence the day after her funeral in Ireland. It was while the family solicitor, that's a lawyer to you, was going over mother's will."

"What did David see?" Samantha asked excitedly.

"Nothing much," Clarissa continued. "He felt her presence. He said he could see her face in a faded painting on the dining room ceiling at my family's old house. He said she looked younger and very happy."

"Spooky! A bit like the Cheshire Cat." Samantha smiled, making a face that somewhat resembled Lewis Carol's famous feline. "Did anyone else see her or feel her presence?"

"No, only David, but it becomes more complex, because Mother appeared in my past life dreams later. David's also seen Mother again, but in his case she was never a person of the past, but living as we remember her. David's not heavily into reincarnation, Samantha. We have fierce discussions about my belief in past lives."

Samantha grinned. "He'll come round," she said. "Your mother seems to be giving you a great deal of energy. It's almost as if she's the one who's leading you both into these experiences."

"Maybe," Clarissa agreed, "but it was a long time before she came to me despite my having been so close to her."

"That's probably why," Samantha said as she got up and walked around the room with her hands behind her back. "You had to clear the blockages of your deep, personal grief, you know, like I said, balancing some karma."

"I always felt a little guilty that I chose to leave Ireland and make a new life for myself in America," Clarissa admitted. "I know it hurt both my parents very much when I gave up a secure, orchestral career in Dublin to strike out on my own."

"That's exactly what I mean, Clarissa. You've had to work off this karma, but after their deaths this became easier. They were no longer there for you to feel your guilt. And in time the blockages caused by that guilt have worn off. Now your mother's energy has access."

"I see what you're saying," Clarissa said slowly. "You know that's the greatest help to me."

"Well, now that your channels of access have been cleared, what's been revealed?"

"Well, David and I met this interesting guy. His name's Jeremy Dyson. He's just recently moved to Minnesota. He's an architect and amateur archaeologist. He's also into past lives and I immediately connected with him. As usual David was more skeptical. Anyway, Jeremy thinks he knew me in the First Century - two thousand years ago!"

Samantha drank from her coffee mug. "So who does he think you were?"

"He thinks I was a Jewish woman living in Marseilles. He calls Marseilles by some other name, but it escapes me."

"That's in France, isn't it?"

"Yes. France was apparently called 'Gaul' in those days. Anyway, Jeremy thinks he was a Roman soldier named Remus. He saw me in Marseilles. Although we didn't appear to speak, he knew my name."

"Your first century name?"

"Yes. He called me 'Maria'. He thinks I might have been Mary Magdalene!"

"Wild!"

"You see, there's this legend that Mary Magdalene went to Gaul with Joseph of Arimathea after Jesus was crucified. I had two sons in those days, Samantha. Joseph of Arimathea might have been the father of one of them, but according to another revealing dream I had, it appears that David's brother-in-law, Dr. John Bishop, was the father of my other son."

"Who was this Doctor John?"

"A Roman, Samantha. A man called 'Antonius'."

"Was he also in Gaul?"

"I don't think so. I saw him playing with my son Marcus on a pebbly beach beside a lake. I think it must have been in the 'Holy Land'."

Samantha got up again. "More coffee?" she asked. "This is becoming very interesting."

Clarissa handed her mug over. "Yes please. I think I need it."

"Now, where does your mother fit into all this?" Samantha asked as she went back into the kitchen.

"My mother, or more correctly the incarnation of my mother, came to me as a first century Jewess."

"Also in the dream state?"

"No. It was more like a trance. If you keep this strictly to yourself, Samantha, it's my belief that she was the Virgin Mary!"

"So, you think you were Jesus!" Samantha shouted excitedly.

"Good heavens, no! But it seems that Jeremy might be right. I could have been Mary Magdalene."

"Jesus' girlfriend!" Samantha shrieked.

Although nervous, Clarissa couldn't help laughing at Samantha's reaction.

"I'm not so sure about being Jesus' girlfriend," Clarissa cautioned as she joined Samantha in the kitchen. "Apparently I was friendly with several men in those days."

"A femme fatal!" Samantha teased. "I suppose that fits the traditional image of Mary Magdalene." And then she too burst out laughing.

"No, you have to be serious," Clarissa insisted. "Some of these other men have been revealed to me as persons who I've met in this life."

"You mean, now?"

"Well, actually I really like this Jeremy guy," Clarissa said with a beguiling smile. "If I didn't love David so much I could go for him."

"So, you had a mad, passionate affair with this Roman," Samantha said nonchalantly. "You could still have been Jesus' girlfriend beforehand."

"That's my point, Samantha. I'm not sure that I was Jesus' girlfriend. I jumped to that conclusion when Jeremy came up with the revelation about Mary Magdalene or Maria of Magdala as he prefers to call her. But now that it looks as if I might have been married to Doctor John two thousand years ago and that Simon Bishop might have been our son Marcus, I'm not so sure."

"Maybe you weren't, but you must have known Jesus."

"Oh I did. I'm sure of that. I guess if I was Mary Magdalene I must have. I have an uncanny feeling that I remember that story about anointing Jesus. David and I looked it all up in the Bible. But, back to Mother. It's been revealed to me that my mother knew Joshua."

"Joshua?" Samantha asked quizzically.

"Yes, according to Jeremy that was Jesus' real name."

Samantha roared with laughter. "Well, she'd better have known him if she was the Virgin Mary!" she squealed. "Really, Clarissa, this is getting more intriguing by the minute. Now tell me about your mother's involvement?"

"It happened in New Hampshire at David's family home. We slept in this cozy, attic room with beautiful views over the countryside up to the mountains. There was a full moon."

"Romantic!" Samantha commented, still teasing Clarissa as she looked at her through those great, green eyes.

"I heard what sounded like my mother's words and the room became very hot and muggy. Mother was talking to Joshua and me about the man in the moon."

"What!" Samantha exclaimed. "Now you have flipped!"

"No, I'm serious," Clarissa pleaded. "She really was talking to us about the moon. She was telling us that the face of the man in the moon is like the face of God. If, after looking up at the moon, we shut our eyes and pray, we might hear the voice of God calling back to us. Joshua was only a little boy in the vision. I think mother was teaching us how to access God. She said something about how she had prayed in the moonlight at the House of the Virgins. She told us how her angel, Gabriel, had come to her in the moonlight and told her that she would have a child and that he would be a son of God. Then, she told Joshua, in front of me, that he was that child and that he would be a prince of peace. At that point I came out of my trance."

Samantha's expression had turned serious. "Extraordinary," she said.

"Later that night David saw Mother," Clarissa continued. "He saw her in the moonlight at the window. She repeated the words of a letter she wrote to him the day we got married. It was a beautiful letter. It said something like this. 'I'm so very glad to have met you and to know that Clarissa found you. I will not be here much longer. I am ready to go into the other worlds, but I now know that I will do so in the knowledge that you and Clarissa will be together in the light of Christos'."

Samantha sighed. "That is beautiful."

"I can show it to you sometime," Clarissa suggested. "David had it framed. It's at our house. Anyway, David woke me up. He tried to show me where my mother was standing in the moonlight by the window. I was half-asleep. I couldn't see anything, but he was most insistent. 'I'm telling you, I heard your mother's voice and in the moonlight I swear I saw her face!' he said. It's not like David to be so insistent. He doesn't really believe in these things."

Samantha remained quiet for a moment with her eyes on the empty, coffee mug that she was rotating in her hands. Then she looked up. "Of course you were there! There are too many coincidences. All of you have become focused on this past energy that you share. But you haven't mentioned David, other than the fact that he dreamed of your mother, who as I said, could be the initial key to opening you up to your past lives. Who do you think David might have been?"

"I've no idea. David sort of half goes along with us," Clarissa answered. "I mean, as you say, he was the one who dreamed of Mother, but he doesn't really believe in past lives. He finds Jeremy Dyson interesting because of his knowledge of history and geography rather than for his revelations about past lives. And yet, you know Samantha, I have this gut feeling that he is a part of all this. Simon Bishop's his relative, not mine, and I do feel drawn to Simon in this strange way."

"Your first century son Marcus?"

"Yes. And another thing, Samantha, the mere fact that you predicted our marriage long before it happened; I mean I'm not sure you just predicted the future."

"What do you mean?"

"I think it was somehow meant to be that David and I would meet. Perhaps it's because we knew each other two thousand years ago - the attraction of similar energy as you call it?"

"Perhaps," Samantha said without commitment. She knew from her experience of discussing past lives with all sorts of people that Clarissa really wanted a reassurance from her. "You have to be very careful to who you say these things."

"I know," Clarissa agreed. "But I don't have anyone to share them with. You're my best friend, after all."

"Your secrets are safe with me," Samantha assured her. "You probably were all together in the First Century. But you're close to sacrificing a sacred cow here. You could have insights into the life of Jesus Christ himself."

Clarissa laughed. "That's funny," she said. "Today's supposed to be his birthday."

Later, after Clarissa had driven home through the crisp, new snow, there was a telephone message waiting for her. When she punched the button on her answering machine she heard David's voice.

"Greetings from the 'Prince Regent.' Happy Christmas, darling. A happy New Year to us both. And by the way, a very happy birthday to you on January fifteenth just in case you thought I might forget. God knows when I can call you again. Good luck on the 'Ulysses' cruise. I love you."

"Damn it, David! I missed you!" Clarissa yelled.

· · · · · · · ·

Ten days later, Clarissa flew to San Juan and joined the 'Ulysses' on a cruise through the Caribbean, the Panama Canal and up the Mexican Riviera. The heat in Puerto Rico was a shock after the cold conditions of Minneapolis.

The 'Ulysses' was old. The walls of her hull showed rivets crusted over by years of rust and paint rather than the more familiar, welded plates of ships built in the last quarter of the Twentieth Century. This ship, however, had a reputation for presenting successful, classical music themes. For several years now, Clarissa had agreed to at least one cruise a year as a guest artist.

A gang of young Filipinos were busy loading provisions while a Greek Officer in a pristine uniform stood with his hands behind his back, looking disdainfully at their progress. Other Greeks, less splendidly attired, shouted orders, but rarely lent a hand. There was nobody to carry Clarissa's bags. She approached the officer.

"Excuse me, sir," she asked.

The officer smiled, but said nothing.

"Do you think someone could help me with my bags? I'm one of the guest artists."

The officer clicked his fingers and shouted. One of the lesser Greeks looked up, gesticulated with his hand and yelled at two of the Filipinos.

The Filipinos then came over to Clarissa and her bags. They smiled politely, gestured for her to go ahead up the gangway, picked up the bags and followed.

Clarissa's cabin was small, but she knew from past experience that this would be so. There was no room for a tub in the minute bathroom. Passengers and artists who travelled on the 'Ulysses' came for the concerts - not for the comfort. There was a printed program on her dresser. She noted that she was to perform three times, once the night after Aruba, again the night before Acapulco, and finally, en route to Los Angeles. She set about unpacking her clothes. There was no room in the wardrobe to properly hang her concert gowns, so she hung three of them in a garment bag on the back of the cabin door.

Clarissa knew most of the other guest artists as they got together in the Trojan Lounge for a welcome reception. Most of them were asked back year after year. Opera, baroque chamber music, classical guitar, string quartet and a brass ensemble were all represented, presided over by a larger than life conductor whose fans booked passage as much for his amusing anecdotes and flair as for the wide variety that was offered. This year, as a special feature there was something different - a glass harp trio from Switzerland.

Clarissa sipped on a 'Mimosa' that barely contained champagne and struck up a relationship with the glass harpists. They were touring in the United States, but didn't speak much English. "It's very rare to find a team who play the glass harp," Clarissa noted. "How long have you been together?"

"Five year," the younger of the two girls replied. "My father, he play zee bottles and taught me ziss technique. In my childhood he used to visit fairgrounds and circuses with zee bottles. I was struggling viz zer violin in college. Zere I met Kurt and Elsa. We ver all playing fool with zer wine glasses one day. Zat vas it. Zer glass harf vas born."

"And your name?" Clarissa said as she started to look through the program.

"Ursula."

"So you still play the bottles and Kurt and Elsa the glasses?"

"Yes."

"Ah, I see you perform before me. I'll look forward to hearing you play. The glass harp's something completely different," Clarissa acknowledged. "I've only once ever heard one played in concert. That was at a symposium in the Black Forest. The sound moved me very much. So, tell me. Where have you been touring?"

"Vee performed at Zer Sviss Embassy in Vashington first," Ursula informed Clarissa. "Zen before Kristmas vee had concert in Chicago, St. Louis and Memphis. Over Kristmas vee ver in Atlanta, Georgia and ver invited down to zis beautiful island on zer coast. It iz a very special place called Zee Island. Vee performed at zis unique hotel, 'Zer Cloister', in zis incredible room like a old Spanish baronial hall. Everyone zere vas very formally dressed."

"You should have seen zee Kristmas trees they had zere and zee decorations. It vas like a fairyland," Elsa added.

Kurt grinned. "Zee food vasn't bad either."

"Vee will never forget performing zere," Ursula continued. "Vee have performed in many great concert halls."

"And some pretty dreadful one's ven on zer road," Elsa added.

"But zis place, 'Zer Cloister', had to be one of zee most unusual," Ursula said enthusiastically. "It vas like performing for a old aristocratic family zere. I kept thinking I vas at zer Clara's house in 'Der Nussknacker' especially viv zee huge Kristmas tree in zee corner totally dominating zis amazing room."

"It sounds incredible," Clarissa agreed. "By the way, that's my name - Clara, Clarissa Peterson. I'm the solo pianist. I grew up in Ireland."

"Vee have played zer glass harp in Ireland," Elsa informed her. "Actually it vas zer nearest experience to zis place in Georgia. Vee played at zer two old castles."

Somebody clapped their hands loudly and Francesco Lovello, the flamboyant conductor, started to make a welcome speech. The 'Ulysses' music cruise was officially opened.

Later that night Clarissa took a walk around the Boat Deck. It was a warm and balmy, tropical night. Nobody else seemed to be about. She stood at the rail and looked at the long ribbon of fractured moonlight on the ripples of the water. She thought of David and cupped her hands to blow him a kiss. She knew that he had done just the same on New Year's Eve. 'We are on different ships in different oceans,' she thought, 'but the waters unite us.'

• • • • • • • •

During the glass harp concert Clarissa sat with her dining companions, Frank and Jesse from Oklahoma, and Jim Barton from San Francisco. Francesco Lovello came out on stage to introduce the artists. As always, he received loud applause from the audience.

"Tonight, Ladies and Gentlemen," Francesco said, as he flamboyantly adjusted the silk handkerchief in the breast pocket of his tail coat, "we truly bring you something different. I believe this is the very first time that our Ulysses concert season has presented this particular instrumentation." He paused and looked around at the audience. "Some of you may remember blowing into bottles when you were young."

There was a ripple of laughter.

"I see you know who you are," Francesco quipped. "Some of you may also remember irritating everyone else in the restaurant by rubbing your finger around the rim of your wine glass to create a musical note."

There was louder laughter.

"I've done it myself," the maestro admitted, to even further applause. "Few of you, however, have heard this taken to the highest art form, the glass harp. There are indeed, only a handful of glass harpists who are treated seriously by the music profession, but it is my belief that when you hear the trio who will be performing for us tonight, you will rank them among the world's great performers. This is magic to the ears, nectar for the soul. Ladies and Gentleman, from Switzerland, currently on tour in the United States and en route with us for further concerts in Los Angeles, San Francisco, San Diego and Sacramento, will you please welcome 'The Helvetia Trio'."

The curtain opened on Ursula, Kurt and Elsa. Ursula was stage left, seated on a stool behind a table of assorted, green bottles which represented the bass harp. On a long table, cleverly affixed in tiers, were an assortment of crystal wine glasses and goblets into which had been poured exact measurements of water. On the count of three, Elsa and Kurt began to rub the rims of the glasses with wet fingers while Ursula blew over the mouths of the bottles. The music of Johann Strauss filled the Trojan Lounge in a manner in which it had never been heard before. Then followed Dvorak's New World Symphony, works by Stravinsky, Mozart and Bach, the performance ending with a piece entitled 'Harmony in Crystal'.

It was the trio's own composition and it was questionable whether the work was truly classical, but it had the audience enraptured. It was the music of the spheres brought to a new perspective in the incredible tones of the glass harp.

Clarissa felt links with the great impressionist composers that she liked to play, Grieg and Debussy. But the unique decibels and tones of the harp turned those impressions into a new reality. The music was at first romantic, bringing her thoughts of David as she sat and listened. She could see the contentment on his face in the garden. She could imagine him talking to the plants. That was when she loved him most - when she saw him alone in the garden. There, in harmony with nature, he was stripped of all pretences. Clarissa could feel that contentment and it glowed within her as she felt a oneness with her man. She closed her eyes and David's image swirled into a kaleidoscope of happy colors in harmony with the rising tones of the glorious harp. Then she saw a young Roman contorted in ecstasy. She thought he felt like an incarnation of Jeremy Dyson, but he didn't have a beard. His Roman pride completely succumbed to her in its moment of weakness. She could hear him laugh in the high notes, she could feel his flesh in the low notes, and then it was over. The harmonies changed and the kaleidoscope swirled in soft greens and blues revealing the face of a woman she didn't recognize. The music didn't give Clarissa time to reason, question or wonder why. This woman's face meant sweetness and love that she had never known before. There was a tenderness here - a gentle submission to another's touch. It was Clarissa who received the caresses. It was she who became the object of love. But this was not passion. This was not triumph. It was a gentle beauty that matched the music, soaring into a deeper emotion, more settled, more permanent, more secure. The lips, the face, the loving eyes, mingled with smooth flesh, white breasts and soft hands in tender caresses. Then, the heavenly music paused. The deeper, bass tones of the bottles took over, changing the image to a reflection of David's brother-in-law Doctor John. Softness merged with kindness as she saw him in the flowing folds of a toga. It was his face, but his self-centered character changed in the beauty of the tones. The image was fading in shafts of light that flickered in the rising scales. Gaseous swirls of water and fire intermingled. The light pulsated, there were dancing leaves, and then, total joy. The music soared, the light increased, the sound was all around. She saw a bearded face. Who was this in the final image whose visage became lost in the brightness of the light? Was this man or was this God? There was no describing the glow within, the power of the light and the ringing sound of the music that encompassed all.

Slowly Elsa and Kurt lifted their fingers from the glass rims as Ursula blew the last chord. 'Harmony in Crystal' was completed. The Helvetia Trio stood and took their bow.

First in hesitant groups, then in massive response, the audience rose to their feet. They had heard the music of the spheres.

"That was unbelievable," Frank drawled in his southern accent as he turned to Clarissa at the end of the applause.

"I was transported into another world," his wife agreed.

Clarissa was really lost for words. It was almost as if she had been through a time tunnel. The music had swept her up in unknown emotions from the past. These were echoes of that first century life. The images were only vague, but the emotions carried with the sound in that swirling light, had drained her. "Yes," was all she could reply to her companions.

Jim Barton leaned back in his chair, looking intellectual. "Quite amazing," he said. "The tonal quality of that music is unreal."

Francesco Lovello was already out on stage eulogizing the performers and their work. Nobody was really listening to him. The sound of the glass harp had transported them to other dimensions and continued to ring in their ears.

In the quiet of her cabin, Clarissa struggled to write down the patterns of the visionary experience she had undergone while listening to the harp. She tried to rationalize the different faces. David was obvious. The young man was probably Remus Augustus, the Roman reincarnation of Jeremy Dyson. 'Was he also my lover?' she thought, knowing that she couldn't deny that she found Jeremy Dyson very attractive in this life. The woman intrigued her. Clarissa knew that she had been the recipient of much love from this woman, but had no idea who she might have been. Reflection on the emotions that this image, created by the music, had churned, were warm and inviting. Clarissa felt no shame at this revelation, only a softening sense of endearment. Next came the encounter with Doctor John. This one baffled her most. She sensed such a different personality in John's Roman guise. Was he Anthony or Antonius as Jeremy had suggested? In many ways he was still a nameless face of the First Century, but yet seemed to be the father of her son. She didn't want to think of him as her husband, but she felt drawn to his Roman personality. She sensed in his image all the opposite traits to those she had encountered in David's brother-in-law. Here was warmth and affection, caring love and selfless giving, that were so different to Simon's father.

'Can someone, once so close to perfection, be reincarnated at a lesser level,' she thought. 'Lucifer was one of the angels of Christian myth, but became the devil.' She sucked on her pencil and pursed up her lips. 'No, I mustn't think this way,' she concluded. 'Perhaps I just don't know Doctor John very well. I just couldn't feel the warmth that he perhaps holds deep within. Maybe it's just his material success that hides his soul.'

Clarissa started to write up the last encounter. It was more one with the light than a personality. As Clarissa wrote in her journal, vague images showed through the light of recent memory. His was the only bearded face. His were the most penetrating eyes. Could this be her encounter with Jesus himself - Joshua of Nazareth? She wrote down this possibility, although as with the others she had no clear insight as to a First Century name to fit the face.

Deep in thought, still moved by the musical encounter, Clarissa closed her journal, put it on the floor beside the bed and switched off the light. She needed a good night's sleep. She was to give her first concert the following evening.

The glass harp music, however, continued to reveal its truths to Clarissa in her dreams. She felt a deep contentment as her next vision opened ....

A dark-haired woman sat beside her on a hillside. Below them was a lake of which the far shore showed as a purple haze on the horizon. There were rocks, goats, and wild flowers. Clumps of cypress trees stood like sentinels among scattered olives. To the right there were vineyards, villas and a town that tumbled down to the water's edge. To the left the hills rose up to a ridge that met the blue of the sky. The dark-haired woman kissed her ear and caressed her back.

Clarissa started to giggle. "No, Delilah," she said. "That tickles me."

Delilah didn't stop. The tickles tingled and turned to joy. "How much longer do you think we can live here with Antonias?" Delilah whispered.

Clarissa felt the warmth of the woman's lips on her ear lobe. The tingling sensation caused through her soft touch spread throughout Clarissa's body. "Why do you ask?" she responded. "Do you want to leave?"

Delilah was silent for a moment. She dropped her head and let it rest in the softness of Clarissa's breasts.

"You have Marcus, Maria," she answered. "Antonias has been very good to you both. He's given you a home and the stability your child needed. It would have been difficult to have continued the way we did before Antonias came into your life. It was alright when Marcus was very young, but at his present age we would never have managed." Delilah looked up into Clarissa's face. "You need to stay with Marcus and Antonias, Maria, but I need to go back. Maybe the matron at the brothel will let me return, and if not in Tiberias maybe I can go elsewhere, perhaps to Sepphoris."

Clarissa saw herself stroke Delilah's hair affectionately. "You're part of our family," she insisted. "You can't leave us. I love you Delilah. We need each other."

"I know," Delilah agreed as she took Clarissa's hand and guided it to her left breast. "I need you too, but you have Antonias. You've had us both."

Clarissa could feel Delilah's nipples harden to her touch.

Delilah arched her back with pleasure and turned to kneel on the grass in front of Clarissa. She was looking right at her and tenderly touched her face with the tips of her own slender fingers. "Does Antonias know about our secret?" she asked.

"Of course, Delilah," Clarissa replied, chuckling to herself. "Why are you suddenly concerned after all this time?" She held Delilah and found herself kissing her with the softness of her full lips. "Antonias is a very sensitive man. He understands the way we feel about each other. He knew right from the beginning. He knows how close we are. He even wrote a poem about us, but it was hard for me to understand. He wrote it in Greek and tried to translate it for me. Somehow it didn't quite come out right."

"He's too kind," Delilah observed.

"He loves us both in his funny way," Clarissa said as she held Delilah tighter. "He loves me because of the physical love that I have been able to bring into his life, but he also loves you because he knows that you make me happy. We have a triangle of unselfish love between us, Delilah. You are as much a part of it as I am."

Delilah thought for a moment. "I was afraid to tell you before," she said. "There was an occasion not so long ago when Antonias found me alone. It was one of those beautiful evenings with the golden light streaming down to the lake. He held me that evening and kissed me, Maria. I let his hand touch my breast and I could feel his excitement. He was so gentle."

Clarissa smiled. "He is, Delilah. He's so different from all the men that I've had before. He's always more concerned about my feelings than his. I think that's why I haven't tired of him."

"You don't mind then?" Delilah asked somewhat surprised that Clarissa showed no resentment over Antonias' actions.

"No, Delilah. You don't have to explain to me. That's probably not the only time he's held you, is it?" She laughed, "Actually, Delilah,

I'm glad Antonias has shown you some affection. I'm glad that you've been able to share in some of my joy. Goodness, we've had to share enough men in the Tiberias brothel! How beautiful it is that we can share real love here."

Delilah expressed her comfort in this discussion by tightening her own embrace around Clarissa. "I love you," was all she could say. "Maria, you're a real friend."

"I love you too," Clarissa replied as she ever-so-lightly brushed her lips against Delilah's. "You're not going to leave us yet, are you?"

"Not as long as both you and Antonias want me to stay," Delilah replied.

"Good, then you're staying and that's the end of this talk," Clarissa said with authority. "Now let's go back down and see how Marcus is doing with his lessons. Antonias tries to teach me Greek, but I just don't seem to be able to learn. Thank goodness Antonias speaks our language."

"It helps," Delilah agreed as they stood up, held hands and started to walk down the hill. "Remember that I always spoke some Greek. You really should make more effort, Maria. If we're going to stay with Antonias we should speak Greek. Anyway, you have a Greek name, 'Maria'. If my name was Greek it would be similar to yours - 'Delia'."

They reached the villa and the boy who looked like David's nephew, came running out. Clarissa greeted him. "How was your lesson today, Marcus?"

The boy just grinned in response. He looked more Roman than Jew, wearing a clean, white tunic bordered in a golden, Greek-key design.

The man whom she remembered envisioning on that pebbly beach and who had the face of a younger version of Doctor John, followed him out. He was also dressed in the Roman style.

"Antonias, it's such a lovely day," Clarissa said to him as she hugged Marcus.

Delilah spoke to Marcus in Greek.

The boy looked at her and screwed up his eyes. "What?" he said.

Delilah tried to repeat her question, but obviously the child had no idea what she was talking about.

Clarissa began to laugh loudly. "So much for your Greek, Delilah," she teased.

They both laughed together and Clarissa awoke ....

Clarissa sat up in bed. "Antonias!" she shouted. "His name was Antonias - not Antonius! Doctor John was Antonias! And the nameless woman was Delilah!"

She reached down for her dream journal. 'I must write this up before it goes.' Clarissa recorded as much as she could remember of what Delilah had revealed to her about Antonias and the boy Marcus.

'Simon had to be my son,' she mused. 'Everything's beginning to fit together. Simon was Marcus.'

She put the pencil down and lay back on the pillow in the rather narrow bed that took up most of her cabin on the 'Ulysses.'

'Antonias was the father of my son, Marcus. That's why Marcus had a Roman name, just as Jeremy Dyson said,' she mused, then, sitting up, she started to write again. 'Delilah was my best friend and also my lover. There was something very tender and special about this lesbian relationship. I don't feel guilty about it. Delilah somehow softened me and made me a wiser woman and a better mother.'

Clarissa heard the familiar sounds of a ship docking. The 'Ulysses' had arrived in Aruba. One good thing about performing after a day in port was the ease with which she would find time to practice. The passengers would all be going ashore. She could use the piano on which she would be performing - the 'Yamaha' in the Trojan Lounge. The tuner wanted to go snorkeling and had said that he would work on the piano at three o'clock. That left the instrument free for Clarissa all morning.

She stretched and started to get up with a deep feeling of internal contentment.

•••••••

C larissa's first concert in the 'Ulysses' series was well received. The usual knot of admirers gathered around after the performance to congratulate her on her sensitivity and technique, whatever that should mean. Clarissa had played on ships enough times to know that the best way to win a shipboard audience is by choice of material rather than technical skill. She realized that much of any artist's true sensitivity and technique becomes enveloped by the acoustics and reverberating sound surfaces of a ship's lounge, most of which in her opinion did not even begin to resemble those of a concert hall. But Clarissa loved the enthusiasm of the audiences on these special music voyages. Unlike on a regular cruise, these passengers had all booked because of the artists and the music program being presented. They were captive and responsive.

The following day, January the fifteenth, was Clarissa's birthday. She would be thirty six. The ship would be calling in at Cartagena in the afternoon, so in the morning she decided to indulge herself and spend a couple of hours on the open deck in the sun. It was hot and humid. As Clarissa lay out in a deck chaise, she was conscious of her body. She didn't look bad for thirty six. Her skin was still fresh, almost like that of a teenager and her bikini exaggerated her well-proportioned breasts. Protected by greasy sunblock, she adjusted her towel and lay back to soak up the rays. She closed her eyes. The strong sun filtered through her lids in gentle waves and she drifted into a warm, glowing world, lulled by the hum of the ship's engines ....

The pulsating light conjured up the bearded face that had haunted her in the finale of the glass harpists' performance. As the image clarified, Clarissa saw the face as if peering from a jeering crowd. Stones, aimed at her, began to fly. Many missed, but a few wounded her in the stomach and bruised her arms. One grazed her cheek, drawing blood.

The man with the light-colored beard stepped forward, shielding himself from the missiles. "What has this woman done to deserve this?" he cried.

A voice yelled back, "She's an adulteress - a wicked woman!"

A man in a colorful robe came forward. "Who are you to interfere with the justice of God!" he shouted. "This woman is an adulteress who was caught in the very act. She's broken God's sacred Laws and we condemn her in the name of the Lord!"

"You're right, sir," the bearded one replied firmly. "This woman has broken the Law. Whoever here has never broken any part of the Law, should be the next to throw a stone."

The two men stood staring at each other, fury in the face of the one and quiet authority written across the face of the other. The man who had come to Clarissa's rescue then knelt down and turned his attention to clearing some of the fallen pebbles from the parched earth.

Clarissa tried to speak, but no words would come forth. Her mouth was gagged.

A single stone flew through the air and hit the mystery man on the shoulder. He looked up and spoke again, calmly and with that same authority. "You heard what I said. If there is one of you here without sin, go ahead and cast your stones. If however, any of you have sinned, and I suspect that applies to most of you, disperse and leave this woman alone. Rest assured that your Father in heaven knows what this woman has done and he will be her judge."

There were shouts of "Blasphemer!" and several more missiles hit Clarissa and the stranger.

"What do you say to this, Obadiah?" the principal agitator shouted to the man in the colorful robe.

Obadiah looked puzzled, even afraid. "Leave it alone, Joab. This man's dangerous. His authority sways the cowards. God's justice will be done in God's own way."

The mob began to disperse leaving Clarissa with the stranger who was making letters in the dirt with a jagged stone. Clarissa could read what he wrote. It was the name 'Joshua.'

He turned to her and untied the dirty rag with which her accusers had gagged her. "Woman," he said, "where are those who condemned you now?"

"They're gone," Clarissa whimpered faintly.

"It seems then that you are not condemned," he affirmed. "I don't condemn you either. But, let this be a lesson to you. Whatever you've done against the laws of God see that you don't do it again." Then, untying her arms, he continued, "Come with me. There's more joy in heaven over one sinner who repents than over ninety nine just persons. I can make you whole. What's your name?"

"Maria," Clarissa replied.

The scene filled with light and the bearded man's face disappeared ....

The light became so bright that Clarissa was forced to open her eyes only to see herself staring upward at the full orb of the sun which had risen above the shield of the ship's upper superstructure. She reached beside her deck chaise for her sunglasses in order to cut out the glare. In a moment she was lulled back to her dozing comfort. Images returned ....

Clarissa now imagined, or dreamed, that she saw the same man whom she had thought to be Jesus and who had revealed himself to her as Joshua. He was sitting in a shallow stream. She felt the gaze of those deep, penetrating eyes and there was something very familiar about his bearded face. After the previous revelation Clarissa was more sure than ever that she was experiencing the personality of Mary Magdalene. As such, she saw herself wade into the stream. She felt the pangs of desire. Once beside Joshua, she started to rub an ointment of lye into his hair.

As Maria, Clarissa felt much love as she massaged his scalp to relieve tension and release pressures. As the lather built up, some of the soapy mixture flew into Joshua's eye and made him flinch. Once the pain diminished, Clarissa returned to her task. She sat in the water behind him. At first it felt clammy and cold as the stream rushed past her lower back, causing her skirts to float in folds before her, but that feeling soon passed.

"Lie back now," she asked him softly.

Joshua obeyed and lay his head in her lap as the brook babbled around them.

In her first century body, Clarissa scooped up the water on either side and rinsed his hair. The soapy mixture eased out into the stream.

Joshua looked up into her face as she leaned over him. "Thank you. You do this so well."

Clarissa felt Maria's excitement and pleasure at that moment. "I'd do anything you ask of me," she said. "I love you, Joshua."

Joshua obviously felt the same excitement and gazed at her affectionately. "I know, Maria," he agreed.

Taking his head in her hands, knowing that she was Maria of Magdala, Clarissa eased back. Joshua's head fell between her knees and deeper into the rushing flow. Joshua lay there in the stream stretched out in front of her as the last of the soap washed out of his hair. Clarissa sat back in the water leaning on her elbows with her face turned upward.

After awhile Joshua sat up and shook his head. Again he swept back his hair, squeezing out the water. It hung like a donkey's tail down his back. In her dream, Clarissa reached forward and gently pulled it, releasing the last drops as she wrung it in her hands. Slowly, almost teasingly, she let it go and Joshua stood up, his back still to her, as the water fell from his loincloth. He turned and, smiling, gently offered her his hand to pull her up from the stream. As she rose, her soaking garment clung to the folds of her body and exaggerated the form of her breasts. As Clarissa looked at Joshua she felt the spark of God leap between them. Ecstasy mingled with the mystical in the power that flowed, but it was too powerful to sustain. Clarissa broke the silent bond. "Why don't you wash my hair too?" she suggested. "There's enough lye left in the box."

They walked upstream towards a waterfall. Joshua stopped and took her in his arms. He kissed her lightly on her forehead. With a tenderness within his distant look, he answered her. "You've always managed to wash your hair without me before, Maria."

"I know, but today is special," Clarissa replied. "We're alone here in all this beauty, just you and me. Couldn't you wash my hair just this once? It would give me such joy!"

"Maria, if it will really please you I'll anoint you with lye and water. You once anointed me with oil, it's the least that I can do. You anointed me in spirit, Maria, because you understood me. You understand me more than all the others, even more than Cephas. Because you have faith in me, I'll anoint your head as I wash your hair. It'll be a symbol of the cleansing of your soul. I'll release the power of the Holy Spirit from deep, within you."

Clarissa clung to Joshua in a long, silent embrace. Joshua patted her back as she pressed against him. At length she looked up at him. "You are a son of God, aren't you?"

"There's only one thing that's different about me," Joshua replied. "I know that my soul is the spirit of God. One day you'll know that yours is too, Maria, but sometimes I wonder if the others ever will."

Joshua helped Clarissa pull off her heavy, wet robe, shamelessly revealing her nakedness. They waded back into the stream. Above them, the water tumbled down from a height of about ten feet. Standing close to the fall they embraced. Joshua kissed Clarissa gently on the lips. She could feel the strength of his body against her flesh. Slowly, she pulled at his loincloth which loosened and fell, but as she did so she had this uncanny feeling that they were not alone ....

Nervously, Clarissa opened her eyes. The ship's Officer who had greeted her when she had boarded the 'Ulysses', was looking down at her stretched out in her deck chaise. He had typical, Greek, good looks with curly, black hair and heavy eyebrows. He appeared resplendent, dressed in his full, white uniform, but he exhibited that same haughty pride he had shown at the gangway. "Kalimera!" he said with a confident grin that spread from ear to ear.

'Buzz off,' Clarissa thought as she rubbed her eyes. 'What do you want - my body?'

"A beautiful day we have today," the ogling officer noted.

"Yes, but it's a little too hot. I think I'm going in," Clarissa answered, hoping that this apparition in a white uniform would quickly disperse. The officer took the hint and moved away to try his luck elsewhere. 'It's a funny thing,' Clarissa thought as she picked up her towel, 'you never see these officers in the lounge or at the recitals, but they appear out of nowhere as soon as you stretch out in a bikini on deck! Perhaps David was right, or maybe it takes one to know one!' She laughed at herself - 'Damn it, I married one!'

Clarissa returned to her cabin, convinced of Mary Magdalene's romantic liaison with Jesus Christ. She knew that it was true. There was an envelope from the radio room on the floor. She picked it up and opened it.

'Happy Birthday, darling,' it read. 'It is only six weeks now and I am counting the days. We had a great start to the World Cruise and will be back in Papeete tomorrow. Good luck with the concerts. I love you with all my heart. Much love, David.'

"I love you too!" Clarissa shouted with joy as she kissed the paper. "You remembered my birthday!"

• • • • • • • •

The sun beat down on the 'Ulysses' throughout her transit of the Panama Canal. Clarissa stood at the rail, looking out at the lush, tropical landscape of the Gatun lake. She was wearing a short sunsuit with a straw hat to protect her head. A large group of yellow butterflies flew up from the shore line, shimmied in the sunlight and fell back into the shadows of the undergrowth. The peace and beauty of the scene was disturbed by a voice from behind. "Kalimera," it boomed.

Clarissa turned. There he was again, the same officer who had appeared from nowhere the day before.

"A hot day," the Greek continued, "but you look nice and cool."

'Creep,' Clarissa thought before replying as politely as she could. "Thank you. I always love coming through here. Don't you think the Gatun Lake is one of the most beautiful places in the world?"

"Too hot, but it has a certain beauty," the officer admitted. He joined her at the rail, with a smirk of victory on his face. This time he had struck up a conversation with her.

'It's not surprising you're hot strutting around in that uniform as if you were God's gift to woman,' Clarissa thought.

The butterflies rose up in a cloud from the overhanging jungle once again.

"Butterflies," the officer noted.

"Yes, aren't they beautiful," Clarissa agreed.

"You like butterflies?"

"Yes."

"We have a whole valley filled with butterflies on Rhodos," the Greek explained. "Every summer they hatch out in the valley and they cover every leaf and bough."

"It must be lovely," Clarissa acknowledged politely.

"What's your name?" the officer asked. "Are you one of the musicians?"

"Yes, as a matter of fact I am," Clarissa said turning towards the persistent man. "My name is Clarissa Peterson. I'm the concert pianist."

He introduced himself. "Babis Demetris - Bridge Officer. Very nice to meet you."

"I come nearly every year on the Ulysses Music Cruise," Clarissa explained. "And you - you are from Greece?"

"Yes. From Rhodos," Babis answered.

"Ah, the butterflies," Clarissa said. "Rhodes, where can be found the valley of butterflies."

"That's right," Babis replied, moving closer to her.

'Shall I tell him I'm married now,' she thought.

"Have you spent any time in Greece?" he asked.

"I've been there once or twice. My mother loved your country. She was often at Samos."

Babis grinned. "Samos," he repeated. "My father was from Samos."

"And you are from Rhodes?" Clarissa confirmed.

He laughed. "Born in Rhodos, but from Athens now!" He answered as if Athens was the only place in the world.

"Well, there's a lot more to Greece than just Athens!" Clarissa said with a grin.

"Athens is Greece!" Babis replied pompously and then continued in a more relaxed way. "The politics, the music, the tavernae, the girls, our glorious past - these things are Athens!"

"You must get homesick traveling around the world, then," Clarissa said cynically.

"Sometimes," the Greek replied and turning towards her with a sparkle in his eyes added, "but not when I see a beautiful woman like you."

'Down boy!' she thought, somewhat flattered, but much amused. She had seen this line enacted so many times by the over-sexed Latins that abounded on cruise ships. She turned from him and stared out at the beauty of the lake once more. 'Perhaps he will take the hint,' she thought.

He stood there beside her for what seemed like an eternity, but eventually, realizing that she was not ready to succumb to his charms, pompously excused himself. "Enjoy your day, see you around."

"Probably - I'm not going anywhere," Clarissa replied nonchalantly.

When she thought he was gone she turned around. Babis was engaging himself in conversation with Ursula, the young, Swiss, glass harpist. "Creep!" she muttered.

The 'Ulysses' passed from the Gatun lake into the narrower waters leading in to the Gaillard Cut. The lush vegetation gave way to waving, pampas grass scored by scars of ruddy earth left from recent slides. The official lecturer from the Panama Canal Commission, who had been reasonably quiet throughout the transit of the lake, started to talk again. His voice reverberated from the deck speakers. "We are now coming into the most important part of the canal. This is the area which presented a forty year challenge to its builders. It was here that most lives were lost and the greatest operation in the moving of earth by humankind was achieved."

Clarissa lost track of what he was saying as he started to reveal the incredible statistics of the American achievement. After the beauty of the lake, this section of the canal bored her. She had heard the commentary almost every year out of the past ten. She chose to go to the Lido for lunch.

At the Lido she noticed Babis Demetris coming in with Ursula. Clarissa smiled to herself. 'That was quick,' she thought. 'David was right after all!'

Later in the afternoon as the 'Ulysses' pulled out of the last of the locks to greet the Pacific Ocean, Clarissa turned her thoughts to David. They were now both on the Pacific. He was in French Polynesia and she was off Balboa. They were in the same latitude enjoying a similar climate, but about six hours still separated them in time. 'The Pacific's so vast,' she thought, 'nearly half the surface of the globe. When I join David in Hong Kong we'll still be in the same ocean.' In a strange way the vastness actually reassured her of their closeness.

A refreshing breeze stirred the humid air.

Clarissa's friends from Oklahoma spotted her at the rail. They looked like they had been boiled in a lobster pot.

"What a day!" Frank said, his graying, ginger hair blowing in all directions in the welcome breeze. "We haven't missed a thing. We've been out here from start to finish."

"And burned ourselves to a cinder," Jesse interrupted in her Oklahoma drawl.

"But well worth it," Frank continued. "It's hard to believe that we're now in the Pacific ocean. The canal gives you the feeling that you've crossed from one half of the world to another - from the Western World to the Orient."

"I know," Clarissa agreed. "I was just thinking that we're now in the same waters as my husband even though we won't be together until Hong Kong."

"It sure shrinks the planet," Frank noted.

"Actually, traveling by sea does seem to shrink the planet much more than traveling by air," Clarissa agreed. "In a plane, even though the traveling time is far less, you're taken from one culture right into another without any sense of the gradual change in between. When you travel on the ocean like this, each culture just merges into the next and you do come to realize how small our world really is."

"I hadn't thought of it that way," Jesse said. "That's very true."

Clarissa looked serious. "The world is slowly becoming one despite all the seeming chaos that we read in the news. But looking at this lush jungle today makes you think. We humans had better stick together if we're going to survive. It's not really our planet, Jesse."

"What do you mean?"

"The grass and the trees have been around a lot longer than us. Have you ever thought that when you fly you don't see any sign of humanity? You see blue oceans, white clouds, green forests and meadows."

"That's true," Frank agreed turning back from the railing to rejoin their conversation. "You also see deserts and mountains. Actually that's all you see flying from Oklahoma to Los Angeles."

"Miles and miles of desert," Jesse agreed.

"Exactly," Clarissa continued. "We're just ants on this planet. One day we may be trodden down, but does it really matter?"

Frank and Jesse looked at Clarissa, not quite knowing how to answer her.

"We are only very temporary inhabitants of the Earth," Clarissa went on to say. "My goodness, we were just about the last species to evolve here and yet we look like we might cause our own extinction." She looked out at the passing vegetation. "There are animals and insects out there whose life forms have been around far longer than mankind, yet seem to have adapted to this planet rather better than we. The world will go on regardless of human beings. Remember, the dinosaurs were here a lot longer than us. The creative energy just goes on from one life form to another."

"You really believe in that reincarnation idea, don't you?" Frank acknowledged with a grin.

"But what about our salvation?" Jesse asked. "How can we be saved by Jesus Christ if we are only going to come back again as an insect?"

"I'm not sure Christianity has all the answers," Clarissa replied. "Maybe Jesus meant to teach us that our salvation is within ourselves. Remember that more of the world believes in reincarnation than not."

Jesse looked at Clarissa. "We've had such interesting discussions at the table on this trip. You've really added so much to our enjoyment with all your interesting ideas and your beautiful music. You inspire people. I'm not sure that I always agree with everything you say, but you sure make us think."

"Well, one thing's certain," Clarissa replied. "It is a magnificent planet. Today has been a day to remind us of that. I really think the Gatun Lake with its lush, tropical banks, butterflies and all those islands, has to be one of the most beautiful places in the world."

"Oh, me too!" Jesse agreed.

• • • • • • • •

Clarissa's second concert was scheduled two nights before Acapulco. She put together her best program for this one, knowing that passengers usually relaxed on the easy, three days at sea cruising from Balboa to the Mexican Riviera. Without concern for ports and shopping, they attended the music programs in large numbers.

Babis Demetris, who had sat through the second performance of the Helvetia Trio the night before, no doubt primarily because of his swift conquest of the young Ursula, was in Clarissa's audience. The following day he again approached her on deck. As before, Clarissa was stretched out on a chaise soaking up the rays. This time, however, she was wearing a snappy, one-piece bathing suit.

"Kalimera."

"Good morning," Clarissa replied.

"You played very well last night."

"You were there?"

"Of course. Do you think I wouldn't come to hear you? You played the piano beautifully."

Clarissa was genuinely surprised. "Thank you," she said. "It felt good last night. The audience was most appreciative."

"Forgive me for asking," the Greek continued, "but every time I see you I get this strange feeling that we've met before."

"I don't think so," Clarissa replied. "At least not unless you were on board last year or possibly three years ago. I've been coming on the 'Ulysses' to play for a number of years now."

"No, it wasn't here. I've only been on the 'Ulysses' for six months. Perhaps it was in Greece."

Clarissa's elation dropped. 'When is this creep going to give up?' she thought. 'I've never laid eyes on him before. He's tried all the oldest lines in the book.' She looked him squarely in the eyes. "Look, I don't recall meeting you," she said firmly. "Aren't you seeing the young, glass harpist? You've been running around her like a bee at the honey pot. For your information, I'm married and I'm not interested in any kind of a relationship!"

The Greek looked surprised. "Oh no! I don't mean anything like that! It's just that I have this feeling that we've met before!"

"If we have, I'm not interested now," Clarissa said firmly. "Could you please just leave me alone!"

Babis grinned, saluted her and walked away.

He didn't bother her again, but he did take Ursula out for lunch in Acapulco. Between Acapulco and their journey's end in Los Angeles, Ursula and Clarissa met. Amongst other things they discussed Babis Demetris. Clarissa said nothing against him, well aware that Ursula was enjoying the temporary, romantic illusion. Ursula disturbed her however, as she revealed some of the strange things the Greek officer had told her.

"Heez certain he knows you, Clarissa," she insisted. "He can't remember vere or ven, but he sveres he has met you. Are you sure you have never zeen him before?"

"Ursula, I swear to you, I've never laid eyes on him."

"Vell, he thinks he met you either in zee Greece or zee Israel. Every time he zees you he brings up zee zubject. I really don't think he iz vonting you, he iz genuinely interested in you because he think he know you."

"The only time I've ever been to Israel was to play a concert in Tel Aviv. I was there such a short time - I just flew in and out. Unless he was at the concert he would never remember me," Clarissa insisted.

"Perhaps he vas. Votever, you made a great impression on him."

Clarissa looked at Ursula. She hoped the young girl wasn't concerned because she was afraid that Babis might desert her. She knew how intense these shipboard romances could be. She wanted to reassure Ursula that she had no interest in a relationship with the Greek.

"It's all very fascinating," Clarissa said at length. "But, rest assured I've no interest in striking up any kind of a relationship with Babis. Enjoy him while you can. I'm a married woman and I've no interest in upsetting you or anyone else. If he thinks he knows me, so be it. I can only say that I swear I don't remember him."

Ursula looked relieved.

"Now, to other things," Clarissa continued. "When is your first concert in Los Angeles? I might be able to come. I'm going to be in Los Angeles three days before I join the 'QE2'. Your music is sensational."

"Vee vill be performing at zee Beverly Wilshire for a fund raiser zee day after vee dock, but our big concert iz at zer 'Hollyvood Bowl' a veek from now," Ursula explained.

"That's too bad, I'll miss you," Clarissa noted. "What's the fund raiser? Maybe I can get in."

"I'm not sure," Ursula replied. "Zum political ting."

"Your music really is very, very moving," Clarissa commented. "I can't tell you how pleased I was to hear you. Best of luck to all of you in California. You really have something very special."

"It's our music," Ursula replied. "Vee just love to play."

• • • • • • • •

Clarissa was greeted by Harry Hoven, the suave, English Cruise Director of the 'Queen Elizabeth 2', who welcomed her back on board the world's last, great, ocean liner. There was a dignity about this ship that appealed to Clarissa. Harry Hoven had programmed her for two concerts in the Theater. After the poorly maintained 'Yamaha' on the 'Ulysses' it would be a joy to play a full, 'Steinway' Concert Grand. On her evenings of performance her audiences were appreciative, but not as enthusiastic as those on the Ulysses Music Cruise. The 'QE2' was on her annual World Cruise, but many of her passengers on this segment were only going across to Hawaii. The ship anchored off Ensenada, Mexico, to pick them up and spent three days crossing the Pacific to Maui. Then followed a full day ashore before arrival the next day in Honolulu.

Harry Hoven invited Clarissa to join with other members of the Cruise Staff and Entertainers on board for a lunch outing in Lahaina. Harry had made arrangements through the ship's agent and they reserved the whole terrace of the 'The Smiling Dolphin', a colorful, seafood restaurant in the old, whaling town. In no time drinks were ordered - an assorted mixture of multi-colored, tropical punches, local beers and white wine. The party of fifteen pawed over the extensive menu of succulent seafood. There was a relaxed and carefree atmosphere not always evident in the hustle of on board management.

"So you're off to Japan next?" Harry said to Clarissa, bringing her into the conversation.

"Yes, my agent has me booked for a series. I'm playing in Tokyo, then in Kyoto and Kobe, followed by a final concert in Nagasaki. Actually it'll be my first time performing in Japan. It was convenient, you know, I'm on my way to Hong Kong and the dates fitted in perfectly."

"How long will you be in Hong Kong?" Harry asked.

"About six days - I have some radio and T.V. interviews there. Then, I join my husband on the 'Prince Regent'."

"Of course," Harry said explaining to the others. "Clarissa's husband is the Chief Purser on the 'Prince Regent'."

"Nice ship," one of the entertainers, a male vocalist from England, commented. "I worked the 'Prince Regent' early last summer in the 'Med'. A very comfortable ship. Like the 'Queen', she's a real ship." He turned to Clarissa. "I think I remember your husband. He was about to go on leave to get married. So, you were the bride?"

Clarissa blushed. "I hope so," she said as they laughed and drank to her health and happiness.

"I think I met your husband on the World Cruise last year," Harry suggested. "We were docked together in Hong Kong and a party of officers from the 'Prince Regent' came over to the 'QE2'. I never got a chance to board the 'Prince Regent'. We had so many functions going on, but everyone says she's a lovely ship."

"My favorite, or at least when I'm not on the 'Queen'," Clarissa replied. "But then, I could just be a little prejudiced."

There was further laughter.

"I'll say one thing for the 'Queen'," Clarissa continued, "you do have the best pianos. You should see some of the pianos I have to put up with on other ships."

"And the best musicians too," the male vocalist confirmed, "British of course."

'The cruise ship business is so small,' Clarissa thought. 'Everywhere you go you meet people you've met on other ships or who know friends of yours.'

Platters of assorted seafood arrived, although there was the odd heathen amongst the group who ordered a steak. The lunch continued in a very carefree way until nobody felt any pain and in good spirits, all were ready to tackle any task the ship might present to them.

"See you at the luau tonight," Harry said as Clarissa expressed a desire to disappear into the numerous boutiques along the Lahaina waterfront. "Oh, and don't miss the 'Waki Waki Hula Show' at six. The children are adorable," he called back as he made his way down to the tender.

Harry was right, the children's' hula show that evening was adorable. It received a standing ovation from the passengers in the Grand Lounge - a rare occurrence. The Luau, which was complete with suckling pig, banana leaves and tiki-tiki lights, was an equal success. A Hawaiian band provided the music under a canopy of stars and a clear moon. It was a magical occasion supported by a rare assortment of exotic and fruity, tropical drinks, the sort that look harmless, but come back at you with a kick. At sailing time, Clarissa helped herself to the cheese board at the midnight buffet ready to retire to bed after a truly lovely day. The packing could wait until the morning.

That night Clarissa had another dream relating to the First Century. In the morning she hastily recorded the details in her journal before packing for her evening flight to Japan.

'I had just poured the precious oil the blind man had given me over Jesus' head,' she wrote. 'Two rough men who were close to Jesus stepped forward and caught hold of me. I struggled, but they were very strong. A man who seemed like Babis Demetris, the Greek officer who pestered me on the 'Ulysses,' yelled at me, "What are you doing, woman? Such precious oil could have been sold for up to three hundred denarii!"

A burly man who was also very close to Jesus, joined with Babis, shouting at both Jesus and me, "I agree with you Judas! The proceeds of such a sale could have been used to help the poor!"

Jesus turned on them coming to my defense. "Janus and Jonas, release her! Leave her alone!" he yelled. "Let her go!"

The two men obeyed and freed me.

Jesus calmed down once they had let me go. He put his arm on the burly man's shoulders. "Cephas," he said. "The poor you'll have always." Then he pointed at the man who had the feeling of Babis, whom Cephas had called 'Judas'. "What this woman has done for me may seem a waste to you, but she has expressed a deep love by her action. She'll be remembered for what she has done because she's closer to spirit than most of you. She has recognized the inner love in another." At this point I awoke.

Almost immediately I went back to sleep and the dream appeared to continue where it had left off. I could smell the fragrance of the sweet oil. The character like Babis was now sitting outside a rough, square house, washing his feet with the same men, the ones called Janus, Jonas and Cephas. Jesus, whom they called Joshua, was also with them. I was with my son, who once again felt like Simon, Doctor John's boy. As we approached I heard Babis complaining to Jesus, "What did she do that for?"

I wanted to ask Jesus what was going on, but he was busy calming the others down, so I took my son into the house. From the open door I could hear Jesus admonishing Babis who I can now assume to have been Judas Iscariot. "Many who love me shall come to hate me," he was saying. "The boundaries of love and hate are very close."

"Women!" Babis muttered in response. He pointed at Jesus. "Watch these women, Joshua! They're making you soft." He spat on the ground and stood up. "They only have one use other than the cooking and baking. If only all women could be like Lazarus' sister Martha and not emotional like Mary and your friend Maria, we'd all be better off."

Jesus addressed Babis quietly. "Judas, there is no bitterness in the love of God. Calm yourself."

"So be it," Babis muttered, and again I awoke.'

Clarissa closed the journal and put it in her hand-baggage.

'So Babis Demetris was right,' she thought. 'He had met me, but it was two thousand years ago. He was Judas Iscariot!'

• • • • • • • •

Clarissa read through her dream journal again on the flight to Tokyo. A certain pattern seemed to be emerging. There was absolutely no doubt in her mind that she had lived a past life in the time of Jesus. Every indication seemed to be that she was Mary Magdalene in those days and that she had some sort of special relationship with Jesus. He seemed to be commonly referred to as 'Joshua' in her dreams. This had been corroborated by Jeremy Dyson who acknowledged that Jesus' real, Aramaic name would have been 'Joshua'.

She now knew that she had shared these experiences in some way with several others. Her own mother seemed to take on the role of the Virgin Mary. It was also apparent, again confirmed by Jeremy Dyson, that the Virgin Mary's real name in those days would have been 'Miriam'.

'But why wasn't my name Miriam?' Clarissa thought as she stared at the distant, white clouds forming the horizon against the blue sky beyond the wings of the jet. 'Mary Magdalene seems to always come out as 'Maria' in these revelations. Jeremy says that's the Greek translation of 'Miriam', so why wasn't I called 'Miriam' by my Jewish contemporaries?'

She dwelt on this question for a moment and then considered the role of Jeremy Dyson. The architect was convinced he had lived as a Roman soldier in the First Century. He was sure he had known her then. He claimed that he'd met her in Gaul at Massilia, apparently the Roman name for Marseilles. Perhaps he called her 'Maria' because it was the Roman version of her name more likely to be used in Gaul. But surely before that, in Palestine, she must have been known as 'Miriam'.

She noted on the back page of her journal how she had listed the various characters that had begun to emerge. She looked at what she had written.

'Clarissa - Maria of Magdala. Mother - Miriam (the Virgin Mary). Jeremy Dyson - Remus Augustus. Doctor John - Antonias. Simon - My son Marcus.'

She added in her bold handwriting, 'Babis Demetris (Greek Bridge Officer on Ulysses) - Judas Iscariot,' and then returned to her thoughts.

'It's funny how most of our present immediate relatives seem to have been around in different, but also close relationships two thousand years ago. It looks like I was married to Doctor John, David's brother-in-law in those days. Marcus appears to have been our son. That's very direct - Simon is Doctor John's son. If Antonias and I were married two thousand years ago, Antonias' son could have had the same father as in this lifetime - but who knows?'

Her heart fluttered for a moment. This whole idea of past life, family connections when reviewed sitting in a large jet flying across the Pacific Ocean at thirty three thousand feet, just seemed ridiculous. It made sense when talking intimately to someone like Jeremy Dyson, who himself had the ability to make the First Century come alive just with his historical knowledge, but in a plane with a kimono-clad stewardess offering tea, coffee or soft drinks, it seemed absurd. She tried to think of other things, but the dreams listed in the journal kept returning to her.

'That last night on the ship,' she considered. 'That dream was interesting. In the first part I know it was referring to the time I anointed

Jesus with the oil the blind man gave us. Judas got very upset and suggested to Joshua the oil could have been sold for a large sum of money. Then that burly man called Cephas, took it further and said we should have given the money to the poor.'

She laughed and her cynical smirk caught the attention of the Japanese businessman who sat beside her. 'It's funny,' she thought. 'In these days of Social Security and Welfare States such a consideration wouldn't even cover the administration costs.'

'Then Joshua rebuked them in my defense,' she analyzed. 'In the second part of the dream he was still rebuking them, but the scene was different. Instead of being in an open glade we were outside this smelly, tanner's house. I didn't see what actually happened, but it seems like this must have been the other anointing that the Rector in Laconia was preaching about - the anointing of Jesus by Martha's sister Mary. Judas' reaction was almost the same then. What did he say?'

She opened the journal again and looked at what she had written.

'This is it - "What did she do that for?" Babis or Judas said. Then Joshua rebuked him by saying, "Many who love me shall come to hate me. The boundaries of love and hate are very close." I wonder what he meant by that,' she thought. 'Judas was the one who betrayed Jesus. I wonder if he knew all along that Judas would betray him?'

She read on.

'"Women," Babis muttered. "Watch these women, Joshua! They're making you soft."'

Her mind pondered these words. 'He seemed to hate me. He tried to bad-mouth me in front of Joshua and turn Joshua against me. But in Joshua's wisdom he told Judas that the boundaries between love and hate are very close. He was even jealous of Joshua's popularity. In many ways I feel sorry for Judas just as I felt sorry for Babis. Such people can't help being chauvinists because they are ignorant and insecure. They really need a lot of love. Strangely enough, in my dream that's just what Joshua went on to say - "Judas, there is no bitterness in the love of God. Calm yourself." That's really a beautiful thing to say at a time of resentment and anger.' She stared at the page in the journal again. 'Judas' anger was directed at both of us, Mary and me,' she concluded. 'David was right. He said that both of us anointed Jesus in our own way. He told me there were two stories. Now, both these stories have appeared in my dreams and both have shown Judas Iscariot's hatred of us, indeed his apparent hatred of all women. But then, I suppose we women didn't count for much in the First Century.'

She turned back to the pages she had written about Antonias and Delilah. 'Antonias didn't hate women. He was just as gentle and kind to my friend Delilah as he was to me. He must have been very understanding and tolerant for a Roman. That's sure strange if his soul has really incarnated as Doctor John in this life - His character's completely changed. I wonder if I truly was married to him as Maria? If so, what happened to him? Our son Marcus is with me as an older boy in these anointing dreams, but there's no sign of Antonias.'

Clarissa stared out at the great, blue dome above the clouds, dismissing the in-flight movie that had begun.

· · · · · · · ·

The 'Prince Regent' was sailing in the warm, tropical waters of the Coral Sea having just left Cairns in Queensland, Australia. David hadn't given much thought to first century revelations after he had returned to the 'Prince Regent'. Life at sea was generally far too hectic. Whenever he did have a moment to relax from running his side of the ship's operation, along with the eternal task of handling minor frustrations of inordinate proportions in the world of their spoiled passengers, David tried to escape up to 'Monkey Island', the officer's sun deck, to work on his tan. He wanted to be sure he looked bronzed by the time Clarissa came to join him in Hong Kong. Passengers never ventured into this upper haven, forward of the ship's funnel and set amid the radar globes and various wireless antennae surrounding the mast.

"David! We don't often see you up here!" the ship's nurse exclaimed as the Chief Purser climbed up the steps to this exclusive enclave.

"Hi Fiona. I haven't seen you in days," he replied, "not since Mrs. Heppel passed away. I haven't seen you around."

David pulled up a lounge. They were the only two officers up on 'Monkey Island'. He couldn't help noticing how attractive his old flame still looked in a yellow bikini. Fiona had a much better figure than her uniform ever displayed, but then he already knew that. She had also obviously spent a lot of time sunbathing.

"I guess you must have been working on your tan," David commented. "I've got to work on mine before Clarissa arrives in Hong Kong."

"She's sailing with us?" Fiona asked in a tone that revealed her deep-seated resentment.

"Yes, from Hong Kong to Haifa," David answered nonchalantly.

"That'll be nice for you. Is she going to play for the passengers?"

David tried to be civil. He found it so awkward to talk to Fiona since his marriage. "She's not engaged to play, but maybe the Cruise Director will find a spot for her. She hates coming on and not performing."

He took off his shirt, making himself comfortable on the chaise.

Fiona turned over on her stomach and seductively released her bikini strap to expose her back.

David rubbed suntan oil on his chest and arms.

"You wouldn't mind rubbing some on my back?" Fiona asked.

Reluctantly David obliged.

"You still do that well," Fiona commented.

Ignoring her flattery, David lay down and began to snooze. 'Clarissa should be in Tokyo by now,' he thought. 'It must be cold up there. I'm glad we're not going further north than Hong Kong this year. I really much prefer it in the tropics.'

The sun felt good on his naked flesh.

'Let's see,' he continued in his musings. 'Madang in a couple of days, then a day at sea before Zamboanga where the monkeys have no tails. Another day at sea and it's Manila. Two more and we're overnight in Macau. And then the next day we arrive in Hong Kong. It won't be long. Let me see ... that's eleven days.'

David could hear the hum from the funnel and the gentle rapping of the wireless cables. The sun was strong. His face glowed. He thought momentarily about Jeremy Dyson. It still bothered him that the architect felt this attachment to Clarissa. He accepted that it was all in a past life when Jeremy was a young Roman named Remus Augustus, but he just felt uncomfortable about the way things were developing. There seemed to be a dangerous fusing of their first century and present lives. Perhaps this was enhanced by his own guilt feelings brought about by the presence of the pretty, blonde nurse that now lay sunning herself beside him. He and Fiona had enjoyed an exciting relationship and he knew he had hurt her. He didn't trust Jeremy. He knew his own history too well. Deep down he was not happy about the 'damned Roman soldier' sailing with them from Bombay to Haifa. He drifted into sleep as he mused on these thoughts. He was taken to another time and another place ....

He saw himself climbing over a vineyard wall. He was young, little more than a teenager. It was a hot and sultry day. He was dressed in a simple, white tunic and carried a sling shot. He dropped down from the wall into the cool shelter of an olive grove that ran between the vineyard and the blue waters of a lake. After he landed he saw a naked man running in the opposite direction. He heard a woman's voice yelling abuse at the man in a foreign language which he seemed to recognize. The voice also struck a chord of recognition. Then he saw her. Somehow he felt it was someone he knew, even though she had her back to him. She was completely naked. Her dark hair hung below her shoulders. He advanced towards her. As the leaves crackled under his feet, he hesitated. She looked in his direction. David froze as he gawked at her.

Initially, the woman picked up her clothing and tried to hide her nakedness. Despite her dark hair, he knew, somehow, that this was the embodiment of Clarissa! But she had a beguiling smile which she quickly turned to her advantage. She lowered the garment which she had so hastily wrapped around her flesh and revealed her ample breasts. Then, completely naked, she sat on the garment. She cupped her right bosom in one hand, and beckoned to him with the other.

David could see that this image of Clarissa had the look of a sultry, Hebrew girl. He realized that he was a Roman youth, bronzed from the sun and full of the lust of his young years. Her invitation was too much for him to dismiss. He advanced towards her and with a young Roman's eager desire, he dropped his slingshot, pulled at his belt and opened his tunic. 'She's asking for trouble,' he thought. 'I'll show this Hebrew whore who I am.' David set on her with all the fury of frustrated youth. "I am Linus, the son of Flavius Septimus, you dirty, Hebrew whore," he muttered to himself as he buried his head in her breasts and pulled at her nipples with his teeth.

She pushed him on the shoulders interupting his passion. "You're the Roman's son, aren't you?" she said.

David, in his dream, had no difficulty understanding her Aramaic. "What is that to you?" he replied in the same language.

That beguiling smile crossed her face again. "I want you," the embodiment of Clarissa said simply, taking all the bombastic force out of his attack, and infuriating his young, Roman pride.

"Who are you?" David asked.

"Maria," the woman replied.

"That's a Roman name," David said with surprise.

"My mother's a prostitute in the village. Maybe I had a Roman father and that's why she chose to give me a Roman name. She had many Roman clients."

David fell on the woman. His hands ran all over her curvaceous body. Instead of anguish, however, there was only a look of amusement and pleasure on Maria's face.

"I've always wanted you," she said as she studied him. "I've watched you and your father."

She began to caress him and guided his frenzied movements into her own undulating rhythm. He did not make love to her, she made love to him.

He lay with her in silence after his swift fulfillment. Somehow he knew that he would see her again ....

A series of shrill beeps sharply yanked David back from his dreamy doze.

Fiona MacAllister struggled to reach for her beeper, innocently revealing her pert little breasts.

"Hospital - three one three one," it answered.

"Drat!" she replied as she reached to fasten her bikini strap. "I thought I had the afternoon free. Marcia's down there. What in the world do they need me for?"

Hastily Fiona pulled on her shorts and tee shirt, reattached her beeper and picked up her towel.

"It always happens," she said looking down at David. "It'll be your turn next."

She was gone.

David knew that he had dreamed about Clarissa, but many of the details were fast fading in his return to reality. He felt that he had raped her as a young girl in some far away place. It had excited him and her response had been far from negative. He knew the girl was somehow Clarissa even though she had not looked like his twentieth century wife. His dream had taken him far back in time. Had he been a Roman? He could hardly remember as the sight of the Radar domes and ship's rigging told him that he was definitely on board the 'Prince Regent,' the dream faded rapidly.

'It was just a possessive reaction to my thoughts about Clara and Jeremy,' he concluded. 'Eleven days! I'll see Clara in eleven days!'

* * * * * * * *

Clarissa had left Minneapolis for the Caribbean and a journey across the Pacific and on through the Indian Ocean without thinking that any part of that journey would be cold. She simply hadn't packed for winter. Japan was a surprise. It snowed in Tokyo, although for the most part it rapidly turned into slush. In Kobe, it was just raw. In Kyoto, winter showed its full force, coating the ancient temples and palaces in white and leaving long tendrils of ice on the feathering willows. It was bitterly cold, but enchanting.

After purchasing a heavy anorak for an exorbitant price, Clarissa was able to visit some of the splendid historic sites in Kyoto. The Golden Pagoda beside its frozen lake and the Shogun's Palace particularly impressed her. She caught the Golden Pagoda in the latter part of the afternoon, just as the sun peeked through layers of cloud that sent shafts of light through the winter tracery to hit those gilded roofs. Mingling with the pinks and turquoise fringe of the clouds, the light made the fresh snow sparkle in its late, afternoon glory.

Clarissa stood mesmerized by the pagoda for a long time. It was almost as if God spoke to her in this crystallized moment of beauty, then, in rapt realization, she remembered how she had dreamt about this scene back in the Minnesota fall. "It was a glimpse into the future!" she whispered to herself. "I really did see exactly this scene. It's quite remarkable."

That evening back in her hotel room, Clarissa composed a lyrical piece based on the experience. She called it 'Gilded Snow'. It was not easy to compose on the upright, practice keyboard which the Orchestral Society of Japan had provided for her use in the hotel room, but the music flowed from her as if written by a guiding hand. After midnight she plucked up enough courage to go down to the lobby. The piano that had been in use earlier, was standing alone on an island reached by a little, wooden bridge over a vast pool filled with colorful carp. Clarissa took her scribbled score and boldly sat at the instrument. When she began to play, the sound, although not loud, reverberated in the hollowness of the massive atrium. Late customers in the Lobby Bar turned their heads and kimono-clad matrons stopped in their tracks. Chic, young, Japanese couples heading to the sophistication of 'Koko's' nightclub, stood politely at attention to listen.

Clarissa was lost to them as she saw the images of the Golden Pagoda dance before her in the notes of her music. The building pulsated before her eyes. It became blurred. It changed form from glistening, gilded roofs, merging into a pillar of shining light. White of the snow faded in the brightness of the image and trees merged into shadows. The pillar took on the form of a man standing with his arms outstretched and his head gazing upward. Light surrounded the figure, making his body stand as a silhouette against such brilliance. Clarissa sensed she was there. She saw her first century son, the boy who seemed like David's nephew Simon, run out from their hiding place. She felt her heart tremble. 'Psst! Marcus!' she heard herself whisper in the notes of her composition, 'Come back!' The boy appeared to turn around. He smiled. It was Simon's smile. Then he crawled back. The music began to rise again. From their cover Clarissa observed Joshua's face in the silhouette. She thought she saw his hand just slightly move as if making a gesture for them to go away. She held on to her son tightly. The silhouette clarified as the brilliance faded. Clarissa clearly recognized Joshua, with his sandy beard. He was dressed in his usual, white robe and she knew that she was Maria. Then the white of the robe spilled into the landscape, returning the scene to its original snow. The figure was left standing as a gray pillar, losing its significance. It became the gilded pagoda. A final burst of golden light lit up the snow-laden eaves before the sun moved behind clouds. The temple took on the drabness of winter as its moment of glory became lost. The music ended.

Clarissa took her hands from the keyboard. The Japanese spectators smiled and bowed politely. "It's alright," she muttered to herself. "I can include it in the Nagasaki concert if I work on it tomorrow."

Back in her room she lay down on the bed. 'That was extraordinary,' she thought, 'the music took me back to Palestine. I can't shed this 'Jesus' thing. It haunts me even when I play! He was there in the strange light. We saw him there, standing in the place of the pagoda. My son was with me. Marcus and I stood there in front of Joshua of Nazareth. But there was something secret about it. It was as if we weren't meant to be there. He didn't want us there ... I'd better write this down. It wasn't exactly a dream, but I may need to share this strange experience with David and Jeremy.'

Before she slept Clarissa wrote down the waking dream experience. 'I wonder if it will haunt me again if I play the piece in Nagasaki?' she thought.

The following day she performed the Rachmaninoff Piano Concerto with the Orchestral Society of Japan. Neither at rehearsal nor in the performance was she taken into any visionary trance. Her playing was greeted with overwhelming Japanese politeness just as it had been in Tokyo and Kobe. She took this to be a compliment. It was so different to play for an Asian audience. Clarissa never really knew what their true thoughts were.

Nagasaki was another story. Here, Clarissa had been scheduled to play a more virtuoso concert. She hoped she could include 'Gilded Snow' as an encore. If so, she decided to dedicate the piece to the Orchestral Society of Japan in grateful thanks for the tour.

She felt a wonderful warmth in Nagasaki. After the cold in the other Japanese cities, Nagasaki was mild. The sun shone brilliantly and the city was a real surprise. Despite the holocaust of atomic destruction, much of old Nagasaki had survived and no destructive force of humanity had been able to destroy the exquisite beauty of the narrow harbor and the surrounding hills.

Clarissa climbed the many steps up to 'Madam Butterfly's' house and the scene of 'Major Pinkerton's farewell'. She reflected for a moment there as she stood and admired the view down the harbor out to the open sea.

"You can't stand on this spot and not hear the strains of Puccini's music," she whispered to herself. Within her inner consciousness the aria 'One fine day' reverberated in her ears. 'It's like a call over the water,' she thought. 'If I was to imagine I was singing this aria I wonder if David would hear me across the sea. It's only five days now until we'll be together in Hong Kong.' She hummed a few bars and then blew a kiss to the southwest. 'He must be somewhere between Manila and Macau. I can't wait to see him and share our secrets. I've so much to tell him, not least how that scene at the Golden Temple in Kyoto matched what I saw that night in Minnesota. If future dreams can really be that accurate then surely these past life dreams must be equally so. I wonder if David's had any similar experiences?'

Clarissa leaned against the wooden fence. A line of identically dressed, Japanese schoolchildren came giggling through in their organized way. Their teacher briefly spoke to them. Clarissa could pick up the words 'Puccini', 'Major Pinkerton' and 'Butterfly' as the children looked at the great bronze statue of Major Pinkerton's Japanese lover. The children then all simultaneously looked out towards the harbor just as Madam Butterfly does in the opera.

Clarissa smiled. "David's my Major Pinkerton," she whispered to herself. "One day we'll stop this wandering life and really settle down together just as Butterfly had wished."

She looked at her watch. It was already three o'clock in the afternoon. It was time to go back to the hotel and start preparing for the evening concert.

When the time came and the conductor announced her name, Clarissa walked out onto the stage of the concert hall. The lights blinded her as she smiled out at the auditorium. She couldn't see the faces of the crowd, but she sensed their presence. She felt good. She adjusted her piano stool. She rubbed her hands. Pre-performance nervousness, mixed with that familiar and eerie silence that precedes the first note. She then looked up at the conductor and the Rachmaninoff Piano Concerto started yet again.

Clarissa knew she was playing well. Perhaps it was because she was full of anticipation and hope. This was the last concert of the tour. David was waiting across the water. When the concerto ended the applause was more than enthusiastic. She knew that in Nagasaki she had cracked the Japanese. 'They'll love the new piece,' she thought.

As she worked through her program of Grieg, Listz, Debussy and a couple of Japanese composers, she looked forward to her possible encore. This was not a stuffy audience of social climbers doing their bit to support the classic arts. This Nagasaki audience loved romantic, impressionist moods.

She finished her official program with a fiery rendering of Listz's Hungarian Dances. When she stood to take her bow the audience was ecstatic. She couldn't see if they were on their feet in the blinding lights, but she felt they were. The conductor confirmed her feelings. He had a genuine smile that spread across his face and broke the bounds of oriental politeness. He pointed his baton at Clarissa when she took her second bow. The encore was in.

When that special silence hushed through the hall again, Clarissa found it hard to concentrate. Deep down she knew that she had other motives for playing the piece. Would the same images haunt her?

She poised herself and began. The special mood of the music called on her from deep within. The Kyoto experience was repeating itself in Nagasaki! She clearly saw the pink and turquoise clouds send those rays of golden light through the crystalline tracery of the winter trees. The gilded pagoda shimmered in the snow. As the music changed so the pagoda changed. First it blurred into that pillar of light and then took on the form of Jesus. The snow melted away from the landscape and the trees softened into timeless olives. Then, Clarissa saw Marcus run out and felt Maria's fears as she called him back. She saw the look of concern on Jesus' face as he waved them away. The crescendo followed, leading to the metamorphosis. The brightness of the sunlight pulsed around Joshua, burning his image in her mind, and then faded.

The white of his garment slipped quietly into the snow. The image of the Christ turned back into the grayness of the temple pagoda as the rays of light withdrew into the folds of the pink and turquoise clouds. Clarissa played the final phrase slowly and deliberately. She felt drained and yet full of emotional energy. The mystical images that had come to her through her musical insight of the Kyoto shrine in the snow, had made a sort of photographic imprint on her brain. She knew that every time she played this piece the images would be relived.

When she stood, the audience also stood. Whatever the music had revealed to Clarissa had not marred the natural beauty of the piece with its extraordinary descriptive power. She received her bouquet. She took two more bows. The Nagasaki concert had been a resounding success.

• • • • • • • •

David couldn't sleep. The 'Prince Regent' was rolling and pitching as she crossed the South China sea. Although the officers' accommodation was in an enviable part of the vessel, forward and topsides was not the best place in a storm.

'This might delay our arrival in Macau,' he considered as he looked at his watch. It was two-forty in the morning. He was expecting the agents to come on with the pilot at six.

The 'Prince Regent' had run into rough seas about ten in the morning. The crossing from Manila to China was often a bad one. Many passengers were seasick. There had been no chance to catch the last of the warm sunshine on 'Monkey Island'. Whatever suntan he had now was what he would have for Clarissa.

As he tossed and turned he was eventually lulled into a shallow sleep and a world of dreams that took him back once more to Roman times ....

He saw himself as a tribune. He was surrounded by the splendor of gleaming, white marble. Golden eagles of Imperial power stood on pillars, catching the setting sun. Boxed, miniature, cypress trees graced the terrace where he sat.

A clean-shaven official in a pristine toga, whose face reminded David of that stamped on Roman coins, poured him a goblet of wine. "What do you know about these Nazarenes?" the man asked.

"Not much more than you, Pilatus," David answered.

"But more than me?" the official pressed.

"What do you mean?" David asked feeling a little afraid of his superior. He could tell from the man's tone that this official somehow knew that their thinking was not in tune on this particular subject.

"Why are you so cautious?" the man David had addressed as Pilatus continued. "It's obvious that we have another of these Jewish political movements here which will only end in a bid for freedom and fateful retribution. At least Caiaphas and his Temple hordes have the sense to see that."

"You may be right with reference to the Nazarenes, if you mean by them the general mass of peasants that follow their way," David agreed. "But, I have to say that I'm not sure that I share that view with reference to the leaders, especially the one referred to as the 'King of the Jews' whom we crucified."

"Why, Linus Flavian?" Pilatus asked with assertiveness, but without looking at David or taking his eyes from the view across Roman Jerusalem.

"I met the one called Joshua long before we crucified him. He was a healer in Galilee and in desperation I sought him out to heal my father's steward, Demetrius," David explained.

"And," said Pilatus nonchalantly.

"He healed him. In fact he never even touched him. He merely said that my faith in coming to him was enough to heal him. By the time we arrived at my father's villa above Magdala, Demetrius had recovered."

"Coincidence," Pilatus said staidly, still not taking his gaze from the view of the setting sun over the city.

"It could have been," David admitted, "but I don't think so."

Finally Pilatus turned and looked straight at David. "And why not?" he said firmly. "What was so special about this 'Galilean' that makes you doubt this rather obvious coincidence?"

"In Galilee I witnessed too many miracles performed by this healer. He was a man of extraordinary love with a commanding, but humble presence. I saw him raise a cripple from his pallet. I saw him cure blindness and heal other diverse diseases. The people said that he had even raised a man from the dead!"

"There are a multitude of such 'magic' men in our world," Pilatus assured David. "Many are charlatans, but some do have a measure of success. You'll find them in Rome just as you will in Jerusalem."

"I know, sir. That I can't deny. But this man was different. You found it hard to press charges against him yourself when the High Priests sent him to us."

"I really can't remember," Pilatus answered. "I presumed he was just another, political trouble-maker."

"There was trouble after we crucified him. There was a clash between those who believed in this man, and the Temple authorities."

Pilatus nodded. "Ah, yes. The crucifixions two years ago."

"Correct, sir. There was a clash between these people and the Temple. I believed that their differences were purely to do with interpretation of their religion. I think the High Priests used us to quell this movement because they didn't like the threat to their own religious security. I don't believe these Nazarenes, or at least those who were the actual disciples of the miracle-worker, had any political desire to overthrow our authority."

"So you think we miscarried justice?" Pilatus stated severely.

David sipped on his wine nervously. "I think we might have been just a little hasty in condemning the healer to the cross."

"Sometimes we have to put expediency before true justice in order to maintain law and order," Pilatus reminded David.

"That's just what my father said," David recalled.

"Your father Flavius Septimus is a wise man. It's a shame that he retired from public life so young. Alright, Linus Flavian, you've been honest with me so I'll be honest with you. I'll always put the good law and order of the Prefecture first, but I'll accept that your theory may be right. The High Priests are trying to use us to gain their desires. It may be the High Priests that we should observe more carefully. Now, what about the Roman Jew, Saul of Tarsus?"

"You mean the High Priest's representative?"

"Yes," Pilatus confirmed.

"He's a clever man - well educated. But he's a man who has to be watched. He'll try hard to gain his own way against great odds. I think he used us, sir. There's no hidden leader in the wilderness. The ghost of Joshua, the 'King of the Jews' is their leader. I've met them since, when I was up in Galilee. They have quite a following in Capernaum, the town where Joshua lived."

"This following - did it exist before he came down here challenging the authority of the High Priestly hierarchy?"

"Yes," David acknowledged before continuing his revelations. "Some of them think they've seen Joshua in their dreams and that he can still guide them in some spiritual way."

"Amusing," Pilatus concluded.

"I think it's quite probable," David said with greater commitment. "My mother was sick and his spirit came to them in this way and she was healed."

"You mean one of them communicated your mother's needs in their dreams and she was healed?"

"Something like that."

"Well let's hope that these Nazarenes can restrict their work to such healing practices and not become the objects of High Priestly wrath that provokes them to rebellious action thus calling on our wrath," Pilatus said, letting David know that no matter what either of them thought, it was the safety of the State that had to come first - Roman duty as opposed to human sentiment.

"Let's hope so," David agreed as he tried to smile off the disclosure of his sentiments.

Pilatus raised his goblet.

"Don't worry, Linus Flavian," he said. "Your secret feelings are safe with me just as long as we serve Caesar, Syria and the Prefecture. To duty, Linus!" ....

"To duty!" David shouted out as he came from dream vision to full waking. Reality returned in a breath as he rolled from one side of his bed to the other. There was a crash as toiletries fell to the floor in his bathroom. He heard a drinking glass break.

The ship rolled the other way and there was a further crash from the bathroom. 'That was a big one,' he thought. 'God knows what the office will look like in the morning. I think the girls had everything taped, but things are really shifting.'

He thought about that for a moment until the ship lurched again. Some trays clattered in a pantry.

"Jesus Christ!" he cried out. "Why can't someone calm the waters?" Then he laughed at his own joke.

His dream went round and round in his head as insomnia continued throughout the storm. He didn't remember all the minute details, but he was again aware that he had been a Roman. This time he was sure that he'd been a tribune named Linus Flavian and he realized that he had known Pontius Pilate.

At four in the morning he called the Bridge.

"What's our ETA?" he asked.

"We're running about two to three hours behind at the moment, David," the First Officer answered. "The 'Old Man' thinks we should be picking up the pilot just before nine and alongside about ten-thirty."

"That'll mess up the tours a bit," David noted. "It'll leave us with lunch problems. We'll be ready at eight just in case you make up time. We're not getting much sleep here anyway. Thanks for the info."

"You're welcome," the First Officer replied.

He called the Crew Purser.

"I hope I didn't wake you Paddy, but I doubt it," he said when he heard the Crew Purser's Irish brogue. "New ETA for pilot is eight-forty five. We'll be ready at eight. If it calms down a bit you have an extra two hours."

"Thanks a bunch!" the Crew Purser replied. "I haven't slept a wink. How's your cabin?"

"Not too bad. Something's gone down in the bathroom."

"Chaos here," the Crew Purser said laughing. "My best whiskey's gone. The whole place reeks like an Irish bog!"

"See you at eight," David said and hung up.

Next he called the Manifest Officer. She was awake and even thinking of getting up.

"I'll have them all ready by eight," she responded. "I hope the drawers held in the office."

"Thanks. See you there," David replied.

He saw no point in trying to get to sleep. He decided to get up and do some work. Maybe if he cleared his desk now, even though the ship was still bouncing around, he might get to see something of Macau. He was planning on dining out with the Hotel Manager in the evening. They had planned that a long time ago. David wanted to get off in the afternoon and just walk about for an hour or two to check out some of the old, Portuguese architecture. It wasn't often that they came into Macau because of its proximity to Hong Kong.

The office wasn't too chaotic. A few, surface papers were lying on the floor, but most drawers and doors had held. His staff had done a good job. 'I owe them one,' he thought, and he began to go through his files.

As they approached land, the seas abated. Things began to come back to normal.

• • • • • • • •

Clarissa arrived on schedule in Hong Kong two days before the 'Prince Regent'. When she came through Customs she looked around for her contact from 'Global Artistes', her London-based

Agency. They had set up the Japanese tour and arranged for her television performance and radio interviews in Hong Kong. They had also informed her that Gloria Ainsworth from Hong Kong Radio would meet her. Finally, in that sea of humanity that always seems to be milling around in Hong Kong, she saw a label displaying her name - 'Clarissa Corrington'. She never could quite get used to the reality that for eight months now she had been Clarissa Peterson. She had performed as 'Clarissa Corrington' all her life. The alliteration seemed to suit the classical music world. She pushed her baggage cart in that direction.

Holding the sign was a lady in her forties. She was wearing a chic suit of Asian design, but it was obviously not Chinese. Of medium build with strawberry blonde, close-cropped hair, she looked the part of a female executive.

The lady extended a hand. "Clarissa Corrington?" she asked.

"Yes, that's right. You must be Gloria?"

"Welcome to Hong Kong," Gloria replied with a clipped, British accent such as is rarely heard in the mother country any more. "Did you have a good flight?"

"Very good."

Clarissa realized Gloria was sizing up her baggage wondering how they would manage. It was all on one cart, but the three bags were large and looked heavy. "It is rather a lot for one person," Clarissa admitted. "I'm traveling around the world. I started out on a music cruise through the Panama Canal, then took the 'QE2' across to Hawaii before flying to Japan. From Hong Kong I'll be continuing the journey with my husband on the 'Prince Regent', finally getting off in Israel. Unfortunately I really need a lot with me apart from the concert dresses. There's so much music."

"We'll manage alright," Gloria said. "Plenty of room. I'll have to fetch the car, so wait for me on the curbside just through the doors there. I'll be back in a jiffy. It's not far."

Gloria Ainsworth moved into the sea of dark-haired Asians, her blonde head bobbing between them until she reached an escalator and disappeared. Clarissa pushed the heavy cart through the doors and out into the pick-up area. Traffic controllers blew whistles, frantically pointing taxis to the curbside. Buses roared, brakes squealed, children yelled. There were people everywhere. Clarissa knew from the hustle and bustle that she was back in Hong Kong.

'David will sail in the day after tomorrow,' she thought as she waited.

Gloria wasn't long. Her blue hatchback pulled up. A curbside superintendent helped load the bags. In no time the car was moving out into the heavy traffic of Kowloon.

"We'll take the tunnel," Gloria said patiently. "It'll be easier on the other side. It's always jammed over here."

Once they were in the tunnel and moving at a reasonable pace, Gloria started asking Clarissa some of the questions that she knew would eventually come up in their interview. "Now, the agency told me you were from America - from Minnesota. You don't sound like an American?"

"I'm not," Clarissa replied. "I've lived in the United States for many years, but I was brought up and raised in Ireland."

"Southern Ireland?"

"Yes - County Tipperary."

"Goodness gracious! You don't say! What an incredible coincidence! My family were from Tipperary. They came from Neenagh."

"That would be North Tipperary," Clarissa noted. "My family are living further south - outside Ardfinnan between Clonmel and Cahir."

"Ireland is such a gorgeous country. I used to visit my granny in Neenagh, but unfortunately we never lived there," Gloria explained. "Daddy was in the Guards and we lived in London. Eventually he was posted here in Hong Kong, so I came out when I was nineteen. I've never regretted it. I love Hong Kong. Anyway, that's enough about me. How did you come to leave Ireland?"

"Opportunities just opened up for me in the Americas," Clarissa explained. "And I was at school in England."

"Where?"

"West Heath - I hated it," Clarissa replied.

"I don't believe it! I went to Benenden," Gloria revealed. "We were in the same part of the country. We used to play hockey and lacrosse against you."

Clarissa laughed. "I'm afraid I hated games. That was the worst part of school for me. I don't know why so many people say school days are the best years of your life. I couldn't wait to get back home to Ireland for the holidays. Apart from my music, horses were my only interest in those days."

"And so how did you get started on your music career?" Gloria finally asked.

"It was very competitive as a student," Clarissa explained. "I won a place at the Guildhall School of Music in London. I played at Wigmore

Hall and with the London Symphony at the Festival and Royal Albert Halls after I finished at Guildhall. I was lucky. That opened up a career for me in the great concert halls of Europe. But in a way I got that out of my system. I toured with the Dublin Philharmonic. You know, it seems classical musicians the world over seem to want to play in Paris, Vienna, Salzburg, Berlin, Prague and Munich. It's great training to play at the hub of the music world, but you have more freedom to express yourself elsewhere, where the competition for classical perfection is less. When I was invited to tour in America I just felt I had found that freedom that I couldn't find in Europe."

"More so than London?" Gloria asked as they left the tunnel and passed through the 'Central' district before climbing up from Victoria to the 'Peak'.

"Funnily enough, I never played much in England when I was touring in Europe. I went back to London from the United States. Now, I play in London at least twice a year. Actually I'm doing a video series in England later this year."

Gloria started to point out the landmarks as the road wound its way up past the sunken bowl of Happy Valley Racetrack and skirted the more lavish area of the 'Peak'. It crested to reveal views over Repulse Bay across to the outer islands and the open sea. It was not long before they pulled in to the garage beneath the tower block where Gloria lived with her husband Patrick and their Irish setter.

The flat, as Gloria called their apartment, was on the eighteenth floor. A Filipino maid opened the door.

"Hello, Millie," Gloria said in her hearty, English way. "Sorry we were a bit long. The traffic was beastly in Kowloon. Is Mr. Ainsworth back yet?"

"No ma'am. He called and said he would be back about six-thirty."

Gloria introduced Clarissa. "Millie, this is our special guest, Clarissa Corrington."

The maid smiled.

"The porter's bringing up her bags," Gloria continued. "Clarissa's a very well-known pianist. She's going to do a piece for us on the telly tomorrow and we'll be talking on the radio show."

Millie nodded politely. "Shall I open the kettle for tea?" she said.

"That would be wonderful!" Gloria agreed.

Millie went to the kitchen.

The views were stunning from all the windows. The back of the apartment looked up into the craggy heights behind Repulse Bay and the big, picture windows all along the front, looked out over the water to the outer islands.

"The ships must have to come past here on their way in to the harbor?" Clarissa suggested.

"All the large ships approach Hong Kong harbor this way," Gloria replied.

"My husband will be coming in on the 'Prince Regent' the day after tomorrow. Maybe we'll see his ship?"

"Almost certainly, my dear. The 'Prince Regent' is a luxury cruise ship isn't she?"

"Yes. My husband's the Chief Purser on board. It's the ship I'll be joining."

"Oh that's right! You told me. The ship that's taking you to Israel. We should see her. They usually come by about seven-thirty in the morning."

They walked over to the window. "They come quite close to this side of the bay," Gloria explained. "We should see her come round from behind those three islands and right up past Aberdeen." Gloria looked down as they admired the view. "Right below us is the old Repulse Bay Hotel. That tall block beside us is built up from the shell of the old hotel. They restored the terrace and facade when they pulled the old building down. It's a wonderful club now. We thought we'd have dinner there tonight. If Patrick's back at the usual time, we should be able to have drinks on the terrace before sundown. It's one of the great experiences of Hong Kong."

The doorbell rang. Millie opened it and the porter brought in Clarissa's bags.

"Let me show you your room," Gloria suggested.

The porter followed them.

The guest room only had a partial view of the bay and mostly looked out on the side of the hill. It was comfortable, however, and Millie had placed an abundance of towels in the bathroom.

Gloria left Clarissa to refresh herself. Soon Clarissa heard a dog barking. The Irish setter had been released from somewhere.

"Tea's ready!" Millie shouted out from the kitchen.

Gloria knocked on Clarissa's door. The dog made a great fuss of Clarissa when they sat down for tea in the living room.

"Millie," Gloria called out softly. "You don't need to stay tonight. You can leave now if you like, but could you take Brewster out first."

"Alright ma'am."

Millie took down the dog's lead from a hook by the front door. In a bound Brewster was beside her. The door closed and Gloria and Clarissa were left to themselves and their steaming cups of English tea.

"Millie's wonderful," Gloria said. "She's just a super girl."

Later, after Patrick had come home, they went down to the Repulse Bay Club for dinner. The view from the terrace after the sun had dropped behind the hills, was everything that Gloria had described. So was the immaculate service of the club stewards and the impressive menu that combined French and Oriental dishes.

"Clarissa goes to Israel from here, Patrick," Gloria explained after they had exhausted the normal topics of conversation about the club, the food and Hong Kong life in general.

"Well, by way of Bangkok, Bali, Singapore, India, Africa and the Suez Canal," Clarissa said with a chuckle. "I'm sailing with my husband. He's Chief Purser on the 'Prince Regent'. The ship's on her annual World Cruise."

"How long will she be in Hong Kong?" Patrick asked.

"Four days," Clarissa replied.

"Maybe you and your husband would like to join us Saturday night at the farm?"

"Why not? What a great idea, Patrick," Gloria echoed. "We have this old farmhouse in the New Territories where we hide on the weekends. It was pretty run down when we bought it, but Patrick's been restoring it. It's not really a farm now, but it does show another side to Hong Kong other than shopping and hotels. We love it there. It might be a nice break for your husband."

"I'm sure we'd love to," Clarissa answered. "Perhaps we can let you know once I've found out what David's plans on the ship are in Hong Kong. They get terribly busy on board and he may not be able to sneak away overnight, but it would be nice for him if we can."

"Well, tell us about Israel?" Gloria continued wanting to get back to the subject. "That's such a fascinating part of the world."

"Gloria has this notion she lived there once before," Patrick interjected.

Clarissa gulped. "What!" she blurted out as if she didn't believe what she was hearing.

"Yes," Patrick continued. "She's into this reincarnation bit. It's something that's grown within her ever since she interviewed a lama."

"One of those monks from Tibet?"

"Yes. It was quite an event in Hong Kong," Patrick explained. "Most the monks fled Tibet when the Chinese moved in, so to have one on the show roused a lot of curiosity and some heated discussion. There was considerable interest in Hong Kong at the time."

"Tell me about your past life in Israel?" Clarissa asked Gloria enthusiastically.

"I believe I lived there in the time of Christ," Gloria answered in a matter of fact sort of way. "I saw Jesus. I followed him out to Golgotha the day they crucified him."

"Do you remember what he looked like?"

"He had extraordinary eyes even as he carried his crossbeam. His face and hair were all matted with the blood from the thorns that they stuck in his head, so it's hard for me to recall much more about him facially. But he'd undergone a dreadful whipping. The welts on his back were unbelievable. He fell down close to where I was standing and he looked straight at me as if pleading for me to help him up. The Roman soldiers kicked him, trying to get him to stand again, but he just lay there helplessly. A stranger close to me ran out to assist him. The Romans yelled at the man and seized him. Then, they forced him to carry Jesus' crossbeam."

"That was Simon of Cyrene," Patrick added, just in case Clarissa was not familiar with the Bible story.

"Quite a crowd had gathered along the death walk," Gloria continued. "Some jeered and threw rubbish at him, but there were a good many who wept and called out to him with compassion. Some shouted his name, but it wasn't 'Jesus' as we know it. They shouted 'Joshua!' which was his real name at the time. Jesus is just a Greek and Latin translation of the Hebrew name."

"Yes. I'm interested in this first century period myself," Clarissa revealed cautiously. "I know about the name 'Joshua'."

Patrick smiled.

"Did you follow them to the crucifixion?" Clarissa asked eagerly. "Did you see them nail him to the cross?"

"I went with the crowd. I was curious. The rumor was that Joshua had upset the Temple authorities. He'd caused some kind of a riot with the moneychangers."

"That hardly seems enough to merit crucifixion," Clarissa continued.

"Some said he was a zealot leader which would have bothered the Romans. They were very suspicious of anyone who set himself up as any kind of a leader that was not sanctioned by the Temple hierarchy. The Romans really controlled the High Priests at the Temple. Many Jews, including my own first century parents who were wealthy merchants, were quite happy with the Roman presence. It gave us security and prosperity. The fanatics called us 'Herodians' or 'Roman Jews'."

"Did you think Jesus was a troublemaker at the time?" Clarissa asked.

"I'd never heard of him until I found myself face to face with him in the street," Gloria admitted. "But I heard much more about him after his death."

"What do you mean?"

"Joseph of Arimathea was a friend of my father's. He visited us several times before he left Jerusalem. He mentioned Joshua. He said that he was convinced Joshua was a Holy man. He was healed by him from an almost certain early death. He was apparently riddled with worms. Somehow, Joshua healed him."

"He was the man who gave Jesus his tomb," Clarissa said vaguely remembering the details of the Easter story.

"Yes. He was a wheeler-dealer like my first century father. He had connections all over the Roman Empire. Not long after Jesus' death he left Jerusalem and we never saw him again. He said he was going to Gaul. Apparently he had some sort of an illicit relationship with one of Joshua's girlfriends and finding out he'd got her pregnant, fled Jerusalem with her. It was something of a social stigma. The woman was an uneducated Galilean."

"How do you know all this?" Clarissa asked after one of the stewards poured them all after-dinner coffee.

"Most of it was revealed to me in a regression session I had with a psychologist I interviewed," Gloria explained. "He offered to lead me into a past life experience if I was receptive. Apparently I was, but it took about three sessions to come out with all the details I've just told you. During the first session I only regressed to my great grandfather's time in Ireland. Then at the next session I was taken back to a life as a Portuguese trader. That was when I first encountered the Orient. It wasn't until the third session that I worked my regression back to these revelations about Palestine in the First Century. I told the therapist much the same thing I've told you."

"Fascinating!" Clarissa exclaimed. "And you really believe all this?"

"The man told me after the last session that he was quite sure I was really there. I believe him. A lot of things have come to me in dreams since."

"Have you met many other people who can recall their own past lives?" Clarissa asked.

"It comes up quite often on the radio show," Patrick intervened. "Whenever Gloria delves into matters of the occult this subject of past lives seems to surface."

"Yes. It's all part of reincarnation," Gloria explained. "If you believe in the soul's advancement through many lifetimes you are bound to become curious about your own past lives. After interviewing the lama I became fascinated by the whole reincarnational process. After all, it's all around us in the traditions of Asia."

Clarissa sipped on her coffee, subconsciously looking around at the other tables before she plucked up courage to bring up her own experiences. "I find this whole subject fascinating. Would you think it just a coincidence, or some sort of divine guidance if I were to reveal to you that I too have had first century, past life revelations from Israel?"

"Not at all," Gloria answered in a sincere and interested tone. "That's often how Spirit works."

Clarissa hesitated. "Well, you'll never believe this, but I think I knew Jesus too." She blushed. "I believe I was Mary Magdalene."

Gloria looked at Patrick. "I don't believe this!" she exclaimed excitedly. "How was this revealed to you?"

"Mostly in dreams, but also in certain visions and mutual dreams with other people. It seems that I keep meeting people in this life who I knew in that first century past. It's like a great jigsaw puzzle that is slowly coming together."

"I believe we all have the potential to tap into our past lives," Gloria confirmed. "If something really powerful bound us together in the past it's highly probable that we'll be united again. Perhaps one could describe it as the life energies combining the same chemistry again and again."

"Jesus might have had such energy," Clarissa noted.

"Exactly. Maybe the energy that was focussed in Jesus, touching lives in the First Century, might have acted as a force through to the present day. Possibly that's what we're now experiencing and possibly that's what brings us together."

Patrick shook his head. "Steady, Gloria," he warned her. "Let's not go in too far with this. Let's just leave it that you both lived past lives at the time of Christ."

Gloria had a faraway look. "Well, I'm not sure," she said. "I think Clarissa and I should talk some more, but right now perhaps we should make a move. We have to be at the studio early in the morning."

Patrick took care of the check.

"It really is very lovely here," Clarissa acknowledged as they looked out at the twinkling lights of passing junks among the cargo vessels in the harbor passage.

· · · · · · · ·

As Clarissa slept in the Ainsworth's guest room, so first century images returned. She dreamed she was on a sailing vessel ....

A well-dressed man, who she instinctively knew to be Joseph of Arimathea, stood on the deck beside her. Her son, Marcus, was with her as in past revelations.

"Gaul," Joseph said as they looked up at light-colored cliffs. "It won't be too much further now."

"I can feel the baby," she said. "He's kicking me, Joseph."

"Don't worry, Maria," the older man reassured her. "Your child will be born in Massilia. I'll take care of Joshua's son" ....

Clarissa awoke, her heart pounding. "Joshua's son!" she shouted as she sat bolt upright in the darkness. She switched on the bedside lamp and reached for her dream journal.

'February third,' she wrote. 'Tonight it was revealed to me that I was to be the mother of Joshua's child.' She then recorded as much of the dream about Joseph of Arimathea as she could remember. Turning to the last page she added to her list of names - 'Gloria Ainsworth - Friend of Joseph of Arimathea.'

Clarissa's brain was in turmoil. It was a long time before she slept again that night. It seemed no sooner had she dozed off then Gloria came in, waking her with a refreshing cup of tea.

"Did you sleep well, dear?" Gloria said as she put the tray down on the bedside table.

"Very well," Clarissa lied sleepily. "What time is it?"

"Ten past six," Gloria announced as she went to the window to open the drapes. "We must leave by quarter past seven. They expect us in the studio at half past eight and the traffic is simply dreadful at that hour."

The studio was at Broadcast Drive in North Kowloon. Clarissa was to take part in a cultural program featuring various visiting artists from around the world. Gloria knew all the people in the studio which made the preliminary work easy. Then followed the long sessions in make-up and the slow laborious technical rehearsal, which left only a minimum of time for Clarissa to try out the concert Grand. When all seemed to be in order, there followed that typical, broadcasting phenomenon of hurry up and wait. When she was called to perform on camera it was already three-thirty in the afternoon. Once out there, the time flew by as Clarissa became immersed in her music. In this particular recital she had been asked to incorporate one of her own personal compositions. Since there was no studio audience, she had to rely on the smiles and thumbs up symbols of the cameramen to measure her standard. They seemed impressed. She hoped the producers on the other side of the glass were equally as pleased.

"That was wonderful," Gloria said as she greeted Clarissa after the performance. "They loved it."

"Are you sure?" Clarissa asked, being just a little nervous about the rather esoteric and personal nature of the last piece, an 'ode to love' that she had actually written for David shortly after they'd become engaged.

"I was with the producer while you were playing. He was enchanted," Gloria assured her. "Now, when we do our interview on the radio tonight you won't mind if I ask you about that piece?"

"Of course not, Gloria. It means a great deal to me."

"Why don't we take tea at the Peninsula Hotel next? It's time for a break," Gloria suggested. "We can prepare ourselves for tonight's program after that."

They hadn't eaten all day other than a slice of toast with marmalade before they had left the apartment in the morning.

It was only a short taxi ride to the 'Peninsula'. Afternoon tea in the foyer was rather a formal event and a meal in itself. In this respect Clarissa realized that some aspects of Hong Kong life were entrenched in British traditions. There was a trolley of assorted teas. Gloria made their selection. Delicate cucumber sandwiches, and finger's of Gentlemen's relish followed. Fruit cake, manageable meringues, scones and strawberry jam were also offered. As an extra, one could order fresh strawberries and cream. Gloria did. All was served to the strains of a string quartet that intermingled popular melodies from Noel Coward and Ivor Novello with the lighter side of Mozart and Bach. It was all frightfully genteel.

"I like to indulge myself here once in a while," Gloria said as she tackled one of the gooey meringues. "Your visit to us gives me the perfect excuse."

"Hong Kong is such a bustling city," Clarissa had to acknowledge. "It really has something for everybody. Here one can eat in the best restaurants of the world, buy every kind of clothing available or escape to the more primitive, but nonetheless charming world of the Chinese river people. It's all here. Right now we could be at the Ritz in London."

"That's what I like about Hong Kong," Gloria agreed. "Almost everybody who's anybody at some point comes through the city. I've probably had more opportunities broadcasting here, where the lifestyle is so much more pleasant, than I would have had in double the years in London. Remember, here I pretty much have a monopoly on who's news."

Clarissa laughed. "So I'm news!" she exclaimed.

"Certainly!" Gloria replied. "Not only are you a magnificent pianist whose work deserves to be heard, but you also have these fascinating insights into the past. You don't mind if we touch on that tonight, do you?" She raised her eyebrows with a genteel concern that could only beg the answer 'Yes'.

"Well, er ..." Clarissa stammered. "Well only in a very general way, Gloria. I mean, I believe I lived in the First Century. I believe there is some strange force that is bringing me together with others who I might have known in the First Century. But I can't very well tell your listeners that I might have been Mary Magdalene!"

Gloria smiled. "I don't expect you to," she said reassuringly. "The interview will focus mostly on your music, especially on your own compositions. I would like to tie that in with your husband's arrival in Hong Kong tomorrow on the 'Prince Regent' - that's local news. You did say that the 'Ode to love' was dedicated to him at the time you became engaged."

"Yes."

"So you don't mind us chatting about that?"

"No, of course not. I'm proud to talk about our love."

"Good. Now, after we've explored all that, you'll have a chance to play. Incidentally, that should be a short, lyrical piece - not too classical."

"No problem," Clarissa chipped-in excitedly. "I have this new composition that I premiered in Nagasaki last week. It's quite short and got a standing ovation in Japan. It's a piece about a winter scene at a Kyoto temple pagoda. I call it 'Gilded Snow'."

"Sounds perfect," Gloria agreed. "Now, it's after you've played that we'll move into the reincarnation area. I'll tell you why I want to bring this up. I have three other guests tonight. One of them is a Chinese local government official who has been on the show before. I know that he's willing to speak about past lives. The subject underlies a lot of Chinese thought. What happens is I try to establish a dialogue with the listeners at home. Some will call in, but I also try to be on the pulse of what I believe they'll be thinking. I then try to draw my guests into the discussion. You'll be on last, so we can explore past lives in a general way as our post interview, ongoing discussion. I don't like to structure things too much as it kills the spontaneity, but do you catch on?"

This wasn't exactly what Clarissa had expected, but somehow she felt protected and secure in Gloria's hands. "Yes. I'll go along with whatever you say," she replied.

"Good. I think we're going to have an exciting evening," Gloria intimated as she reached for the silver teapot. "Now, can I pour you another cup?"

"Thanks," Clarissa nodded. She felt strangely exhilarated. She could see that Gloria usually got her way, which was probably why she was such a success on Hong Kong Radio. There was something very comforting in Gloria's confidence. Clarissa was also glad that she was going to get another chance to play 'Gilded Snow'. She was really pleased with the composition and looked forward to hopefully recording it on a new album in the not too distant future.

· · · · · · · ·

C larissa had felt a little nervous sitting through Gloria's interviews with the other guests. But when the time came to bring her 'on the air' she relaxed, warming to Gloria's smile.

"My next guest on this evening's edition of 'The pulse of the Fragrant Harbor' is world-renowned, Concert Pianist, Clarissa Corrington," Gloria announced. She turned to Clarissa. "Welcome to the show."

"It's a pleasure to be here."

"Clarissa Corrington has just completed a very successful tour in Japan, her first tour in Asia for some time," Gloria continued. "Earlier today Clarissa recorded for Hong Kong Television and that brilliant recital will be broadcast on Sunday, but tell us first what has motivated you to bring your talent to the Orient?"

"My agency, 'Global Artistes' based in London, set up the tour," Clarissa explained. "They knew that I needed to be in Hong Kong at this time in order to meet up with the luxury cruise ship the 'Prince Regent'."

"She comes in to Kowloon tomorrow?"

"Yes."

"And you'll be sailing out from Hong Kong on her in four days time?"

"That's right."

"I should explain that Clarissa is a regular traveler on the high seas. Her husband, David Peterson, happens to be the Chief Purser on board the 'Prince Regent' and every year the ship completes a cruise around the world. Some of you may see the ship come in tomorrow morning and some of us may be lucky enough to be going on board. How long will you be sailing?" Gloria asked.

"About six weeks. I leave the vessel in Haifa for a concert in Jerusalem."

"Well, let's look at your music," Gloria continued as she moved into the more serious part of the interview. She wanted to know how Clarissa saw herself in the concert circuit as a cross-over artist.

As best she could, Clarissa went through the old territory of a classical upbringing and orchestral success, but how she had always felt that there was a more personal way for her to express her music. She indicated how the great, impressionist composers had inspired her and how later the Orient had influenced her. She told the listeners how she had been invited to tour in China and had become impressed by the philosophy behind traditional, oriental music. "Music should interpret the reaction of one's heart and be carried by one's soul," Clarissa explained. "It should represent the vibration of the universe."

"You mean the old, medieval term becoming one with 'the music of the spheres'," Gloria suggested, trying to assist Clarissa in the depth of this rather esoteric discussion.

"Precisely. All music is vibrations and the 'music of the spheres' is only the vibration that holds the universe together. So you see, to some people music becomes an access to the light and sound of God."

"And does it for you?" Gloria asked.

"It should. I'm not sure that all music does. If melody is subjected too much to repetitive rhythm this chance to soar seems to become lost. Some of the over-structured classics are that way which is why I like the romantics and impressionists. Mind you the strict classics are good training in discipline," Clarissa added with a chuckle. "It's hard to become an accomplished pianist unless you've subjected yourself to that classical discipline." She didn't want to give Gloria's listeners any notion that she was opposed to the classics. "Really what I would like to say is that rhythms should become melodies. The rhythm of nature becomes a melody. The rhythm of the universe becomes the music of the spheres."

"I think you've said it beautifully," Gloria stated sincerely. "Do you think you could share one of your own compositions with us?"

"I'd love to. Actually, I'd like to share with our listeners a piece that I wrote only last week during my Japanese tour. I was inspired by a snow scene in Kyoto. The snow contrasted with the sparkling gold of a temple pagoda. Late, afternoon sun was breaking through gray clouds in a luminous patch that became a kaleidoscope of yellow, pink, green and turquoise. It was almost as if God had opened a window in the sky to illuminate those gilded roofs. While the window was open I became spellbound and uplifted into other worlds. It can be a crystalline moment when music causes you to soar with heart and soul, but you have to catch it while you can. Even in my vision at the pagoda, eventually the cloudy drabness returned. I'd like to play for you 'Gilded Snow'."

Clarissa then played.

Gloria could see that her Chinese guests, who had said nothing during her preliminary interview with Clarissa, were impressed. There was something about this piece that had the timeless, ethereal quality of Debussy's 'Clair de Lune'. It was on Clarissa, however, that the music had the greatest effect. The identical vision of the illuminated Christ returned just as it had on the other occasions.

The piece completed, the three Chinese gentlemen clapped loudly. Clarissa returned to her seat beside Gloria.

The local government official congratulated her. "Velly good Miss Collington - Beautiful, beautiful music."

Clarissa smiled. "Thanks. That piece surprises me. It actually moves me very much ... and I wrote it!"

"We should feel very privileged in Hong Kong," Gloria continued in her general broadcast to the listeners. "That's only the second time this piece has been performed in public. It was only written last week. I'm sure we'll be hearing it again as it makes its way around the world." Then Gloria turned back to Clarissa. "What is it that really surprises you about this piece?"

"It transports me in time whenever I play it," Clarissa explained. "I have this strange vision that takes me back two thousand years."

"To a past life?" Gloria asked excitedly, but with enough sincerity to reassure Clarissa that it was all right to bring up the topic now.

"I suppose you could say that," Clarissa admitted. "As the sun from this opening in the clouds sheds this amazing kaleidoscope of light on the pagoda, the whole scene changes before my eyes. I didn't write it this way. I wrote about the light on the pagoda. That's what inspired me in Kyoto. But, when I play the piece, a different image comes to me. The pagoda becomes a sort of beacon of light as a metamorphosis takes place. The snow melts away to dry, dusty earth beneath a grove of ancient, olive trees somewhere in Biblical times. I'm there, hiding behind a rock with my son, Marcus. The pagoda becomes Joshua, the Christ."

"Why 'Joshua'?" Gloria asked slowly.

"Because that was his real name. 'Jesus' is only a Greek translation. I'm sure the person standing in this shaft of brilliant sunlight is Joshua," Clarissa insisted with a certain knowingness.

"And Marcus ... you know your son's name was Marcus?"

"Yes. But, Joshua doesn't seem to want us there. When Marcus runs out he signals to him to go back."

"Who tells you his name is Marcus?" Gloria repeated.

"Nobody, Gloria," Clarissa said in something of a daze. "I just know."

"Well, there we have something," Gloria acknowledged openly to her audience, "an extraordinary revelation from an extraordinary musician. I think what Clarissa has shown us is that music can become a channel leading us from the reality of our present experience, whether through beauty or emotion, to a spiritual experience or contact with that music of the spheres, where perhaps for a moment we can leave these shackles of time." She addressed Clarissa again who looked a little shattered that she had allowed herself to reveal so much. "Obviously you believe in reincarnation?"

"Yes. I've certainly come to believe in past lives although I can't say that I was brought up in such a tradition." Clarissa laughed as she looked at Gloria. "It wouldn't exactly have sat well with the staid congregation of the protestant Church of Ireland and certainly not with the Catholics."

Gloria agreed. "No, I can relate to that myself," she admitted, "but on the other hand we Irish do have a Celtic mystic streak which may be why we've found it easier to adapt to these things once we're free from local convention. But back to your recent revelation. You believe that this is about a past life when you might have lived at the time of Christ?"

"Yes, it does seem that way," Clarissa answered somewhat hesitantly.

"Have you any recollection of past lives in other centuries?"

'Thank goodness she's steering me away from Mary Magdalene,' Clarissa thought before answering. "Yes I do remember other past life experiences. Once I was a Mongolian warlord and was put to death in front of the Emperor of China when I was trying to rescue my wife from her captors. All I remember is this flashing blade and that was it. In a medieval lifetime I was a bee keeper at a monastery in England. That's interesting because I was a man in that lifetime. I don't have recollection of too many other past lives, but that doesn't mean I don't believe I've lived them." Clarissa hesitated. 'I don't think I should say too much about being a prostitute slave in India,' she thought, abandoning this part of the discussion. "If soul goes onward in a journey to perfect itself so to become one with God, it must progress through many lives. Most of the time, however, we are blind to what's been in our past or what even might be in the future."

Clarissa's casual mention that in the past she had once been a man, caught the interest of the listeners. They began to call in. From here the interview opened into the general past life discussion that Gloria had wanted and the subject became objective enough for Clarissa's fears to become abated. Listeners exchanged past life experiences and the three Chinese gentlemen became engrossed in discussion with Gloria and her American-Irish guest.

· · · · · · · ·

After dining in the officers' mess, David went back to his cabin for an early night. He knew he would have to be up at the crack of dawn, although the worst of the paperwork had already been cleared by the Hong Kong immigration officials who'd boarded the 'Prince Regent' in Macau. He had barely turned out his light when the phone rang. "Drat it! Whose that!" he said as he reached for the handset.

"David old pal! Martin here - the boxing kangaroo! I'm back in the radio room. I thought you might be interested to know your wife's on local radio."

"Clara?" David shouted.

"Yes. Clarissa Corrington. That's her stage name isn't it?"

"Yes! That's her! What station?"

"Channel seven - It's coming through loud and clear. We're off the outer islands now and can pick it up easily."

"Thanks for letting me know. She said something about recitals and interviews in Japan and Hong Kong."

David tuned in.

The interviewer's voice came over the air. "Back to you over in Lantana. Did you learn of your past life experience through a dream or through revelations?"

"It was initiated in a dream," a well-educated voice returned. "At first I just thought of the experience in that way. I dreamed I was a French soldier in the colonial wars in North America. I became separated from my fellow soldiers and eventually made my way to a log cabin where an English family of fur trappers were living. They took me in and I lived with them for about six years. During that time I became quite friendly with one of their daughters, a beautiful, young girl in her early teens."

"And you now think you've met this girl in the Twentieth Century?" the interviewer interrupted.

"Yes, she's my wife."

"So what you're really saying is that the love which was kindled, but not fulfilled in the Eighteenth Century, has now continued in the Twentieth?"

"That's exactly how it is," the man replied. "My dream was a window into that past life."

David heard Clarissa's voice as she joined in the radio discussion. "Marriages are sometimes brought together in ways that seem beyond our control. My own marriage was predicted by a close friend of mine three years before I ever laid eyes on the man who became my husband. She told me his name, David Peterson. I'd never met anyone of this name, but she had a dream about our wedding. She was one of the guests. For three years I really laughed at her, but sure enough when I met the man I was to eventually marry, his name was David Peterson."

"And he's now the Chief Purser on a ship arriving at Ocean Terminal tomorrow, the 'Prince Regent'," the interviewer, now turned moderator, interjected.

"That's right, and I can't wait to see him!"

David's heart jumped with anticipation and excitement. He felt Clarissa's love over the air waves.

"Well, I'm sure you'll both have a very happy reunion tomorrow," the moderator continued. "We certainly all wish you such from Hong Kong Radio. But, tell us before we close, how can you be sure that you would have fallen in love with this man and married him if your friend had not shown you the way?"

"It's not like that, Gloria. Samantha didn't show me the way. I really didn't believe her at the time she told me and even less as nearly three years went by. When I did meet David, the last thing I thought about was Samantha's dream. It wasn't until after we became interested in seeing each other that I began to associate David's name with the dream. Even then, I had to confirm it. Samantha writes down her dreams and that's not a bad practice for all of us, otherwise we forget them very quickly. Dreams really can lead to an awakening of our soul memory."

"What did your husband think when you told him?" Gloria asked.

"Well, I didn't tell him for a long time. I guess I wanted to be absolutely sure we were in love." Clarissa laughed, "I didn't tell David until after we were engaged!"

The phone rang. It was his friend Martin again.

"What did I tell you? This is your life!"

"I haven't said a word," David replied. "All I can tell you is that what Clara has just said is true."

"Heavy stuff, pal," Martin replied. "And so who were you two thousand years ago?"

"I'm not sure, Martin. But if per chance I was a Roman Captain of the Guard, I think now is about the time I would choose to lock you up. Clara takes all this stuff very seriously. Besides, since I've met her, I've been drawn in to some extraordinary coincidences that truly might add up to something in this reincarnation business. There's more to it than you think."

"I know, David. I realize that. I was only kidding. You missed her playing. She played something she'd written herself about a snow scene in Japan. It was one of the most beautiful pieces of music I've ever heard. Hopefully you can get her to play it for us when she's on board. Maybe we can have a Ward Room recital?"

David laughed. "On that old upright? It's completely out of tune!"

"I can arrange to have it tuned. Really, David, many of us would like that. It's something different and you say she's not traveling as an entertainer."

"No, but the Cruise Director might be able to squeeze her into the program. The 'Lookout' or the Pavilion Lounge would be rather better than the Ward Room!"

"Fair enough! Have a good time in Hong Kong, old chum," his Australian mate returned. "The interview was top notch, but I can tell her that myself after she comes on board. Sweet dreams!" He hung up.

On the radio, Gloria Ainsworth was still rapping up the discussion. "Not only has Clarissa Corrington shared with us her enormous talent this evening, along with my other distinguished guests, Mr. Wang Ho, Joseph Bond and Mr. Andrew Choy, but she brought about through her music, a subject that never ceases to fascinate us all - past lives. Do we remember our past lives and how they are revealed to us? I would particularly like to thank those of you who called in with your own fascinating and inspiring stories on this subject. It takes courage to share these things, but there's a rising consciousness in the world today that seeks a new truth. There are many seekers, perhaps in our small way we have been able to set some of you on the road to self-discovery."

There was a brief pause and then the moderator signed off. "This is Gloria Ainsworth on Hong Kong Radio's longest-running, talk show, 'The Pulse of the Fragrant Harbor', wishing you all a pleasant night until we talk again."

Play off music came over the air and on the dot of Eleven, pips sounded the reading of the late News.

"I missed most of it," David sighed. "I wish I'd heard it all."

He found it hard to sleep. He realized that he truly was in this first century past life experience with Clarissa. There could be no turning back.

'Why did she say so much?' he questioned. 'Did she tell them she was Mary Magdalene? They'll kill me in the mess if she did. Fiona will tease me unmercifully.'

He was so excited at the prospect of seeing Clara! Hearing her voice had brought her so close. He wondered if she had experienced even more first century visions? He suspected she had. This was going to be a reunion! At last, he slept.

• • • • • • • •

Clarissa was up early and kept looking out at the gray light of dawn to see if she could see the 'Prince Regent' approaching. Perhaps she had slipped in before daylight and was already berthed.

Gloria was making toast. "Medium light for you, dear?" she asked cheerfully.

"Yes please," Clarissa answered.

It was seven-twenty and the rising sun was just beginning to silhouette the outer islands across from Repulse Bay. A large ship appeared from around the headland. She was quite close in, just as Gloria had suggested.

"I think this is her now!" Clarissa shouted, causing Brewster to bark and rush to the window.

Sure enough it was. The 'Prince Regent' came into full view. Her decks were still illuminated and many of her portholes showed light where eager passengers were no doubt looking out to glimpse their first impressions of Hong Kong.

Gloria Ainsworth, wearing a rather tatty bathrobe over what looked like an expensive negligee, drew to Clarissa's side.

"Isn't that ship beautiful?" was all Clarissa could say as her heart thumped with the knowledge that she was so close to her loved one.

The ship did look stately as she slid past Repulse Bay and on towards the jumble of junks that make up the harbor of Aberdeen. She had classic lines - a long, dark hull with a long, white superstructure and a great, big, black funnel with gold rings, right where it should be, in the very center of the ship.

"They don't build ships that look like that any more," Clarissa explained. "They just build floating 'Hyatts' today. Hardly any of the new ships have a proper funnel."

"I agree," Gloria sighed. "We see so many of them here in Hong Kong, but truly the 'Prince Regent' and the 'QE2' are about the only two left with those classic lines. Some of the new ones have no funnels at all."

The sun was up above the islands now and caught the stern of the 'Prince Regent' full on, before the ship disappeared beneath the cliffs of the Peak to make her turn towards the main channel.

"It looks like they were right on time," Gloria said as she started to butter the toast and pour out cups of tea. "They should be docked by eight o'clock. What time would you like us to run you down? The traffic's not so bad on Saturdays."

"David will be busy most the morning. There's usually a horrendous stack of company mail in Hong Kong. I can go whenever you want to leave. Don't let me hold you up. I can be ready any time."

"Well, we usually leave for the farm about ten o'clock if that's alright with you," Gloria hinted. "Now, don't forget we really want you both to stay. We could either come back for you tonight or pick you up tomorrow sometime."

"I'll ask David as soon as I'm on board," Clarissa promised, while Gloria scribbled down their New Territories number on a piece of paper in the kitchen.

Patrick took out Brewster.

• • • • • • • •

Patrick tried to find a porter at Ocean Terminal who might help them with Clarissa's bags. The terminal is designed in such a way as to allow passengers to walk off a ship straight into the shopping mall that seems to cover the entirety of Kowloon's downtown district. It is not easy to find a way through that shopping jungle with three large suitcases and an assortment of hand baggage. Clarissa and Gloria stayed with the car at street level for fear that the Hong Kong police might move them on. Gloria kept looking at her watch. At length Patrick returned with a baggage boy and a handcart.

Clarissa kissed Gloria affectionately and shook Patrick's hand. She was just as anxious to get on board as Gloria and Patrick were to get to their farmhouse. She followed the porter into the labyrinth of the lower levels of Ocean Terminal. Eventually, finding themselves at an old elevator they were slowly raised to the more familiar floors of the shopping mall. From there Clarissa followed the porter out to the upper level dock-side, adjacent to the superstructure of the 'Prince Regent'.

They were stopped by security guards before being allowed to proceed, but she was in good hands. David's department prepared the lists of boarding passengers for security. Naturally Clarissa Peterson's name was there.

Once Clarissa was on board it didn't take long for the news of her arrival to reach David in the purser's office. Dressed in his white uniform, he was up and out in the foyer before he had time to comb his hair. "Clara, darling!" he shouted when he saw her with the porter.

They walked towards each other and fell into a fond embrace.

"I've missed you so much," Clarissa said. "I've lots to tell you."

"Me too," David agreed. "Now, let's get these bags to the cabin."

He tipped the porter who saluted him gratefully. At last David and Clarissa would have time to themselves.

"I heard your talk show last night," David said as they began to unpack Clarissa's bags. "You were great."

Clarissa felt some relief. She had been worried as to whether she might have said too much. She certainly hadn't anticipated David hearing the broadcast.

"It came through loud and clear as we approached the outer islands. It's a very easy run up from Macau. Incidentally, it was great to see Macau. The architecture's spectacular. I guess Hong Kong once looked something like that although less baroque." David turned back to the broadcast. "But how on earth did you get into that discussion on past lives last night?"

"Did you hear the part where I played?"

"No, unfortunately I missed you playing," David reported. "I tuned in when you were all discussing dreams. This guy called in saying he had fallen in love with some colonial teenager in backswood America and that he had married her in this present lifetime."

"Oh, you missed a lot, David, apart from my playing," Clarissa said slowly. "But did you hear the part about Samantha's dream and us?"

"Yes, I heard that. That was all true."

"Everything we discussed was true," Clarissa said defensively as she looked up in to his eyes. "You do still believe in this first century connection, don't you?"

He kissed her. "Of course I do, Maria," he said. "I just don't know that we should broadcast to the world about these things."

"I was worried about that too," Clarissa agreed, "but fortunately Gloria Ainsworth was sensitive enough to keep off the subject of who we might have thought we were."

"Does she know?" David asked with some concern.

"Yes. But Gloria and Patrick are genuinely fascinated by our whole story. They actually would like us to visit them tomorrow and stay overnight. Do you think that might be possible? On the weekends they live out on a farm in the New Territories, but the past two nights I stayed with them at their flat in Repulse Bay. They want us to come out to their farm."

"What if they blab our story to the newspapers?" David warned. "We need to be very careful. As Mary Magdalene you might have been very close to Jesus. You two might have even been lovers!"

"More than just lovers," Clarissa replied slowly.

David had been picking Clarissa's things out of her suitcase as she hung them up. "What do you mean?" he asked as he held up a blouse.

"In my most recent revelations I see evidence that we actually had a child."

"What!" David shouted, dropping the blouse, "You think you and Jesus had a baby!"

"Don't worry! I didn't say anything on the radio about that," she assured him. "I didn't say anything about Maria."

"Thank God!" David exclaimed. "They'd have crucified you!"

"They did crucify Joshua," Clarissa said lightheartedly as she hugged her husband. "But first things first - I need you." She pulled him down on the bed and they embraced with the passion of teenagers, scattering articles of Clarissa's clothing in their frenzy.

"Don't you think we'd better finish your unpacking first?" David suggested.

"Only if you promise to make love to me as soon as these things are put away."

They finished unpacking.

"Tonight I've arranged through the agent for a quiet table for two at 'Gaddi's'," David said as Clarissa undressed. "It's a superb restaurant in the Peninsula Hotel. I always wanted to go there. It's pretty formal, but we can dance there too, I'm told."

"That sounds wonderful," she said as she stood in front of him in her underwear. "Actually Gloria took me there for tea."

"Yes, but not to 'Gaddi's'," David assured her.

Clarissa snuggled up to her husband. "Now, let's make love!" she suggested.

As they lay in bed, full of the joy of their reunion, Clarissa reminded David that they had to let Gloria and Patrick know about their plans. "Would you be able to get away tomorrow night?" she asked.

"Oh, to stay with your friends in the New Territories?"

"Yes, David. You'd love Gloria and Patrick. They're expecting us to say 'Yes' unless you have something important happening on the ship."

"Actually, I'm free. You might have to let me back in the office this afternoon for a while and up till around eleven tomorrow morning, but after that I should be free."

"Good. Let's call them," Clarissa suggested. "Here, I have the number in my purse. I presume you have outside lines?"

"No problem. Give me the number and we can dial direct from here."

The Chief Purser requested an open line and dialled the Ainsworth's New Territories' number.

Gloria answered.

"Hi Gloria, this is David Peterson from the 'Prince Regent'. Clara has told me so much about you."

"David! Welcome to Hong Kong! We watched you sail in this morning. Clarissa's told us so much about you too," Gloria reciprocated. "Now, are you going to be able to stay over with us tonight or tomorrow. We've plenty of room and we're dying to meet you."

"Tomorrow would be fine," David replied. "By the way we heard most of the interview and discussion on board. It was very interesting."

"Clarissa's so fascinating. I can't wait to hear more of her stories. We feel like we know you too, even though we've never met. Clarissa told us so much about you. Can Patrick pick you up about ten o'clock?"

"Eleven would be better," David suggested. "I really need to do some work in the morning."

"Good, eleven o'clock then. Patrick will probably drive up to the Ocean Terminal car park on the top level. He'll meet you up there."

"You must be my guests on board, Monday," David announced in invitation. "We'll bring passes for you both."

"Oh, that would be wonderful!" Gloria said excitedly, although she had anticipated the possibility. "Do you mind if we do a little interview for the show. Maybe I could also get to talk to the ship's Doctor, the Chef de Cuisine or the Cruise Director if they are around when we come on board?" she asked with that reporter's cunning.

"Alright, I'll see what I can do," David agreed.

"See you at eleven o'clock."

"Top car park."

"Jolly good. Cheerio."

"Bye."

David hung up the phone. "We're going," he said to Clarissa. "She's quite determined isn't she? She wants to get some shipboard interviews!"

Clarissa laughed, "She always gets her way. I warned you, didn't I? I hope you like them though. She's sharp as a tack - doesn't miss a trick."

"It'll be interesting," David said as he lay back with a satisfied smile. "You're gorgeous, darling. As good as you were two thousand years ago! How was I so lucky!"

"What do you mean?" Clarissa asked with surprise.

"I've had some dreams too!" David revealed. "I've dreamed about us two thousand years ago!"

"You and me?" Clarissa asked enthusiastically.

"I believe I might have been a Roman. I met you when we were teenagers. We had a mad, passionate affair just like that Frenchman with his colonial 'homecoming queen'!"

Clarissa laughed. "Well, you haven't lost your passion, but be serious!" she said. "How did we really meet? Who were you?"

"I was a Roman, just as I said," David replied. "I am being serious, Clara. I was an arrogant young Roman and I took advantage of you in an olive grove."

"I hope it was worthwhile," Clarissa teased seductively, not really believing him, and in her own arousal trying to bring back his passion.

"Yes! It was, but as for now, let's save that for tonight. I have to go back to the office - remember? I could stay here all afternoon, but if we are going to be away most of tomorrow and overnight, I had better get busy now."

He kissed her, dressed and left the cabin.

Clarissa showered and washed her hair for their evening at 'Gaddi's'.

'I don't believe it,' she thought as she held up the drier, 'David's really changing. He's much more aware of his dreams now! No wonder it's so good between us.'

• • • • • • • •

It was only a short walk through the Ocean Terminal and along the waterfront to the 'Peninsula'. Wealthy passengers might avail of the hotel's Rolls Royce, limousine service to take them the five hundred yards, but the walk through the lower environs of the terminal to the chauffeur park was almost further than that along the street. David hoped that there would not be too many passengers dining at 'Gaddi's', at least tonight. Anyone who had asked him or his staff about dining at the 'Peninsula' had been steered towards the equally prestigious 'Terrace Grill'.

Clarissa looked lovely as always. Her hair was a little longer than three months before and fell in rolling, blonde curls over her shoulders. She wore a blue cape and white, three quarter length dress. In the artificial street light David could see how it could conjure up an image of first century Biblical dress. It was something to do with that all-enfolding cloak.

They turned into the more brightly, illuminated forecourt of the hotel just as one of the famed, green, Rolls Royce courtesy cars pulled out. At the entrance doors, young page boys with pill box caps and white gloves, greeted them. Inside, they stood looking up at the great, gilt and white plaster ceiling of the foyer where Clarissa had sat with Gloria for afternoon tea. Around them wafted the echoing strains of a string quartet playing in the gallery.

"Good evening, David. Is this your lovely wife?" a voice questioned.

David went on red alert! 'There are passengers in the foyer,' he deduced. 'I knew there would be. They seem to mingle here all day on the ship's stopover in Hong Kong. They 'nickel and dime' us over cabin discounts and yet spend thousands in the Peninsula boutiques for grossly marked-up products available in other markets of Hong Kong at one third the price.' He looked to see who was speaking to him.

"Good evening!" David replied.

He introduced his wife politely. "Clara, this is Mr. and Mrs. Achenbloom, regular World Cruise passengers."

"On your way to 'The Terrace'?" Mr. Achenbloom asked.

"No, 'Gaddi's'," David explained.

"Oh! You'll love it. Have a wonderful evening," Mrs. Achenbloom proffered, as if 'Gaddi's' were some sort of a secret that only the Achenblooms of the world should know.

Soon David and Clarissa were away in the special elevator that took them up to the restaurant. David was delighted to see that at least on first glance there was nobody there whom he recognized.

The Maitre d'hotel showed them to a beautifully set table for two in a romantic alcove. This was the perfect spot for David and Clarissa's reunion dinner. After they had ordered, they stepped down onto the little dance floor to enjoy a pre-dinner rumba. As they held each other to the gentle sway of the trio's music they looked every bit the honeymoon couple that they still felt they were.

"Oh David, so many things have happened since you left," Clarissa said at length when they had returned to the secrecy of their booth.

"You mean on this first century mystery?" David asked with a grin.

"Yes. A couple of other significant characters have walked into the scene. The first was a macho Greek officer named Babis Demetris who I met on the 'Ulysses'."

"One of the Greek white sharks!" David teased her.

"Yes, he found me lying in the sun in my bikini."

David laughed. "Well, what did you expect, then!"

"No, you've got to be serious now, David. I had a dream in which Babis appeared as Judas Iscariot."

"Really! The plot thickens." David paused for a moment. "Seriously, Clara, I've also had some experiences or revelations as you would say." He looked around to see that they would not be overheard. "I really did dream that I was this young Roman boy and I found you in this olive grove. You were naked in my dream and you didn't look the same, but I knew it was you."

Clarissa smiled at him across the table. "How was I different?" she asked.

There was something about her smile that reminded David of the young girl in his dream and brought back the details. It was beguiling, the smile of a temptress.

"That smile was the same," he acknowledged, reaching across the table to take her hand. Then, he became very serious. "You had long, dark, wavy hair and a fuller figure."

She laughed as she saw him looking at her cleavage. "Bigger boobs!"

"Yes, Clara, but you have to be serious and listen to me. Your name was 'Maria'. Now, I don't think that was any coincidence. I really do believe you were Mary Magdalene."

"Yes, but who were you?"

"I was this young Roman, as I said. I think my name was 'Linus'. Anyway, I thought I could satisfy my young lust on you right there in the olive grove. I felt superior to you and only wanted to use you."

Clarissa looked at him directly in the eyes. "And so you raped me?"

"Well, not exactly, Clara. That is what was so strange. I thought I was going to rape you, but it almost turned out to be the other way 'round. You took possession of me."

Clarissa batted her eyelids. "I was quite a femme fatale!"

This time it was David who laughed as he squeezed her hand. "Yes, as a matter of fact you were. But there's more. I dreamed I was this Roman again. Linus now seemed older. He was with Pontius Pilate. As Linus I called him 'Pilatus' and we discussed the crucifixion. I can't remember all the details, but I got the feeling that neither of us thought Jesus, who I called 'Joshua the miracle-worker' deserved the death penalty, rather it was something that we had to do for political expediency."

"Really!" Clarissa said seriously. "So you believe that you knew about Jesus then, and that you might have also known Mary Magdalene?"

"It seems that way," David admitted, "but I don't remember everything in my dreams. I just remember certain key points, but almost immediately forget the rest. You seem to remember much more than I do, so tell me about this macho Greek, Judas Iscariot?"

"Babis Demetris," Clarissa reminded him. "He's a Bridge Officer on the 'Ulysses'. He tried to chat me up when we were going through the Panama Canal. He lay this typical line on me and in essence I told him to 'buzz off'."

David grinned. "Good for you."

"Later he got lucky with a brilliant, young, Swiss entertainer. She was a glass harpist. Anyway, Ursula kept telling me that this Babis creep thought he had met me before, either in Greece or Israel, and that he was intrigued by me."

"You really are a femme fatale!" David teased.

"Well, not exactly, as it was revealed to me later. I dreamed about the anointing scene where Mary Magdalene poured the precious oil on Jesus' head. Judas Iscariot yelled at me something about wasting the oil and that it could have been sold for a lot of money and distributed to the poor. Jesus' disciples had taken hold of me. They were all against me, egged on by Judas who seemed to hate me. In my dream Judas' face seemed like that of Babis Demetris."

"And that's why you think the Greek was Judas Iscariot in a past life?"

"Yes," Clarissa answered. "I continued to dream about him. I watched and heard Jesus rebuking him. 'Many who love me shall come to hate me,' Jesus said. 'The boundaries between love and hate are very close.' Judas Iscariot cursed and spat on the ground. He glared at Jesus. 'Watch these women, Joshua!' he said, 'they're making you soft.' He called Jesus 'Joshua', David, just like Jeremy Dyson. It's all in my dream journal."

"Interesting," David admitted, "but don't you think you might have conditioned yourself into thinking this way, Clara? If your friend Ursula kept telling you her Latin, lover-boy had met you in Greece or Israel, you might have just built this meeting into your dream state. As far as the rest of it is concerned, well, we spent a lot of time researching this business of Mary Magdalene anointing Jesus. That scene is pretty well ingrained in your brain."

"Don't be so skeptical, David, there are other things. I've had several visions that have shown my relationship with Jesus."

At this point Clarissa looked around. Two waiters were heading their way with soup plates under large, silver covers. She waited for them to serve the lobster bisque.

Ceremonially the two waiters raised the gleaming lids at the same moment, revealing the plates of steaming broth. "Bon appetit" they said in their best Chinese-French.

"As I was saying," Clarissa continued. "I have had a number of visionary experiences involving Jesus or Joshua."

David looked at her intently. "Alright, carry on."

"Well for a start, let's talk about what really set off the discussion on reincarnation last night on the radio show."

"Yes, you never did get around to explaining that. Somehow we got sidetracked!"

"I wrote a lyrical piece a week ago in Japan. It was very cold in Kobe and Kyoto. In Kyoto there was quite a snowfall. I must say the old temples and palaces really looked very mystical in the snow. I visited the Golden Pagoda Temple. At that time the late, afternoon sun just caught the gilded roofs in a kaleidoscope of magical light. That became the inspiration for my piece. I liked it and tried it out as an encore at the Nagasaki concert. Would you believe it, David? It got a standing ovation!"

"Well done!" David encouraged her. "Bravo!"

"That was the piece I played on the radio show last night."

"But what has that to do with past lives?"

"It's something that has happened to me every time I've played this piece. Incidentally I played your piece, 'Ode to love', on the T.V. show. Actually, I believe that screens tomorrow night. We might be able to see it when we are at Gloria's."

"So what happens when you play this new composition?" David asked as he tried to bring Clarissa back to the point.

"I get transported back to the same scene two thousand years ago. The gilded pagoda sparkling in the snow becomes Joshua standing in a shaft of brilliant light."

"What!" David exclaimed.

"Yes. I see him standing with his arms outstretched in prayer in this grove of old, olive trees. The snow in the foreground just melts away into this dusty ground scattered with stones and boulders. I'm hiding behind a large rock and I instinctively know I'm Maria of

Magdala. My son, Marcus is with me. He feels like your nephew Simon."

"Doctor John's eldest boy? The one who had a crush on you at Thanksgiving?"

"Yes, but now I think I know who his father was. Strangely enough he was the same person two thousand years ago, it was your brother-in-law Doctor John. He was a gentle Roman in the First Century. His name, according to my dreams was 'Antonias'. He was a good father to Marcus. He was everything that Doctor John doesn't appear to be, gentle, shy and unassuming."

The waiters returned to simultaneously remove the soup plates. With an equal flourish to that which had accompanied the soup, the main course dishes were exposed. Clarissa had chosen turbot and David the rack of lamb.

"So back to your composition about the pagoda," David said as he reached for Clarissa's hand under the table. "You had explained how this gilded pagoda flowed into an image of Christ standing in a shaft of light with arms outstretched in prayer, at least that was before you got sidetracked into all this stuff about Doctor John. Doctor John can wait. What else happens as you play this piece?"

"Marcus runs out during a certain crescendo," Clarissa explained. "Joshua sees him and quietly shoos him away. Obviously we're not meant to be there even though he knows we are. I try to call Marcus back and shortly after he rejoins me, the shaft of light illuminating Joshua's figure fades. For a moment his visage is quite clear to me before he metamorphoses back into the gilded pagoda. I get this uncanny feeling that behind the parted hair and straggling beard masks the soul who is now Jeremy Dyson."

"No, Clara!" David whispered with strength. "Don't turn this mystery into some sort of an ego trip. We know Jeremy was a Roman, but not the Christ! What was his Roman name, I can't remember?"

"Remus Augustus," Clarissa reminded him.

"Yes, that's right. He wasn't the Christ!"

David looked over his shoulder again. He truly hoped nobody could hear what Clarissa was saying. "Now, back to the main point," he continued. "What happens as you play the last part?"

"The brilliant light that shone through the clouds onto that Kyoto shrine fades and a gray sadness ends the piece," Clarissa said looking at David a little afraid of his reaction. "The piece is all about this special light catching the snow, but somehow this other image showing Christ's light, keeps creeping in."

"It sounds a bit like the 'Transfiguration' to me," David suggested.

"What's that?" Clarissa asked.

"Sometimes I forget how you Anglo-Irish Protestants were abandoned in your Christian upbringing in Catholic Ireland," David teased. "The Transfiguration was a miraculous transformation of Jesus that took place on a high hill in Galilee. It was only witnessed by Peter, James and John, Jesus' inner three disciples. Jesus' clothes became a luminous, shining white and Moses and Elijah appeared with him."

"Oh, yes. I remember something about that," Clarissa admitted.

David smiled. There was a warm compassion on his face that mingled with a deep-rooted love. "You and Marcus weren't meant to be there, Maria," he continued. "You weren't there in the Bible."

"But maybe we were there two thousand years ago," she insisted, not taking her eyes off her husband's face. She reached out for his hand again. "You were in Palestine two thousand years ago. If we really did have a mad, passionate affair as teenagers, do you think you ever met me again in those days?"

"I don't know," David answered quietly. "Maybe that's yet to be revealed to us, but let's certainly hope so."

"I guess some things will just have to remain a mystery," Clarissa said triumphantly. "Now, let me tell you about this other extraordinary revelation."

"There's more!"

"Oh yes, David, a lot more."

"Well, first explain how playing this piece on Hong Kong Radio got you onto the subject of past lives last night."

"It was like I said. I told them that every time I play this piece I'm somehow transported back into the same moment in the past."

"Marcus running out in front of the transfigured Christ?" David asked for confirmation.

"Yes. Marcus running out in front of Joshua while he was praying in the light."

"I believe you, Clara, don't doubt me. I'll accept that you were there. But what are these other revelations?"

"Well, they involve Gloria Ainsworth. It's probably best if she shares some of them with you tomorrow. She has this notion she also lived in first century Palestine. She mentioned it when I told her I was getting off the ship in Israel."

"It seems like everyone we meet is involved in this," David acknowledged with no small amount of concern.

"That's becoming more and more apparent," Clarissa admitted, "now that we've made some inroads into understanding this mystery. It's almost as if through a series of coincidences we've all tuned in to the same wavelength."

"So, who did Gloria think she was?" David asked.

"She saw Jesus on the way to his death. I'm not sure whether she actually saw him die on the cross, but her father was a friend and business associate of Joseph of Arimathea, the man who gave his tomb for Jesus' burial."

"And wasn't he also the man who Jeremy Dyson thinks was the father of your other child?"

"Yes, but as I told you, I'm not sure about that any more. After Gloria introduced the idea of Joseph of Arimathea to me, I dreamed about him. That was just two nights ago here in Hong Kong. In the dream I was on a small boat with Joseph that looked a little bit like a Chinese junk. Anyway, Joseph seemed to be looking after me. I knew I was pregnant and in my dream Joseph clearly said that he would take care of Joshua's baby." She stared blankly at David awaiting his reaction. "David! In this dream it was revealed to me that I was carrying Joshua's child!" she repeated. "Jesus may have had a son!"

"Jesus Christ!" David exclaimed. "So you were being serious about having this baby with Jesus! Do you know what you're saying!"

Slowly Clarissa and David let go of each others' hands and looked down at the plates on the table. They remained silent, both deep in thought as they began to eat.

'Is this about letting go of concepts?' David asked himself. 'Can we let go of our expectations of things we hold dear, and still love them?' Nodding with a smile, he looked up at Clarissa, "It's hard to let go of our long held traditions, but sometimes we have to." He took her hand. "Before we have dessert, let's dance. I think that's enough of the heavy stuff for tonight."

For the rest of the evening they dropped the subject of first century past lives and enjoyed the elegant atmosphere of 'Gaddi's'. They danced until the trio stopped playing. They were the last to leave.

"I love you, David," Clarissa said as they walked back along the waterfront towards Ocean Terminal and the 'Star' ferries. "Whatever may have been our purposes two thousand years ago I'm so glad we have each other now. Despite the past let's live in the present."

"You don't have to sell me on that," David whispered, "but I have to admit the past does seem to be getting more and more fascinating!"

They kissed each other in front of the bow of the 'Prince Regent' before going up the steps into Ocean Terminal to make their way to the gangway.

· · · · · · · ·

The following morning, being Sunday, most the shops in Ocean Terminal didn't open for business until ten. Clarissa went out to buy flowers for Gloria. She had noticed a florist on their way in the night before. Finding the place open, she made an appropriate selection and had them gift-wrapped for presentation in that traditional fashion that is typical of Asia.

David was ready to leave by eleven and they made their way up to the car park.

Patrick Ainsworth was already there. "Over here!" he shouted as he waved his arms frantically.

Clarissa waved back with her free arm as she clutched the floral bouquet. They walked towards him.

"Gloria didn't come," Patrick said as he took their small bag from David. "She's working on lunch."

"These are for Gloria," Clarissa said.

"She'll love them," Patrick assured her. "I think I'll put them in the boot with your bag. There's not a lot of room in my little car and we wouldn't want them to get crushed."

David smiled. "The boot," he whispered to Clarissa as he climbed into the back seat of the 'Austin' mini. "He sounds just like your brother in Ireland."

"Well, the trunk if you must be a 'Yank'," Clarissa whispered back.

"I just keep this little run-about at the farm," Patrick explained. "Gloria so often takes the hatchback and I hate to be immobile."

Very soon they were on their way leaving behind the labyrinth of Kowloon's shopping streets with their tracery of billboards in assorted, Chinese characters. They crossed the flyovers that surrounded the approaches to the Lion Rock Tunnel and drove through to the New Territories. On the other side they passed the Chinese University campus before heading out through a jungle of high rises into the hills.

"Our house isn't very big," Patrick explained. "It was an old, pig farm on the outskirts of a Chinese village. We've just retained the farmhouse and one of the yard buildings. Bit by bit I've restored them, opening up walls and turning tiny rooms into an open plan."

"Sounds delightful," Clarissa said enthusiastically. "What sort of a village is it today? The New Territories have built up so much."

"Yes, many of the old duck farms have gone, although there are more where mainland China meets the New Territories. Actually, the part of Ho Tai Tsuen where we live is still quite quaint," Patrick explained as he pulled off the motorway on to a regular highway. "You could almost say our village has remained fairly rural, but it sits just off an expanded new town that has, like so many, developed along the railway."

About ten minutes later, skirting around the town to which Patrick had referred, they arrived in Ho Tai Tsuen. There were many, traditional, blue-gray tiled, single story houses hiding behind endless walls. Circular, Chinese doorways led into little courtyards where old men with white beards and traditional robes, watched their grandchildren running around in bright teeshirts and dungarees. The children smiled and waved at the 'Ainsworth' car as Patrick drove by on a road that was becoming more narrow at every turn. Dogs ran out and barked. A family of ducks marched courteously in a line down a muddy path. Gaunt, but strong, Chinese laborers, carried huge loads on their backs, baskets of choy greens, bundles of wood and panniers of mudbricks. Bicycles lay against walls. There was a smell of ripe onions in the air.

"This is more like old China," Patrick said as he saw how fascinated David and Clarissa were with the sights and aromas. "This is why we like it out here. Hong Kong isn't really about fancy shops and de luxe hotels, it's about the Chinese people. These people are civilization's great past, but they also represent our future. China will never go away. China existed as an organized people long before the 'West' and will, by my prediction, dominate our world again in the Twenty first Century. There is an innate wisdom here. The Chinese are no fools. They know their time has come. But it is here in the villages that the continuity between past and future can best be seen."

"The Chinese believe in reincarnation, don't they?" Clarissa asked.

"Yes. But it's not so much that they believe in reincarnation. Actually, it means little to them intellectually," Patrick explained. "They really wouldn't understand why we're so excited about our past lives. If you asked a Chinese man to explain reincarnation, he would laugh and not consider it important. But the principles of Asian philosophy that drive all the Eastern religions have their origins in China. Many Chinese don't know that they carry this secret, but intrinsically they do. Their timeless past may well become our future. Their untapped inner knowledge is the same as that which fascinates the more enlightened of us who come from the Western traditions."

"Fascinating," David acknowledged as Patrick swerved the car around a pot-hole and nearly ran into an oncoming cyclist. The bicycle wobbled, but the Chinese gentleman just grinned as Patrick drove on.

"In many ways they're like children," Patrick continued, "but to quote Jesus Christ, 'out of the mouths of babes and sucklings shall wisdom be revealed', well something like that."

Patrick turned down a muddy lane with stone walls on either side. It was very narrow, but opened out just below the village in a lush, green area where banana trees competed with tall bamboos and flowering blossoms. There was a pond on the right of the road covered in waterlilly pads. Several were in bloom displaying pink flowers. Ahead was another high wall with a half-moon gate.

"Welcome to the pig farm," Patrick said as he stopped to open the grill.

Through the gate they found themselves in the remains of an orchard. Down a short drive was the Ainsworth's country cottage. Gloria stood on the patio terrace. She still looked very chic for her rural surroundings and was excitedly talking to a large cockatoo in a cage.

"Say hello to our guests," she said to the bird, but the cockatoo made no response.

As David and Clarissa got out of the car, Gloria came over. She kissed Clarissa before shaking David's hand politely. "You must be David," she said warmly. "We've been so looking forward to meeting you. It's wonderful that you can stay with us."

"Oh, it's so nice to be here," David replied. "It's a whole different side of Hong Kong. It's beautiful."

"It's very peaceful after the bustle of the city and yet we can be back in the center in forty five minutes," Gloria agreed. "We just love it here. Now, let me show you around."

Gloria took them into the house. Inside was an extraordinary, eclectic collection of Asian and Western art, furniture and ornaments.

"You have such beautiful things here," Clarissa noted having observed that the Repulse Bay apartment had been strictly Western.

"We tend to keep our treasures here," Patrick explained. "One, they are safer. Theft can be quite bad in Repulse Bay and on the Peak, but away from the city in this village we never have to lock a door. We only have the grill at the gate in order to keep Brewster in when he's down here, but we left the hound with Millie this weekend. More important, however, we really want this to eventually be our home. When we retire we'll live here and give up the flat in Repulse Bay."

"Now, let me show you the pigsty," Gloria said with a grin. "We always put our friends up in the pigsty."

They went outside into the garden. As they passed the cockatoo, the bird surprised them. "Hello, I'm a silly old fool," he said.

Clarissa was fascinated. "He talks!" she exclaimed.

"Well, only to people he likes. He's very choosey," Patrick informed her. "You're privileged."

Gloria led the way to the bottom of the garden. "This is it," she said proudly as she opened the double doors into a sumptuous room with a King-size bed over which hung mosquito netting held back by large, tasselled ropes. "We converted this old pig house into this guest suite."

There was a Chinese carpet on the floor and two, antique, bedside tables that looked like they had come from a Tai-pan's mansion. A bookcase displayed various collectibles and a comfortable armchair with a footrest gave a place to read.

"The bathroom's down here," Gloria told them as she led the way through a door on their left. This opened into a passage. Off to the right was a toilet with rather antiquated plumbing and a wooden seat on a spring. "The thunderbox," Gloria explained.

"Be careful of that seat," Patrick added. "It can be a trap for unwary players! It'll spring back and hit you on the bum if you're not careful."

Beyond the toilet were two or three other small rooms.

"These were the sties," Patrick explained. "The bedroom was the feedhouse. There were six sties in this bank, but we knocked three of them down to make this substantial bathroom."

The bathroom was spacious, but again the plumbing looked ancient. The tub was huge and there was a large washbasin and dressing-table. One corner of the bathroom was also taken up by a shower cubicle.

"I think you'll find there are plenty of towels," Gloria said, "but if you need more just let us know. We've plenty up at the cottage." She went back into the passage and opened the door into what would have been the last two sties. "Laundry and ironing," she announced. "Actually this is the utility room for all of us so I hope you won't mind if I occasionally pop in through the back door here. Now, is there anything we can get you? I left fruit and bottled water in the bedroom. It's best to use the bottled water. We're not on the mains here and the well is a little uncertain."

"I think we'll be very comfortable," Clarissa answered. "Everything looks lovely."

"It's very peaceful at the bottom of the garden," Gloria admitted, "but you might find the birds quite loud first thing, especially after being at sea."

"We'll like that," Clarissa replied. "It's one of the things we like most when we come home to Minnesota."

"Good, well let's all go back up for a quick drink before lunch. I've made it very simple, lots of rice, stir-fried vegetables and our special meatballs."

"You're privileged," Patrick informed them. "You're getting the meatballs!"

They walked back up to the cottage. The sun was in and out, but at that moment caught the blossoms of the flowering Bohenia trees, contrasting them sharply with the lushness of the greenery.

"I'm a silly old fool," the cockatoo repeated as they passed his cage.

• • • • • • • •

Gloria didn't bring up the subject of the First Century until after lunch. When she had poured the coffee she came directly to the point. "David, I hope you won't mind, but I'm completely fascinated by Clarissa's first century, past life experiences. I don't know whether she's told you, but I believe that I also lived at that time."

David grinned and caught Clarissa's eye. "Yes, she did say something to me," he admitted.

"Do you both believe that you were together before?"

"If we are to believe all the extraordinary dreams and coincidental meetings that we've experienced since this whole thing started, yes. It looks as if we met at least once, two thousand years ago," David explained looking at Clarissa rather uncomfortably. "But I don't think we knew each other very well." He certainly didn't want to share with Gloria the intimate details of his romp in the olive grove.

"So where do you fit in?" Gloria asked.

"I think I was a Roman administrator of some sort. I seemed to know Pontius Pilate as if I was part of his entourage in Jerusalem. But, I had a sympathy with Jesus. I discussed my opinions with Pilate after the crucifixion. Jesus apparently healed some of my family members from sickness of some sort. I respected the miracle-worker. Maybe I became one of the Nazarene's followers."

"Jesus is the common link between us all," Gloria admitted. "Did Clarissa tell you I believe I saw Jesus on the way to his crucifixion? It was revealed to me in a dream some time ago. At first I didn't understand it, but the more the subject of past lives came up on my show the more intrigued I became. Now I'm totally fascinated."

"Can you tell David what you saw?" Clarissa asked.

Gloria sat up and adjusted her skirt. "There were a lot of people cramming the street I needed to get down," she said. "It was such a jostling crowd I decided to wait until the wretched prisoners had passed. They passed very close to where I was. Jesus fell right in front of me. I could see his eyes clearly. He looked right at me."

"Did he say anything?" David enquired.

"No. He just looked up at me with these pitiful eyes. But even in his agony there was a dignity. His eyes were mystical, deep and penetrating," Gloria explained. "A young man ran out to help Jesus, but before he could get to him, the Roman soldiers had brutally kicked him. The young man quickly backed off and then the soldiers went after him. Jesus just lay there crumpled up in front of me. Then the soldiers grabbed the young man and forced him to carry Jesus' crossbar."

"That was Simon of Cyrene," David said, becoming more interested. "You witnessed a scene straight out of the Bible, Gloria. Maybe you just imagined it because you know the story well?"

"Why do you always say that?" Clarissa complained. "What about your dreams? You always suspect others, but what about you and Pilate?"

David was relieved that Clarissa had not referred to the scene in the olive grove. "Well, I'll try to be scientific," he said. "Nothing is proved, but I'm open to the possibility that we might be sharing some common, past life experiences."

"I used to think just like you," Gloria admitted. "The funny thing is, however, that I've had the same dream many times. That scene left a great impression on me. The other interesting thing is that in my dream I never seem to know for certain that the prisoner is Jesus. It's only after I'm awake and think about the scene that I realize this had to be about Jesus and Simon of Cyrene."

"That's interesting," Clarissa interjected. "That might be true with all of us if names aren't mentioned in the dreams."

"But in your case, Clarissa," Gloria noted, "names usually seem to have been revealed."

"True. I can be pretty sure about my own name as 'Maria'. It used to confuse me that I appeared as Maria in my dreams because I think of Maria as Mary Magdalene which is somewhat awesome, but it became even more confusing when I started to have dreams about someone called 'Mary'. Both of us appeared to anoint Jesus with perfumed oils. But that seems to have resolved itself. There were two Marys - Maria of Magdala and Mary the sister of Martha, and Judas Iscariot seemed to have hated them both."

"Have you discussed Babis Demetrix, or whatever his name was, with Gloria and Patrick?" David asked picking up on Judas.

"No, not really," Clarissa admitted.

"Tell us, then," Gloria pleaded. "Who is Babis?"

"He was a macho Greek who took a shine to Clarissa," David chuckled. "Actually, Clarissa thinks he was Judas Iscariot."

"Judas Iscariot!" Gloria said excitedly. "Judas could be the key to lots of things in this story. He's a bit of an enigma."

"I met this officer on board the 'Ulysses'," Clarissa explained. "His name was Babis Demetris. He was a good looking Greek who seemed to be harassing anyone under forty who was traveling alone. That is any girl, I should say. I told him to get lost, but he came back to me in the dream state. He appeared to me as Judas Iscariot. It was interesting, because it all happened in this double dream about the anointing of Jesus. At first I saw myself anointing Joshua with this oil that a blind man whom Joshua had healed, gave to Marcus, my son. Judas criticized my action vehemently. He obviously didn't like me. He yelled at me and said something like, 'What are you doing that for, Woman?' One of the others, called Cephas, joined in as two of Joshua's fishermen friends grabbed hold of me. This Cephas man, a big, burly fellow, suggested that the fragrant oil could have been sold for money that they could have given to the poor. Joshua rebuked them, telling them that there will always be poor people, but that what I had done was an act of love. Actually, if I get my dream journal you can see exactly what they all said. I'm just giving you the gist of it."

"Cephas," David murmured. "That rings a bell with me."

"Cephas was St. Peter," Patrick interjected. "Sometimes in the Bible he is Simon Peter, sometimes plain Peter and occasionally Cephas. If I remember rightly, 'Cephas' is Hebrew for a rock and 'Petros' is the Greek. The name Peter or Cephas was probably the name the early Church gave to the Apostle with the idea that he was the 'rock' on which Jesus said he would build his Church."

Gloria raised her hand as the professional moderator. "One thing at a time," she stated firmly. "I want to know the rest of Clarissa's story about Judas Iscariot."

They became silent and Clarissa continued where she had left off. "I woke up for a moment, but when I returned to sleep the dream continued. The characters were the same, but the scene was different. Judas was yelling at Jesus this time. First he shouted, 'What did she do that for?' and then repeated Cephas' statement about selling the fragrant oil for money. He cursed women. He said they were making Joshua soft. I wasn't sure what had just taken place because I had been with Marcus, but when Judas mentioned both our names, 'Maria' and 'Mary' and suggested that Mary would be better off if she stuck to her household chores like her sister Martha, I realized that this had to be a different anointing. There's actually a second anointing story when Martha's sister anoints Jesus." She looked at David. "That was the story the Rector at your mother's church spoke about when we were there for Thanksgiving."

"Yes, it was," David admitted. "Well, perhaps we gleaned something out of the sermon after all."

"What interests me," Gloria said as she poured them all more coffee, "is that you encountered someone in this life who was none other than Judas Iscariot at the time you were Mary Magdalene. Somehow all the central players in the Christ story seem to be coming together again."

"What about your connection with Joseph of Arimathea?" Clarissa asked.

"Well, I was just thinking about that as we sit here. I mean this is a powerful group. We have an aide of some sort to Pontius Pilate, we definitely seem to have Mary Magdalene and I believe that I knew Joseph of Arimathea."

"Tell us more about that?" David asked, raising his eyebrows.

"He was a friend of my father's. We were from wealthy, Jewish families living in the patrician circles of Jerusalem. Unlike my father, who wasn't very religious, Joseph was an influential member of the Sanhedrin, the high council of the Temple hierarchy. He was a pretty sick man, suffering from internal disorders common at the time, especially among people of our class. Miraculously, Jesus healed him. At least that's how Joseph described it. Anyway, just like the Bible says, he managed to persuade the authorities to let him bury Jesus' body in his own tomb rather than in the common, criminals' pit. The Roman officer in charge agreed. In fact, he and Joseph became friends. One night before Joseph left Jerusalem, we all dined at his house and the Roman tribune was there. I can even remember his name, and that's interesting because his name doesn't appear in the Bible. He was 'Linus Flavian'."

"Linus Flavian!" Clarissa gasped.

"Yes, I'm sure that was right. He was a senior member of Pilate's government."

Clarissa's jaw dropped as she looked at David.

"That's who David thought he was!"

"Yes," David agreed. "That was the Roman's name in my dream. Pilate addressed me as 'Linus Flavian'."

Gloria sat back in her armchair rubbing her hands. "Fascinating! You should write this whole thing down. It has all the ingredients of a great story!"

"We are," Clarissa said slowly, knowing that she was recording as much as possible in her dream journal. "Now, Gloria, what about the part of the story where Joseph tells your family he's leaving Palestine?"

"That was the last time I saw him. After Jesus was crucified, it seems that Joseph of Arimathea took care of Mary Magdalene. Now, as I explained to Clarissa the other day David, the rumor was that he took just a little too much care of Mary Magdalene to the point where Mary became pregnant. In the Hellenist circle in which we lived, this would never have been accepted. With respect, Clarissa, Mary Magdalene was not of the same class. In order to save them both from disgrace, he left Jerusalem and took Mary Magdalene with him. Legend says they went to Gaul."

"Gloria, I'm going to have to interrupt!" Clarissa abruptly interjected. "I really haven't had a chance to discuss this with you yet with all the excitement of the recording and the radio show, but the night after you told me that story about Joseph of Arimathea, I had a very strong dream about him. We were on a ship with one, big sail. We were close to a land of craggy, light-colored cliffs. I felt the baby kicking in me. Joseph hugged me and told me he would always take care of me and 'Joshua's' baby. The child I was carrying was not his, it was Jesus' child!"

David caught his breath and stared at his shoes.

The revelation even silenced Gloria.

Patrick scratched his head. "Before we all get sentenced by the Inquisition," he said with that little touch of humor that was needed to break the tension, "don't be too sure that this was Jesus' child. Joseph of Arimathea told you he would take care of 'Joshua's' child?"

"Yes," Clarissa said firmly.

" 'Joshua' was a common Jewish name. Maybe there was another Joshua?"

Clarissa's thoughts were at the waterfall in the stream where, as Maria, she had washed Joshua's hair before persuading him to wash hers. "My Joshua was Jesus, Patrick. If I was pregnant I'm sure it was by him and not by anyone else."

An awkward silence followed.

"Tell me something," David said at length to Gloria. "How do you remember so many details? I find it quite hard to remember my dreams unless I write them down, and even then some of the finer details such as you've described are gone."

"Most of my revelation didn't come in dreams, but in regression sessions," Gloria explained. "You see, when I had the lama on the radio show, someone called in about past life, regression therapy. This is a relatively new psychology field and there are therapists who can lead you back into your past lives, so I tried it. Now, I believe this has helped in solving extreme problems of unresolved karma."

"You mean imbalance in relationships from the past?" David queried.

"Precisely. The balancing of soul energy is no less an important subject than the ancient balance of 'Yin' and 'Yang', or the matter held together in delicate balance by the energy around us."

"Now, 'Yin' and 'Yang' are not to be confused with good and evil?" David continued with his rhetorical questioning.

"No. That's usually so hard for the Western World to understand, but it's second nature to the Asian community. All things seek an eternal harmony, that is, ideal balance. 'Yin' and 'Yang' are like the positive and negative forces in a battery. They're not good and bad, yet you must have plus and minus for the battery to work - so it is with the eternal harmony of life."

"A good analogy," David agreed.

" 'Yin' represents the dark, cool, damp, soft and mysterious elements and 'Yang' the hot, fiery, fast, hard and straightforward elements.

Everything is composed of both, but if one set of elements outweighs the other the result is usually a cycle of imbalance that we label bad. Though the imbalance can lead to what Westerners call evil or even sin, Asians might prefer to just call it bad luck. Often the imbalance is beyond our personal control because we are only a small part of the ongoing attempt to find balance between all living creatures."

"I've never really heard it explained so simply," David said in admiration. "Now, in that light, karma as it is called in the East, is not necessarily evil or bad, but simply an imbalance that has to be corrected?"

"Exactly," Gloria said with a satisfied sense of achievement. She loved getting into these philosophical discussions. "Maybe sometimes karma spills over from our past lives. And it could well be that is what is bringing us all together now! Maybe Jesus was never meant to die the way he did, but the fact that he was crucified by the Romans caused a certain imbalance in all our lives we are told, which we're now working out two thousand years later."

"You mean for humanity or just us?" David asked.

"Well, I meant just us, but that's an interesting thought," Gloria noted. "Maybe Christ has to come again to put the record straight."

David pulled his chair a little closer to Gloria's. "You don't really believe that Jesus died to save us from our sins, do you?"

"Well, that's the Church's belief, but I don't personally," Gloria admitted. "I believe that Jesus, was a great teacher and healer. He was just behaving in the right way at the wrong time. Naturally crowds gathered around him. The Romans didn't like crowds. Religiously, motivated crowds were threatening to Roman peace. I remember my father discussing these things with Joseph of Arimathea - that was also revealed in the regression session."

"So tell us about the past life, regression program?" Clarissa asked, pleased to see that the philosophical discussion was winding down.

"She went bananas!" Patrick echoed with his customary, good humor. "I had to take her to this Indian guru over on Lantana. He looked the part alright - one of those weirdos with long, white hair and a face like a prune. She tried to get me to go through with it too, but the guru wouldn't take me. He said I wasn't ready!"

"Well, you weren't dear," Gloria replied. "You have to believe in this kind of thing in your heart. You didn't then, even if you do now."

David couldn't deny his curiosity. "This is interesting. Tell us more. Do they hypnotize you?"

"No. They say there's no hypnosis. You're wide awake throughout and you speak for yourself. The therapist just leads you into the scenario," Gloria explained. "The really vital thing is to say absolutely the first thing that comes into your head, however stupid that may seem. If you start to think, you can block out the soul memory with too many thought patterns from your present life. Once you've plugged in to a past life, it'll start to flow. Keep talking, sometimes you might seem a little spaced out, but just keep describing the first thing that comes into your mind. You're somehow tapping in to your soul records. I can't explain it and it doesn't work for everyone, but it worked pretty well for me. Once I found myself face to face with Jesus on his way to the cross, everything else followed."

"Does the guru share your experience?" David asked.

"No. He just guides you. He prepares you with some relaxation exercise. It's not hypnosis, but he might ask you to imagine you are looking at a painting in a gallery or the scene from a window. Something to just lead you into the first, visual image you have."

"How do you feel afterwards?" Clarissa asked.

"Completely normal except that you have added to your twentieth century brain all the images that the session has unearthed. What's more you seem to retain a clearer memory of those facts from then on than your normal retention. I can't tell you why, but that just seems to be so."

Patrick glanced at his watch. "I don't wish to say anything," he said cheerfully, "but if we're going to get out at all this afternoon we'd better get a move on. It's already ten past three."

"We thought you might like to go out to the duck farms and see some of the border villages, but it's a good, forty minute run," Gloria suggested. "Then tonight we thought we'd take you to the Golf Club. It's not far from here and they have a good buffet on Sunday nights."

"Sounds great," Clarissa agreed although she would have been quite happy to have just returned to the pigsty for the rest of the afternoon.

"Your concert is on Channel Five at seven," Gloria continued as she organized their day. "We booked a table at the Club for half past eight so we can all watch you on the 'box' first."

"Right, expedition duck farms!" Patrick commanded. "Select a pair of 'wellies' each from the patio. It can be a little muddy there."

"Let me just run back down for my camera," Clarissa said as David helped himself to a pair of the rubber boots.

Patrick went to start the car.

When Clarissa came back she selected a pair of shiny, red 'wellies' from the patio. The cockatoo put his head on one side. "Silly old fool" he said.

"And you too!" Clarissa replied, delighted to know she had passed his test of approval.

• • • • • • • •

The hills on both sides of the border between the New Territories and Canton, looked pale blue, almost ethereal in the late, afternoon light. The great slabs of water, home to thousands of birds, reflected the pallor of the sky. There was not a sound other than the quacking of the ducks as they waddled along earthen dikes between the ponds, leaving narrow tracks of mud, feathers and poop.

Patrick and Gloria led David and Clarissa out along the ridges.

"Look at the babies!" Gloria exclaimed as a mother duck shook its wings and dropped down into the pond. Eight little ones followed her, falling over themselves as they slid into the water as little bundles of down.

Clarissa took a photo.

"A Kodak moment!" David teased.

The ponds looked like flooded, rice paddies. Along their edge they were connected by bridges of planking to the old Chinese village where most of the duck farmers lived.

"We should walk back through the village," Gloria suggested. "That'll give you a real taste of rural China."

There couldn't have been a house of less than two hundred years of age in the village. Every roof was sealed by dusty, gray tiles fixed on their angles by elaborate gargoyles and terra-cotta spirits. The walls were dirty white. Mud abounded in the streets. Ducks waddled up and down as if they owned the place and there was a pungent odor of farmyard manure. Here, the Chinese wore three quarter length trousers and traditional wide hats made from bamboo just as seen in the classic paintings of the nineteenth century. Their clothes were a dull blue and gray, but their eyes seemed to sparkle with the wisdom of centuries. Some were starting to cook; others were idly smoking their long bamboo pipes. Children with round faces and rosy cheeks, laughed as they played. One fishermen proudly brought in his catch, only to find when his back was turned that the benefactor was a village cat. Patches of bamboo and willow sprung up wherever the ground was rich enough to take their roots. A street divided to accommodate their growth. Tits flew above while mice roamed below.

"Timeless China," Gloria repeated as they climbed from the village back to the narrow road where Patrick had parked the car.

A heron stood by the willows, watching them, then gracefully flew up into the evening light to a better perch from which to fish.

"I'm glad we had these rubber boots," David admitted as they took off their 'wellies' to throw them in the trunk of the car. "You were right about the mud."

"It's so peaceful," Clarissa said. "Thanks for taking us here."

Patrick started the ignition and drove them home. They had about half an hour to change in order to be up at the cottage to see Clarissa perform on television.

Crickets and bullfrogs were now tuning up in the evening shadows of the garden. The sty looked invitingly warm.

"I could do without the formal bit at the Club tonight," Clarissa said. "It's so romantic here."

David agreed as he kissed his sweetheart. "I guess the romance will just have to wait until later."

Later came after they had watched Clarissa's performance and waded through a heavy buffet at the Hong Kong Club. The place resembled that of a country club anywhere in the world. It was a mixed haven for golfers and socialites. Gloria introduced David and Clarissa to many British ex-pats and various Tai-pans. It was almost like being back on board ship and going into 'smile' mode. There was little opportunity in the slightly, artificial environs of the club, to investigate the stimulating discussion of the afternoon.

"Gloria would make an excellent Cruise Director," David said as he and Clarissa reached the sanctuary of the pigsty. "She's a real, people person."

"She's interesting," Clarissa agreed. "I thought you'd like her. The thing is, she really likes us and she's genuinely fascinated by what we have to say. She may be opinionated, but she certainly knows how to get the very best out of anybody. That's why she's so terrific at her job. I loved doing my interview with her. I felt completely relaxed when we were on the air."

There was a warm, pinkish glow to the bedside lamps in the pigsty. It caught the folds of the mosquito net that was raised to look like the rear canopy of an Empire-style bed. The light also reflected the burnished gold of the antique, Chinese wall carvings.

"It's lovely here," Clarissa said as she melted into David's arms.

"Very romantic," David agreed. "Let's light the candles in that old candelabra by the fireplace."

They lit the candles and prepared for bed. They both knew that they each wanted to celebrate their love. Clarissa struggled with the ancient shower while David languished in the huge bathtub. Their bodies warmed by their recent ablutions, they came together in the coziness of the sty. The bed was soft. The room glowed, and their love was fulfilled.

• • • • • • • •

The following day, David and Clarissa entertained Patrick and Gloria to lunch on board the 'Prince Regent'. Their new-found friends were impressed with the gracious, old-fashioned atmosphere of the ship. As promised, David also arranged for Gloria to interview the Hotel Manager and the Cruise Director. Just before their guests were due to leave, they ran into Fiona MacAllister.

"This is the ship's nurse," David said as he introduced the lithe blonde.

Clarissa kept her thoughts to herself as she observed David's ex-flame.

"Gloria Ainsworth is a well-known, radio personality here in Hong Kong," David explained to Fiona. "Could you spare a few minutes to give her some anecdotes and information on the ship's hospital?"

Gloria and Fiona chatted for about ten minutes in the busy ship's lobby.

Hong Kong tailors were beginning to bring on their clients' completed clothes. Passengers were greeting these merchants like old, personal friends, although in reality they were little more than another number in their tailor's book. At six in the evening the 'Prince Regent' would sail. The three days of frantic shopping were nearly over. It would be on to Thailand and Bali, before docking in Singapore for the next round of serious buying.

In the frantic atmosphere of the lobby, David and Clarissa hastily said goodbye to the Ainsworths. David needed to get back to his desk.

"Keep in touch," Gloria insisted. "We were all meant to meet. It's been absolutely marvellous. Don't forget what I said, you should write everything down. It's quite fascinating. It would make a tremendous book."

"We'll send you the first copy," Clarissa said as she hugged her hostess.

"Signed?" Patrick added as he extended his hand to say farewell. "By the way that nurse is a knock out."

David escorted them to the gangway. "Thanks for all you've done for Clara here. She loved it."

"She's so good," Gloria said. "We've got to get her music out. I'll make sure the radio station keeps plugging her C.D's. Send me a copy of the new one when it comes out, the one that's going to include 'Gilded Snow'."

"We will," David assured her as they shook hands.

"Goodbye!" Clarissa shouted over his shoulder. "Remember me to Millie, Brewster and the cockatoo!"

"We will!" Gloria called back as they waved from the end of the gangway before turning back into the frantic, shopping crowd roaming Ocean Terminal.

• • • • • • • •

At midnight, on February the thirteenth, the night before the 'Prince Regent' anchored off Bali, David whispered his secret to Clarissa. "Happy Valentine's Day!" he announced as he handed her a rose which he had hidden under their bed.

Clarissa took the flower, smelled it and turned towards him in the bed. "Oh! David! How romantic!"

"That's not all," David continued. "I've arranged a very special stopover for us in Bali seeing this is Valentine's Day. We're staying overnight and we're going to 'Amandari'."

"What's that?" Clarissa asked excitedly.

"According to our agent it's Bali's most romantic hideaway. I've known the agent here for years. He's arranged it all for me and they've given it to us complimentary because the agent told them we're on our honeymoon."

"We are, David," Clarissa said as she stroked his chest. "Life with you is one, long honeymoon. In fact the little breaks only emphasize that. Whenever we're reunited it's another honeymoon!"

"Well, for our honeymoon, an 'Amandari' car will pick us up at Padang Bay around ten-thirty. They'll bring us back here the next day by noon. We sail at two. It'll be a wonderful romantic getaway for us. I've arranged for everything to be covered in the office, but it may mean we won't get much time off in Singapore."

"I'd rather have the time with you on Valentine's Day!" Clarissa said lovingly as she threw her arms around his neck and smothered him with kisses.

David was true to his word. The ship's agent confirmed that a car from 'Amandari' would be on the dockside at ten-thirty. It was about a ten minute boat ride from the ship to the pier at Padang Bay. David and Clarissa left shortly after ten.

It was hot - very hot. On the pier, Balinese traders were busy trying to sell anything for a dollar. No sooner had passengers walked down the gangway from the little shuttle boat than they were besieged. Postcards, woodcarvings and batik cloth were thrust at the bemused visitors. Prices rapidly reduced as bargains were made. Hanging down over the scene like great lanterns were decorated palm fronds and bamboo poles from which hung mobiles to protect everyone from evil spirits. Beneath them, David spotted their driver. The man held a placard that simply said 'Amandari'.

"Is this the car for the Petersons?" David asked.

"Mr. and Mrs. David Peterson," the young Indonesian, dressed in a white, safari suit, confirmed.

"You're going to drive us to the Amandari?"

"Yes. Please come this way."

David and Clarissa followed the man to a gray, Japanese, 'Grand Rover', a rather smarter vehicle than the general collection of worn out taxis and mini-vans whose drivers were shouting business. In no time they left the mad scene on the pier and the shops of Padang village to reach the timeless beauty of the real Bali, untainted by the commercial greed of the tourist trade.

Lush, green fields and paddies of rice fell away from the roadside. Smiling natives, carrying water jars and huge platters of fruit offerings for the gods, waved at the jeep as it passed. At every bridge and before every house stood a statue decorated in checkered cloths and eternally plied with the produce of the land. In the villages, more bamboo poles hung over gateways in festive decoration.

After a while, traffic increased and Bali's driving nightmare became more apparent. Motor scooters vied for space with bicycles, heavy trucks and overloaded buses. The scene became more urban. There were walls everywhere, many under repair and frequently opened up by elaborately carved gateways leading to nowhere of great significance. Temples abounded.

This semi-urban sprawl, interspersed with lush areas of rice paddies, was old, dusty and colorful. There was little evidence of twentieth century architecture. Everything was patched in traditional style, giving a permanence to the unique Balinese way of life.

At length, after nearly an hour's drive, they came to the village of Ubud, a long street of busy shops selling all manner of art, crafts, clothing and leather goods. "Just ten minutes more," the driver said.

Above Ubud the road took two or three, right-angle turns around the brick walls, until the jeep found the narrow opening that led down a paved lane to the masterpiece of Balinese architecture that is 'Amandari'.

The Manager greeted David by name.

Clarissa was impressed.

After a few, simple, registration formalities, they were escorted to their villa by a beautiful girl in a gorgeous sarong.

"Your first time in Bali?" she asked.

"For my wife," David replied, "but I come here most years. This is the first time I've stayed on Bali, though. I'm usually aboard ship."

"In Padang?" the girl with sultry, beautiful eyes asked.

"Yes, one of the cruise ships," David answered. "I work on board."

They walked between walls harboring bowers of bourganvillea and alamanda flowers, spilling down in cascades of pink, purple and yellow. The roofs of the villas that peeked out from above these walls were thatched in grass and shaped in pyramids, each topped by an elaborately woven crown. The path was steep. Each villa had its own separate gate, guarded by a divine statue and lit by lanterns. The Balinese girl with a figure that glided on air, stopped in front of one. "This will be your room," she announced. "Please come in."

Through the gate was a garden of lush, tropical plants. Flagstones led to an intricately carved, double door that took them into the huge room that made up the ground floor. Two, large divans gave the impression that this was both the sleeping and living area, but David and Clarissa were soon to learn that this was not so.

"Please let me show you upstairs," the girl said.

They followed her into an elaborate dressing room on the lower level. At one end there were doors out into a private, walled court in which was a sunken, marble bath tub. Surrounding the tub were plantings of foliage. At the other end was a spiral staircase that led up into the bedroom. The bed was canopied and the views were spectacular. To the left, one could see the gentle, Balinese landscape folding its way down to the distant sea. To the right, dodging between puffy clouds, were the mountain heights of the hinterland. Immediately below them was a deep and spectacular gorge with lush paddies climbing down to a river of muddy, white water.

"This is paradise!" Clarissa said excitedly. "This has to be the most beautiful hotel room I've ever seen!"

"You like it?" the girl asked.

"Yes, very much!" Clarissa repeated.

They followed the girl back down to the lower level. A house-boy had arrived with complimentary drinks and a huge plate of elaborately carved and beautifully presented fruits. "We wish you a very happy time at Amandari," he said as he bowed and placed his hands together.

The two Balinese servants then left and David and Clarissa were alone.

They ran into each others arms.

"It's perfectly lovely, darling" Clarissa said.

"Happy Valentine's day, Clara," David replied.

After a while, they walked back down to the main area of the hotel to have some lunch. The dining room looked out over the swimming pool which was at the top of the gorge. It merged with the landscape. A small pavilion built on a little promontory at the far side reflected its columns and grass thatch in the pool's placid waters. Beyond were lush, rice paddies and feathering palms.

David and Clarissa sat at a table in the open room overlooking this spectacular scene. The perfume of plumeria greeted their senses as they ordered nasi goreng and gouda gouda.

Clarissa reached across the table and took David's hand. "Thank you for bringing me here," she said. "How can we be so lucky to be so happy?"

"It's because of our love," David replied.

In the afternoon they swam and lay for a while in the sun, but by about three-thirty the blue sky was swallowed up by advancing monsoon clouds.

"I think it's time to return to the villa," David suggested as he felt the first drops of rain.

By the time they got back inside, it was raining hard. The sound of the rain beating on the grass thatch only added to the romance. They followed the advice of nature and joined themselves in the passion of love before falling asleep in each others arms.

Dusk descended. The rain stopped. It was nearly seven-thirty when they awoke.

"Let's take a bath in that marble tub," Clarissa suggested.

The air outside smelled fresh after the rain. The light in the wall above the bath, illuminated the lush plants in the bathing courtyard.

Clarissa started to fill the tub and added bath foam. The foam grew as the water level rose. By the time David came down from the upper level, Clarissa was already seated in the tub.

"You look like an advertisement for soft 'Camay' soap," he teased as he saw only her head and arms above the bubbles.

David stood with just a towel around him. "Is there room for two?"

"Of course, my love. Do you think I drew this bath just for me! This tub is like a small swimming pool. Come on in."

Clarissa reached for David's towel and pulled at it.

"Clara!" he yelled.

The towel fell away leaving him naked.

"Come on in!" she repeated.

David joined her in the bubbles. They caressed each other and kissed as the Balinese moon began to peek out from the recent rain clouds.

"I love you so much!" Clarissa whispered in his ear.

"I love you too, Clara."

The sounds of grasshoppers and frogs greeted the moon with their nocturnal chorus.

As the water cooled, Clarissa removed the bath plug. They stood up, dripping foam. "We'd better take a shower," she suggested, but her thoughts somehow connected with that day two thousand years before when she and Joshua had washed each other's hair and the bubbles from the lye soap had filtered into that Galilean stream. Finally they had stood naked together under a waterfall. As she held David's hand and led him to the shower she felt she was with Joshua.

David sensed something strange in her. "What's got into you?" he said with a grin.

"I had this really sensuous dream about Maria and Joshua," Clarissa revealed. "I haven't told you about it yet, but this place has somehow reminded me of it."

"So what happened?" David asked as the jet streams from the shower bounced off their flesh.

"I washed Jesus' hair in a stream, then he washed mine. It was a beautiful scene. After we had washed each other's hair we walked upstream to a waterfall. There, we stood together and embraced."

David caressed Clarissa's body in the warm water of the shower. "That's not terribly surprising if you were Mary Magdalene," he noted.

"No, David, but we were naked just as we are now. Somehow our nakedness and the warm sensations that I felt in his presence, made this moment incredibly sensual."

David kissed Clarissa. His growing erection was obvious. "It makes this a pretty sensuous moment too," he said.

Clarissa caressed him in the warm stream as they continued to kiss in the light of the Balinese moon.

In the brightness of the interior they dried themselves off on luxurious, bath towels. Clarissa looked at her husband. David had a fine physique. There was not much sign of middle-aged spread on his forty plus old body. His legs and arms were hairy, but his torso was smooth.

"You have a beautiful body," Clarissa said as she put her arms around him again. "But we'd better 'get on with it' as your mother would say. It must be well into dinner time by now."

David picked up his watch. "My God! It's already eight-thirty!"

Clarissa wore a simple, lace dress and David a silk shirt and white pants. They made their way down the alleyways between the Balinese walls to the dining room. The Maitre d'Hotel took them to a romantic table for two overlooking the pool. The haunting sound of gamelan and gongs drifted up from the pavilion, competing with the sounds of the crickets and bullfrogs. The whole scene was bathed in the moonlight.

"The passengers will be getting this for local entertainment tonight," David mentioned. "It's always such a hassle getting all the gamelan and gongs on board. It's so much better to hear this as we are now, in its natural setting. To be honest, on board it sends most of the passengers to sleep after five minutes. It needs the competition of the crickets and frogs, the light of the moon and a romantic dinner, to make the magic happen."

"I agree," Clarissa said as she smiled at him in the candlelight. "But here, it is magic."

The rest of their time at 'Amandari' was further magic.

"I could have stayed here a week or more," Clarissa noted, as she packed their few things back into their overnight bag. "This was the most beautiful Valentine's gift we could have shared."

"It was wonderful," David agreed. "I'm so glad you came into my life, Clara."

By midday on February the fifteenth, they were back on board the 'Prince Regent'. The ship's agent came by to pick up the last collection of mail from the Purser's Office. "How was 'Amandari'?" he asked David.

"Perfect. It couldn't have been better. We don't know how to thank you enough for making it all happen."

"We'll see you next year," the Balinese gentleman replied as David gave him a carton of American cigarettes.

Within half an hour the ship's engines started up and the 'Prince Regent' sailed out from Padang Bay. The monsoon clouds gathered to bring their daily afternoon rain.

• • • • • • • •

The bus bounced down the dusty road that led to the entrance to Fatepur Sikri. Jeremy Dyson mopped his forehead. Dark patches of sweat showed through the khaki linen of his safari shirt. He was almost the only white man on the bus. There was a young Canadian couple sitting several seats down on the opposite side, who were backpacking on a two month tour of India, but aside from these two, they sat amongst an overfilled bus of dark, brown-skinned Indians. The motley-dressed locals were making their way out from Agra home to their various outlying villages and farms. Monkeys, in family groups at the roadside, watched them pass and periodically the bus was obliged to give way to a snail-paced, buffalo cart or working elephant. Clouds of fine, red dust, tenacious flies and oppressive heat also accompanied them every minute.

Jeremy could have taken a taxi from the Oberoi Intercontinental, but he preferred to experience the local color. He learned at the bus depot that he could return at five. This would give him six hours to explore the ghost city of the Moghul Emperor Akbar. After the Indian experience on the bus, he felt a little cheated when he arrived at the great gateway into Fatepur Sikri only to be confronted with the tourist trappings of Western society. Along with a Coca Cola stand, merchants were selling 'Moghul' tee shirts and filigree trinkets of all sorts made from cheap, Indian silver.

Standing in a uniform that was far too hot for the climate, a gatekeeper took Jeremy's money and handed him back the few crumpled rupee notes that were his change. "We close the main gate at six," the official said.

Once away from the great gateway, Jeremy switched his mind back into archeological mode as he began to interpret sixteenth century Fatepur Sikri. As David had suggested, there was a great romance about the place. The magnificent buildings competed with the rich growth of jungle and were the demesne of large lizards and camouflaged snakes. Jeremy trod with care. He was almost alone in the majestic glory of Akbar's short-lived capital. It was so different from the crowds who had thronged the Taj Mahal in neighboring Agra.

'David Peterson was right,' he thought. 'This is a fascinating place.'

He ventured from the main square with its magnificent gateway symbolizing the deist fusion of India's faiths, and past the elaborate, marble tracery of a prophet's tomb. As in digs of Greece and Israel, he wanted to see the streets and imagine them alive with the life of a bygone era. He became immersed in imaginative reconstruction and marvelled at the beauty of the red stone.

Flamboyant, green parakeets played in the foliage and a giant, yellow and black butterfly spread its wings in the heat of the day.

'I wonder if they ever knew the glory of this place in their previous incarnations,' Jeremy thought. 'Such majesty as this butterfly could only belong in the opulence of Moghul glory.'

He sat in a shady corner of what had probably been a tradesman's store. 'Reincarnation is the wheel of Indian life,' he thought. 'I haven't really considered it much since my discussions with the Petersons. I wonder if they've had any further revelations about our first century connections? Many have subscribed to the theory that Jesus came to India and like Akbar adopted philosophies. Perhaps it was this that made his teaching so dramatically different and brought the wrath of the Jewish hierarchy upon him. Maybe he came to believe in reincarnation and assuredly here he would have learned meditation and healing skills very different from those accepted in Palestine.'

A monkey screeched. Jeremy reached into his knapsack for his water bottle and took a few sips. An Indian boy, dressed in nothing but his dhoti, entered the building. Jeremy stood up as the boy approached. The youth was thin and emaciated, but had an engaging grin. He pulled on Jeremy's arm. "Mister, I show you temple. You want to see."

Jeremy followed the boy back out into the deserted and overgrown street that sloped down into the surrounding jungle. They turned a corner and there before them was an exquisite, little, Jain temple. Elephants jousted with each other in the carved stonework that rose up like a squat obelisk. The boy looked in at the entrance and beat on the stones with a stick. "Snakes," he said knowingly.

Jeremy stood back. A long, thin snake wriggled out of the cavern. The boy poked it with his stick picking it up and throwing it to one side where it slithered into neighboring ruins. The youth was grinning, obviously realizing that his bravery was impressing the foreigner.

Jeremy tried to grin while the boy beat with his stick on the entrance stones again.

"Grass snake," the boy said. "No bad snake in here." He beckoned for Jeremy to follow him inside.

The cavern was dark and cool. Jeremy lit a match. In the fluorescent glow of the flame he saw that the inside walls were as elaborately carved as those on the outside. The boy was beaming with pride.

After visiting the Jain temple, the boy lead Jeremy through many buildings before they arrived back in the main square. A few Indians were already waiting for the bus as the golden light of the plateau hinterland told that evening was near. Half an hour late, the decrepit bus pulled up outside the entrance. There were men sitting on top of the vehicle amidst bundles and baskets and it didn't look like there was much room inside. Jeremy was lucky. He took the last seat. His grinning boy looked up at him from the dusty street below. Jeremy reached into his pocket and found some dirty, old rupees. He passed them down. Other boys appeared as if from nowhere. Faces became desperate. Scuffles and fights broke out. The bus pulled away in a swirl of smoky dust.

As the bus approached Agra, darkness enveloped them. The smells and aromas of spices and curry, mingled with those of filth and dung. Bicycles moved everywhere, many with no lights. Oil lamps began glowing softly in the hovels where the teeming masses lived. Then the squalor changed to splendor as the facades of Shah Jehan's monuments and the floodlit walls of the Red Fort loomed before them. From the bus depot Jeremy Dyson took a taxi to his hotel. Boys in livery, with plumed hats and gold braid, opened the doors into the Oberoi Intercontinental's air-conditioned world. Fountains played, marble gleamed and illuminated, plastic, precious stones sparkled from the walls. Close to the elevators was the elaborate entrance into the Moghul Restaurant where waiters, in larger versions of the bell boys' splendor, carried trays of silver bowls and steaming dishes.

The hostess was dressed in the finest, silk sari in colors of red and green patterned in gold. "Will you be having your dinner with us tonight, Mr. Dyson?" she asked.

"In about half an hour," Jeremy replied. "I must just go up and change."

The hostess smiled. "We'll have a table for you."

Later Jeremy did dine in the Moghul Restaurant. The food was beautifully presented and he had been hungry after his long day out at

Fatepur Sikri. He couldn't help but be amused by the note that he read on the bottom of the check that the waiter had handed him to sign. 'If you did not feel like a Moghul Emperor in our Restaurant please let us know'.

'Such contrast,' Jeremy thought.

Tired, he went to bed. In his dreams that night he saw himself as a young Indian boy ....

The sun beat down and dust swirled in the streets that were filled with putrefied dung. The streets didn't look dramatically different from those with which he had become familiar. Painted elephants guarded the doorways into houses and stores. People mingled with sacred cows that had bells around their necks. But there were no bicycles, no motor scooters and no rusting cars. No overcrowded buses honked their horns to clear a passage. Bullock carts were more numerous, elephants were more in evidence and camels abounded. Yet the people looked much the same. Their clothes were little different - great color mingled with dirty rags. Graceful women carried water pots and baskets on their heads. Men sat squatting in doorways watching the world go by while others drove their beasts onward with sticks and shouts. There were beggars with crippled limbs and monks with shaven heads. The monks wore long, yellow and brown robes. Artisans sat under colorful awnings spinning and weaving, shaping clay and working wood. Boys like Jeremy seemed everywhere. Some were thieving, others just playing and laughing, running about without any apparent purpose. Jeremy sensed himself amongst them. He felt a compassion for these street companions. They seemed to respect him and called out to him by name. "Ravi! Ravi!" they shouted. They called to him because he was their leader. He brought water to the beggars and had a kind word for the cripples.

Then, as 'Ravi' in his dream, Jeremy turned from one of the side streets into a more major thoroughfare that led down to the river. The road was teeming with life. People were running, many were laughing and farther up Ravi could hear the trumpeting of elephants. The elephants moved into the crowd clearing a path through 'the untouchables' as Ravi knew his kind were called. Ravi watched as they passed. The giant beasts were decorated with golden tassels and the Maharajah's coat of arms. Heavy bells hung from their sides clanging with the elephants' ungainly motion. Royal guests, including white rajahs in elaborate nineteenth century uniforms, swayed in their howdahs, while boys little older than Ravi sat behind the elephants' ears. The boys wore fine clothes and held their heads up high as they swatted flies away from the elephants' hides. Other boys held colorful umbrellas above the howdahs to protect His Royal Highness' guests. After the elephants there seemed to be a pause in the royal parade. People began to mingle in the street again waiting for the Maharajah's carriage. Ravi joined them. Many hoped that maybe a few silver annas might fall from the royal hand, while others, who revered the Maharajah as close to heaven, just wanted to touch his carriage with its gilded frame.

Four, sleek, black horses pulled the open 'landau'. The crowd pushed and shoved. Ravi found himself in the front. Then one of the lead horses shied. It reared and as it fell knocked Ravi to the ground.

Ravi could hear the shouts of those around him. He felt a pain in his ribs. Then he was kicked again. He cried out in agony. He heard the rumble of the carriage wheels. He was trapped, crushed, and then his world blacked out.

Ravi now saw himself above the carriage. As it passed, he saw his frail body mangled by the wheels. Nobody stopped. Nobody cared. The crowd continued to follow the procession and his broken body was left to bake in the sun. There was no pain now, only an increasing light that pulsated and intensified as the scene below him disappeared. He was content, free! He felt like he was traveling down a dark tunnel toward a swirling light that became brighter and brighter ....

Jeremy awoke in the air-conditioned comfort of his twentieth century 'Moghul' palace, the Oberoi Intercontinental of Agra. He was not dead - he was alive!

In the morning he took the train from Agra back up to New Delhi. The following day he was in conference with the Rajpath Hotel Group, assisting in the creation of their twentieth century restoration of Moghul splendor for present day tourists. As he sat at the boardroom table he couldn't help but think of those illuminated, plastic gemstones in the marble walls of the Agra Intercontinental. He chuckled as he recalled the words on the foot of the restaurant check, 'If you did not feel like a Moghul Emperor in our restaurant please let us know.'

In less than a week he would be flying down to Bombay and joining the 'Prince Regent'. He looked forward to sharing his India experiences with David and Clarissa.

● ● ● ● ● ● ● ●

From Singapore to Bombay it had been a relaxing and calm voyage on board the 'Prince Regent'. The Cruise Director managed to squeeze Clarissa in to his scheduled entertainment. She played a recital in the 'Lookout' to an appreciative audience. At the end she performed 'Gilded Snow'.

Clarissa had not been haunted by her first century revelations since Bali. When she played 'Gilded Snow' the old images that had come to her in Japan and Hong Kong, returned. When the piece reached that point where the glowing light faded to reveal a more detailed look at Joshua, she swore that his face was Jeremy's face. But before Clarissa could be certain the image returned to that of the Japanese shrine in the snow.

The audience loved the piece just as they had in Nagasaki and Hong Kong.

After the performance she sat with David in the bar. "Every audience for whom I've played 'Gilded Snow' seems to have liked it. It should do well on my new C.D."

"I like it too. All those remarkable colors you describe seem to come through. But, tell me something, Clara. Did you have the same experience this time as in Hong Kong and Japan?"

Clarissa put down her glass of sherry and looked at David. "Yes, the vision was just the same. But there was something else I noticed."

"What?"

"For a brief moment in the crescendo when I see Joshua I felt I was feeling the presence of Jeremy Dyson."

"Jeremy!"

"Yes, David. I've never been certain before, but tonight I was sure that Jeremy and Joshua were of the same soul. Perhaps it was just an illusion created by Joshua's strident tone and bearing, but there was something that definitely reminded me of our friend."

For some reason David felt disturbed by Clarissa's observation. It dawned on him that Jeremy would be sailing with them in just a couple of days. He couldn't bring himself to express to Clarissa his mistrust of Jeremy Dyson and the inner pangs of jealousy that he felt when she discussed him. "Why, Jeremy?" he repeated. "Haven't you already established that he was this Roman soldier who had the hots for you in Gaul. He couldn't have been Joshua."

Clarissa twisted the stem of her sherry glass between her thumb and forefinger. "No, you're right," she said. "It's impossible. If Jeremy Dyson was that 'damned Roman soldier' Remus Augustus, he couldn't have been Joshua." She smiled at David as she raised the glass to her lips and took a sip. "I'm so pleased you like the piece," she said. "This is exactly the kind of music that I most want to play. The beauty of nature can be depicted in sounds to make our hearts soar - filled with divine love. I'll play it in Jerusalem at my next concert."

"Global Artistes really did a good job on this tour," David noted, "all those concerts in Japan, the television job and the radio interview with Gloria Ainsworth in Hong Kong, and now this concert for you in Jerusalem." He paused as he thought of the Holy city. "I wish I could be with you in Jerusalem. I know you'll find the city very impressive," . he said regretfully. "But whereas I'll miss Jerusalem, you'll miss Ephesus. I'm really looking forward to seeing Ephesus again. I'm determined to get out there when we're docked at Kusadasi, especially after all the things your friend Jeremy had to say about the ruins."

Clarissa frowned. "David, he is your friend too! And talking about that, have you been able to upgrade his cabin?"

"I must look at that in the morning," David replied. "I've suddenly realized it's only two days away. The new download will be coming in on the Marinet. I can sort it out then. It won't be any problem. You know I'll work out something for him."

"Thanks," Clarissa said. "Won't he be surprised when he hears all our revelations? I can't wait until you get home at the end of the World Cruise and we can all sit down with Samantha. Now, if we could just beam Gloria Ainsworth in for that reunion we would really have something to talk about."

"Watch it, Clara!" David warned. "You're getting a little spacy. Let's just take one day at a time."

"I always feel high after I've been playing, especially when there's such good response," Clarissa replied. "But you've got to admit those three together would make this story hum."

David's 'Aussie' friend, Martin the Radio Officer, came up to them. "If you're buying, I'll join you for a drink."

"Of course," David agreed. "Pull up another chair."

Martin sat down, took Clarissa's hand and kissed it. "You were magnificent. That piece about the snow was a bloody ripper! What in the world is someone of your talent doing hanging out with this Purser fellow."

"I guess he's my inspiration, besides he keeps me grounded," Clarissa replied reaching for David's hand.

Martin ordered a beer.

180

• • • • • • • •

Jeremy's taxi took him the short distance from the Taj Mahal Hotel to Ballard Quay in Bombay. As always it was hot and humid. A heavy haze hung over the harbor where rusting, cargo vessels that tramped their way around the Indian Ocean, lay silently awaiting their next load. In dramatic contrast, the 'Prince Regent' gleamed with fresh paint. "Nice boat," the turbaned driver noted as he drove his taxi right up to the gangway.

A security officer checked Jeremy's ticket. Two Filipino bell boys came down the gangway and reached for his baggage. Jeremy paid the driver. An officer greeted him at the shell door, and Jeremy was aboard.

He presented his passage ticket at the Purser's Office and signed his registration.

"You've been upgraded," the receptionist noted when she saw his 'EE' ticket. "We've given you a Boat Deck cabin. I hope you'll like it. If not, please come back and we'll see what else we can offer you."

"'B' Sixteen," the young, Scandinavian girl announced to the Filipino bellboy who by now had Jeremy's bags on a trolley.

"The boy will take you up to your cabin, Mr. Dyson. We hope you enjoy your cruise."

Jeremy followed the bellboy. He was taken up to the Boat Deck and found his cabin to be very much bigger than he had anticipated. 'David must have done this for me,' he thought. 'This must cost far more than I paid.' He gave the Filipino five dollars. Now alone, he took a good, long shower.

Jeremy's phone rang shortly after he had changed. It was Clarissa. "Is that you, Jeremy?"

"Yes," he replied. "My God! It's you! I didn't recognize your voice!"

"Welcome aboard! How was India?"

"Wonderful. I achieved everything I needed to do in New Delhi, and just as David said, Agra and Fatepur Sikri were marvellous."

"Great! I wish we could have been with you. By the way, how's the cabin? David did his best for you."

"Unreal!"

"Good. When can we get together?" Clarissa asked eagerly.

"What do you suggest?"

"How about meeting up in the Lookout Bar at six?"

"Where's that?" Jeremy enquired.

"Forward and one deck up from your cabin."

"I'll find it. See you at six."

At five past six Jeremy found his way to the bar.

Clarissa was already waiting. She stood up as Jeremy approached. "Jeremy! It's great to see you! It's so good that you're on board!" Jeremy greeted her with a kiss and Clarissa felt the whiskers of his beard. She was not used to beards, but there was something about the sensation that felt strangely familiar. "David can't get away yet," she explained as they sat down, "but he might join us before dinner. The officials should have left by now. We'll be sailing any minute."

A waiter came up to their table. Jeremy ordered a whiskey. Clarissa already had an orange and soda.

"How can you drink whiskey in this heat?" she asked.

"It doesn't really make much difference in this air-conditioning," Jeremy noted with a grin.

The ship started to slip away from Ballard Quay. In the tropical, evening light, the rusting cranes and Victorian, stone buildings took on an iridescent glow.

The waiter returned with Jeremy's whiskey.

"Happy days!" Jeremy said.

"Cheers", Clarissa replied as they chinked glasses.

"So how was your concert tour?"

"It went very well. On the 'Ulysses' I met this wonderful glass harp trio from Switzerland. Their music was so special. It really moved me."

"Glass harp?" Jeremy repeated quizzically. "What exactly is a glass harp?"

Clarissa dipped her finger in her soda and then rubbed it lightly 'round the rim of Jeremy's whiskey tumbler. A low hum started to ring from the glass.

"That's a deep note," Clarissa explained. "Your glass is still pretty full. Now, imagine a whole table of glasses of differing sizes and containing different amounts of water. You could have two or three octaves. Then add an octave of bottles over which you can blow to create the bass sounds and you have the glass harp."

Jeremy started to rub the rim of his glass. Nothing happened. "It doesn't seem to work for me."

"Make sure your finger's wet enough," Clarissa advised.

After several attempts Jeremy managed to get his whisky tumbler to play a note. By now, others in the Lookout Bar had started to do the same and a gentle, telepathic hum was moving through the room, interspersed with laughter and mirth.

"Extraordinary!" Jeremy remarked. "It seems to be contagious."

Clarissa laughed. "We do seem to have started something, but you'll note it works best with the wine glasses."

Fiona MacAllister walked in to the humming bar and passed by their table. She was dressed in her nurse's uniform. Momentarily she stood there amazed at what was going on. She giggled as she joined one of the Bridge officers at a nearby table. Her white skirt rose up to show rather more leg than it should have.

Jeremy couldn't help but notice her. "One of the lady officers?" he asked.

"The nurse," Clarissa replied. "Actually, she's an old flame of David's."

Jeremy grinned as he looked over in Fiona's direction. "He had good taste."

"Hopefully he still does," Clarissa said firmly.

"Oh, unquestionably," Jeremy admitted as he turned the gaze of his sparkling eyes back from Fiona to Clarissa. "Now, where were you after the 'Ulysses'?"

"I crossed to Hawaii on the 'QE2' and then flew to Japan. The concerts in Japan went very well and from there it was on to Hong Kong. I had a television spot in Hong Kong and a fascinating interview on this radio talk show. Actually I stayed with the talk show host there. David met her too. She was most interesting. Like us, she believes in past lives."

Jeremy sipped on his whiskey and leaned towards Clarissa. "Go on," he said. "Did you tell her anything about your own revelations?"

"Yes. She believes that she was also around in first century Palestine. She said she knows that her father of that time was a friend of Joseph of Arimathea."

Jeremy raised an eyebrow. "And you were a friend of Joseph of Arimathea. In fact, if you remember, I thought I first saw you and your son when I was a young, Roman soldier in Massilia."

"Marseilles."

"Yes, Marseilles today, but Massilia two thousand years ago."

The 'Prince Regent' pulled out into Bombay Harbor. The Gateway to India arch and the facade of the Taj Mahal Hotel came into view. The windows of the hotel glinted from the red, setting sun and the city took on the splendor of the days of the British Raj.

"A country of such contrasts," Jeremy observed. "Magnificence stands beside appalling squalor, and yet unlike South America say, where the wealth and poverty seem segregated, in India they seem almost fused. They seem interconnected."

"Reincarnation," Clarissa replied. "They don't believe in reincarnation in South America. In India, a wealthy man is always aware that he was probably once a poor man."

"Or even a sacred cow or an insect!" Jeremy interjected.

"Yes. Do you ever remember being an animal in a past life?"

Jeremy laughed. "Actually no, but that does not mean that my soul energy was never around in another life form. I just don't recall it."

"Well, let's just stay with the First Century," Clarissa continued. "I've experienced a few more revelations since we last met. How about you?"

"Funnily enough, I really haven't had any more first century experiences, but I did have a strange dream in India that took me back a hundred years or so. I was a poor, Indian boy who was trampled to death by the horses of a Maharajah's carriage. Maybe it's because I had spent the day in Fatepur Sikri with this Indian boy. Perhaps that triggered me into the dream. The contrast between the splendor and the squalor somehow reminded me of this past life when I was killed at about that boy's age. What about you? Have you had any more revelations?"

Clarissa looked around to see if anyone was listening. Most were busy exchanging stories of their adventures in India, the poor quality of the bargains they had bought, the discomforts of the buses on tour, the flies, the dirt, the poverty and their great joy to be back on board ship. She caught Fiona's eye. The nurse gave a caustic smile and turned back to her officer friend. Nobody seemed interesting in prying into their conversation. "Yes. Several," Clarissa answered Jeremy. "Do you think there were any other occasions that we met in the First Century, or just that one time in Marseilles?"

"Massilia," Jeremy corrected her again. "Possibly. You do seem very familiar in some inexplicable way. From the very first time we met I've sensed this bonding with you. Why do you ask?"

"Well, when I listened to the glass harp on the 'Ulysses', the music conjured up several images. At first I saw David in the present, and then, in a sort of kaleidoscope of colors that swirled me back in time, I sensed him as a Roman youth. The strange thing is that I felt your energy in David's face."

"We are rather different!" Jeremy exclaimed as he stroked his sandy beard. "For one thing, David's clean shaven."

"I know, Jeremy," Clarissa agreed firmly as she was reminded of those strange, tingling sensations that she had felt when he had kissed her in innocent greeting. "That's what was so strange. In the image that came to me within that sound, I knew I was with David, but he had your appearance. He was a young Roman just like you have described Remus Augustus to have been, and he ..." Clarissa looked around again, "he was very passionate if you understand me."

Jeremy looked away. He desperately wanted to disguise any real feelings that he might have for Clarissa. He saw Fiona MacAllister and was surprised that he found himself starting to make comparisons between the lithe nurse and David's wife. "I don't recall great passion," he replied, "but I do believe that I was attracted to you. Clarissa, I was only half your age! You had a son my age!"

Clarissa grinned. "So, I was pretty good for my age," she teased. "No, the reason I asked was to confirm something else. David thinks he was a Roman in the First Century, some sort of an assistant to Pontius Pilate."

Jeremy pushed his whiskey tumbler aside and put both his hands on the table, leaning towards Clarissa. "Really!" he exclaimed. "Since when?"

"He dreamed about Pontius Pilate and himself discussing Jesus' crucifixion. He also had this strange dream about raping me as a Roman youth. I think that's what I tapped into when I listened to the glass harp, but somehow I confused my first century experiences with the two of you. David's still very skeptical about all this, but he knows that he dreamed about some sort of torrid scene between us."

"Between us or you and David?" Jeremy asked for clarification.

Clarissa smiled. "I was too old for you, 'Remus'," she said. "Linus was more of a contemporary. Perhaps I did meet him when he was a youth."

"Linus?"

"Yes, that was David's name back then. At least that's what Pontius Pilate called him."

"I see. So you think you met us both in the First Century?" Jeremy started to laugh. "I guess this Linus was the lucky guy!"

Clarissa blushed. "Well, maybe that's why we're married today," she replied. "Perhaps there was some unfinished karma created in our first century lives that has been working out since, even now." She looked Jeremy right in the eye. "But why do you think I saw David with your face as I listened to the glass harp - your eyes and sandy beard?"

"I don't know," Jeremy answered seriously. "Possibly it was just a stage in your recognition of David as a young Roman. Your only image of a young Roman at that point was the one I had described to you - our meeting in Massilia. But it's unlikely that a young Roman would have had a beard."

"There's more," Clarissa revealed.

"About David?"

"No. There was more revealed to me in the extraordinary tones of the glass harp. After seeing this passionate scene with the young Roman, I found myself in the arms of a woman. Jeremy, I've never had a relationship with another woman, I mean a sexual relationship."

"Not in this life," Jeremy reminded her. "Carry on, I'm fascinated."

"The woman had short, curly, dark hair. She had a face of classic beauty and bright eyes, but she was so loving in her tender touch. I've never told David about this. He might think me odd or something. I'm trusting you to keep my secret. But I have to admit it seemed a beautiful experience."

"This was also in the First Century?"

"Yes. More was revealed to me later. The woman's name was Delilah." Clarissa looked at Jeremy nervously. "I'm embarrassed. I really shouldn't be telling you about this."

"So you had a lesbian relationship in the First Century," Jeremy repeated in a matter of fact sort of way. "Not unusual. Women had no status in the First Century and were often ignored. Sometimes they could only express tenderness and love through physical contact with each other. Homosexual relationships between men were also common."

"Actually, I don't think we were real lesbians," Clarissa said in defense. "Delilah was a prostitute. In fact I think I was too."

Jeremy laughed. "You should have been if you were Mary Magdalene!"

"Shhh!" Clarissa whispered. "Someone'll hear you." She looked around again to ensure their privacy.

Two ladies at the next table were busy vociferously complaining about the tour to the Elephanta caves - something about too hot and too many steps.

'No doubt David will get a complaint form later,' Clarissa observed. 'The Chief Purser is supposed to turn the temperature down for the tours in India! And they were all warned about the steps by the Shore Excursion Manager. Really at times, I just give up.'

"Actually, most Roman men were not truly homosexuals either," Jeremy continued, bringing Clarissa right back to their discussion. "In fact they were pretty adventurous lovers by all accounts. That legend lives on in the reputation of the Italians to this day."

"True," Clarissa acknowledged. "I got my bottom pinched in Rome only last year!"

They laughed and sipped on their drinks.

"There was one other thing that sprang from the glass harp experience," Clarissa continued. "After seeing myself with Delilah, the scene moved on to Doctor John."

"Doctor John?"

"Yes. David's brother-in-law. The man we told you about, the surgeon from New Hampshire."

Jeremy leaned back in his chair. "Ah yes. I remember. Wasn't he the father of the boy who had a crush on you?"

"That's right. Simon Bishop. The boy was my son in the First Century. If you remember he had the Roman name Marcus, and you told me that he probably had a Roman father. Well, he apparently did, at least if my vision during the music of the glass harp reveals any truth. His father's name was Antonias and you'll never believe this ...."

"What?" Jeremy asked.

"I'll swear Antonias was Dr. John Bishop, even though he didn't look like him!"

Jeremy leaned forward again with one finger scratching the corner of his mouth. "So what you're saying is that Simon's father today might also have been his father when he was your son in the First Century?"

"It seems that way, but there's more. Delilah seemed to reveal to me that I was married to Antonias or at least that we were living together. Delilah was living with us too."

Jeremy smiled and took hold of Clarissa's hand. "So you were a sort of triangle, a menage a trois - you, Antonias and Delilah?"

David Peterson walked into the bar. The room was very full by now, but he saw where Jeremy and his wife were seated not far from Fiona MacAllister. As he approached he noticed Jeremy and Clarissa were holding hands. It bothered him. He approached their table. "Jeremy," he said with a discernible chill.

Clarissa and Jeremy looked up and instinctively let go of each others' hands. Jeremy stood politely. "David!" he exclaimed. "Good to see you!" He slapped him gently on the back. "Not over worked I hope? Clarissa and I have just had a most interesting conversation. It seems we all have a lot to catch up on. It's so good to be here!"

"Welcome aboard!" David replied artificially in his official capacity. "Please sit down." David drew up a chair. He pointed at Jeremy's almost empty, whiskey glass, "I see that Clara's been taking care of you. Won't you have another?"

"I will if you are."

In no time a waiter took their order.

"Many thanks for the cabin. It's wonderful, far beyond my expectations," Jeremy said politely.

"We do what we can," David answered. "So what were you discussing?"

Clarissa laughed. "Past lives! What else? I just told Jeremy about Linus."

Somewhat relieved David looked at the architect. "Oh! Don't take all that too seriously," he said. "There may be something in it, but it's more likely that I just caught the bug from Clara here. She's the one who really dreams. Has she told you about Judas Iscariot?"

"No," Jeremy said as he turned to Clarissa. "What's this about Judas?"

"Clara met this macho Greek on the 'Ulysses'," David informed him.

"Babis Demetris," Clarissa continued. "He was a real creep, but he appeared in my dreams. I saw him with Jesus. As Judas Iscariot, or at least 'Judas' was the name Jesus gave to him, Babis Demetris complained bitterly about me and other women in our group. He said we were pulling Jesus down and making him soft. As Judas, supported by a burly fellow called Cephas, he said that the oil that I had anointed Jesus with could have been sold for a fair sum of money and the coins distributed among the poor. But Jesus supported my actions and rebuked Judas."

"Clara's convinced she was Mary Magdalene if she lived in the First Century," David interjected. "Did she tell you about the stoning?"

"Not yet."

They both looked at Clarissa.

"Oh, that was another dream. It was also on the 'Ulysses'. The 'Ulysses' seemed to have a peculiar effect on me. Anyway, I saw myself in the stoning pit. They actually started to throw stones. One hit my head and I was partially concussed. The spokesman for my attackers seemed to be an older man named Obadiah. Anyway, just as in the Bible, this other man who looked somewhat like you, Jeremy - he had a similar, sandy beard and your deep, penetrating eyes - came forward."

"Don't build Jeremy up too much," David observed. "The beard was about the only thing they had in common. You don't want to turn him into a mystical Rasputin." He felt rather pleased with his analogy.

Jeremy laughed. "Certainly not. Actually, Clarissa's describing a fairly, standard vision of how people think Jesus looked. It may be completely wrong, but it's the image we all have and so it's not really surprising she sees Jesus this way in her dreams. I should be flattered really. People have often said I look like Jesus Christ because of this beard, but in reality none of us have the slightest idea what Jesus really looked like. This sandy beard image is merely the way medieval artists portrayed Jesus, drawing on the fashions of their own times."

"Interesting," David noted. "So Jesus may not have had a beard at all."

"Who cares?" Clarissa continued. "Jesus rescued me! I knew it was him because he wrote his name in the dirt. He wrote 'Joshua', the name you always give to Jesus."

"That's right," Jeremy agreed. "He was Joshua."

"But Clarissa already knew that Bible story," David interrupted again. "We all know that story. I'm not convinced that it was a past life revelation. It was a rehash of something that we already know."

"Is Obadiah in the Bible version?" Jeremy asked. "I don't remember."

"I don't remember, either" David conceded, "but is that really important?"

Clarissa sat up straight, but with her eyes cast down in thought. "Why do you say I'm conditioned by the Bible version of the story? I've hardly ever read the Bible."

"You probably heard the story as a child in Ireland," David persisted.

"Well, if you can prove Obadiah was Mary Magdalene's persecutor, fine!" Clarissa agreed. "But if he's not mentioned in the Bible you'd better think again!"

"We could always look that up," David suggested.

Jeremy nodded in agreement.

Fiona had finished her drink with the Bridge officer. She got up and walked to their table. "Hi David!" she said giving him a knowing wink. "Glad to be out of India?"

"Definitely," David replied. "It'll be your turn next when they start coming down with the 'Delhi belly'!"

Jeremy stood up grinning like a teenager, begging for an introduction.

"Meet Jeremy Dyson here," David said. "He's a friend of ours from Minnesota. Jeremy's with us to Haifa. Jeremy, this is Fiona, the ship's nurse."

"Terrific!" Fiona replied. "We'll see you around."

"Pretty lady," Jeremy said as he sat back down.

Clarissa caught David's eye. "Yes," was all her husband gave away in response.

A shrill voice interrupted them from behind, "David!"

The Chief Purser turned around. It was their dining companions, Dorothy Connolly and her sister Michelle.

"We just wanted to come over and tell Clarissa how much we loved her recital the other night," Dorothy said. "My sister and I particularly liked the last piece you played. The piece that you said you wrote in Japan. It was so different."

Clarissa beamed. "Thank you."

"You're such a lovely couple. We feel so privileged to be sitting at your table."

"Meet a friend of ours. He's just joined the ship today," Clarissa said.

Jeremy stood up and extended his hand.

"Won't you join us?" David asked.

"We'd love to," the ladies replied.

A waiter came over and pulled up two extra chairs. He put down two more napkins on the table. "What can I get you?"

"A gin and tonic for me, and a stinger for my sister," Dorothy requested.

The elderly lady then looked at Jeremy. "How long will you be with us?"

Jeremy proceeded to explain his commitments in India and Israel and how convenient it was that the 'Prince Regent' could carry him between engagements.

"Will Mr. Dyson be able to join us at the table?" Dorothy asked.

"Let me have a word with the Maitre 'D'," David suggested. "They will be quite pushed to add an extra place."

"Oh, we can all squeeze up a little," Dorothy said enthusiastically. "We have such an interesting table and I'm sure Jeremy would be a great addition."

"Alright then, take it as done," David agreed. "Jeremy can eat with you ladies tonight. I can't be in this evening, but I'll make sure John Pierro has an extra seat there for tomorrow night."

"Tomorrow night is the night of the 'Rajah's Ball'," Michelle reminded them. "We should all be dressed as if we were at a Maharajah's court. We'll have a chance to wear our saris. You should see what Dorothy and I found at 'Burlingtons' in the Taj Mahal Hotel."

Later, when David and Clarissa were alone in his cabin, Clarissa started to laugh as she undid the package that she too had bought at 'Burlingtons'. She held up a blue sari and loosely wrapped it around herself. "What do you think?" she asked.

"You bought that for the ball?" David responded incredulously. "Can you dance in it?"

"Of course."

"The color's beautiful," David admitted. "I wonder what Dorothy and Michelle will look like in theirs. They're such nice people. They love you Clara. They're so genuine and they involve themselves in everything. Wouldn't it be nice if they were all like that."

As they prepared for bed, Clarissa brought up the subject of Jeremy. "You were a little cold towards him," she said. "He asked me at dinner what he had done wrong."

"I know. Sometimes he just rubs me up the wrong way. It's silly really, but I guess I just got a little jealous. I mean, he's really hung up on this idea that he knew you two thousand years ago. He's quite open about it. I'm sure he believes you were lovers."

"Maybe we were, although it seems he was rather older than me."

"Damn it, Clara! Are you insensitive to how I feel about all this! How do you think I felt when I came in the bar and found you two holding hands and looking into each others' eyes?"

Clarissa walked over to him. "David, darling. It's not what you think. There's nothing between us. We were just engrossed in the mystery of our possible past." She put her arms around him and he felt her tears. "Jeremy said he thought that's what had upset you. He was really very concerned."

David sat down on the bed. He sensed Clarissa's love and felt his own shame at his jealousy. 'Why am I so untrusting?' he thought.

'Clara's so loving, so giving and I am always so ...' He, then started to cry.

"David, we mustn't let any of this come between us," Clarissa said comforting him as she held him close. "Our union is a divine union. We were brought together by Spirit. Remember how Samantha predicted our meeting? Remember, how it was when we first met?"

"It was your music, Clara. It was so different. I had never heard anything like it. I felt I was in the presence of an angel when you played."

"I don't think so," Clarissa said as she held him tighter. "My music only awakened a spiritual response in you because you were ready. The music became a channel between your soul and God. You're different, David, although sometimes you don't know it. That's why I fell in love with you. I recognized your inner spirit."

David smiled at her comforting words.

"You sometimes find it difficult to show your inner self around people. God knows, I can understand why. Look at what you have to deal with here. You know, there was somebody complaining before you came into the bar tonight that the Elephanta caves were too hot and there were too many steps! Of course, it was all the ship's fault."

"It always is," David chuckled. "They hate India, but they would also complain if one year we didn't come here. They wouldn't be able to buy their saris!"

"But, David, I've seen your inner spirit, even if they haven't," Clarissa continued. "Look how nature moves you. Remember the horses with Mother in Ireland? I think that's when she really accepted you, when she saw how you loved her horses. Or, what about the peace that emanates from you when you're in the garden at home? Those moments are every bit as important as my musical moments when the soul soars and the God-spark is released."

David kissed her. "You're my guardian angel," he said. "Now, how did it go at dinner? What did the others think of Jeremy Dyson?"

"He was a hit," Clarissa admitted. "You can't deny, David. He's very charming."

"He's an enigma," David said as he stood up. "I'm sorry, darling. I didn't mean to upset you or him. It was silly of me. Please forgive me."

That night they did not make love. Rather they held each other in a spiritual embrace that took them to a higher state of union than they had yet known. Before they slept Clarissa whispered in David's ear. "I can feel your love, darling. It radiates from your heart."

"Yours too, my dear," David replied.

• • • • • • •

Jeremy next encountered Fiona three days later on a beach in the Seychelles. David and Clarissa had brought him out to the far side of Mahe by taxi mid-morning. They had enjoyed lunch at the Moon Bay Resort, a simple, rustic place that served good, grilled seafood. It was about two thirds the way down the sweeping bay of deep yellow sand fringed with tropical lushness. High, cliff-like hills rose up behind, catching the billowing white clouds and a lone church tower marked the far end of the bay where was situated a native village. After lunch David had needed to get back to the ship. Clarissa wanted to take the opportunity to get in the Theater to practice. So, Jeremy said he would stay a while to swim and that he could pick up a taxi later. As he walked down the beach from the hotel he passed Fiona sitting alone on a 'Prince Regent' towel, soaking up the rays.

Jeremy had to admit that she looked stunning in her white bikini complimented by her well tanned skin. The lights in her short, blonde hair gleamed. He approached her. "Hi, you're the nurse from the ship aren't you?"

Fiona took off her sunglasses, "Yes, and you're David Peterson's friend."

"Yes. I met David and Clarissa in Minnesota. Actually they've just gone back to the ship. We had lunch together at that hotel back there. I decided to stay to walk on the beach."

"You should swim. The water's wonderful," Fiona intimated.

"Yes, I'm going to take a dip. Maybe I'll see you on board."

"No doubt," Fiona replied before putting back her shades.

Jeremy walked up the beach towards the village. On his way back he turned towards the surf and soon was in to his waist. Fiona had been right, the ocean was as warm as any he could remember. He plunged forward and swam out beyond the waves. After a while he heard Fiona's voice echoing across the water from behind him. "I told you it was wonderful. This is the Indian Ocean at its best."

Jeremy turned around. Fiona was standing in the ocean, her hair all wet. She splashed her way towards him. Her nipples showed as dark aureoles against the constraints of her slightly translucent bikini. Her firm, pert breasts were more than obvious.

"Oh, hi there," he said nonchalantly, trying not to reveal any interest in her body. "You're right. It's wonderful."

When Fiona reached him she asked how long he had known David Peterson.

"Not long. We met about five months ago. We became friends immediately. Actually, it's a strange thing, but we all think we knew each other in the past."

"What, in your childhood?"

"No. In the past. At some other time in history," Jeremy explained.

Fiona screwed up her eyes. "How weird. David and I used to be pretty close. He never suggested any of that stuff in those days. I guess it's his wife's influence."

"I take it you don't believe in past lives then?"

"Not really. I can't say I've ever given it much thought. It sounds like trash-tabloid reading to me. I suppose I'm open to anything, but it's not something I've ever considered." She laughed. "Who do you think you were then, Napoleon Bonaparte?"

"I don't recall much of my past lives," Jeremy admitted, "but I do have this strong feeling that I was around two thousand years ago as a Roman soldier. I'm a part-time archaeologist and I work a lot in that period. Maybe it's just association, but there have been some strange coincidences in my life and meeting David and Clarissa has been one of the most interesting."

A large wave took them by surprise. They fell into each other's arms as they struggled to maintain their balance. Jeremy could feel Fiona's flesh, its smoothness exaggerated in the salinity of the ocean. "Sorry," he said apologetically, as he quickly released her. "That one caught us off guard."

When Jeremy engaged a taxi back to the ship he shared it with Fiona. Jeremy felt Fiona's sensuous youth as he sat beside her. 'So this was one of David's bachelor day flames,' he thought. 'He was a lucky man.'

The next day Fiona invaded Jeremy's sub-conscious mind as he sat on deck in the hot, tropical sun. He had spilled the fruity contents of a cooling punch over his white shorts. Cursing silently, he rubbed the sticky liquid away as he lay back in his chaise. The sun beat down upon his face as he drifted into another time and place ....

He saw himself dressed in a dirty, white robe that showed the stains of grapes. Fiona was there with him. He knew it was her, although she was different in many ways.

She appeared to be laughing, her clear skin protected in the folds of a blue headdress, as she squatted by a millstone grinding corn. Two hawks flew overhead, circling above a rocky terrain. Below them, vineyards folded down a hillside towards a verdant plain, the other side of which rose brown hills that faded into the heat-haze of the distant horizon.

"They're looking good, Joanna," Jeremy observed as he surveyed the vineyards. "I think we'll do well."

"These vineyards were nothing before you took them over from Father," Fiona, who Jeremy had noted to be Joanna in this place and time, informed him. "You've worked so hard. They've never looked better."

"Jon's been a big help," Jeremy acknowledged. "He'll be coming over from Grandfather Joachim's house this afternoon. I told him we would thin part of the lower section today. Is Rachel coming to join you?"

"I never know, Josh. I think she feels a bit lonely sometimes. James is always so busy."

In his dream Jeremy realized that Fiona, with wisps of dark Semitic hair peeking from her headdress, as Joanna, was his wife of long ago. He took the metamorphosis in her hair color for granted. As Joshua, he kissed her lightly on the cheek. "Is there any fresh bread?" he whispered.

She pushed him away. "Josh! You and Jon are terrible. If I go on letting you eat our fresh bread every afternoon I'm going to have to bake an extra loaf for us each day. Now, help me sort out the bad grains here before I grind more. That's the price you're going to have to pay. Only then will I fetch the new loaf."

Jeremy suddenly realized Fiona was calling him 'Josh,' an abbreviation of Joshua. He saw himself helping her sort through the grains. They tossed aside those that came from the dreaded darnel weed. It was easy to miss them because they looked like the spelt and barley, but they could quickly sicken the stomach.

"I love it here, Joshua," Joanna said. "When we start our family it'll be so great to know that our children will be born in our own house overlooking the vineyard and the valley. We have the same magnificent view as Joachim Ben Judah."

"How soon will that be?" Jeremy asked, wondering if his wife of that time was pregnant.

"Whenever it's God's will," Joanna replied.

"Joanna, you're not going to have a baby are you?"

She lay back on the ground looking up at him, her eyes sparkling mischievously. "I don't think so," she teased him.

As Joshua, Jeremy lay down beside this dream version of the lithe nurse and took her in his arms. "I love you, Joanna," he whispered in her ear. "We will have a family. Our sons will look like me and the girls will look like you."

"All Levis and Judahs, Josh," she said, pinching his beard. "But you've got to let me finish grinding today's corn first. If you really want some of the fresh bread you'll find it inside. Help yourself before Jon gets here. He'll eat it all if you don't. I left it out for you anyway."

Jeremy gradually opened his eyes. It was still very hot, but the deck chair under his body gave the first hint of his current reality. "Joshua?" he muttered. "Would that be so strange if I really was married to Fiona as a Hebrew?" He lay there thinking as details of the dream began to fade. 'Maybe this would explain why as a Roman soldier I had such a fixation about Clarissa who appears as this older, Hebrew woman. If Fiona and I were married at some point in Jewish history and I had got a taste for Hebrew women, perhaps that desire carried on into the First Century. Joanna and I an item ..." He laughed. "Joshua and Joanna ... it sounds Biblical."

Jeremy got up from his chaise and took a dip in the pool. Not only did the cooling water refresh him, but it took the sticky punch out of his shorts.

• • • • • • • •

Much though David would have liked to have gone on safari in Africa he had to resign himself to remaining on board. Mombassa was a major turnover port on the World Cruise. Many segment passengers were scheduled to leave and join the 'Prince Regent' there.

Apart from their growing friendship, Clarissa was glad that Jeremy was on board. It gave her someone to go out to Tsarvo Park with on one of the scheduled tours. East Africa was new to them both.

"I wish I could come with you," David said as he kissed Clarissa goodbye after an early breakfast in the officers' mess. "Take plenty of pictures, especially of the lions."

David disappeared to handle the multiple problems of dealing with African officials. There were the immigration and customs formalities to complete, the 'gifts' for the officials to be arranged, which somehow quickened this process, and the agent to be informed how the ship wanted to process disembarkation and embarkation procedures. David could be sure that the way the agency had set things up would be far from satisfactory. Finally, there was the need to check on the transport for the air/sea package flying out of Nairobi. The previous year they had got shafted on this and had to put the passengers up in Mombassa an extra day. Flight arrangements between Mombassa and Nairobi seemed to be 'by chance'.

There were a number of announcements about the forthcoming safari tours. It seemed like almost all passengers sailing beyond Mombassa were traveling up to the various game parks.

Clarissa called Jeremy's cabin at eight-thirty.

Fiona answered!

"Is Jeremy Dyson there?" Clarissa asked somewhat taken aback.

There was a silence, then she heard Jeremy's voice.

"It's me Clarissa," she said. "They've changed the meeting point from the Theater to the 'Lookout'. I'll meet you there at nine."

"Really?" Jeremy said with surprise.

"Yes, they've just announced it, but maybe it didn't go through the cabins."

"There have been so many announcements I just tuned out," Jeremy replied. "Okay, I'll meet you in the Lookout Bar in about ten minutes."

Clarissa hung up. "I just tuned out!" she repeated. "Like hell!"

David was not happy about Clarissa and Jeremy sharing accommodation at the lodge, but there really wasn't much choice. Clarissa had a complimentary ticket as his wife. That was a substantial saving. Staff, complimentary ticket holders had to share accommodation. Likewise Jeremy, as a passenger, would have to pay substantially more for single accommodation, but at the price he had paid, he would have to share double accommodation. Jeremy wasn't anxious to join a fellow passenger and Clarissa wasn't enthusiastic to share accommodation with a staff member. It had been a mutual decision that they would take a room together, thus resolving their separate problems. Of course, they had consulted with David and he'd agreed. David had been afraid to reveal his true feelings. He had tried to put on a brave front for Clarissa, but deep down he still mistrusted Jeremy.

Jeremy and Clarissa met with their fellow travelers at nine. They were in the 'Blue Group' traveling to Salt Lick Lodge. There was an interesting assortment of dress. Some, like Jeremy, were in khaki safari suits, although they didn't all display a flamboyant cravat. There were ladies in broad-brimmed hats that looked more appropriate for a society race meeting than the game parks. Others were in jeans and tee shirts. Some favored animal prints, blouses featuring elephants with rhinestone eyes, that might make a good talking point when back home at the Country Club, but were out of keeping with the rugged nature of their upcoming journey. There were men in shorts, others in sweats, and ladies with pocket books that could be carrying their cabin sinks. Almost everyone was festooned in cameras from small instamatics to sophisticated camcorders. Clarissa was traveling in light pants and a white tee-shirt with pale-blue flowers across the front. The ensemble was simple and complimented her.

"You're coming with us?" a voice asked from behind a well-made-up face. The lady wore a safari suit that looked like it had been designed for a 'Broadway' musical rather than the real thing. Her husband was in a lightweight two piece, expensive and Italian looking. They were carrying no less than three 'Louis Vitton' bags. Clarissa recognized them as Mr. and Mrs. Achenbloom.

"Yes," Clarissa replied. "I've always wanted to do this."

"You'll love it dear. Last year we saw a whole pride of lions. But that was in 'Masai'. Our best experience was at 'Treetops'. There you could see all the game just from the balcony of the room. The safari vans are so dusty and uncomfortable. Is your husband traveling up-country with us?"

"No, he's too busy. Mombassa's a hectic stopover for him."

"Oh, you must travel with us in our car then," Mrs. Achenbloom proffered. "The Office arranged a limo to take us up."

"Thank you so much," Clarissa replied, "but unfortunately I can't. I'm escorting. But, no doubt we'll see you at 'Salt Lick'. You'll probably get there before us."

"There's a nice little bar there," Mr. Achenbloom advised. "We'll be making a head start on the 'Jumbo' martinis."

After they had moved on, Jeremy looked at Clarissa in a bemused way. "Who were they?"

"Mr. and Mrs. Achenbloom," Clarissa informed him. "David says they are very regular, World Cruise passengers. They pretty much own the ship and everyone gives them exactly what they want."

"Including limos on African safaris!" Jeremy noted. "If she walks out into the bush in that outfit she'll be eaten by a lion!"

Clarissa laughed. "And if you insist on wearing that red cravat you might get trampled on by a rhino!"

"Blue Group Section One," the Tour Manager announced before he started to read off names. Naturally there were stragglers who were still missing. Some hadn't heard the announcement and had headed off to the Theater.

At length all were assembled and the safari adventure began.

Mr. and Mrs. Achenbloom's limo turned out to be a black and yellow taxicab of about nineteen sixty five vintage that looked like a bumble bee. To Clarissa, the 'Land Rover' safari vans were much more inviting. 'The price of privacy,' she thought.

Dockside traders were busy setting up their wares. A wooden menagerie of African animals was spread out for the tourists. Elephants and giraffes were the most numerous and came in every conceivable size. Impala and gazelle followed in popularity and competed with rhinos, spears and shields, boxes and trinkets, statues and chess sets in assorted colors and woods. Carved ivory, whether false or real, attracted much attention, despite David's warnings to passengers that real ivory is banned in the United States. Crew members were already out there bargaining for spoils.

"I bought two elephants in Delhi," Jeremy informed Clarissa. "They were too big to fly down to Bombay so I arranged to have them shipped to Minnesota. God knows when I'll see them."

"David bought elephants in Madras a couple of years ago. You might remember them on either side of the fireplace in our living room. I hope he doesn't do something stupid like buy one of those giant giraffes while we're away. People go crazy over these animals. Apparently on board they have to have a sale at the end of the World Cruise because passengers find out how hard it is to get their bargains home!"

They settled into one of the safari vans that was labelled for 'Salt Lick'. There were five other passengers with them and a guide.

The architecture on the road out from Mombassa was mostly Moslem and the guide explained how much of the East African coast was settled by Indians. Further inland everything changed. The low undulating hills covered in sporadic patches of bananas and clutches of coconut palms gave way to grander country. The light became more intense, bringing out the purples and blues in the vast landscape. Huge plantations of sisal, like regiments of spears, waved ungainly heads to the sky. Distant hills marked the horizon where the vast azure dome with its dramatic cloud formations met the glory of the inner continent. The road narrowed. The soil became red and the bush more remote.

"We will enter 'Tsarvo East' soon," the guide explained. "From then on you should watch out for elephants. They might surprise you. They're red."

"Isn't it a bit early in the day for pink elephants?" a joker in the party named Sam, jested.

"It's the earth. The elephants are covered in the dust of the red clay," the guide explained.

Elephants were the first game to be spotted. There were three of them standing in the shade of two lone trees in the scrub. They were a ruddy brown. The van stopped so eager photographers could take their first pictures.

At 'Voe', a lodge overlooking a cliff that dropped down to a muddy watering hole, they broke for lunch. Salad and various suspect meats were served. The passengers ate little and talked much. From this outlook, the real vastness of the African bush lay before them in a wide panorama. Here too, was their last chance to buy film. The kiosk at 'Voe' was soon depleted.

It was another two hours driving through 'Tsarvo' to Salt Lick Lodge. Along the way they did see eland and zebra and at one point a lone giraffe, but for the most part it was the vast landscape that impressed.

'This is what David would love,' Clarissa thought as they bounced along the dirt road. 'I can sense his awe of nature here. We are in God's country, untamed and untouched - a land that belongs to nature and not to man.'

The safari van pulled into 'Salt Lick' about three-thirty in the afternoon. It was hot, but not as oppressive as on the coast. The lodge stood like a series of mushrooms on stilts in the untamed bush. These mushroom-like rooms were united by walkways that led to the dining room, bar and reception in a rustic, stone building. Two other safari vans from the ship had already checked in, but there was no sign of the Achenbloom's taxi.

Jeremy laughed. "That bumble bee's still on the road."

The guide gave them all keys to their rooms. "Let's meet here in an hour," he said. "Four-thirty should be a good time to set out on our evening drive. Bring along your bug spray."

Jeremy and Clarissa followed the signs to mushroom number twenty five. It was well out from the center block and had commanding views from its balcony over the vast panorama.

"It's magnificent here," Clarissa commented as she stood beside Jeremy who had started taking photographs. "You can hear the sound of silence."

Clarissa went inside and took two bottles of spring water out of her knapsack. She put them in the bathroom which was a small division within the round room. Otherwise all she unpacked was a toothbrush and paste. There were twin beds veiled in mosquito nets. The floor was of plain boards. Two native African throw rugs ran along either side of the beds. It was rustic and simple. Clarissa lay down to rest.

When Jeremy came in, he sat on the side of Clarissa's bed. "I haven't had a chance to tell you about Fiona yet," he said.

"Fiona?" Clarissa repeated quizzically as she tried to disguise the fact that she knew David's old flame had apparently spent the night with him.

"Yes. Fiona MacAllister, the ship's nurse."

"What about her?" Clarissa asked nonchalantly.

"I dreamed about her the other day."

"What is it about this woman that has you all ogling at her?" Clarissa snapped. "It seems the whole ship's in love with this nurse!"

"I didn't say I was in love with her."

"Well then, why did you dream about her? I don't imagine you usually dream about a woman unless you feel something for her. I saw how you looked at her when she came by the table the other night, and what was she doing in your cabin this morning?"

Jeremy blushed. "It's not what you think, Clarissa," he stated as calmly as he could. "Why did I dream about you?"

Clarissa felt a little uncomfortable. She was reminded of David's feelings and she didn't want to fall into the same trap. Jeremy was also somewhat of an enigma to her. She knew deep down that there was a great attraction between them that possibly did spill over from the First Century into the Twentieth. That, she felt obligated to suppress, yet she realized she was feeling the pang of jealousy .

"But there is something funny about it," Jeremy continued. "When I dreamed about Fiona she was no bikini-clad beauty such as I saw on the beach in Mahe, so don't think I'm on some sort of an infatuation trip. She was a Biblical character from many centuries ago. Her name was Joanna. My name was Joshua."

"So what? Joshua seems to have been quite a common name in our past lives," Clarissa stated. "If I was Mary Magdalene and Joshua is Jesus' real name, I also knew a 'Joshua' many centuries ago."

"Yes. That's precisely what I meant about it being funny," Jeremy continued. "In the First Century I feel like I knew you when I lived that life as a young Roman in Gaul named Remus Augustus, but in another past life, if my most recent dream really is a revelation, I was married to a Jewess, this time probably in Palestine. As I said, her name was Joanna. I saw her grinding corn outside our little house above a vineyard. I swear to you, Clarissa, Joanna was Fiona in my dream. Truly! Just as I know that the woman I saw when I was Remus Augustus in Massilia was you!"

Clarissa was miles away. She thought of David's countenance in the vision of the glass harp and then compared it to her sense of Jesus at the transfiguration as it appeared to her every time she played 'Gilded Snow'. 'Could this really be Jeremy's soul,' she wondered. 'Could Jeremy have been Joshua?' "You are quite sure that you were this Roman, Remus Augustus?" she asked.

Jeremy smiled. "Yes, at least as sure as I am of anything in this past life mystery."

"But you also think you were Joshua?"

Jeremy laughed. "Well, not at the same time. If I was this Joshua guy married to Fiona, the Joanna of my dream, it would have had to have been before or after my life as Remus. Why do you ask?"

"The name 'Joshua'," Clarissa said slowly. "It was Jesus' name. I just wondered if there might be some connection."

Jeremy laughed louder. "Impossible! Jesus wasn't married! My goodness, the Church would never have stood for that! Maybe he would have married Mary Magdalene or Lazarus' sister if he had not been crucified. Who knows? But he didn't. He died on the cross."

"We might know," Clarissa said slowly. "Maybe between us this mystery will be revealed."

Jeremy appeared to lose some of his confidence. Clarissa had thrown out a challenge. "You really are taking this seriously, aren't you? Can you imagine what repercussion such a discovery would have on the world?"

"Pretty frightening," she admitted. "But something deep down just tells me we are a part of this."

They sat in silence for a moment. Jeremy trembled when he looked at Clarissa's face. "Something mystical is drawing us together," he said slowly. "Our casual meeting in Massilia wasn't the only time we met two thousand years ago, was it?"

"No," Clarissa replied.

Jeremy reached for Clarissa's hand. They stared at each other for what seemed an eternity. "Look, I'm going outside," he said at length. "This is all a little heavy." He released his hold on her hand and looked at his watch. "Meet me down in the reception area in about twenty minutes. I don't want to miss the first game drive." He took his cameras and left.

Fifteen minutes later, Clarissa found Jeremy talking to their guide. All their party were anxious to get out on their first drive. They climbed into a 'Salt Lick' jeep and in no time were out in the wilderness following a rough track through the bush. The light was more golden than earlier in the day. The purples in the rolling hills were deeper and the red earth more vivid. In short order they had seen plenty of zebra, but as they rounded a hummock, the guide stopped the jeep. Ahead of them, standing quite alone, was a hartebeest.

"He's guarding his territory. Any member of his family could make a lion's dinner," the guide noted. "Two days ago there were lions in this area."

He drove very slowly, edging close to some tall grass. The vehicle came to a halt and he turned off the ignition. There was complete silence under the big sky. They could hear each other's breathing as they waited in anticipation.

The guide slowly stood up and peered through his binoculars. "On the right," he whispered. "You can just see the tops of their heads."

Clarissa looked towards the right side of the tall grass. She couldn't see anything.

"Where?" asked Sam the joker in his Texan drawl, as he sweated profusely around the neck.

The guide pointed in the direction that Clarissa thought she had scouted. "Just beyond that second clump of grass and to the left of the dead tree. You can see their ears. There are three lionesses."

They all craned in the right direction.

"I see them!" Jeremy exclaimed.

One of the lionesses shook its head. The movement made her more obvious.

Clarissa saw her too.

Cameras clicked, although it was fairly obvious that even with a pretty powerful telephoto lens not much would come out except grass and ears.

Then the lioness stood up, tossed its head, stared at the safari jeep, turned and slowly meandered off deeper into the tall grass.

"God dammit!" the Texan yelled. "A perfect shot and I was too mesmerized to take it."

Jeremy laughed. "You're not alone Sam. I don't think any of us got anything but her backside. We were all too busy watching."

Clarissa smiled. 'Well done you beautiful lioness,' she thought. 'You beat us all at your own game.'

The hartebeest saw the lioness and ran with the speed of a gazelle. The lioness wasn't interested.

"They must have had a kill," the guide explained.

While they all watched the hartebeest make its dash to safety the other lioness' moved away. The safari party turned back just in time to see the rump and stringy tail of the last beast.

"God dammit!" Sam roared again.

Clarissa chuckled. "The lions are smarter than we think," she said.

The guide then started up the jeep and they moved on to look for their next opportunity. They didn't have to wait long. As the track took them over open grassland Sam's wife shouted out, "Are those two black flamingos?"

"Ostriches," the guide explained. "Look how fast they run."

The two ostriches were broadside and actually overtook the jeep.

"Did you get them, Sam?" the Texan's wife drawled excitedly.

"I sure did, darlin'," her husband answered. "Jesus Christ, Trudy! Those guys are bigger than 'Big Bird'!"

"So are their eggs," the guide explained. "Ostrich eggs are some of the biggest you'll ever find. They're often likened to dinosaurs' eggs. But look at those two, they must be running at thirty miles an hour. They won't keep it up for long. They soon tire."

A large herd of zebra approached from the other side. The red dust on their white stripes gave them a strange lustre in the golden light.

Cameras clicked again.

"Those guys seem to be everywhere," Sam noted. "Doesn't anything attack them?"

"They have few predators," the guide informed them. "Zebras are increasing throughout the park."

"They're beautiful," Clarissa observed.

"Can you ride those babies?" Sam asked.

The guide grinned through his teeth. "Although they look very docile, in reality they're far from tame. It's very hard to break a zebra. They won't let you touch them, believe me."

Telephoto lens at the ready, Jeremy was busy photographing the striped, horse-like creatures.

Later on the drive, they encountered giraffe and a large herd of eland. The jeep stopped again. The guide peered through his binoculars. Among the eland were some tiny dik diks.

"If you've got bino's take a look," the guide said. "If not, pass 'round mine."

Sam and Jeremy looked through their binoculars while the guide passed his to a widow from Arkansas. At their distance the beasts were so small that it was hard to pick them up.

"Look carefully at ground level. They're only the size of a large hare," the guide suggested. "Dik diks are pretty rare. They usually run with eland for safety. These are the only ones that I know of in this part of the park. They were highly prized in the days of the hunters, and that, combined with their convenient size for a solo prowler, has almost eliminated them. We may be the only party to see dik dik today."

"They're just like baby elands, Trudy," Sam observed as he passed his expensive binoculars to his wife.

"That's why they feel safe with the eland," the guide repeated.

Jeremy passed his 'binos' to Clarissa. "Have a look. They're like miniature antelopes."

"My great uncle used to shoot them," Clarissa said when she zoomed in on the little bucks. "It's funny, but that animal's name has stayed with me since childhood. In our old house in Ireland all my great uncle's hunting trophies hung in the back hall. There were all these great horns covered in dust mounted on dark, wooden shields. The only one which was close to my height in those days was the dik dik's. I could read the inscription in gold leaf. I can remember it plainly - 'Dik dik G.E.A. 1910'."

"G.E.A." Jeremy repeated. "What did that stand for?"

"German East Africa."

"Oh, of course! It was before World War One! Germany had quite an empire. It was only after the war that this area became British. It's funny when you think about it Clarissa, none of those empires lasted anything like the timespan of our Roman Empire."

Clarissa put down the binoculars and looked at Jeremy. "True," was all she said. As they stared at each other she couldn't help being reminded once again of that feeling from Joshua in that moment of metamorphosis that haunted her when she played 'Gilded Snow'. Deep down she believed Jeremy was Joshua. She felt an awe in her stomach.

As Jeremy looked at Clarissa he also felt drawn to her in an indescribable way. He knew that they had not just seen each other in the streets of Massilia, but that they had been lovers.

For what seemed eternity they both remained locked in their moments of past time when indeed the legions of Rome did rule the world.

The guide started up the jeep again. "We might still find some elephants," he said. "They're usually close to the lodge. They like the shade and the watering hole."

Sure enough, where the density of the scrub increased as it dropped down in front of 'Salt Lick', an elephant family showed themselves. They were less dust covered than those at 'Voe' and their great gray silhouettes and floppy ears showed up mightily against the declining light of the wide horizon. They were a perfect photograph.

Inside the lodge Mr. and Mrs. Achenbloom had taken up residence at a table in the bar. "Come and join us, dear," she said to Clarissa. "How was your tour?"

"Wonderful!" Clarissa admitted. She truly had thoroughly enjoyed the experience.

"Jumbo martinis?" Mr. Achenbloom asked as Jeremy joined them.

"Well, I'd rather a whiskey," Jeremy answered.

"And me a soft drink," Clarissa requested. "I'm really thirsty."

For the next ten minutes Mrs. Achenbloom monopolized the conversation. She discussed the ship and how various aspects of food and service just weren't as good as they had been on previous years.

"Why do they come on safari?" Jeremy asked Clarissa as they went back to their room to shower before dinner.

"I don't know, but there are lots of others just like them. David could tell you a story or two. You wait, Jeremy, tomorrow the Achenblooms will buy up almost everything in the shop here so they can take back gifts for their friends and say they got them on safari in Africa."

They both burst out laughing.

"Well, whose first for the shower?" Jeremy asked.

"Ladies first," Clarissa answered as she flashed a sultry smile at Jeremy. "Now, are you going to let me get ready or am I going to have to get naked in front of you?" She surprised herself with her own brazenness.

Jeremy blushed. "Oh, of course, Clarissa, I'm sorry. I'll just go outside and look at the landscape until you're ready."

"I'll give you a shout," she replied.

Camera in hand, Jeremy left and leaned over the rail of the verandah. The sky was streaked in aqua and yellow as the last rays of the sun filtered through horizon clouds. Overhead the first of the stars began to twinkle in the great, night canopy. The sounds of crickets and frogs drifted up from around the watering hole.

'It's magnificent country,' Jeremy thought. He felt a deep contentment. He was glad that he could share this experience with Clarissa. They seemed so in tune with each other. He pointed his camera, focused on the horizon and took a slow exposure of the vastness at sunset. 'Everyone has heard of sea and sky,' he thought. 'This is land and sky.'

By the time Clarissa called out from the room it was almost dark. Jeremy returned. She was already dressed, but her hair was still wet.

"There's no dryer," she said. "But if I go outside it should dry off pretty quickly. I guess it's my turn to give you the privacy."

"Alright, but close the door. The bugs are starting to come in."

They were. Several large moths were fluttering around the room.

"You'd better take the spray can with you," Jeremy added as he entered the bathroom. "I think the first of the mosquitos were trying to nip at me when I was out there."

Jeremy undressed and turned on the shower. The water wasn't very hot, but as he stood there he felt a strange closeness to Clarissa. He imagined that she was beside him standing naked in the flowing water. He closed his eyes in his fantasy....

Jeremy could feel the water freely flowing from his head and running through his beard. He could hear it dropping down into a pool below. It was as if he was standing under a waterfall and he knew that he was with Clarissa. He could almost hear her laughter and feel her flesh against his. His body responded to his thoughts and he felt his man-flesh spring to life. Then, guilt overtook him and he tried to banish such thoughts ....

Jeremy opened his eyes and reached for the bar of soap in its plastic tray. He soaped his body and washed it off. He turned off the shower and grabbed the only large towel left in the bathroom. It was not very thick, but he quickly dried off, put on his undershorts and with the towel draped over his shoulder returned to the bedroom. He let Clarissa in.

"How was it?" she asked.

"The water was only tepid. You must have got all the hot water."

"I must have. It was hot for me."

Jeremy reached for his bag and pulled out a clean shirt and white pants. "Well, I don't suppose it's a formal night tonight," he teased, "but at least I have a clean shirt."

"I'm afraid you'll have to put up with my same tee shirt," Clarissa replied, "but at least I did bring a change of underwear."

Jeremy blushed. "Me too, but that will have to wait 'til tomorrow."

When dressed he combed his hair. "Well, ready for dinner?" he asked.

"Yes, but please, please, please make sure we don't sit with the Achenblooms?"

• • • • • • • •

Clarissa and Jeremy sat with Sam and Trudy over dinner. The food wasn't bad for a safari lodge. The salads seemed fresh and there were healthy things like yoghurt for those who didn't want to sample the stew that could have contained any kind of African vermin. Actually, it tasted pretty much like familiar beef and Jeremy enjoyed a couple of helpings. Clarissa stayed with the salad and yoghurt. Sam and Trudy elected for ribeye steaks which they found to be rather overdone.

After dinner Clarissa and Trudy had a quick look at the shop. There was a smaller selection of most the things that had been displayed on the dockside in Mombassa plus a number of items made from skins and hides. Just as Clarissa had predicted, Mr. and Mrs. Achenbloom were busy buying. Clarissa bought a small ebony elephant for David.

"Make sure you oil it well, dear," Mrs. Achenbloom advised. "If you don't, these woodcarvings crack as soon as you get them home. We had terrible problems with the ones we bought in Bali last year."

"David warned me about that," Clarissa said. "I know you have to be careful."

Jeremy was waiting for Clarissa outside. "Let's take a look at the watering hole," he suggested. "There's a tunnel out to a viewing platform. They say quite a lot of game come down here in the evening."

Carrying her elephant in a plastic bag, Clarissa followed Jeremy through the tunnel that led from the lower lobby to a grilled-in cave right above the watering hole. Floodlighting was very cleverly installed in such a way as not to frighten the animals, but on the contrary to drive them towards the hole. Two or three other game watchers were already in the cave, pressed against the railing, cameras at the ready.

An eccentric looking, well-preserved, English gentlemen complete with monocle and moustache, had set himself up at the far end with his 'Nikon' on a tripod. "Have you thousand ASA film?" he asked Jeremy.

"No. Only four hundred."

"Sorry, old chap," the Englishman informed him, "but that won't work. You can't use flash here and only one thousand will pick up in this light." He could see that Jeremy's camera was not the tourist instamatic that was the cause of so many wasted photographs in the cave. "Here, take this," he said as he reached into his pocket. "You don't look like an amateur."

Jeremy was most surprised, although not too pleased to have been called an 'old chap'! "Why thanks," he said. "That's very nice of you. You're right, this needs one thousand ASA film."

"Now let me give you a hint or two," the professional know-all whispered in his upper crust English. "If you wait patiently on this side and watch the water just to the left of that tree, you might see a hartebeest. He was there about fifteen minutes ago. They're getting quite rare now. The damned Germans hunted them almost to extinction."

"Really, we saw a hartebeest this afternoon."

"You were lucky. Very lucky. Now watch carefully, this could even be the same beast."

Quite slowly the distinctive, curving antlers of the hartebeest came into the floods. The light caught the animal's eye which glowed red in the darkness. The beast lumbered forward and put its head down to drink. It's antlers were almost iridescent against the dark background. Then all of a sudden there were two, three and eventually four sets of antlers. Jeremy and the British photographer clicked away.

"They look so mystical in the night," Clarissa observed as she leaned against Jeremy to get a better view. He put his arm around her and squeezed her waist gently.

"To them this is just another day," Jeremy whispered, "but for us, to see them come down to drink is the thrill of a lifetime."

"The others don't know what they're missing," Clarissa agreed.

When the Englishman had taken as many photographs as he needed, he turned to them. "I've waited up four nights for that. Well worth it, wasn't it? By the way, Jobson's the name, James Jobson. Is this your first safari?"

"Yes," Clarissa replied. "I'm Clarissa Peterson and this is a friend of mine, Jeremy Dyson."

"Americans?"

"Well, yes," Clarissa answered, "but I was originally from Ireland. We both now live in Minnesota."

"Jolly good! Ireland eh! What part?"

"Tipperary. My family has lived there for generations."

"I used to fish at Knocklofty on the Suir. Very pleasant spot. Donoughmore had a wonderful ghillie there. Declan Breen, that was his name."

"No kidding," Clarissa said. "My family lived further up the river from Knocklofty, between Ardfinnan and Cahir."

"Where?"

"Ballyporeen House."

"Oh, I knew folks out your way. Let me see," he said tapping his temple. "It'll come to me. Must be twenty years ago at least. Major John Corrington, I think that was the name. Nice property looking out over the Knockmealdowns."

"That was my father!" Clarissa said, nonplused by the coincidence.

"We knew each other back in the guards," James Jobson revealed. "So you are Jack Corrington's daughter? Well, bless my soul. There's a coincidence."

"Yes, I am. I don't believe this. You were a friend of my father and we meet here at a watering hole in the African bush!"

"Quite remarkable, quite remarkable," James repeated. "We'd better go back on up and have a drink."

"Really, I can't believe this," Clarissa repeated. She looked at Jeremy.

"Life for us seems to be full of strange coincidences," Jeremy observed. "At this point very little surprises me. There seems to be a destiny governing our lives."

"So, when did you leave Ireland?" James asked Clarissa as he packed up his tripod.

"About fifteen years ago. I made my career in England and America."

"Clarissa's a concert pianist," Jeremy explained.

"Jolly good! Well done!" the eccentric man applauded. "Minnesota eh! Isn't that Red Indian territory?"

"It was," Jeremy answered.

Clarissa was reminded of Dr. John Bishop. 'It's funny how people always have this same reaction to Minnesota. Ours is a beautiful state of rolling hills, trees and lakes and Minneapolis is one of the greatest, cultural centers in the country,' she thought before answering. "I work quite a lot with the St. Paul Chamber Orchestra and they're highly regarded. There's a lot going on in the 'Twin Cities'. The 'Indian Territory' as you call it, is further west in the Dakotas."

"Jolly good!" James Jobson repeated as they started back up through the tunnel leading to the lower level of the lodge.

In the bar, at a table lit by a mock oil-lamp, James offered to buy them drinks. Some of the 'Prince Regent' crowd were seated on wicker chairs at other tables, but most had retired early, knowing that the morning drive would start shortly after dawn.

"Ballyporeen House," he repeated after they had ordered. "Your mother kept pretty good horses if I remember - rode out with the 'Tipps'."

"That's right," Clarissa confirmed. "I rode to hounds myself during winter holidays, but Mummy hunted all her life. Sadly she passed away a few months ago."

"Oh, I'm sorry," James said in a more sombre accent. "And your father, Major Corrington?"

"Daddy died four years ago. My brother and his family live at Ballyporeen today. I'm kind of the black sheep - the one who went to America."

"Quite, quite," James mumbled as if he had marbles in his mouth.

The houseman brought over their drinks, two scotches and an orange soda.

James raised his glass. "Cheers!"

"Cheers!" Clarissa repeated, but Jeremy fell into his more customary "Happy days!"

James looked at them intensely. "You know this is such a coincidence, but I'm sure we were somehow meant to meet. I don't really believe in coincidences."

"Nor do we," Jeremy interjected. "We believe in a certain destiny brought about by our past associations."

"Jeremy's a part-time archaeologist when he's not busy building hotels and universities," Clarissa explained.

"Yes. Working with history makes us appreciate how much influence the past actually has on the present," Jeremy suggested. "That's why I don't really believe in coincidences. There's always some reason for events - old karma, cause and effect, call it what you like, but there's always a reason why we interact with people the way we do. It's our energy fields interacting. After all, we're only vibrating energy."

"Interesting. Quite fascinating," the Englishman said as he leaned back and put his monocle back in his shirt pocket. "Our energy creates our destiny?"

"Yes, in a nutshell," Jeremy agreed.

James sipped on his whiskey. "That's exactly the way I've always felt. I'm afraid that's one of the reasons why people call me 'Batty'

Jobson, but it's true. That's why there are no coincidences. You can call it the hand of God if you like, but unfortunately God is perceived by different people and different religions in so many ways. It's better not to humanize God. Call God the energy."

"You're our kind of man!" Jeremy exclaimed excitedly. "That's it precisely!"

"When you've knocked about the world as much as I have - India before the war, South Africa, Australia, and sadly, but interestingly, a spell as an advisor to Australia in Indo-China during the French pull out that led up to that Vietnam fiasco - you come to terms with the limits of individual religions and the oneness of this universal energy."

"We couldn't agree more," Clarissa interjected. "That's just how we feel."

They chinked glasses again.

"You see it's not just a coincidence that we are sitting here talking," the old boy continued. "It wasn't by chance that we met at the watering hole. I knew your father, Mrs. Peterson. Who knows, I might have met you in those days."

Clarissa smiled. "I was only in Ireland for school holidays. After I left school I went to college in London. I was back in Dublin for a while with the Philharmonic there, and then in Europe my career took off."

"The important thing is there was some special energy that drew us together. We share these same feelings," James continued. "If we never see each other again we'll still have enriched each other's lives in this discovery. You see there are no coincidences."

Jeremy liked the old boy, but he really wondered where this conversation was leading. "Do you believe in past lives?" he asked boldly.

"Reincarnation, eh!" James repeated. "No experience of it, but the oldest and deepest philosophies in the world accept it. Yes, I suppose in theory I do. Past energy does seem to haunt us. Why not past lives as you Americans say. You do have funny ways of expressing things - Past lives, eh!"

Jeremy grinned. "Well, what would you say?"

"Don't know really ... I suppose we always say 'reincarnation'. Past lives just seems a little strange to us." He drank the last of his whiskey and put down his glass. "You know something, it's not reincarnation that's really important, it's how the energy of past incarnations or earlier experiences even in our present life, affects the here and now. The past affects the present and the present creates the future. Past, present and future are all interconnected. That's the way I see it."

"Maybe that's what we mean when we say time is an illusion," Jeremy agreed.

"Perhaps," James nodded. "It's all very deep and fascinating, but I'd better not keep you chaps up if you've got a game drive in the morning. They have no mercy here. They leave right on time and if you're five minutes late you'll miss it."

• • • • • • • •

B ack in their room, Clarissa and Jeremy prepared for bed. Clarissa brushed her teeth using the bottled water in the bathroom. When she came out, Jeremy was sitting on his bed wearing just his boxer shorts. She couldn't help noticing his bronzed body. There was no doubt about it, the architect attracted her. 'Latent energy,' she thought. 'We had to have known each other pretty well two thousand years ago. We must have been lovers.'

Jeremy got up and went to the bathroom. Clarissa took that opportunity to get undressed. She stripped down to her rather delicate bra and panties, a recent gift from David in Singapore. She climbed into her bed and closed the mosquito netting, pulling up the sheet for modesty. There was no air-conditioning and it was muggy.

About five minutes later David returned, turned off the only light and climbed into the other bed, fighting with its mosquito netting in the dark.

The night sounds of Africa drifted in through the screened louvres and the pale glow of moonlight fell in streaks across the room.

"Goodnight, Jeremy," Clarissa whispered. "I hope you don't snore!"

"I'll try not to," he answered. "Sweet dreams!"

But they couldn't sleep. It was too warm. Clarissa kicked back her sheet.

Jeremy could see her flesh highlit in the pale moonlight through the fuzz of the mosquito netting. There was something incredibly erotic to him about this glimpse of Clarissa lying in her lingerie. He was reminded of that moment in the ocean three or four days before when he had encountered Fiona in her translucent bikini. 'David's two women,' he thought. 'What a lucky man.' He turned away and tried to sleep.

All of a sudden Jeremy became aware that Clarissa was getting up. She had opened her mosquito net and started to walk across the room. The moonlight was now brighter and Jeremy caught his breath as he saw Clarissa. Every aspect of her became sensual in the opaque light enhanced by the mystery of the muslin material of his mosquito net. He tried to suppress his feelings. He imagined she was Fiona, anyone but David's wife. But he could see that she was not Fiona. In the exaggerated moonlight her silky bra revealed much fuller breasts and her form was generally less boyish and more sensually soft. He heard her pour water in the bathroom as she took a drink to quench her thirst. Then she was back. Her face caught the moonlight and she climbed into her bed and curled up again beneath her net in the hope that soon she would sleep.

At last, they both drifted into slumber ....

In their dreams they saw each other. This time they clearly knew each other. Clarissa looked into Jeremy's face and Jeremy into Clarissa's. They were standing under the same waterfall that Clarissa had seen in her vision of Maria washing Joshua's hair. It was the waterfall that Jeremy had imagined when he had stood under the shower earlier in the evening. The water poured down from a ledge of rocks, falling into a pool that bubbled downstream towards a great lake. There were palms in the grove and aspens along the river bank. The sky was azure and the sun was hot. They were, in that unique time and place, Joshua and Maria. Maria had released Joshua's loincloth and they were both standing unashamed in their nakedness. Birds sang to them. They could sense the spark of God flowing between them in this moment of pure joy and selfless pledge. They were innocently one. Their nakedness was natural. As their flesh touched, Jeremy didn't feel the guilt pangs that had attacked him when he'd seen Clarissa walk across the room half-naked in the moonlight. Nor did Clarissa feel the censored rejection that she had been forced to apply when she had leaned against Jeremy at the watering hole, or seen his bronzed body as he had sat in his boxer shorts on the edge of his bed. In the world of their joint dreams they touched each other in total freedom ....

When they awoke they lay silently looking up at the rafters and woven thatch of their circular room. The moonlight had given way to the light streak of dawn. The telephone rang.

Jeremy struggled out of his mosquito netting. "Yes," he said sleepily.

"It's four-thirty, this is your wake-up call," a native voice answered. The phone cut off before Jeremy could answer.

Clarissa modestly pulled up her sheet to hide her semi-naked flesh. Jeremy stretched and went to the bathroom.

• • • • • • • •

The morning game drive was not as rewarding as had been that of the previous afternoon. However, the sight of a muddy hippopotamus down at a small creek satisfied the photographers.

"Look at that baby yawn!" Sam yelled as he caught the hippo opening his jaw.

"It's enough to make us all yawn," the widow from Arkansas commented. "I don't know about the rest of you, but I didn't sleep a wink. It was so hot in my room."

"It was warm," Clarissa agreed. "I found it hard to sleep too. I only caught an hour or two."

"Let's hope they have a good breakfast for us," Sam commented. "After this early morning nonsense, I'm ready for a 'steak and western'."

"That does sound good," Jeremy admitted.

The safari jeep left the hippo's creek and drove on through the vast landscape. There were more eland, ostriches and zebras, but no exciting elephants or giraffes to enhance their experience.

"Can we return to the lions?" Jeremy asked the guide.

"I was planning that on the way back. There's a good chance they'll be in the same area. They usually stay in their territory."

The lionesses were there, and with them, the king himself. The lion was perched on a hummock above the tall grass.

Sam was speechless for the first time on the trip. Only clicking cameras broke the silence as they all got their shots. It didn't matter now if none of them ever saw another animal. Their safari had been rewarded and they had an African memory that they would never forget.

It was about three in the afternoon when they got back to Mombassa. David was in the midst of embarkation. Clarissa wrapped up the carved elephant in some pretty paper and wrote a card which she left for him. 'To my beloved David, with all my love forever, Clara.' Then, she went down to the spa and soaked in a jacuzzi. The bumpy jeep rides and lack of sleep at the lodge, combined with the early start in the morning and the long drive back to Mombassa had exhausted her.

'It's funny,' she thought as she lay back in the hot, swirling water, 'we never saw James Jobson today and yet I feel we met him yesterday for a reason. I'm not sure exactly what. We didn't even get his address, but that dream last night seemed to fit his theory. The past does affect the present which does shape our future. We create our own destiny. Jeremy had to be Jesus. If Jeremy was Jesus, I'm almost certain we were lovers. After what happened at the waterfall we had to become lovers. It's awesome. How can I discuss this with either Jeremy or David? Jeremy might take advantage of our situation. He really is a ladies' man! God damn it! He had Fiona in the sack within three days! But I'm also afraid to tell David. I'm not sure he'd believe me. He wasn't happy about Jeremy and I sharing a room in the first place ... But, nothing happened, at least not outside the dream state.' Then she smiled as she reflected on the experience, 'My God, was it powerful!'

The echoing sounds of others in the spa brought Clarissa back to reality. She felt afraid. She didn't believe much in prayer, but she went through the motions in her despair. 'Please God, don't let Jeremy break up my marriage! I love David! If I loved Jeremy two thousand years ago, don't let me fall for him now!' She thought about James Jobson's interpretation of past lives. 'Don't let the present coincidences built on the past, shape our future,' she pleaded. 'I'm happy in the present. I love David. I want to live with David forever.'

During the next few days she avoided Jeremy, although she laughed when she saw the Cruise Director sentence him to appalling punishment at the 'Equator Crossing' ceremony during the visit of his Most Noble Majesty, King Neptune of the Deep.

Jeremy must have sensed her fears, as he likewise avoided her. On more than one occasion Clarissa saw him talking to Fiona out on deck. Clarissa's mind welcomed the detachment, but her heart pulled for her love at the waterfall. Emotionally, it was difficult for her to keep the past from the present.

David was too busy to notice. The period between Mombassa and Suez was traditionally known to ships' heads of departments as 'Hate week' - six boring days at sea with the excitement of Africa over. The coming interest of Europe still seems far away. The long term passengers have had too much of the ship and too much of each other. The result is a pile of senseless, niggling complaints that all have to be handled by the Hotel Manager, the Chief Purser and the Cruise Director.

• • • • • • • •

This was the first time Clarissa had sailed through the Suez Canal. After the beauty of the Gatun lake in Panama, she felt a profound disappointment as the ship moved through this desert ditch.

"It's really very boring," she said as David tapped her on the shoulder during his lunch break. "It has none of the beauty of the Panama Canal."

"Actually I much prefer traveling to South Africa on a World cruise," David admitted. "The Mediterranean is a snare and an illusion in March. It can be quite cold. When you think about it, the Suez Canal really divides the world. At its northern end there are seasons and at its southern end is the eternal warmth of the Indian Ocean. Personally I like the warmth of the Indian Ocean."

Clarissa agreed. "After all, we met in the Indian Ocean the first time I came on board the 'Prince Regent'."

"And it took me nearly two weeks to talk to you!"

"Ah, but you had Fiona trotting after you. It was difficult to attract your attention. But I knew Spirit would lead you to me. I recognized your name. Samantha had already told me."

"It took me a long time to break up with Fiona," David admitted. "It was very difficult at the time."

"But you have no regrets?"

"None, Clara."

They watched the passing desert.

"I wish you could come with me to Jerusalem," Clarissa said.

"I wish I could, but you win some and you lose some. I wish you could be with me in Ephesus, but in less than a month we'll both be home in Minnesota. Do you think the snow'll be gone by mid-April?"

"It should be. Actually, soon after you come home, the fresh, new leaves will begin to break, and in May the lilacs will be in bloom. You'll love the lilacs, David. I'm really looking forward to our summer on the lake."

"Me too," David agreed as he left to return to his office.

'I might as well start packing,' Clarissa thought, and she went down to their cabin to start tackling the task.

Two days later the 'Prince Regent' was docked at Haifa. Jeremy had a long-standing invitation to go out to the archeological dig at Sepphoris and left right after the ship had docked. However, over rather superficial farewell drinks the night before, they had all agreed that he should share Clarissa's taxi when she left for Jerusalem. She didn't have to be in Jerusalem to meet with the Israeli conductor until the following day, so David took the opportunity of an open day to take Clarissa to Nazareth and the Sea of Galilee.

They were more than a little disappointed as they visited the vast Church of the Annunciation. It occupied the central area of town where Nazareth's well and Joseph's carpenter's shop had possibly been located in the time of Jesus. Now, however, the place was swamped with tourists, many of whom were nuns and priests or church groups from around the world who believed in the purported authenticity of every detail. If the guide said this is where the Archangel Gabriel visited the Virgin Mary and told her she was going to have God's child, they believed it.

"It's way too commercial," Clarissa stated as they passed the souvenir stalls. Statuettes of 'Blessed Mary ever Virgin' and local olive wood, rosary beads and crucifixes were everywhere. Deep down, however, there was something else that bothered Clarissa. 'If my mother really was Miriam, the mother of Joshua, two thousand years ago,' she thought, 'I hardly think she would have approved of all this. Mother was always for simplicity. She was such a humble and unassuming person. I'd rather think of the Virgin Mary in her image.'

The taxi driver was surprised that they returned to the parking lot so quickly. It was now about eleven-thirty in the morning. "I can take you to Mount Tabor on the way to Tiberias," he suggested

"What's there?" Clarissa asked.

"The Church of the Franciscans. It's very peaceful," the Israeli explained.

"We're not too big on all these churches," Clarissa replied. "What was Mount Tabor famous for?"

"The Transfiguration of Jesus Christ."

Clarissa looked at David. "That could be interesting."

"Okay, let's go to Mount Tabor on our way to the Sea of Galilee," David confirmed.

They discovered that Mount Tabor was quite close to Nazareth. As they left the town they could look down on the valley of Esdraelon where all manner of fruit was growing in neat orchards of irrigated bushes. Off on the left was a strange outcrop rising up from the valley. According to the taxi driver that was Mount Tabor. Along the road descending from Nazareth to the valley were many spring flowers. White Nazareth Irises abounded. In clefts of rock, colorful pink cyclamen bloomed. Lower in the valley wild hyacinths added a touch of blue.

"Is the roadside always so colorful?" Clarissa asked.

"No, you've come at the right time," the driver-guide explained. "Those blue flowers are often called the 'lilies of the valley' in the Bible. They only bloom in the spring."

It wasn't long before they were driving up the winding road that made its way to the top of Mount Tabor. There was a silent stillness in the air outside the hilltop monastery sitting perched among cypress and olive trees.

"Do you think this could be the place that I see when I play my piece?" Clarissa suggested to David, as she saw how shafts of light played through the branches. "Perhaps this is where Joshua prayed as he stood in that extraordinary light."

"It's very peaceful up here," David admitted. "This place could be an inspiration to anybody. One can almost sense a spiritual presence."

From the top of Mount Tabor there were magnificent views down the valley towards the distant coast. One could also see across to the rolling hills of southern Galilee and on into ancient Samaria.

A Franciscan brother in his brown habit came out from a door in the great sandstone facade of the monastery. A bell started to toll. The brother greeted them, "Shalom!"

"Good morning," Clarissa replied.

David looked instinctively at his watch. Surely it had gone twelve by now. It had, it was nearly one, but it was still before lunch.

The brother smiled at them. "American?" he asked.

"Yes," David replied.

"I was born in Illinois," the Franciscan informed them, his Israeli accent taking on an American tone. "Why don't you come inside? There are beautiful frescoes in the church that depict the scene of Christ's transfiguration." The man's face seemed to glow as he spoke to them. "Come with me," he said proudly.

He took them in to the cool of the monastic church. Unlike most churches, the building was fairly new and there was much light inside that reflected off the yellow sandstone. Beautiful modern frescoes did indeed adorn the walls.

The face of the transfigured Christ dominated that over the wide chancel. As Clarissa stared at the image she felt Jeremy's presence, just as in the vision that recurred each time she played 'Gilded Snow'. But as always, she couldn't be sure. The longer she stared at the face, the more it seemed to pulsate. It didn't always seem like Jeremy. Sometimes it seemed like David and then sometimes it looked like the face of that smiling Franciscan monk.

On either side of the central fresco were white-bearded representations of Moses and Elijah, also bathed in brilliance. In another were Jesus' apostles, Peter, James and John. David and Clarissa looked up from afar at the shafts of light in which Jesus and the two ancient prophets of the end time stood. The inscription beneath said 'Let's make three tabernacles, one for Moses, one for Elijah and one for the Lord.' Clarissa couldn't help noticing in this giant painting that there were many rocks strewn around in the area where the inner three disciples knelt. She trembled as she squeezed David's hand. "I was there" she whispered. "I was hiding behind those rocks."

It was doubtful if the Franciscan brother could hear what she had said, but he turned towards her. A glowing warmth emanated from the man and Clarissa felt that she was in the presence of Christ.

"Thank you for visiting us," the monk said as the bell continued to toll. "Our service will start in about ten minutes. The brothers are starting to come in. You're welcome to stay."

David glanced at his watch again. "We have a driver waiting outside," he said politely. "I think we'll have to go."

"Shalom!" the monk returned, as he bowed humbly. He left them and vanished through an inside door.

When David and Clarissa went outside David admitted that there was an awesome peace in the church.

"I felt strangely transformed myself," Clarissa agreed. "I felt the presence of Jesus in that kindly monk. It made me glow."

"Perhaps that is what the 'Christ' should mean," David said philosophically. "Perhaps we should look for the Christ-likeness in all whom we meet. Maybe there's a little of the 'Christ' in all of us."

"Especially in you," Clarissa said as she squeezed her husband's hand. "Remember what my mother wrote, 'I am so glad to know that you and Clarissa will be in the light of Christos'."

As they drove from Mount Tabor across the more arid landscape to the shores of the Sea of Galilee, they continued to feel that glowing presence.

When they descended to the blue waters of the inland lake, the vegetation became more lush. Vineyards abounded and rows of fruit trees replaced the barren, rock-strewn hills.

"We can stop for 'Peter' fish at a little restaurant on the waterfront in Tiberias," the driver announced, seasoned to taking tourists on the Galilee route.

"What kind of a fish is 'Peter' fish?" Clarissa asked.

"It's a flat fish, rather like a plaice. It's the main fish of the lake and very good - beautiful, white flesh. They say it was the principal fish that Saint Peter and the apostles used to catch."

"Will we still have time to go to Capernaum?" David asked, becoming just a little anxious.

"Oh yes. You can't come to the lake and not visit Jesus' town. I'll get you back to Haifa by six."

"Well, no later than six," For some strange reason as a senior officer of the ship David always felt guilty taking time ashore. But he had wanted to spend this day with Clarissa knowing that soon they would be separated for another month.

The driver stopped outside a little shoreside restaurant. There were tables on the pebbly beach under an awning of palm fronds. The pebbles curved away from them to the right leading to a little promontory that jutted out into the lake. Along this shore, a few small fishing boats were pulled up, much as others must have been two thousand years before.

"This was a thriving, Roman town in Jesus' time." their guide explained after he had ordered 'Peter' fish for them. There's not much evidence of its Roman past today, but it's still a popular place. Many Israelis have expensive homes here. It's quite fashionable."

To David and Clarissa the Tiberias waterfront didn't look very fashionable. It was one long line of fish restaurants somewhat similar to the rustic one in which they sat, but when the 'Peter' fish came, it was well worth it. The white flesh looked succulent. Fresh lemons and olives gave it a bitter-sweet taste.

'So this was the Roman town on the lake' Clarissa thought. She looked along the sweeping curve of the pebbly beach. 'Is this the place where Doctor John carried our son? Is this where Marcus played as a little boy? Why haven't I had any further revelations or feelings about Simon's father? I wonder what happened to Antonias? After I joined Joshua's group he seemed to fade away.'

The driver was anxious to move on. He had got the message that David was concerned they might be behind time. David paid the bill and they left the restaurant to drive north towards Capernaum.

The road skirted the lake. Vineyards and olive groves, interspersed with patches of citrus fruits, grew on the left. After a few miles the shingle beach reappeared on the right. A large group of cypress trees grew along this coast and the hillside became steeper as it rose up from the lake.

"They think the Biblical village of Magdala was about here," the driver said. "The Romans called it Tracchea. It really wasn't famous for anything other than being the home of Mary Magdalene, the prostitute who Jesus rescued from seven devils. Do you mind if I stop here for gas?"

Clarissa looked out at the lake from the flat beach area. She could imagine the fishing boats lined up there in Jesus' time. She could almost smell the fish drying on mats in the sun. There was no village now, only a shack beside a gas station.

The driver stopped the taxi for a fill-up. Clarissa chuckled to herself. 'I wonder what he would think if he knew that he was driving Mary Magdalene today?'

David heard her giggle. He smiled and reached for her hand. "Penny for your thoughts?" he asked. "What's so funny?"

"You heard what the driver said. This place wasn't famous for anything except for being the home of Mary Magdalene. What if he knew?"

"About you?"

"Yes."

"Well, don't tell him. I think we'd better keep quiet about that 'round here."

"It's interesting," Clarissa observed. "No great church has been built here to commemorate Maria."

"Perhaps that's deliberate," David suggested. "Christianity has difficulty recognizing Mary Magdalene. It complicates things for Jesus to have had a girlfriend, besides as our man said, the Church sees her as a prostitute and a sinner." David rubbed his hand over her thighs, "But I'll tell you one thing, if I'd been here two thousand years ago I think I'd have paid for your services!"

The tank filled, the driver returned. "Alright, Capernaum next," he said as he drove away.

About three miles further on from the probable sight of Magdala, the road crossed a flat bridge close to an area where a shallow, but fairly wide stream made its way into the lake. The land around the stream was surprisingly lush. Willows and fan palms followed the banks and not too far away one could make out some waterfalls where the stream tumbled down from rocks above. There was a Hebrew inscription on a camping sign beside the bridge. Underneath the Hebrew letters the word 'Gennesar' was painted in English.

"Can we stop for a photo here?" Clarissa asked. "That's a really pretty spot."

"It's popular with students and families," the driver informed them as he slowed down. "It's strange, but there are no tents up today. There are usually four or five."

Clarissa took her photograph.

"How long will it take to walk to those falls?" she asked.

"Clara, we haven't time," David said a little impatiently.

"About ten minutes," the driver informed her, "but as Mr. Peterson says, we are a bit pushed for time."

"I must walk up there David," Clarissa pleaded. "It's my destiny. I must see that waterfall!"

David looked at his watch. "What is it, Clara?" he asked noticing the sudden desperation in her voice.

"It's something I haven't told you yet, David. I've been afraid to tell you, but come with me. I've got to see that waterfall."

David bowed to her wishes. "Alright darling, but twenty minutes, that's it. I must be back by six-thirty at the latest."

They started to follow the stream towards the falls. When they were out of sight of the taxi, Clarissa stopped.

"Do you know where this is?" she said.

"Gennesar according to the notice back there. Look, Clara, what's all this about?"

"You see that wide, pool area? That's where I washed his hair."

"Oh, I see. You think this is the place you dreamed about when Mary Magdalene and Jesus were bathing in the stream."

"Yes, but it's more than that, David. This is what I haven't told you. I'm almost positive Jeremy was Joshua. I see him in the metamorphosis every time I play 'Gilded Snow', but when we were on safari in Africa I saw a vision of him right here at this waterfall. We stood naked together. Jesus and me. Jeremy was Jesus."

"But Jeremy thinks he was this Roman guy, Remus whatever his name was," David insisted. "He can't have been Jesus as well."

"I agree, but nonetheless I'm almost positive he was Jesus. I'm not nearly so sure about Remus Augustus. I've never had any revelation that I knew this Remus guy two thousand years ago, but I certainly seemed to know Jesus, or Joshua. Almost all my revelations are with Joshua. Maria of Magdala was supposed to be with Joshua. And now, I'm quite sure that Jeremy was this Joshua."

"What's Jeremy got on you," David said scornfully. "Why this change all of a sudden? What happened in Africa? Did he make mad, passionate love to you? What's this about standing naked together? I knew you shouldn't have shared a room with him. You space cadets are all the same, you just bend your emotions to suit your dreams. I wish we'd never started on this past life nonsense!"

Clarissa looked scared. "It's not nonsense. I love you David," she pleaded. "That's why I didn't tell you."

"Didn't tell me what? That this bearded creep was screwing your ever-living brains out!"

She started to cry and looked up at him with appealing eyes. "No, David. I swear nothing like that ever happened. Jeremy never touched me in Africa. He was a perfect gentleman. The revelation was only a dream and we didn't make love, we just stood together in a magic moment from the past." She pointed at the falls. "It happened right there. It wasn't Jeremy and me. We were Joshua and Maria. Past energies may bring us together in the present, but we are not the people we were. I'm your wife, David. I love you, and the past is not going to destroy our future."

David calmed down. He put his arms around Clarissa. "I'm sorry," he said. "I love you too. Why am I so tormented by this? I get so possessive. I don't really trust Jeremy. He's a ladies' man." He frowned ... "Haven't you noticed how he's been chatting up Fiona?"

Clarissa laughed through her tears. "So you're a little jealous. The ghost of Fiona still walks."

"Of course not, Clara!" David exclaimed. "I love you! Fiona's completely a thing of the past." He paused and squeezed her hand, "But you do remember the good times," he added.

"Exactly, David. That's why I remember this waterfall. Joshua's in the past, but like you I do remember the good times."

They hugged each other in reconciliation as David tried to hold back a tear. "That, that's not really quite the same," he stammered. "We just mustn't let these past life experiences destroy what we have. I love you, Clara."

"Alright, Linus," Clarissa said tweaking his nose. "Don't forget that you've had some revelations too!"

"Then let's have a pact," David suggested. "We mustn't hide anything from each other. We tell each other everything."

"I'm sorry. I was afraid," Clarissa admitted. "I knew you weren't happy about Jeremy and me having to share that room in Africa."

"I wasn't, but I shouldn't have said what I did. We mustn't let anything come between us. Now, let's take a look at this waterfall. We might as well seeing we've got this far."

They walked to the falls. Water tumbled over a ledge in the rock just as Clarissa had seen it. Looking back downstream they could see the palms and the aspen willows leading to the Sea of Galilee.

"It's awesome," was all Clarissa could say.

"I'm so sorry," David repeated. "I should never have yelled at you like that. It is beautiful. I'm glad we came."

Ten minutes later, their upheaval settled, they were back in the taxi and driving to Capernaum.

Modern Capernaum turned out to be a small, seaside community at the northern end of the lake. At the approach to the town, feathery palms fringed the waterfront, hiding white buildings much as David and Clarissa might have imagined them to have been two thousand years before. Farther on, an incongruous billboard announced their arrival in 'The town of Jesus'. But modern buildings detracted from the Biblical look of the older one's. Schools and gas stations also undermined the mystical feeling of time past. Army jeeps gave a sense of life in Israel as it is today, where northern Galilee guards her borders in uncertain times. It was only close to the shore that there was any real sense of the past, an area of dark stone ruins that the driver informed them was the town where Jesus had lived. In the center of the site were some upright columns of Corinthian design holding up a section of architrave in front of a dressed stone wall.

"The ancient synagogue," the driver said.

"Where Jesus preached?" David asked.

"Yes, this was Jesus' town," the driver repeated as if the billboard and other sundry notices hadn't got the message across.

Around the ruins of Capernaum were the usual collection of tourist shops selling everything from tee-shirts depicting 'Jesus' town, to prayer books and Bibles cased in olive wood. David and Clarissa only had time to glance at the ruins. Neither of them were very impressed. As in Nazareth, there was something very artificial about the whole presentation. Different denominations of the Christian Church all seemed to have their pitch. There were churches of the orthodox Greeks and even a small Russian chapel. The Roman Catholics had a convent close to the gates where pilgrims could stay and the Protestant churches from Anglican and Lutheran to Scottish Presbyterian all had their niche.

David bought a blue guidebook. "We can read about it later," he said. "Perhaps we should drive on."

On their way up from the lake, they passed a little gazebo-like monument that the driver said was the place of the 'Beatitudes', and just beyond that there was yet another church, rather beautifully set among cypress trees on the hillside. It had a Renaissance look to it, with fluted columns and a delicate facade.

"Here Jesus performed the miracle of the loaves and fishes," the driver explained.

"Let's get out for a moment," Clarissa suggested. She was not particularly interested in Jesus' miraculous feats or the comforting words of the 'Beatitudes' from the 'Sermon on the Mount', but there was something about the peace and beauty of that hillside covered in wildflowers that was in deep contrast to the artificiality of Capernaum. "Take a picture of me with these flowers?" she asked David.

"Consider the lilies of the field," David said as he set the camera. "I'm telling you that Solomon in all his glory was not arrayed like one of these. You look beautiful, Clara, more magnificent than Solomon. One, two, three," and he pressed the shutter.

"What was that you said about the lilies?"

"Oh, that was something Jesus said on a hillside above Capernaum," David explained. "I always remember that quote. It's one of the more sensible sayings of the Bible. We can learn so much about the real presence of God from the great beauty of nature. A place like this means far more to me than Nazareth or Capernaum. Here God's presence can be felt."

"That's beautiful," Clarissa said. "Would you like me to take a photo of you with the flowers?"

"Alright, but make it quick," David said as he posed for her.

On their way to Haifa, Clarissa dozed while David read the Capernaum guide book. At one point he looked up. "You remember the remains of the synagogue?"

"At Capernaum?" Clarissa answered sleepily.

"Yes ... It says here that the building dates from the time of Hadrian in the early part of the Second Century. It wasn't the building Jesus knew."

"Really," Clarissa yawned. "Do you think all those tourists realized that?"

"I doubt it. There are so many things about Jesus and his times that have become twisted to suit the whims of the Church. I'm rapidly concluding that Jesus wouldn't recognize his life or message if he were to return today and see what Christianity has made of them."

The sun was setting over the Mediterranean as they drove down from the high ground through the city of Haifa to the waterfront. It was six-thirty five. The 'Prince Regent' was waiting for them. Reunited in their love, they had just one night left to celebrate.

· · · · · · · ·

D avid helped carry Clarissa's bags to the taxi. Clarissa showed the driver the letter she had from Global Artistes. She was to stay at a convent on Mount Zion. Jeremy was booked at the King David Hotel. Clarissa was to contact Maestro Goldstein shortly after she arrived. His number was on the sheet.

"Do you know where this convent is in Jerusalem?" she asked the taxi driver.

The man studied the letter. He held out his hands and shrugged his shoulders. "No, but don't worry," he answered. "I'll get you to Jerusalem. I'll take you to the 'King David' first. They'll know this address and can direct me there after we have dropped off Mr. Dyson."

Clarissa wondered where Global Artistes had placed her, but felt she was in safe hands. She turned to kiss David goodbye. He was dressed in his uniform. She started to laugh.

"What's so funny?" he asked.

"Your uniform reminds me of Babis Demetris, but you're a lot more handsome."

They kissed.

"I'll call you from Piraeus," David said. "Good luck in Jerusalem."

"Thanks for everything, David," Jeremy spoke from the back seat. "I'll see you again in Minnesota."

"I hope all goes well for you here. Glad you could sail with us," David said cordially, trying to conceal his recent feelings of animosity.

David stood and watched as the taxi wheeled around and drove out through the dock gates. When he could see the car no more he returned to his duties in the Purser's Office.

· · · · · · · ·

"H ow was Sepphoris?" Clarissa asked Jeremy, trying to be polite on their journey.

"I was amazed," he revealed. "So much has been done since I was last out here. But I had the strangest experience there, Clarissa."

"What, another revelation?" she asked almost skeptically as she tried to suppress her curiosity.

"Yes. I felt I was there two thousand years ago."

"As Remus Augustus?"

"No. As a slave named 'Joshua'."

"What!"

"Yes. I was examining one of the excavated streets. As I sat by the base of one of the pavement pillars, I had this vision, a sort of daydream. I was back in Roman times again. I was tied to a post and a soldier was whipping me with a flail. It was very painful and I could hear myself screaming. Then it stopped. A voice shouted out in Latin, 'What has this man done?' I turned my head and could see the Commander on a white horse talking to the officers who were responsible for my punishment. 'He was idling on the job,' one of the Romans informed the Commander. My torturer then started to beat me again, but after only three strokes, the Commander ordered him to stop. He spoke to me himself in Aramaic."

"What did he say?" Clarissa asked.

"He told me not to idle on the job and that if I did I would be punished severely, but he also arranged for my release. He said something about Roman justice and discipline and that an honest day's work would be rewarded honestly. He seemed like a good man, Clarissa. He wasn't a typical brutal Roman."

"Perhaps you have guilt feelings about your own brutality when you were that Roman soldier called Remus Augustus," Clarissa suggested. "This daydream as you call it, might just be a way of working off your karma from that life."

"I don't think so," Jeremy said slowly. "I think this was from an earlier lifetime before I was Remus Augustus."

"As who?" Clarissa asked wondering what he would say.

"As a Galilean vine-grower named 'Joshua'."

Clarissa could hardly contain her excitement. "Jesus' name!"

"It was, but as I've said before, it was not an uncommon name," Jeremy replied, turning his head towards her. "I don't think we should talk about this now. I'll tell you about it when we stop for lunch."

Jeremy looked at the passing scenery for a moment or two and then returned to the subject of Roman brutality. "I thought I could overhear that Roman Commander talking with his officers in my daydream. The Commander told them to see that the men were not too brutal with us. The officer shouted back at the Commander, 'Is Rome going soft?' 'No Marcellus,' the Commander answered, 'but this time we intend to establish our rule permanently.' He went on to explain something about the weakness of the Herodians and that all real government in Palestine was now Roman. The officers applauded that, but this remarkable man Flavius Septimus went on to say, 'We want these people with us, not against us. We must be firm, but we must also be fair'." Jeremy looked at Clarissa like an academic professor. "You see, there was Roman justice in the brutal world of the First Century after all."

Something about the Roman name 'Flavius Septimus' seemed to register with Clarissa. "What did you say this man's name was?" she asked for confirmation.

"Marcellus called the Commander 'Flavius Septimus', at least I think that was right, but you know how it is in dreams."

"I thought that's what you said. I've heard that name somewhere," Clarissa intimated. "I can't remember where, but I've heard that name before."

"Sounds like he was a member of the famous Flavian family of Rome. They were quite powerful in the last days of the Republic," Jeremy suggested in his professorial tone.

When they stopped for lunch and were alone, Clarissa reminded Jeremy that there was more to his Sepphoris experience that she wanted to hear.

"There's something that I've never had the opportunity to tell you," Jeremy said. "I think I might have been married to a Hebrew girl at one time before I was Remus Augustus. That's when I might have been this Hebrew slave named 'Joshua'."

"When?" Clarissa asked.

"Possibly, as Joshua, I was working on the reconstruction of Sepphoris under forced labor. The Romans did that. They rounded up Jewish peasants during troubled times and put them into work gangs. In my vision it seemed like there had been a great fire in the city. Actually I was shown carbon from damaged buildings of the Great Rebellion while I was in the museum yesterday."

"What was the Great Rebellion?"

"One of the many Jewish revolts, but Sepphoris was burned badly in about thirteen A.D. Now, if I had been married to this girl Joanna before the Great Rebellion, it's possible that is how I ended up as a slave in Sepphoris."

"What makes you so sure you were married to this Joanna?" Clarissa asked, her pride slightly hurt as Jeremy revealed secrets that destroyed her belief that he had known her as Mary Magdalene in the First Century.

Then Jeremy dropped his bombshell. "I think that nurse on board the 'Prince Regent' was Joanna, the one David used to know, Fiona MacAllister."

Clarissa was stunned. She said nothing, but just stared straight ahead.

"I didn't think you would be very pleased to hear that," Jeremy continued, "but it came to me in an extraordinary revelation after we left the Seychelles. I couldn't bring myself to tell you about it while we were in Africa. I don't know why, but I had all sorts of confusing thoughts at that time. Anyway, I dreamed about Fiona, but she appeared as this young, Semitic girl named 'Joanna' and it seemed then that we were married. We had a vineyard and I just had this fleeting vision of Joanna milling flour outside our little house among the vines. She made very good bread, just not enough of it."

Clarissa sniggered. "Fiona's probably a better cook than I am."

Jeremy reached out for Clarissa's hand. "Don't take this personally. I still have this uncanny feeling that somewhere in the First Century we met. Now, I just don't know whether it was as Joshua or Remus."

"How could you be both people?" Clarissa said sarcastically, no longer wanting to be hurt by Jeremy's revelations.

"If I died about twenty eight A.D. I could have been reincarnated as Remus Augustus in time to have been the young soldier who saw you as Maria in Massilia," he suggested.

In her disappointment, Clarissa quietly realized that she could not suppress all her feelings for Jeremy. 'The past effects the present which moulds the future,' she kept repeating to herself as she thought of James Jobson. 'I won't rest until this mystery is solved. Jeremy Dyson played a part in my first century life. He was with me at that waterfall, Joanna or no Joanna - Fiona or no Fiona. He was Jesus! I know he was Jesus!'. But, there was no way that she could confront Jeremy with her inner feelings as they drove on to Jerusalem.

When they reached the 'King David', Jeremy asked for the time of her performance.

Clarissa gave him the details. "If you come, do make yourself known at the stage door. I would love to see you. Maybe we could have a bite to eat afterwards if Maestro Goldstein doesn't monopolize me." She hastily wrote Jeremy a note and gave him her card. "Present this at the door, it might help in letting you in."

• • • • • • •

C larissa arrived at the Carmelite Convent on Mount Zion about four o-clock in the afternoon. A Deaconess in an old-fashioned habit, showed her to her room. It was clean and surprisingly well-furnished. There was a comfortable bathroom and plenty of towels and amenities.

"This is a very good location," the Deaconess explained. "The Upper Room is very close to here. You can also easily walk into the Old City and up to the Temple Mount. It's well worth visiting. The old, sacrificial rock of Mount Moriah is incorporated in the present Dome of the Rock. It's a very sacred place to Christians, Jews and Moslems."

"How far is the wailing wall?" Clarissa asked.

"Not far. It's the only visible part of the Temple Jesus knew that can still be seen. Everything else was destroyed by the Romans in seventy A.D."

The wailing wall was the main place that Clarissa knew about. The taxi driver had talked about it coming down from Galilee. She knew it was the most sacred place to the Jews in all Jerusalem.

"Now, you should visit the Church of the Holy Sepulchre," the Deaconess continued. "I take it you are a Christian."

"Anglican."

"Nothing wrong with that, my dear," the Deaconess said condescendingly. "We are all one in the Lord Jesus."

Clarissa changed the subject, not really considering herself anything. "Where can I practice?"

"Oh yes," the Deaconess answered thoughtfully. "We have a Grand piano in the Refectory. You may use it any time other than meals. The Refectory is the large dining hall off the reception area. Dinner tonight will be at seven, but you can have your meals sent to your room if you would prefer."

"Thank you for all your help and advice," Clarissa said politely. "There's just one more thing - can I make telephone calls direct from the room? I need to call Maestro Goldstein right away."

"No problem my dear. Just dial nine and you'll get an outside line."

Clarissa was pleased when the Deaconess left. Although the room was very comfortable, she felt there must be a certain similarity between this and the convent schools that her Catholic contemporaries had all attended in Ireland. 'Thank God I didn't have to go to a convent school,' she thought. 'There were some advantages to being a backsliding Protestant in southern Ireland.'

She dialed Maestro Goldstein's number.

"Hello," the Maestro answered with a deep, Prussian accent.

"Clarissa Corrington here. I just wanted to check with you about the concert tomorrow."

"Ah, Fraulein Clarissa Corrington," the Maestro repeated. "Velcome to Jerusalem. Vee are honored that you can play viv us. Now, you have zer program. I believe vee vill start with zee Rachmaninoff and then play zer Grieg and Debussy. Between the Rachmaninoff and zer Grieg vee'll be featuring a young Israeli cellist who'll be playing a new composition by our national composer Herr Samuel Horowitz. It's quite a modern piece and vill contrast vell with your verk."

"Will I be closing?" Clarissa asked, becoming a little concerned that she might not be able to play 'Gilded Snow'.

"Oh yes. You're our star, Fraulein. I look forward to conducting you. Can vee meet in my office at nine-thirty tomorrow morning? I vud like to talk to you before vee go into rehearsal. Zee orchestra call is for eleven."

"I'll be there. I'd like to show you this piece I recently performed in Nagasaki and Hong Kong. If I have a chance I'd like to include it as an encore."

"Bring it my dear. I vud like to look it over first."

"I'll see you tomorrow," she concluded.

"Buggatoff," the Maestro responded. "Shalom!"

"Shalom!" Clarissa repeated.

After she had put the phone down she was forced to laugh. 'What was that he just said to me? "Bugger off!" It can't have been. It must mean something else in Hebrew.'

Clarissa was at the Maestro's office right on time. He greeted her cordially. He was the typical, European conductor with a large mass of unruly white hair, a wrinkled forehead and angular chin, atop of a wiry, lean body. He looked over her manuscript of 'Gilded Snow'.

"Interesting," he said at length. "It vud orchestrate vell. Maybe you should consider zat."

"I'm not sure," Clarissa said hesitating. "It's really a lyrical piece."

"You may play it as an encore," he agreed. "Zere vill be two curtain calls before zee encore. I vill take the second call and then call you back. Now, vud you like coffee?"

As they enjoyed two mugs of coffee Clarissa began to warm to the Maestro. She plucked up courage and asked the question that had haunted her all night. "What exactly does 'Bugger off' mean?"

The Maestro laughed. "Buggatoff! You haven't heard much Hebrew before?"

232

"No," Clarissa admitted. "I was only here once and that was many years ago when I played in Tel Aviv."

"You must have thought I told you to bugger off," he said with laughing eyes. "Zat's the reaction of most foreigners. It merely means Good Evening. 'Buggatoff Shalom' is just our vay of opening or closing a speech. It's a little more formal zan Shalom."

"Well, I guessed it was something like that," Clarissa said with a smile. "It just sounds so strange when you first hear it."

"Oh, there are a lot of strange verds in modern Hebrew. Many of our new Hebrew verds have come in to zee language viv zee immigrants. They are old German, French, English and Russian verds that have become Hebrew."

Clarissa grinned, "I don't think 'Bugger off' is one of them."

"No, zat's more traditional Hebrew," the Maestro admitted.

The rehearsal went well. After a lunch break they reconvened and Clarissa played 'Gilded Snow' through for Maestro Goldstein to hear properly. As always the images of Joshua and Marcus returned. More than ever before, she was convinced that she saw Jeremy's face where Joshua stood.

Maestro Goldstein was a popular conductor and drew a packed crowd to the Symphony Hall. The Rachmaninoff was well received as always. After the cello piece, the Grieg and the Debussy brought back the lyrical mood. Fiery Listz Hungarian dances concluded the concert, bringing out the similarities between some Israeli music and that of gypsy Europe. The crowd stood for the curtain call. Clarissa received her bouquet. Maestro Goldstein came out one more time to thunderous applause, and with all standing, he invited Clarissa back to play 'Gilded Snow'.

The piece was greeted with the same success as in Nagasaki. The audience stood. Maestro Goldstein winked at Clarissa and held out his hand for her. They took a final bow. But as they left the stage the strength of the familiar images stayed with Clarissa.

There was a knock at her open dressing room door, as Clarissa sat taking off her stage make-up. She turned around.

"That was marvellous," Jeremy said as he came over and kissed her lightly in congratulation. "It sounds so much better in a real concert hall."

"You came," Clarissa said softly. "You really didn't have to."

"I wouldn't have missed it for anything," he assured her. "Have you eaten?"

"No, I never do before I perform."

"I suspected that. Why don't we have that late dinner together?"

"Thanks. That would be nice." After the drive up from Haifa to Jerusalem Clarissa felt a lot more comfortable around Jeremy. She felt more trusting in her own emotions and therefore, more secure in her relationship with David.

"Good," Jeremy announced, "because I've made reservations at this late night Bistro." He stood up and bowed. "Whenever the star is ready this stage-door-Johnny is at your service."

"I'll be five minutes," Clarissa said. "I've got rid of the stage make-up, but now I'd better put on my regular face."

"You look beautiful all the time," Jeremy stated.

When Clarissa was ready, they took a taxi to a little bistro set beside the city walls outside the Jaffa Gate. The restaurant looked out over a rock-strewn, grassy area between the highway that skirted the medieval walls. The King David Hotel was only a couple of blocks away. They sat at a cozy table inside the bistro. It was too cold to sit outside on the terrace. Jeremy ordered a small bottle of Chianti wine although Clarissa only had a few sips. Soon they were enjoying plates of pasta with wonderful sauces that would probably make them feel like they were dreaming all night.

"I have all day tomorrow before my flight leaves," Clarissa said, after Jeremy had paid the bill. "Why don't we explore some of the sights together?"

"I'm free. I don't start at the Hebrew University until Thursday. Where would you like to go?"

"Well, I suppose we should go to Bethlehem, but I find all these religious sights terribly commercial. I'd really rather just go out to the Mount of Olives and the Garden of Gethsemane. The nuns at my lodging tell me it's very peaceful and that there's a church there dedicated to Mary Magdalene."

"Good, then that's what we'll do. Why don't you come over to the 'King David' when you're ready in the morning? Bring your baggage with you and we can store it so it'll be easy to take out to the airport. We can just take a taxi from the hotel and do whatever we like. Why don't you walk over to the hotel with me and I'll get you a taxi to the convent?"

They walked along the path that took them through the parkland in front of the bistro and across to King David Street. At the hotel, Jeremy arranged a taxi for Clarissa and they said good night.

Later, while sleeping at the convent, Clarissa dreamed about Fiona MacAllister. She didn't actually see Fiona in her dream, but she knew she was dreaming about Joanna, Jeremy's wife back in the First Century ....

As Maria, she was with Jeremy who once again seemed like the man who always appeared at that metamorphic moment when she played 'Gilded Snow.' He was dressed in a dirty, white robe and they seemed to be in some run-down vineyard on the outskirts of a dusty, Palestinian village. Tares grew freely among the vines and twisted columbines clung to the arms of the past season's growth. Clarissa could see the disappointment on Jeremy's face.

"I used to work this vineyard, Maria," Jeremy confided. He pointed up the hill at a little, stone house built beside the boundary wall. "This was my home." It was derelict. He put his arms around Clarissa's shoulders and they slowly walked towards the house. "I was married once, Maria. My wife, Joanna, died here when the plague came to Nazareth."

Clarissa saw tears welling in Jeremy's eyes, but couldn't reconcile herself to her own emotions, let alone his. Becoming semi-conscious in her slumber, Clarissa's mind took over from the dream ....

'Jeremy was married to Fiona MacAllister two thousand years ago after all,' she thought as she fought those pangs of jealousy.

Momentarily the figure of the lithe nurse danced before her. In her mind she saw Jeremy chatting her up on deck. She thought of David sharing his love with this 'babe'. Then she comforted herself. 'She's dead. As Joanna, she died two thousand years ago.'

Drifting back into sleep, she picked up her dream as Maria in the First Century ....

'Why is it when I have had so many men fall at my feet that this one man whom I really want eludes me? Is it because he has already given his love to this woman? Holy Moses! He accepts my caresses of comfort and he treats me with deep respect, but I just don't seem to be able to arouse his passion. Joshua spends much of his time with me, but the union for which I so long seems constantly denied me.' Maria looked at the unkempt vines and the crude, stone house. 'Perhaps this is the reason. Perhaps this old vineyard and its memories are what stand between us.'

Jeremy, who Clarissa so certainly identified with the Jesus figure of 'Gilded Snow', led her up to the house. They peered into the gloomy interior. They saw some scattered, broken shards, the evidence of wandering inhabitants. Along one wall there were a few pots and jars.

"I built this house for Joanna," Jeremy said. "We were so happy here. Joanna was always laughing. Now, it seems to be only a place for itinerant peasants."

They stepped out into the light again.

"I buried her by the wall up there," Jeremy said, pointing up from the house. Wild flowers were growing among weeds that ran along its base. "Do you mind if I pick some of these and leave them at her grave?"

"Of course not, Joshua!" Maria said, delighted that he was at least sensitive to her feelings.

As Joshua, Jeremy stooped and picked the prettiest of the flowers and then placed them in a small bouquet on a ledge in the wall. "For you, Joanna," he said quietly. "It was not God's will that we could stay together. God set me a different task which is yet to be fulfilled."

Clarissa could see that as Joshua, Jeremy was crying.

"I loved you," he whispered, before turning to hold her, seeking comfort in his Maria's arms ....

Clarissa awoke sobbing tears of joy. She felt a great relief. The load of her jealousy somehow had been taken from her shoulders. She rejoiced in the love that Jeremy must have had for Fiona in their first century lives, but she also knew that the last barrier had come down in the mystery of Joshua and Maria. Jeremy Dyson was assuredly the man whom she had loved two thousand years ago when they had stood beneath the waterfall of Gennesar. Although she still could not prove it to others, she had no doubt that his soul had been that of the Christ, the transfigured man who haunted her in the music that she had created. Hastily, she recorded everything she had experienced in her dream journal for fear that this moment of recognition might become lost. She turned to the page where she had listed the characters. She put a question mark after the entry 'Jeremy Dyson - Remus Augustus' and added underneath, 'Jeremy Dyson - Joshua (Jesus Christ)' and beneath that, 'Fiona MacAllister - Joanna (Jesus' wife)'. 'I suppose it might be possible that Jeremy could have been both persons,' she reasoned. 'Soul energy never dies.'

Early the following day, Clarissa repacked her bags. Her flight from Jerusalem to London was not until eleven in the evening. She checked her tickets. At London's 'Gatwick' she would change to 'Northwest' for the direct flight to Minneapolis and St. Paul.

She took a taxi to the King David Hotel.

Jeremy was waiting for her in the lobby.

The road from the Damascus Gate of the Old City curved round to the right to follow the contour of the Kidron valley just as it had two thousand years before. The valley was still an open space between the outer areas of Jerusalem and the Old City. The Mount of Olives continued to dominate the landscape to the east. Much of the mount was barren, although patches of wild flowers lent color to its upper slopes. The Kidron Valley itself was a mass of colorful blooms and attracted migrating birds flying up from Sinai to greet the European spring. Between the valley and the upper reaches of the mount was an area of trees, gnarled olives, probably up to a thousand years old. Just below the olives Clarissa and Jeremy could see the Church of Saint Maria Magdalena. The building's facade reminded Clarissa of the Franciscan monastery on the top of Mount Tabor. Colorful frescoes filled the pediment above a colonnaded porch. The onion domes behind, however, bore witness to Russian Orthodox caretakers. A few minutes later, the taxi halted in the forecourt.

Clarissa and Jeremy peeked inside the building. Unlike the Franciscan Church on Mount Tabor, it was dank and dim. Heavy incense hung on the air and they could hear the chant of Russian priests. Candles burned in large numbers in front of ancient icons and gold leaf was encrusted on the screen that separated the priests from the people.

Clarissa thought of the Jesus of her visions. 'No way would he recognize what the Churches have made of him,' she thought. 'He has only appeared to me as a man of light - not this sombre darkness. He has come to me as a man who carried his light in his heart, touching all whom he met with an inner power. He encouraged us to reach for that light. David described it so well the other day. What did he say? The Christ-likeness is within us all if we will just open our hearts and let that light show.'

A priest pulled on a heavy, incense censer so that it swung across the chancel. Blue-gray smoke followed its path. The pungent, sickly-sweet odor filled Clarissa's nostrils. It was heavy, so heavy.

"I can't take it," she whispered to Jeremy. "This church is dedicated to my past life. How dare they interpret the beauty of my friendship with the Christ and our love for light and nature in this oppressive way."

Clarissa ran from the church back out into the open air where she could breathe freely and feel the warmth of the spring sun.

"Had enough?" the taxi driver said in a thick accent.

"No! I want to stay here, but in the garden!" Clarissa stated. "That's where people might find the Christ. Not in the dark caverns of that somber place, but in the light of the grove amid the sound of the birds."

The taxi driver could see that Clarissa had become a little emotional. "You want me to wait?" he asked.

"No, that's alright. We can pick up another cab from the rank here. How much do we owe?"

The taxi driver gave her the amount. "Are you sure you don't want to go on to Bethlehem?"

"No. These religious shrines are all the same. If Jesus came back he would be appalled by what he would find. We would rather stay here, and walk out in the hills among the wild flowers. For us that's much closer to God," Clarissa said firmly as she gave him the necessary shekels.

She could see that the taxi driver was a little upset.

"You don't like my country?" he asked.

"It's nothing personal," Clarissa explained. "I love your country. I just prefer nature to churches."

The cab driver shrugged his shoulders and drove away.

"I think he was Russian," Jeremy said. "He was disappointed that you didn't like the Russian Orthodox Church."

"I shouldn't really have said what I did," Clarissa admitted, "but I just don't think this is what Jesus would have wanted. What do you think, Jeremy? If anyone should have an opinion, you should."

"Some churches are very beautiful. I'm not religious, but I can appreciate their architectural merit. Through the ages Western architecture developed for the most part through church architecture."

"The buildings are alright," Clarissa agreed, "but it's all this mumbo-jumbo that goes on inside them. I'm sure Jesus never meant us all to go about with sombre faces and call ourselves miserable sinners. He was a man of emotion and love, light and laughter. If you were Jesus two thousand years ago, Jeremy, you were married. You knew how to love in flesh and blood. You knew how to laugh. You knew how to cry."

"But I never said I was Jesus," Jeremy corrected her.

"But I believe you were, Joshua," Clarissa said looking Jeremy straight in the eye. "Let's go in the garden. I need to talk to you."

As they walked towards the entrance gate to the Garden of Gethsemane, Jeremy felt like a schoolboy being led to his headmaster. He felt just a little frightened. Clarissa had suggested so emphatically that he was Jesus two thousand years ago. The mere thought felt like a religious crime. But he knew in his heart that this possibility had crossed his own mind many times since Africa. He'd just been afraid to really confront it. But on the other hand, in Sepphoris he had seen himself as a Hebrew slave named 'Joshua', working under the Romans. There was nothing in the Bible about that in the life of Jesus. The Bible had never said Jesus was married. Yet he was quite sure that Fiona had been his first century wife. But something had sparked Clarissa off. Something had made her the headmaster he was being led toward.

They walked down through the wrought-iron gate that was labelled in both Hebrew and English, 'The Garden of Gethsemane'.

The garden was really a series of terraces. Young olives were growing in lines. Clarissa began to walk from one terrace down to the next as Jeremy followed. Below the terraces she could see there was an area of lush vegetation. Willows, various palms and a host of blooming iris grew. The water that was channeled along each terrace from a stream above, emptied into a babbling brook that ran out into the colorful carpet of the Kidron Valley.

Clarissa was surprised and pleased that there were so few people in the garden. Perhaps she had picked a moment between tour buses. The nuns had said that the garden was a popular place with tourists of all denominations. She sat and looked out through the trees. She could see the mosque at the Dome of the Rock. Jeremy joined her.

A strange sense of peace descended on Clarissa and she closed her eyes to the warm sun.

Clarissa imagined herself to be back in the First Century. She felt the presence of her man standing beside her in that grassy glade. She was convinced that it was Jeremy's soul, in his incarnation as Jesus, that stood there ....

"I love this place," the man said. "Higher up beyond the olive groves you get an even better view of the Temple and the city, but it's prettier here."

Clarissa looked across the Kidron. The mosque of the Dome of the Rock had disappeared. A larger, even more splendid building stood in its place. The city walls, which looked much the same, were mounted by a white marble colonnade of Greek design. Behind them rose up a great Temple Sanctuary with a Semitic facade. Huge bronze doors caught the sunlight. Where the Dome of the Rock had stood, greasy smoke from a pyre drifted upward into the heavens. To the right and of a slightly different hue, a fortress tower rose to a height that almost rivalled that of the great sanctuary. Otherwise, the domes and roof tops of the surrounding buildings had that common, but beautiful glow that emanates from the yellow limestone. On the far side, behind the Temple, Clarissa thought she could see what appeared to be a Roman aqueduct in two or three tiers of even arches, snaking its way through the western city.

Knowing that she was Maria of Magdala, Clarissa could feel the pressure of the man's embrace and nestled her head against his shoulder. She knew he was Jesus and was overcome by a sense of submission and inner peace.

As Jesus, he was pensive and silent. Maria sensed an apprehension and could see in his gaze an uncertainty. "Don't be afraid, Joshua," she said lovingly. "Let me soothe you and calm you. I know what you like best. Whatever is causing you to feel afraid, take this moment to relax and melt into my arms. Nobody can harm us here."

"The birds sound so lovely, Maria," Jesus said at length releasing his hold and taking Clarissa's hands so that they could stand and just look into each others' eyes.

As Maria of Magdala, Clarissa instinctively knew that at least this once Jesus wanted to share his ultimate love with her. Something was holding him back, but she pressed herself against him to reassure Jesus that she also wanted him. To consummate their union would not destroy the deep spirituality that had grown up between them, but on the contrary, Maria felt it would only bond it. She stroked his hair. "None of them can see us here," she whispered in his ear. "We can be ourselves. We can freely share our joy."

Jesus' anxious gaze melted at her words. He put his arm around her waist and walked her down to the flat part of the glade beside the babbling stream. There they lay together.

As they soothed each other in gentle caresses of love, both their passions rose. There could be no turning back. Their union became complete in the secrecy of the grove. They became truly one. Maria felt more sexually fulfilled than at any time in her life. She had felt the spark of God in their lovemaking. Joshua's divine presence had never seemed so real or so close. In the warmth of that afternoon sun they were transported into an ecstasy that rose above all worries and took them to a place of heavenly bliss. They shared with each other their ultimate joy, and yet as their ardor cooled in the aftermath of their passion, worries returned. "Thank you, Maria," Jesus whispered in her ear as he stroked her hair nervously. "I've so longed to be with you ever since we left Gennesar. In Bethany I began to despair that we could ever again experience the love that we began to share in Galilee." He looked away for a moment. "I'm not sure we should ever have left Galilee."

"Why, Joshua?"

"It's dangerous for me here, Maria. I've come to realize how much I've changed," he said sadly.

This caught Maria off guard. They both sat up. Maria rested her head on Jesus' shoulder. "In what way have you changed?" she asked. She could only sense how much this fulfillment had caused their love to grow.

Jesus began to cry. "Jerusalem is not ... not the same," he stammered slowly as he looked at the city through the trees.

"Don't weep," Maria said as she wiped away his tears. "What makes you cry? Is it something I've done? Do you regret what we've just shared?"

She imagined the worst. 'What if he leaves me now like so many other men? Was I too demanding? Am I ... ?'

Jesus looked at her and tried to smile as he felt her concern. "It's not you, Maria. I weep for Jerusalem. I used to love Jerusalem. The city was a source of much inspiration for me. There was a sense of excitement in the learning here and a spiritual aura at the Temple. Like the Sadducees and Temple Pharisees I used to feel a great pride in our traditions and institutions. It was a privilege and joy for me to teach in the Temple court." Silently he stared ahead. "I sense big changes in Jerusalem," he said at length. "I see fire and complete destruction."

"Why?" Maria asked somewhat relieved that he had not expressed guilt over their recent passion, or its possible consequences.

"The Temple has lost its God-center, Maria. I used to feel the power of the Holy Spirit within the Temple courts. Now I only sense commercialism, power and greed. Maybe it's just within me, but the Temple doesn't seem to belong to us anymore. Perhaps it's the Roman presence, the great tower fortress that has been built overlooking the sacred courts. But equally it has to be our High Priests and Sanhedrin leaders. They have made the Temple their own. They have made our Holy place into their personal powerhouse." Jesus turned and looked right into Maria's eyes. "They're jealous of me," he said. "They see how the people flock to me because many have more confidence in my healing power than in sacrifices at the Temple. The Sanhedrin Council is also afraid of me because they think that every time I draw a crowd the Romans will be suspicious that I'm inciting rebellion. So, I've become a source for a greater fear and hatred that they wouldn't otherwise have!"

"You, Joshua?" Maria laughed. "You've never encouraged anyone to rebel against the Romans!"

"True, Maria, but how do they know that?"

He kissed her lightly on the lips, cupping her face in his hands. "You know my intentions are only to spread our divine love," he said, "because you understand me better than anyone else, better even than Cephas. You are the only one, Maria, who really understands the power of this divine love within."

Maria's stomach pulled as her body glowed to his words.

"But why do you say that you've changed?" Maria asked, bringing Jesus back to his original concern.

"Because I can no longer put my faith in our old ways, Maria. Tomorrow I'll make my Passover sacrifice at the Temple, but it has somehow lost its meaning. I was looking forward to the celebration of Passover with James, Rachel and Mother, but now I'm not sure. We Jews have always been very confident in our traditions and institutions, but I'm losing that confidence. I'm outwardly a Jew, but inwardly I'm no longer a Jew."

Maria was puzzled. "What do you mean?"

"God didn't just choose us Jews to be his people. We are all God's people. All of us have the divine spark within us - the Romans and Greeks as much as us Jews. I've seen how some Romans have opened their hearts to God and allowed their divine love to show through. Romans have come to me to be healed and some have shown greater faith than righteous Pharisees."

"But they don't obey our Law," Maria observed.

Jesus laughed. "So? Who among even the most righteous of Jews or Gentiles have actually found their way to the heart of God by slavish obedience to the Law? If they had they wouldn't expect a savior. Doesn't following the Law then, mean that anyone can follow an even greater law - God's law of love? Did the Law ever mean that much to you, Maria? But I've never felt that your ignorance of the Law has ever held back the inner love that radiates from you. You're a spark of God. The divine light shines from you. That is the law of love."

Maria felt herself blushing. "Maybe, but not as much as it shines from you, Joshua. When we were making love just a short while ago I could feel the power of God flowing between us."

He squeezed her hand. "And so it is."

They sat in silence for a while. Jesus stared through the trees at the city. "Why can't the others understand that we all share the natural love of God?" he said at length. "I have spent so much time trying to teach them the reality of their own divinity. If they can see the divine love in me, why can't they see it in themselves?"

"Perhaps it's because they only see your God-like powers in your healing hands, Joshua," Maria answered with surprising acumen. "I have had the chance to see that divine love in our intimacy."

"My powers are not 'God-like', Maria," he clarified tenderly. "My powers are directly of the essence of God. Our God has sent me into the world so that I can make others realize that their souls too are expressions or sons of God. I was afraid at first, when I began to realize that we are sons of God. But I understand that so much better now. God showed me his power when he allowed me to raise Lazarus from the dead, but he has shown me the soft intimacy of his heart in the divine love that I have found in you. It's the same power, Maria, but somehow the divine love that can radiate from our hearts has a greater strength than the miraculous forces that have caused my name to be bandied about by many people. That's what the others still fail to understand. God is everywhere, Maria. He was there in the total freedom of our lovemaking, but he is also in all the little things of life we share with each other every day. The Law sometimes strangles us so that we lose sight of our real, divine strength as we search for the illusive miracle."

Maria gave a bemused smile as she looked up at Jesus in response. "I'm not sure what you mean, Joshua," she said, "but I know that if the light shines from me it's because of you. You've changed my life."

"I know," Jesus agreed, "but what I may have awakened in you has lived and still lives. Keep feeding on God's love with me Maria, for my strength is your strength. Everyone who believes that my powers are from the Holy Spirit that dwells within me can bathe in the same light and hear the small, still voice of God within themselves. They'll have the power to do greater things than me."

"You give me such strength," Maria said as she put her arms around him. She began to kiss him.

Jesus responded by gently caressing her ....

A glorious peace flowed through Clarissa as the image of Jesus faded. She looked out through the trees at the view across the Kidron.

The Temple was not there, only the golden dome and blue walls of the great mosque that stood on the site of the sacrificial rock.

"What happened?" Jeremy asked. "You look like you've been in a trance!"

Clarissa sat and stared vacantly. The special glow that emanated from deep within reminded her of those early pangs of teenage love that somehow with maturity become lost. She wrestled with it, but wanted to keep it forever.

"What's wrong?" Jeremy repeated.

"Nothing," she replied at length, as she turned and lay her head on his shoulder. "Nothing is wrong. I couldn't be happier. Jeremy, you were Jesus."

Jeremy was less afraid. He could see the great calm that had come over Clarissa. "Why do you think that?" he asked.

"Last night I dreamed about us. Don't be scared, I'm not suggesting anything about our present relationship. But I dreamed about us in the First Century. We were in your vineyard, Jeremy. You showed me the house you built for Joanna. You were sad because the vineyard was neglected and the house had been abused by itinerant peasants. Then you showed me Joanna's grave. You picked wild flowers and put them where you'd buried her. You explained to me how Joanna had died when the plague came to Nazareth. You lived in Nazareth, Jeremy. Your vineyard was just outside the village. You were Joshua of Nazareth."

Jeremy felt a tear fall slowly down his rugged cheek into the folds of his beard. "Joanna died?" he said slowly.

"Yes," Clarissa confirmed, "but there's lots more."

"What?"

"Something happened the night we were together in Africa. I couldn't tell you about it at the time. I was afraid. It was stupid really. Somehow I was afraid that the past might disrupt the present, but it doesn't. The past might reflect the present, but it can't change it. In the same way we think we can anticipate or influence the future now, but when that future comes and is of its own, what we've done will have no further influence."

"Very philosophical, Clarissa," Jeremy said, "but what happened in Africa?"

"I dreamed I was with you, Jeremy. We were naked together under this waterfall. I was Maria and you were Joshua. It was one of the most erotic and sensuous dreams that I've ever had and it gave me these terrible guilt feelings. That's why I hardly spoke to you on the way up through the Red Sea. I was afraid, Jeremy."

Jeremy put his arms around Clarissa and gently kissed her. "I can't believe what you've just told me," he whispered. "I had the same dream. Forgive me Clarissa, but it was very hard to share that room with you. I think I fell in love with you that night. I watched you Clarissa, as you crossed the room in the moonlight. I saw you as you lay beneath your mosquito net like Aphrodite. I wanted to suppress my feelings for you, but I couldn't. And then, I dreamed about you. Just as you've said, we were together. We stood under a waterfall touching each other in a magic moment of love. I was Joshua and you were Maria, but when I awoke I didn't really believe we were Joshua and Maria. I was ashamed of my own lust. I felt like I'd committed adultery even though I'd never touched you."

"Me too," Clarissa admitted, tears of relief forming in her eyes. "I felt I'd betrayed David and yet, at the same time, when I saw you with Fiona I was jealous. It was a terrible week. That's funny actually, because it was the week that David always calls 'Hate week' - the most difficult point on any World Cruise."

Clarissa hugged Jeremy as tears streamed down her face. "I saw us together again just now," she revealed. "We were together here two thousand years ago. Joshua and Maria made love in this very place. It was beautiful, Jeremy. It was the fulfillment of everything that we felt for each other at the waterfall in Gennesar. That really happened, Jeremy. I was at Gennesar with David when you were in Sepphoris three days ago. That waterfall is still there."

They held each other in silence for a long time. Both of them now choking on their emotional tears of joy.

At length Clarissa stood up and blew her nose. "Let's walk down into the glade," she said.

Jeremy got up from the rock. Together they retraced the steps of Joshua and Maria to the flat, grassy area among the palms where they believed Jesus and Mary Magdalene had fulfilled their love. They stood there in silence just holding each other by the hand. Now, in the Twentieth Century, only the migrating birds were witnesses to the drama.

Emotionally drained, they then began to climb back up through the terraces to the entrance. A man in dirty Arabian robes stood by the gate. He looked at Clarissa as she approached.

"Very peaceful," he said as he touched his forehead in salutation.

The man had several missing teeth and a wrinkled face, but in his smile Clarissa saw a fusion of Jeremy and Joshua. He reached out his hand and placed a small metallic object in hers. "This is for you," he said.

Clarissa looked down at the object. It was a small, irregularly-shaped coin.

"Roman drachma," the man informed her. "That is coin from time of Jesus."

Clarissa looked at it closer. She could make out a Roman head with a crown of laurels.

"It could be very valuable," the man continued. "I give it you. Now, you want taxi?"

"Yes," Clarissa answered. "Is there a taxi there?"

The man whistled as if he were a New York controller. A taxi parked by the Russian church started up its motor and drove towards them.

Clarissa and Jeremy got inside.

The Arab stood holding the taxi door and looked in at them with a pleading face. "I am poor man," he said.

Clarissa looked in her pocket-book. She had a ten shekel note and two coins. Otherwise her bills were all large. "Twelve shekels," she suggested.

"You don't have twenty?" the Arab pushed.

"No, only twelve," Clarissa insisted.

Jeremy reached into his pocket. "Here's three more," he said as he passed over three coins.

The Arab grinned as he happily took the money. "Shalom! May Allah be praised!" He touched his forehead again and closed the car door.

"The King David Hotel," Jeremy said.

Over lunch at the hotel Jeremy suggested that they would have time to go to the archeological museum during the afternoon. "I can help make it come alive for you," he said excitedly, "and then, after that, I'll take you to the airport."

• • • • • • • •

During the afternoon of the day that the 'Prince Regent' docked at Kusadasi, David took a taxi out to Ephesus. The cab driver reminded him that the ancient city had been the terminus of major caravan routes passing through the province of Asia and had been a bridgehead between east and west, much as Istanbul is today. David suspected a little local bias in the latter explanation, but seeing that the man prided himself on being an amateur guide, he asked him about the Temple of Diana. "Is there anything left of this wonder of the ancient world?"

"Very little," the driver replied. "It was destroyed in the Third Century. Most the stones were used later to build the Byzantine church of St. John." The taxi was rounding the hill behind Ephesus to drive up to the parking lot where tourists get out in order to walk down through the city. "Look, you can see the marble pillars of the church of St. John over there below the Selcuk fortress," he continued. "The Temple of Artemis was over there, somewhere between the church of St. John and the entrance to the ancient site."

David searched the area to the left. A lone pillar stood in a rock-strewn meadow. The taxi pulled into the parking lot. Most of the passengers had taken the morning tour and so there was not the mass of buses that he remembered from his last visit. A path led off to the left and was marked by a sign that confirmed that the giant pillar in the meadow was from the great Temple of Artemis. The pillar gave little indication as to what the huge structure had really looked like.

David moved to the turnstiles on the other side of the parking area and paid for his ticket. He produced his seaman's pass and got in for half-price. He started on the gentle walk through the scattered excavations of the upper city's state agora, before taking the steeper descent down towards the library of Celsus and the main street. Wild flowers grew in profusion around the marble stones and sprang up in cracked corners of the magnificent, mosaic floors. Shortly after he passed the almost perfectly restored arch of Hadrian on Curetes Street, David wandered into a labyrinth of small shopping lanes. Here, there was more use of Roman brick. He stumbled across the first century public conveniences. There must have been thirty marble seats around three sides of a square. 'Quite remarkable for its time,' David considered. 'The world really didn't catch up in matters of hygiene and plumbing until the Nineteenth Century.' As he looked down into the cavern of the sewage pit below these comfortable seats, he was swiftly reminded that it was an army of city slaves that kept them clean. 'That would be some first century past life,' he thought, 'to have been a latrine sweeper. But somehow nobody ever seems to remember a life like that!'

A little beyond the latrines, he found the back entrance to the principal brothel. It was hard to be sure whether he was in one vast establishment or amongst a mass of small operators in what could only have been described as the 'red light district' of this port city. The low walls of numerous cubicles showed the places of pleasure. Raised divans, some showing preserved wood from first century times, could still be seen against these walls. It was easy to reconstruct the gossamer curtains and note the sickly smells of exotic oils that were the stock in trade of the Roman whore house. In the midst of the brothel complex was the bath for the cleansing of the girls and a marble-pillared hall where clients could wait their turn whilst the tune of a fountain played beneath the open roof. David left the brothel at a lower level, coming out past merchants' stores into the great, wide street that ran from the library, past the principal marketplace, towards the theater and the site of the gymnasium.

This street was paved in smooth, white marble. Three or four steps led up to the pavement with its plinths and statues. It was easy to imagine the architrave that once ran along here to give shade from the Anatolian heat to those who browsed the shops of this expensive district. Opposite, a less elaborate promenade ran beside a wall that had once looked out over the commercial agora to the now land-locked harbor. The present view over grassy meadows, was once open sea filled with ships vying for space in one of the ancient world's most busy ports.

David crossed the marble street in front of the great facade of the library of Celsus and stood in the massive, triple-arched gate of Mazaeus and Mithridates leading into the agora. There, he envisaged the learned men of Roman times sitting in the shade of the portico discussing the important matters of the day. Returning to the main street, he approached the Great Theater. "This was the theater where St. Paul preached to the people," he muttered to himself. "Here, the apostle was lynched for disturbing the trade of Artemis." David could almost hear the crowd pouring out from the building shouting all manner of abuse. Then he heard a familiar voice call his name. "David!" it said. "I knew we would meet again."

He looked around. There were a few tourists climbing up the steps of the theater entrance. A small party of Japanese were some way behind him following a well-mounted pennant.

"Yes. Where are you?" he called back.

"I'm over here," the voice sounded again.

David turned to the left-hand wall. He couldn't believe what he saw. It was a woman in a blue robe with a white headdress. She was gliding, her feet not quite touching the ground and she had the face of Clarissa's mother. Surely it was Margaret Corrington? Around her there was a faint, iridescent glow, similar to that which he remembered when he had seen her face looking down from the painted ceiling of the dining room at Ballyporeen House. "Jesus Christ!" he exclaimed. "If I didn't know better I'd say that was Clarissa's mother!"

He felt he was only about eight feet from this seeming apparition, but he looked around to check if others in the street could see what he thought he was seeing. Nobody else seemed to have heard her or to be taking any notice.

When he faced her again the apparition seemed to say to him, "Take care of Maria, Linus. See that my grandson grows up to be strong, full of the light of his father. Light overcomes all. I am so happy to know that you and Maria also live in that light."

Then, the apparition was gone. There was nobody there. Had there been anything there? All David could see was the old wall and the colonnade of the agora below. He scratched his head. He knew what he had seen and heard, but still he doubted if he could really believe it. 'Perhaps it's the sun,' he thought. 'Maybe I should get one of those hats like the passengers wear.' But the words haunted him. Even if there had been nobody there he had sensed those words. He had at the very least conjured up a vision of his relationship with Maria two thousand years ago. 'Who was the grandson? Did the Virgin Mary have a child other than Jesus, or could it be .... ?' He quickened his pace, afraid of his own thoughts. He wanted to seek the comfort of the milling, tourist crowd and feel his feet firmly planted in present reality. He climbed the steps up into the theater, seeking his escape.

A guide was busy clapping his hands on the stage to show the excellence of the acoustics to a crowd of visitors seated in the middle terrace. David was comforted by the reality and sat and listened to what the man had to say. Apparently, twenty five thousand people had once been able to sit and listen among these stones. The tourists came and went. At length, feeling more himself again, David also left. He followed the harbor street with its tall columns that once had been the entrance to the thriving port area. The lower parking lot was just beyond the gymnasium on the right. David's taxi had driven around and was waiting.

"Do you want to go on to Mary's house?" the driver asked.

David remembered Jeremy Dyson's words - 'a building of the Tenth Century at the very earliest'. "I don't think so," he replied. 'It's still bogus,' he thought, 'although the guidebook actually claims the building to be of the Seventh Century.'

On the short drive back to Kusadasi, David considered the legend of 'Mary'. Jeremy Dyson had said that there was a strong tradition that Miriam, the mother of Joshua of Nazareth, lived out the latter part of her life in Ephesus. The legend was that she went there with John, the beloved disciple. Perhaps it was not so surprising that Margaret Corrington, whose characteristics he had felt in his visions of the Virgin Mary, should have seemingly appeared to him in that Ephesus street. There was such a strong sense of the First Century in every crevice of those magnificent ruins. Yet, he wondered if Clarissa's vision of Margaret as 'Miriam' had felt the same.

That night, after the 'Prince Regent' had left Kusadasi and was sailing towards the Dardanelles to make a stop at Istanbul, David thought he saw Clarissa's mother again.

She had called him 'Linus' when he had seen her translucent apparition in Ephesus. He recalled how he had seen himself as Linus Flavian, Pontius Pilate's assistant. As he thought about this while trying to sleep, he also recalled that Gloria Ainsworth had thought Linus Flavian to have been the Roman at Jesus' crucifixion and the officer with whom her father's friend, Joseph of Arimathea, had negotiated for Jesus' body.

When David did sleep, he felt himself as Linus again. In his dream he knew he was meeting Clarissa's mother, Margaret, in her twilight years. But she now looked like a different woman. She had all the features of those elderly widows from the Florida coast who cruised on the 'Prince Regent' every winter ....

They were outside the impressive Gate of Mazaeus in Ephesus. The forecourt was busy with people who had concluded business in the agora. Clarissa was also there as Maria in his dream. As Linus, David helped Margaret Corrington walk across the main street and up the steep slope of the road that led to the upper level of the city. They walked slowly. It was particularly hard for the old woman to climb up the slippery, marble slabs of the pavement.

"Rest here a while, Miriam," Clarissa said to her mother as they came to the area where had stood Hadrian's arch. The arch wasn't there. There was just a marble bench and a water fountain.

The three of them sat on the bench and looked down at the landscape below. They could see the headland and the open sea beyond. Many ships lay at anchor waiting to exchange cargoes before sailing on to Athens and Rome.

Margaret Corrington, as Miriam, took hold of Linus' hand. "I am so very happy," she said, "to have met you and known you. Soon I will go into the other worlds, but I will do so knowing that you and Maria have found each other. I knew even as your men killed my son, that you had seen his light. It's hard to believe that it has taken so long for destiny to bring you and Maria back to each other, but it was always meant to be. Blessed be God forever! God bless you both!"

"May the light of Christos bless you, Miriam," Linus said. "I thank you for your forgiveness."

As Maria, Clarissa kissed Linus Flavian on the cheek. "I love you, Linus," she said. Then she kissed Miriam. "Thank you for hiding Linus in Ephesus, Miriam. Your light and love has been our inspiration. My only regret has been the fact that you have never met Ben Joshua, your grandson."

The dream faded with the vision of the three of them seated on that marble bench ....

David awoke. The ship's engines told him that they were still cruising through the narrows of the Dardanelles. After crossing the Sea of Marmara they were due to arrive off Istanbul at seven. He still had time to doze a little longer.

• • • • • • • •

Jeremy got Clarissa to the airport in Jerusalem in good time. There was always such a thorough security check for 'El Al' flights. Every bag was hand searched after it had been through the 'x-ray' machine and before check-in at the counter. After check-in, Clarissa was subjected to further searches. A female security agent frisked her. Her hand baggage, strictly limited, was again opened for individual search and again submitted to 'x-ray' screening before she was allowed into the Gateway area.

The flight left on time, right on the dot of eleven. Clarissa could see the twinkling lights of Jerusalem and the illumination of the Dome of the Rock as the Boeing jet wheeled around the city. To the right, she also saw the floodlit facade of the Church of Saint Mary Magdalena above what she knew to be the garden of Gethsemane. As soon as the seat belt sign was off and the Captain announced their flight path, Clarissa took out her dream journal. She hadn't had a chance to write up all the details of her extraordinary encounter with Jesus since returning from the garden at Gethsemane. She had barely completed the task, when the flight attendants came round with plastic trays containing the usual, synthetic-looking food hygienically sealed in foil.

"Kosher or non-kosher?" a pretty, dark-haired Israeli asked.

"Non-kosher," Clarissa replied.

She was served a dish of tasteless-looking chicken and vegetables that really didn't appear to be very different to that of her kosher neighbor. 'It must be in the sauce,' she thought. Although she did notice that he had gefiltefish for his first course, whereas she had aspic, country pate.

When the trays were cleared almost everyone was ready to settle down for the night. They would arrive at 'Gatwick' around six in the morning. There was the option to watch another mindless movie, but hardly anyone was tuned in to their headsets, and those who were appeared to be sleeping through the dialogue rather than enjoying the picture.

Clarissa wrestled with the poignant words she had written in her dream journal. 'God didn't choose us Jews to be his people. We are all God's people. All of us have the divine spark within us, the Romans and the Greeks as much as us Jews. I've seen how some Romans have opened their hearts to God and allowed their divine love to show through.'

'Whoever thought Christianity had an exclusive on the journey home to God,' Clarissa thought. 'My Joshua didn't say that. He asked why his disciples couldn't understand that we all share the power of God. He told me he had been trying to teach them the reality of their own God-spark. What was it he said? - "If they can see the divine love in me why can't they see it in themselves? The divine love that can radiate from our hearts has a greater strength than the miraculous forces that cause people from all parts of the land to visit with me and share their need. That's what the others still fail to understand. God is everywhere. The Law sometimes strangles us so that we lose sight of our real divine strength in search of illusive miracles." Isn't that the problem with Christianity?'

With that thought, Clarissa dozed into that half-sleep which is all that anyone can expect curled up in a jet plane's narrow seat ....

She found herself in a garden of desecrated tombs almost as soon as her subconscious took over. It had been raining and the air was fresh. To her left was a dark, foreboding church with a big dome. She recognized it as the Church of the Holy Sepulchre, although outside the dream state this building wasn't placed in the garden of tombs, but surrounded by the bustle of Jerusalem's old city, the church actually lay within the medieval, Arabic walls. The church frightened Clarissa.

She went inside, but Jesus was not there. All she saw were candles burning before images of his face and the mighty, incense censer swinging from the dome. She could hear priests chanting behind a dark, lattice screen. The building was heavy with the aromatic smoke. She ran from the church back into the rain-washed air. At the bottom of the steps she saw Jesus' burial shroud. As she picked it up she thought she could make out the faint image of his face. It was hard to know whether it had the likeness of Jeremy's face, or that of the Arab at the Gethsemane gate. In the fuzzy image she could also see Doctor John as the Roman, Antonias. For a brief moment she even thought she read into it the face of Babis Demetris as Judas Iscariot, then it seemed as if the face of humanity appeared before her. It was almost as if the cloth was pulsating before her eyes. In terror she screamed, throwing the cloth to the ground.

Clarissa ran, but however fast she moved her legs she remained on the same spot with the church right behind her. A man came running towards her. She stopped in her stationary flight.

"What's the matter?" the man shouted with genuine concern.

At that moment Clarissa somehow realized that she was once again Maria.

"They've stolen his body!" she yelled. "They've taken it away!"

"Whose body?"

"My man's body! Joshua's body! He was murdered by them the other day. He was crucified for no reason!"

But the stranger was immediately distracted from Maria when he saw the desecration of the tombs.

"My tombs! What's happened?" he exclaimed as he surveyed the scene. "Who's been in here sabotaging my tombs?"

"I don't know," Maria answered. "Whoever was here stole Joshua's body."

"What are you talking about, woman? Who was Joshua? I didn't know about his burial!"

"We buried him in this tomb," Maria sobbed as she looked back at the foreboding church. "It was just before the Sabbath. He was crucified just a day and a half ago."

The man calmed down somewhat. "But, that's Joseph of Arimathea's mausoleum," he observed. "You couldn't bury him in there."

"How do you know it was Joseph's tomb?" Maria asked noting that this man seemed to be more than familiar with the burial ground.

"I'm the caretaker," he answered. "Tell me everything. I need to know what's happened here." He held out his hand to her. "Don't be afraid. Tell me the whole story."

The man sat down on a large, flat, round stone. He beckoned to Clarissa to join him. With their backs to the dark church Clarissa recalled what she could remember of all that she had witnessed as Maria. She also revealed her inner thoughts on the love that she had felt for her man. The emotion became too much for her and she broke down and cried.

"I loved him," she sobbed. "I really loved him."

The caretaker put his arm gently around her. "Maria, Joshua will always be in your heart."

As Maria, Clarissa looked at him. There was something strangely trustworthy about his face and around him she felt that she could see the light of God. She picked up the shroud still laying where she had thrown it, slowly unraveling it. "He was buried here. This was his loin-cloth which we used as his burial sheet." A ghostly face was imprinted on the cloth. It was awesome, but at the same time comforting. "Whoever stole his body couldn't take him away from me. He left his imprint behind."

The caretaker didn't know what to say. He stared incredulously at the face on the cloth. "It's unreal. It's as if he is trying to tell us something."

"The love that he gave to all who he met has not died," Maria said as a radiance came over her face. "His love was the love of God and that spark of God can be kindled in all of us. Such love is everlasting and comes from our souls. We are all divine."

Maria's eyes sparkled in the strength of her belief when a sudden warmth spread, first over her smiling face and then throughout her body. 'What if I'm carrying his child?' she thought. 'What greater expression of his eternal love could he have left with me than that?'

The caretaker smiled, unknowing of her thoughts. "Can I take you home? This has been a great shock to you."

Maria looked up at the caretaker. It all came to her in that moment of supreme compassion. She saw in his face Joshua's divine love ....

Clarissa stretched in her aircraft seat as she awoke. She reflected on her dream. 'It was just what I felt Joshua taught Maria in that experience at Gethsemane. Whenever anyone encounters the radiance of another person's divine love they are encountering the 'Spirit of God'. It's just what Jesus tried to teach us two thousand years ago - we are all sons of God, for within us dwells God's spirit. What did Jesus say to his apostles at their last supper? Something like, "Every time you eat and drink, remember that just as this food and drink feeds your bodies, so does God feed you spiritually."'

In the face of the stranger in her dream, who had for no compelling reason shown Maria his compassion, Clarissa sensed Jesus' divine love, just as Maria had done two thousand years before. She had felt a supreme contentment. The dark, foreboding church and the stolen body of her dream no longer seemed important. The importance of a body had been replaced in her mind by the openness of her heart receiving the light of Soul. She knew as she considered the stranger's face that she had found the consciousness of Christ that her mother had so often talked about. She thought of David and her great love for him and she knew why her mother had written, 'I now know that I shall go into the other worlds in the knowledge that you and Clarissa will be together in the light of Christos'.

Clarissa raised her window blind. A gray line of dawn broke the dark horizon. A few minutes later the cloud mass below them caught the first rays of the rising sun. Soon the 'El Al' plane would touch down in 'Gatwick'. It would be a long day, but by evening Clarissa knew that she would be home on the lake in Minnesota.

• • • • • • • •

Clarissa awoke from a deep sleep when the phone rang about midnight.

"Hi darling!"

It was David.

"Oh! Hi..." Clarissa said sleepily. "Are you in Athens?"

"Well, Piraeus," David explained. "It's great here now. They have direct dialing at the dock."

"What time is it?"

"About nine o'clock on a sunny, Greek morning," David said cheerfully. "Sounds like you got back safely."

"I got in about five. I was home by six," Clarissa informed him as she became more alert. "It wasn't a bad flight and 'Northwest' made it direct from 'Gatwick'."

"You're not pregnant are you?" David asked.

"What! I doubt it!"

"Are you sure?"

"Well, considering the number of times we made love over the past month I should be," Clarissa laughed. "But I don't think so. My period started almost the minute I got home!"

"I was just curious," David explained. "You see, I saw your mother in Ephesus. She spoke to me."

"What!"

"Yes. She called me 'Linus', but it was her, Clara. I knew it was her. She was dressed in this blue robe and white headdress. She had an iridescent glow and kind of glided a few inches off the ground."

"Are you alright?"

"I'm serious, Clara. I saw your mother," David repeated. "Well, I'm pretty sure it was her. She asked me to take care of Maria and to see that her grandson grows up to be strong. Well, you are Maria aren't you? That's why I was curious. Are you sure you're not pregnant?"

"I'll be breaking the laws of biology if I am. I'm positive, David. It's impossible. If you had asked me last week I wouldn't have known, but now I can be sure."

"Then maybe she was referring to a child of the First Century. I dreamed about her the same night, Clara. She was old and feeble, but she appeared in a different body-form and was dressed like an elderly Jewess of Biblical times. We were both with her as Maria and Linus. We helped your mother walk up the steep streets of Ephesus. There were two interesting things. We seemed to be a number, Clara - you and I. Maybe I was married to you in those days and we had children and grandchildren, hence your mother's comments."

Clarissa was slow to answer. "Married to Linus, the Roman officer with Pontius Pilate?"

"Yes, but we were older in this dream and we were definitely in first century Ephesus. The arch of Hadrian wasn't there, just a bench where the arch is now, which would have been true. Hadrian lived in the Second Century A.D. We all sat down there to rest."

"Oh my God!" was all Clarissa could say. "I don't believe this! What did Mother think about us being together?"

"She seemed very pleased. She said she knew at the time of Joshua's crucifixion that Linus Flavian had seen the light, even though it was under his command that the death sentence was carried out."

"When do you think we were married?"

"That wasn't revealed, but it looked like a recent match. You thanked your mother for hiding me in Ephesus. I guess that's how we came together. She said something to me that was very similar to what she wrote to me in Ireland. You see I've been writing down my dreams too, Clara."

"Do you think she knew that I was your first, true love in those days and that Marcus could have been our child?" Clarissa asked.

"I don't know darling, but I think it's very probable. Anyway, I just wanted to let you know. This is an expensive call. I can share more with you when I get home."

"I've got lots for you too," Clarissa added. "I had some incredible experiences in Israel. I've written them all down. It sounds like you're ready to join us believers now!"

"Maybe ... " was all David replied.

"Good. We'll have lots to discuss with Samantha and Jeremy."

"Take care, Clara. I love you."

"I love you too," Clarissa echoed. "I can't wait for us both to have a chance to spend some time at home."

"Bye, sweetheart!"

"Bye!"

They both hung up.

'I wonder why my mother told him I was pregnant,' Clarissa thought. 'One day maybe we will have a son, but it certainly isn't now.'

Clarissa drifted back into her disturbed sleep. She dreamed that as Maria she was having a child ....

She was in a sparsely-furnished room with a window that looked out on green hills and light-colored cliffs.

"Catrina!" she cried. "It's coming!"

A sensuous, Latin-looking woman nodded her head and held Maria's arms. "Push!" she cried.

Maria screwed up her sweat-stung eyes and pushed one more time for all she was worth. She tried twisting to ease the pain, but Catrina held her tight. Then there was a strange feeling of relief. Catrina let go and seconds later Clarissa saw her holding up the pink flesh of a baby boy.

Clarissa couldn't believe that all of a sudden the long, painful ordeal was over. There was 'Maria's' son, complete with just a suggestion of dark hair. As Maria, Clarissa tried to laugh with joy, but it hurt too much. "Ben Joshua!" she named the child in relaxed exhaustion.

She watched as Catrina washed the infant in a small bowl of water. Catrina wrapped him in a white cloth and set him down on the couch beside her. Catrina then attended to Maria, cleaning her from the trauma of the birth.

When Maria was comfortable, Catrina called for Joseph and Marcus. Clarissa recognized the face of Joseph of Arimathea and sensed the presence of Doctor John's boy as her first century son. She smiled proudly at Joseph as if he were the boy's father, but in her heart she knew he was not. It was Jeremy's essence that she thought she saw in the baby's face.

Marcus kissed her on her forehead.

"Marcus, this is your brother, Ben Joshua," she proudly announced, as she clutched the bundle of new-born flesh that lay wrapped in a swaddling cloth.

Marcus grinned. "Shalom, Joshua," he said as he greeted the infant, taking hold of his little hand between his thumb and forefinger ....

Clarissa remembered no more, but she knew she had slept soundly when she awoke about three. The jet lag had caught up with her. From then on she tossed and turned until dawn broke. Before she made herself a cup of tea she had already recorded the dream in her journal.

'I can't wait to share this with Samantha!' she thought.

· · · · · · · ·

C larissa met Samantha in a small coffee shop in Ridgedale. They both indulged themselves with a few fresh, home-made pastries.

"It's so good to see you again," Clarissa said as they held their large cups of cappuccino.

Samantha observed Clarissa's sun-bronzed skin from many days in the Indian ocean. "You too, Clarissa. You look so well. I love the tan!"

"It was a wonderful trip. It was so great that I could spend so much time with David. You won't believe some of the things I have to tell you. This was an extraordinarily revealing time for us."

"The dreams?"

"Yes. Sleeping dreams, waking dreams, day dreams - the revelations have been quite remarkable," Clarissa explained. "I've brought my journal. I took your advice. I've written absolutely everything down. David's been doing the same."

"So David has had revelations in his dreams too?"

"Very much so, although he's sometimes still loathe to admit it,"

Clarissa acknowledged. "Our first century past lives seem to have been closely interwoven."

"That's often what brings people together in later lives, Clarissa. There was probably karma to work out."

"Possibly, but this is almost more than karma. Everyone we meet who becomes close to us seems to have been part of our story. Geography seems irrelevant. We've met people all over the world and had experiences in widely different places, but they all seem to have led to first century Palestine."

"Energy fields," Samantha said wisely. "You're giving off similar energies that bring you back to that time when your fields were fused."

"David would say you're getting a bit spaced-out, Samantha. There's one thing I would like to confide in you, though," Clarissa said, looking around in the Coffee shop to see that nobody was listening to them. "The central character in all our experiences seems to be Jesus."

"That's hardly surprising if you're going to regress to the First Century," Samantha suggested. "In retrospect, he's the most famous person of that time."

"Well, it's rather more than that. Do you remember my telling you about Jeremy Dyson?"

"Your architect friend?"

"Yes. Well ... I think Jeremy Dyson was Jesus. He sailed with us from India to Israel," Clarissa whispered, afraid to look her friend completely in the eye.

"So you think you have the hots for this architect? I won't say a word, you can trust me. So it was a rather romantic journey across the Indian Ocean?"

"Oh Samantha! shut up!" Clarissa said desperately. "It was nothing like that at all. If you want proof it's all here in my dream journal. I really believe that Jeremy Dyson was Jesus in a past life."

"Oh! I see," Samantha said shaking her head. "And do you know how many people think they were Jesus in a past life?"

Clarissa looked blank.

"Hundreds that can be spoken of, thousands who would never admit it! In almost every mental institution in the land there's probably someone who thinks he was Jesus Christ."

Clarissa blushed. She felt very insecure. She had been so confident that Samantha would understand. "You don't believe me, do you?"

"I didn't say that. I'm just warning you before we begin," Samantha answered as she finished her coffee. "For all of those who are mentally unbalanced and have hallucinations that they were Napoleon, Ghengis Khan, Buddha or Jesus Christ, there are just as many who are perfectly sane. Most of them keep these thoughts completely to themselves, bottling them up in fear, lest anyone should find out and lock them away. Of course I believe you, Clarissa. Your reaction only makes me believe you more." Samantha reached out across the table for Clarissa's hand and grasped it to give emotional support. "Since that incarnation, there have probably been many lifetimes when Jesus lived new lives. Over the years the soul energy that was present in Jesus has probably been reincarnated in many bodies. If every generation between Jesus' time and the present has potentially raised up the Soul who at one time resided in Jesus Christ, think of the hundreds of times he has been trying to reach humanity through his reincarnations. In a sense the Soul of Christ grows and grows with each generation. The Soul of all our past lives is the soul energy that drives us today."

"Wow! I had never thought of it that way!"

"Sometimes we become too obsessed with all the glorious people we think we might have been in our past lives and we forget all the other little people who have shaped our soul character," Samantha said, releasing her hold on Clarissa's hand. She had a radiant smile. "I'm going to order another cappuccino. Can I get you one?"

"I think I'm ready," Clarissa agreed. "There's so much I want to share with you."

Samantha got up and went to the counter where she ordered the coffees. While she was gone, Clarissa opened her dream journal and started to refresh her memory of some of the most poignant coincidences.

At length Samantha returned with two more frothy cups. "Now, when did you first suspect that your architect friend might have been Jesus?"

"Well, I suppose it starts with me. Everything seems to indicate that I was Mary Magdalene in my first century past."

"Yes, you told me at Christmas. At that time this Jeremy guy thought he was a Roman soldier if I remember. He knew you in Marseilles two thousand years ago, or something like that."

"Yes, he thought he was a Roman called 'Remus Augustus'. He still believes that, but we now think that before he incarnated as Remus Augustus he might have been Jesus. Jesus was crucified just before Remus Augustus would have been born."

"Oh! Wild!" Samantha said excitedly. "So he could have been two different people during your first century lifetime?"

"Yes. What's more, Samantha, I'm inclined to believe now that my son, whom Remus Augustus saw in Massilia that time when he saw me as Mary Magdalene, was actually his son by me from his previous life as Jesus!"

"Run that by me again?" Samantha asked. "I'm not sure whether I got that. It's very confusing, but I think you are saying that you and Jesus had a son!"

"I think I had two sons in the First Century, Samantha. The first was a child who in this life is David's nephew, Simon Bishop. What was even more interesting if you remember, was that I seem to have been married to Simon's father, Dr. John Bishop. Maybe he was a Roman named Antonias, but I'm sure Dr. John doesn't know it."

They laughed.

"I was fairly sure that I was Mary Magdalene when we met at Christmas," Clarissa continued, "but I wasn't so sure that I really knew Jesus. Only the Bible stories told me that, and they don't say much."

"I remember," Samantha said sincerely. "So how have things changed?"

"I've had a number of encounters with Jesus," Clarissa explained. "Jeremy was right, in these encounters he always seems to be called 'Joshua'. I began to sense the presence of Jeremy in Joshua and more recently I even hear Jeremy's viewpoints when Joshua speaks."

"It's highly probable," Samantha reassured her. "If you had some sort of a relationship with this Joshua in the First Century, and tradition seems to say Mary Magdalene did have something going with Jesus, then it's more than likely that there was unfinished karma between you which has brought you together in this lifetime. If Jesus was crucified shortly after you became his girlfriend, it was an unfinished relationship."

"That's really what I'm feeling, but there are a few things that confuse the issue."

"Things that have been revealed to you?"

"Yes. Jesus was married."

"To you?"

"No, to a girl called 'Joanna'. That came to me in the dream state and it was confirmed by Jeremy separately in his own dream! Jesus' wife was also someone Jeremy met on board ship in this life, the ship's nurse, Fiona MacAllister, who incidentally was an old girlfriend of David's."

"No! Intriguing!"

"Well, Joanna died prematurely, Samantha. In one of my dream experiences, Jeremy, who was Joshua in the dream state, took me to their old home, a small, square, single-room house in a vineyard. He put flowers on Joanna's grave and explained to me that she died of a plague."

"So, you became Jesus' girlfriend after Joanna passed away?"

"Yes, but I don't know what happened to Antonias. I mean it looked like we were married, but he just disappears."

"Doctor John - David's brother-in-law?"

"Yes. It's never been revealed to me what happened to him, but if you promise not to say anything, I'll let you into a secret."

"I can't wait. Your revelations are full of secrets!"

"While I was married to Antonias, or Doctor John if you prefer the twentieth century parallel, I had a remarkable lesbian experience. Now, don't get worried, Samantha, I'm not a lesbian, but this experience with Delilah in the First Century was something very special."

"So, tell me about it. Were you lovers?" Samantha asked.

"I suppose so," Clarissa answered slowly. "I mean, I still couldn't tell you what lesbians really do, but whatever, it was a beautiful experience. We touched each other with tender caresses. There was a lot of love, a lot of tenderness." She looked up at Samantha nervously gaging her reaction. "It was very beautiful. Actually a lot more special than most of the 'Wham! Bam! Thank you, ma'am!' men that I've known."

Samantha chuckled. "In this life or the past?"

"Both," Clarissa laughed, her embarrassment abated. "Men can be such jerks!"

"But I take it you still believe that we can't live without them? You haven't become a lesbian have you?"

Clarissa roared with laughter. "Certainly not!" she exclaimed. "David and I have a wonderful sex life. No, forget it! I only mentioned it because I think in a funny sort of way, that my relationship with Delilah somehow softened me for my relationship with Jesus. Don't forget, Samantha, if I was Mary Magdalene I had been a prostitute. Prostitutes are pretty hard people."

"Good point. Anyway, what's all this leading up to?"

"Well, either Antonias died, or we got divorced. I could hardly have stayed married to him and still had a child by Jesus! In my most recent dream I actually witnessed Ben Joshua's birth. I definitely had a son by Jesus in addition to my older boy."

"So you really believe that Mary Magdalene and Jesus had a child? The Churches will go bananas if you say this!"

"I believe it's true, Samantha. If these things had been revealed to me alone, you probably would think me to be some kind of a nut, but they haven't. Things have been revealed to so many different people on our travels this winter, and they've all added to my understanding. I was interviewed on Hong Kong Radio by this Gloria Ainsworth, who's fascinated by past lives. She also seemed to be linked with Jesus in the First Century. She saw him on the way to the cross and her first century father was a close friend of Joseph of Arimathea. Gloria and her husband, Patrick, knew a great deal about the First Century. She and Jeremy would really have a lot in common."

"I'd like to meet this Jeremy Dyson guy myself," Samantha suggested. "He sounds a most interesting man."

"We'll arrange that when David gets home," Clarissa agreed. "You'd get along really well. I can't wait to see him again myself. But now, to other things. David's latest revelation had us married back in the First Century."

Samantha looked wide-eyed. "You and David I hope?" she asked. "We're not back on this lesbian thing are we?"

Clarissa laughed. "Oh, no! Samantha. Of course I mean David."

"How many times were you married in the First Century then?" Samantha asked incredulously.

"Well, I don't know that I was ever married to Jesus, and I can't be certain that I was married to Antonias; actually it has not even really been revealed that I was married to Linus, but it looks like it. My mother appeared to David and pretty much told him so."

"Your Mother!" Samantha exclaimed. "You did say you have this written down, didn't you, because it's hard to follow? Nobody would believe all this."

"It is mind boggling," Clarissa admitted, "but bear with me a minute. Apparently David and I or should I say, Linus and Maria, were married late in life. Linus Flavian was the Roman officer in charge at the crucifixion. It was from him that Joseph of Arimathea got Jesus' body for burial. I have no real recollection of him, but he keeps popping up. He claims to have had some sort of torrid affair with me when we were both teenagers. Also, as I mentioned before, Gloria Ainsworth knew his name in connection with Joseph of Arimathea. David also dreamed about Linus Flavian very recently. He told me about it on the phone the night I got home. That's when he told me about seeing my mother in Ephesus."

Samantha's eyes widened again. "Really! Wasn't it David's experiences with your mother at the time she died that started this whole regression?"

"Yes. My mother seemed to feel something very special about David. I never showed you the letter she wrote him the day we both saw her for the last time? David has it framed at the house. It's quite beautiful. It says something like this - 'I'm so very happy to have met you in this life and to know that Clarissa has found you. I will not be in this world much longer, but I will go to the other worlds knowing that you and Clarissa are in the light of Christos'."

"That is beautiful," Samantha agreed. "I remember you told me that before."

"It was less than a month later that she died," Clarissa explained. "We had only been back from our honeymoon a few days - David had just rejoined his ship."

"I remember," Samantha said comfortingly, "and it was when you were in Ireland at your mother's funeral that David first had these spiritual experiences with her. There's definitely some sort of energy connection between their souls."

"He was the first to see her astral form," Clarissa admitted. "Since then I've encountered her in the dream state, but David was the first."

"Tell me about David's Ephesus experience?" Samantha asked.

"He saw my mother in some old, first century ruins. She called to him and asked him to take care of me and her grandson."

"Oh, Clarissa! How exciting! You're pregnant!" Samantha blurted out.

A couple of customers in the coffee shop looked in their direction.

"No!" Clarissa whispered firmly. "I'm not pregnant. That's just the point," she said as she looked over her shoulder to see if the others were still listening. The interested customers caught her eye and turned away to resume their conversations. "I think my mother was referring to me as Maria of Magdala in the First Century. Remember, I saw her as Miriam, the Virgin Mary, in my early dream encounters."

"That's right!" Samantha noted. "I remember now."

"Well, her grandson as Miriam, would have been Jesus' son."

"That's true if the soul of your mother really was that of the Virgin Mary. This whole story's incredible." Samantha picked up Clarissa's dream journal. "May I?" she asked.

"Go ahead. I would really value your opinion about all this. You're really the only person I can turn to. Even talking to David about this rationally is still a little difficult."

Samantha started to flick through the pages. "You know there is one way we might be able to prove all this," she said. "I have this friend Jim Bodsworth - he's a regression therapist."

"You mean he opens people up to their past lives? That's how these things came to Gloria Ainsworth."

"Yes. It's a serious form of psychological practice today," Samantha explained. "Of course there are some amateur quacks in the field, but I really believe in Jim. He doesn't work on anyone unless he believes in the real validity of the case. He might agree to giving you and David a session, especially if I ask him. We've worked together on other cases. You don't know how many people come to me with their past life fantasies! Jim should be able to lead you into some revelations that might prove to him and to us, the validity of what you claim. Nothing's fool proof, but it's worth a try."

"I hope he agrees," Clarissa said enthusiastically. "You know, David would have laughed at this whole idea a year ago. He was so skeptical about anything unorthodox or not 'main stream' as he calls it. He comes from a very staid background and he lives in a pretty conservative world on board ship. But, he's changing Samantha. He's having as many past life revelations as me these days. I told you he's keeping a dream journal too. I think he's becoming as fascinated by this whole mystery as me."

"Let me talk to Jim. I'll give you a call next week," Samantha said. "When does David get home?"

"April twelfth."

"Two and a half weeks time," Samantha calculated. "That should be about right. We'll be in touch."

They went to the counter and Clarissa paid the bill.

Outside it was a pleasant, sunny day. Little banks of snow still lay around the edges of the parking lot in the plaza, but there were signs that spring was on its way and the eternal, Minnesota winter might be coming to an end. The birds were singing.

• • • • • • •

D avid adjusted his bow tie and checked his dress uniform in the mirror. Tonight was the big farewell party for the World Cruise. The 'Prince Regent' had left Barbados and was on the run up to Ft. Lauderdale. Although David would not be flying home until the ship docked in New York on April the twelfth, many of the World Cruise passengers would be disembarking in Ft. Lauderdale.

The Captain wanted all his senior officers at the party. This was one of the biggest Gala nights of the cruise. David folded the black handkerchief that he customarily wore in the breast pocket of his white mess coat. Just a smidgen showed. He was ready to go down to the Pavilion Lounge. The orders were, 'be there fifteen minutes ahead of the passengers'. The Master wanted a group photograph. David was on time.

The lounge, which was modelled on England's Brighton Pavilion, the fantasy, oriental palace that the Prince Regent of Great Britain had constructed on the south coast of England in the early nineteenth century, had never looked better. Ice sculptures following the general, oriental design of the room abounded. They graced the caviar stands, the smoked salmon booths and the incredible table display that covered much of the ballroom floor. Behind the band stand, huge blocks of ice, illuminated by the colored lights of the stage, spelled out the ship's name. The musicians were already gathered. Tonight they were to play in white tie and tails. The Maitre d'Hotel and the dining room Captains were also sporting tail coats. Tapers in silver candelabra were being lit. Final adjustments were being made to floral fantasies.

The Chef de Cuisine inspected his array of silver salvers laden with canopies, and the warm, chaffing dishes that held fried shrimp, hot quiche and certain oriental delicacies to dip in sweet, exotic sauces. Satisfied, he then inspected his troops - the various chefs in pristine, white coats, aprons and starched hats that were stationed at appropriate places to keep the platters full.

The head wine steward had champagne open and was supervising the filling of the fluted glasses on the first trays. His staff of waiters were standing by in maroon jackets that symbolized their trade. The barkeeper was checking his additional stock to see that those who sought something other than champagne had plenty of spirits and mixes available. A junior barkeeper cut up slices of lemon and lime.

There was a hush as the Captain arrived, followed by a polite round of "Good Evenings" from the officers. The ship's photographer clapped his hands and directed the Captain and his officers to a suitable spot in front of the principal ice sculpture.

"Say Cheese," the brash young man said.

There was a flash.

"One more," the photographer repeated.

David found himself standing beside the Hotel Manager. Fiona MacAllister had eased herself in on his other side.

"The Hotel staff's excelled themselves," David whispered to his immediate superior.

"It's spectacular," the Hotel Manager agreed.

Fiona pinched David's backside. "I liked your friend the architect," she whispered as if he hadn't noticed.

The group photograph over, the Musical Director called the orchestra to 'places'. The Cruise Director and his social staff took up positions with the Captain at the entrance to the lounge. It was five minutes to seven. They could see that many of the passengers were already waiting outside.

"Have you a pig in a blanket?" the Captain asked a nearby waiter who was holding a tray of canopies. "A sausage roll might be all I get tonight."

The young steward grinned as he brought over the tray.

"Are our drinks in place?" the Captain asked the Social Director.

"Right behind you, sir," the Australian gentleman replied.

"Doreen, who's first in line out there?" the Master asked.

"Mr. and Mrs. Achenbloom," the Social Directress confirmed as she stepped towards the Captain waiting to announce names.

"That figures," the Captain chuckled. He swallowed the last of his sausage roll and wiped his hand on a clean handkerchief. "Alright, let's go!"

The Cruise Director signalled across the room to the Musical Director. The orchestra started to play a Strauss waltz. Doreen opened the door. She formally announced Mr. and Mrs. Achenbloom.

The Captain shook hands with the Achenblooms.

"Wonderful Voyage! Superb as always!" Mr. Achenbloom informed him.

The Achenblooms moved on to the Cruise Director and finally to the Social Director. The other passengers then followed in succession for forty minutes without a break.

The splendid room filled with people in unbelievable gowns and colorful Asian and Indian dress jackets that in the latter twentieth century could only be worn in the fantasy world of a cruise ship. It was a splendid party.

"Mr. Peterson," a bald-headed man in a plain, black tuxedo said as he found himself next to the Chief Purser, "I must congratulate you on your staff. You are the unsung heroes on this ship. Any time that Mildred or I have needed to ask for information at the Purser's desk your girls couldn't have been more charming. It's no wonder that this is such a popular ship. You're all so friendly and polite. You never seem to get rattled. We've heard what you have to put up with sometimes. We think you and your team are terrific."

David felt a glow of satisfaction. It was always rewarding to hear the good things. "Thank you, sir," he said.

"Malcolm Streeter," the man introduced himself. "I don't expect you to know my name. We keep pretty much to ourselves, but we've loved every minute of our voyage and hopefully we'll be able to come again next year. If so, I certainly hope you're the Chief Purser and make sure your lovely wife is with you again. We did so enjoy her performance in the Lookout Bar."

The Cruise Director announced the Master who joined him on the band stand to make his farewell speech. Malcolm Streeter moved forward to take a photograph.

"They seem happy enough at this party," the Radio Officer said to David after the Captain had got his customary, World Cruise standing ovation.

"I just met a really nice man, Martin," David answered. "I can't say I've ever noticed him on the voyage, but he's been with us all the way round. He couldn't have been more complimentary."

"Wait and see after the comment cards have been filled in," Martin replied with caution. "You never know."

"No. I really feel good about this one. Clara talks to the passengers a lot and I think we really had an exceptionally nice crowd this year. There are some new, full world cruise passengers and they have been very refreshing - just kind, basic, decent folk."

Nonetheless, David felt a sense of relief as he helped himself to what was left of the caviar as the passengers moved to the dining room for dinner. The World Cruise was winding down and all he had to do was clear his paper work and he would be flying home to Minnesota. Clara would be there waiting for him.

• • • • • • •

Davids's plane touched down at the 'Twin Cities' Airport at five minutes past five. It was sunny and about fifty five degrees. The landscape still looked wintry, but there was no sign of lying snow. Clarissa was waiting for him at the gate.

"I love you," he said as he melted into her arms.

"You're home, darling," Clarissa replied. "I can't believe it. You're finally home."

They held each other for some time, while the passengers on the flight from New York filed past.

"Any more dreams?" Clarissa asked as they started to walk towards the terminal building and Baggage Claim.

"No. Actually, since I called you from Athens everything seems to have gone pretty quiet on that front. I've got my dream journal with me though. We can look at the Ephesus experiences in detail later."

A merchant's floral display greeted them in the foyer.

"Next month I have such big plans for the garden," David said. "I want to plant a whole new border."

They went down the escalator to Baggage Claim. "I have so much to tell you, David," Clarissa whispered. "I think Mother's grandchild in the First Century was Maria's son."

David laughed nervously. "Are you saying what I think you are? What in the world have you and Samantha been cooking up?"

"No, I mean it David. I think Joshua and Maria had a son."

They stepped off the escalator and went to the baggage carts.

"Let's pick up the bags. We'll talk about all this when we get home," David said cautiously. "You never know who's listening."

They were delayed some time in heavy traffic as they set off from the airport. "Why don't we stop off at the 'Two Pandas' for an early dinner," Clarissa suggested as she noticed the time drawing close to six-thirty.

"Good idea," David agreed.

By seven they were sitting at their usual table by the big fish tank. After they had ordered, it was David who brought up their first century revelations.

"You're still sure you're not pregnant?"

"Definitely not," Clarissa replied with surprise. "Are you disappointed?"

"No. I don't think the time is right for us just yet, but if your mother was definitely not referring to us in the present when I encountered her spirit in Ephesus, then she had to be referring to our first century lives. So you think we might have had a child then?"

"You said we had a tumultuous affair when we were teenagers - I suppose it's possible! Maybe Marcus was our son and not Antonias' boy. I'd have much rather had your child than Doctor John's!"

"Yes, that's strange in a way," David admitted, "I have these two visions of us together in those days. The first was when we were young and the next time I saw us together was when we were old. Apart from my being with Pontius Pilate at the time of the crucifixion, we don't really know anything about my life in between. Maybe Marcus was our son. A child of Marcus would have in one sense been your mother's grandson. But there again, that is only by fusing the First Century with the present. You were not Miriam's daughter in the First Century if you were Mary Magdalene."

"No, David. That's why any grandson must have been Jesus' child. The Virgin Mary didn't have any other children. She was ever chaste as they used to say in Ireland. She never had sex, David, not even to create Jesus!"

"Catholic nonsense!" David retaliated. "The Bible says Jesus had brothers and sisters. Now, have you thought of that? Your mother's grandson in the First Century could have been the child of any one of Jesus' brothers or sisters."

"Ah, but the nuns at the convent used to tell my friends when we were children that they were not real brothers and sisters, but cousins, or relatives of St. Joseph."

"You know you are very funny for such an enlightened person. Your Irish background really shows through at times. Even though you were a backsliding Protestant as you say, you were still influenced by this Catholic nonsense." Then, smiling, David took her hand in his. "I love you," he said. "Your Irish background is part of your charm."

"I love you too, David, but why are you fighting the possibility that Jesus might have had a son?"

"I suppose it's possible, but who would have been the mother? Do you really think Mary Magdalene and Jesus had a son?"

"I actually had this dream about his birth!" Clarissa insisted. "I named him Ben Joshua. It's all in my dream journal. You've got to believe me!"

"And Jeremy Dyson was Jesus Christ?" David said slowly letting go of Clarissa's hand.

"Look, I know how you feel about Jeremy, but nothing happened, at least not in the Twentieth Century. Many things came to both of us in Jerusalem. I have so much to tell you. The whole story is coming together."

"I can't wait," David said with a note of sarcasm, still not quite able to shrug off all his fears. "So what happened in the First Century?"

"Jesus was married," Clarissa said with confidence. "His wife's name was 'Joanna'."

"Joanna! Where did she come from?"

"Well, you might find this hard to believe, but you know Joanna in this life. Fiona MacAllister was Joanna in the First Century."

David laughed. "Fiona, married to Jesus! Come on, Clara! This gets more absurd every minute!"

"Both Jeremy and I had dreams about Fiona as 'Joanna'," Clarissa implored. "They were independent dreams. We both tapped into the same thing. The only difference was that Jeremy saw her when she was alive and married to him, whereas in my dream I was with Jeremy and we visited Joanna's grave. Joanna died, David. That's why eventually Mary Magdalene and Jesus were able to get together."

"Clara! Clara!" David shouted. "This whole thing is a complete fantasy! It's gotten out of control!"

Clarissa checked to see that nobody was listening, but they were now alone in the restaurant. "Well, don't you still think of yourself as this Roman, Linus Flavian?"

"That's different," David said slowly. "I'm not claiming to have made love to the Christ!"

"What's different?" Clarissa countered. "You claimed that you made love to me two thousand years ago. It was a pretty, passionate scene if I remember - young Linus in the olive grove with Maria!"

"Well, maybe that's what's brought us together today - karma as you call it."

"Quite, David. And why shouldn't similar karma have brought me and Jeremy together in this century?"

"That's just what bothers me. I mean, you say you haven't made love to Jeremy, but this whole relationships-through-lifetimes worries me."

Clarissa took hold of her husband's hand again and squeezed it. "Oh David! You mustn't worry about that. Look, when we were in

Jerusalem Jeremy came to my concert and we had a bite to eat afterwards. The next day we went out to Gethsemane together. In the afternoon he took me to the archeological museum and then escorted me to the airport. He was a perfect gentleman, David. Nothing happened. But, Gethsemane was a very moving experience. While we were there I had this daydream, a sort of trance as we sat looking across the Kidron valley at the old city. I was taken back to the First Century again. I could see the Temple where the Dome of the Rock mosque stands today. I was with Jesus and he took me down into a glade in the garden. In my vision we did make love, but it was only in my vision. You can read all about it in my dream journal. But after I returned to reality I took Jeremy down to that same spot as it is today. David, that's where Ben Joshua was conceived two thousand years ago! We both knew that this was the place where our first century love had been fulfilled, but honestly, we just stood there in awe, silently holding hands."

"Clara, nobody's ever going to believe all this!" David said, his jealousy somewhat abated. "How can you talk about this to anybody?"

"Samantha knows. She has this friend, Jim Bodsworth. He's a regression therapist."

"One of those people that Gloria Ainsworth consulted?"

"Exactly, David. Samantha thinks she might be able to interest Jim in giving us a session."

"You or me?" David asked nervously.

"I thought you might like to try first. After all, we're pretty convinced that in my first century past life I was Maria of Magdala. We are still not sure about you."

Jimmy Wan came over with their selections in person. He put down the steaming dishes of chicken and vegetables and beef with broccoli. He had not forgotten the special sauce.

"I no forget my most valable customer needs," he said beaming from ear to ear. "Your flend Misser Dyson, he come here offen now. He like 'Two Pandas' velly much."

The Vietnamese waitress arrived with the rice bowls and topped up their cups of green tea.

"Is Mr. Dyson in town?" Clarissa asked, thinking that maybe Jimmy Wan would know.

"He in here two day ago. He no say he going anywhere. He been velly busy on project at Universy," the proprietor informed them.

"Good. We really need to get in touch with him," Clarissa stated. "We're so happy to be home. It was a long trip! We'll both be here for a few weeks now. It's wonderful! I'm sure we'll be coming to the 'Two Pandas' many times."

"Thank you velly much," Jimmy said as he bowed, before leaving them alone. He returned to his desk to welcome other clients to his restaurant.

"So you're suggesting we should see this shrink?" David asked returning them to the subject in hand. "I'm not paying to have my life dissected by a shrink!"

"It might be interesting, David. You might consider thinking of him as a counselor rather than a shrink. I don't think we'll have to pay, either. He's a good friend of Samantha's," Clarissa pleaded. "If this man really is able to regress us back to our first century lives and the stories match up, we would have more backing for our claims."

"Your claims!" David chided. "We'll talk about it later, but meanwhile our dishes are getting cold."

Clarissa and David were hungry. They ate every morsel of Jimmy Wan's Chinese meal. Satisfied, they paid their bill and left for home. It was not long before they were back in the warmth of their house on the lake. Although Clarissa kept the heating at a pleasant seventy degrees, David built a log fire in the living room. There were some things from a New England childhood and years of denial at sea that he just plain missed. The smell of wood smoke was one of them.

• • • • • • • •

Samantha arranged for Jim Bodsworth to come out to the Peterson's house with her. They arrived about three in the afternoon. Clarissa had asked Samantha if Jeremy could attend the session. Jim Bodsworth had agreed. Jeremy was already there.

Jim Bodsworth was very tall, and had a lean and angular face. He wore a comfortable, flannel shirt and a gray sweater over black pants that were slightly flared.

"I want you to meet Clarissa and David," Samantha said as they came over the threshold. "Clarissa is one of my oldest friends."

Jim shook their hands. "Hello. Nice to meet you. Samantha's told me a lot about you both," he said.

Samantha looked at Jeremy. "And this must be their good friend Jeremy Dyson," she intimated.

Jeremy bowed politely.

Samantha was impressed by the architect's old world courtesy.

Jim looked at the cozy, living room, noting the big, picture windows with their view over the sloping lawn running down to the lake. Then, his eye caught the two, carved jumbos on either side of the fireplace. "Nice elephants," he commented.

"Thanks," David acknowledged. "I must say I do rather like them. I got them in Madras a couple of years ago."

"I bought elephants in India in February," Jeremy remarked. "They were going to send them to me, but so far I haven't heard a thing."

"Not surprising," David said grinning from ear to ear. "Dealing with those boys is a slow laborious business. But, they'll arrive. The Indians are hopeless, but you know something, they're basically honest. Your elephants will come. I can't promise in what state, but they'll get here."

"They said it might take three months," Jeremy acknowledged. "I'm really not too concerned. If they make it, they make it, if they don't, they don't."

Jim turned to Clarissa. "Samantha tells me you're a concert pianist?"

"That's right."

"I'd love to hear you play sometime," he continued in his deep and ponderous voice.

Clarissa smiled. "Maybe later," she said, wondering just what Samantha had got them into. She felt there was something a little strange about this fellow. "Can I get anyone coffee or tea?" she asked.

"I could use a coffee," Jim replied.

"Me too," Samantha added.

"How about you, Jeremy?"

"No!" Jim stated firmly. "At least not if we're going to put him through regression. That applies to all of you. Coffee's not good before a session."

"So you are going to put me through a regression," Jeremy said almost relieved to know that the visit was not to be totally in vain. He was nervous and like Clarissa, he had really begun to wonder what Samantha was up to.

"Yes, we can start as soon as Samantha and I have had our coffee," Jim said. "Samantha tells me that you all think you knew each other in some past life. It would be best if we do the sessions one at a time. That way you won't influence each other's minds and pre-condition yourselves. However, I suggest that Samantha acts as scribe. She'll record what you all say. For now, just relax. There's nothing strange about regression. Contrary to popular belief, I won't be hypnotizing you or anything like that."

Clarissa went to make the coffee.

David sensed that it was almost as if Jim Bodsworth wanted to avoid talking to him. Perhaps this was deliberate. 'Maybe he has to remain completely detached from his subjects,' he thought. He walked to the window and looked out at the view. The lawn, so verdant all summer, was still brown. The trees remained lifeless. But he could see ducks flying over the lake in a wedge and the sun made the waters sparkle.

The whistle blew on the electric kettle and Clarissa poured the instant brew. "Coffee's ready!" she called. Jim and Samantha took their steaming mugs. "There's bottled water for the rest of us."

"Right, do you have a simple room with a couch or bed that doesn't look out of a window?" Jim asked.

"Yes," Clarissa replied, "my music room. It's a small guest room, but I keep my racks of music there. It doesn't have a window at all because it's in the basement. You know, we have one of those half-basements."

"Perfect," Jim stated. "Can I look at it?"

Clarissa led Samantha and Jim downstairs to the small, guest suite. Half-windows lit up the living room, but just as she had said, the bedroom was completely in the dark. Shelves of music did line two of the walls which were otherwise blank. There were no paintings and the decor was plain off-white.

"Perfect!" Jim exclaimed clapping his hands. "No distractions! It's perfect!"

"Who do you want to start with then?" Clarissa asked.

"How about your husband?"

"Okay, I'll send him down to you," she replied.

Clarissa saw that David was nervous.

"I've never been to a shrink in my life," he said as they made their way towards the descending stairs. "He's weird."

Clarissa hugged her husband. "Do this for me?" she said. "I think we might find out some extraordinary truths."

David went down to join Jim and Samantha.

"Whenever you feel comfortable," Jim instructed, "take off your shoes and lie down on the bed looking up at the ceiling." Jim set up a small tape recorder. "You don't mind do you?" he asked.

"No," David replied.

"Now, let me explain the process to you. I'm going to talk to you and ask you various questions. Each time I do so you must tell me exactly what you see or hear. Don't think or hesitate, just tell me the first thought that comes into your head. You'll remain awake. There's no hypnosis or deep sleep involved in this technique, just total relaxation - enjoy yourself. Just follow my questions with the first response that enters your head. Do you understand?"

"Yes," David replied as he settled himself down on the bed.

"Imagine you're in a mansion. You've arrived in the entrance hallway. It's rather like an Italian palace. There are many paintings on the walls ... large paintings. Can you see the paintings?"

David imagined the scene in a Palladian villa. He could see shafts of light descending from a rotunda to a hexagon of walls where paintings hung. "Yes," he replied.

"Are you drawn to any one painting?"

"Not particularly."

"Can you see what any of them are about? Are they landscapes or portraits? Perhaps they are abstract?"

David thought about the paintings in those peeling, gold frames at Clarissa's old, family home. "It's hard to tell," he said at length. "The paintings are very dark. Some of them are landscapes and many of them look like they might be of horses."

"Do you ride horses?"

"Not much, that's more Clara's thing."

"Do you think you might have ridden horses much in past lives?"

"I have no idea," David replied, "but if this past life business means anything, then maybe I rode horses when I was a Roman."

"Were you a Roman?"

"I dreamt I was. But it was only a dream."

"And what did you dream?"

David sighed.

"Relax," Jim instructed him. "Take a few, deep breaths."

David breathed in deeply.

"What are you wearing as a Roman?"

"Romans wore togas," David replied.

"Are you wearing a toga?"

"I presume I did. In my dreams I sometimes wore togas. I had three different dreams. In one I was a youth. In another I was a Roman officer and wore uniform, I guess much as you see in the movies like 'Quo Vadis' or 'Ben Hur'. That's when I saw myself with Pontius Pilate."

"And what was your third dream?"

"Well, I was with Clarissa's mother in Ephesus. Clara was there too. We were all much older in that dream and I was definitely dressed in a toga."

"Go back to the paintings," Jim instructed. "Can you see the paintings again?"

David took his mind back to the dining room at Ballyporeen House. He could see the old paintings on the walls. He could envisage the silver laid out on the dark, mahogany sideboard and the crystal chandelier hanging from the ceiling. Up there above him were the frescoes, peeling off along with the cracked plaster. And then, there was Margaret Corrington's face, looking down.

"Do you see anything?" Jim asked after a pause.

"Yes," David replied. "I can see Clara's mother."

"What's she doing?"

"I can only see her face. She's smiling down from the ceiling."

"Is she saying anything?"

"No. She's just smiling, just as she was the day after the funeral when we were all sitting around the table as Mr. Shaunessy read out her will."

"Clara's mother's will?"

"Yes. She looked happy," David noted.

"David, can we stop here?" Jim suggested.

David sat up on the bed. "So is all this true?" he asked.

"I don't know," Jim admitted. "You see, you're not actually going back into any past lives. You're merely recording things for me that are part of your present experience. I'm sure the dreams are true and it is plausible that you might have seen your mother-in-law's face in Ireland, but they are all recollections of experiences you've had in this life. Right now, you're not what we call receptive to regression. This doesn't mean you can't adapt to it another time, but at present there are too many doubts in your mind. You're not able to relax into it so that I can lead you back into your past lives. It's nothing unusual, actually most people are like you the first time." He paused for a moment as David slipped on his shoes. "Now, the dreams you experienced may well be true recollections from the Roman world. In the dream state you were almost certainly more relaxed and more receptive than now. You may well have been a Roman, but I can't prove it at the moment nor can you prove it to yourself. Now, if you want to stay here while we try to regress your wife you'll see what I mean. She might prove to be more immediately open to the experience."

David was mildly amused. 'I never really did believe in this crap,' he thought to himself. 'These people are all the same, spaced-out quacks!'

Samantha went up to call Clarissa.

David watched Clarissa when she lay down on the bed. She looked very intense as if she would be receptive to anything. "I'll bet it works for her," he whispered to Samantha. "I'm just not a space cadet like Clara."

Samantha put her finger to her lips.

After Jim had explained the basics of the session, he began. "Imagine you are on a jet plane," he said slowly. "Can you see out of your window?"

"Yes," Clarissa replied.

"Now Clarissa, in your pocket book you have tickets to any place you can think of in the world. Where are you flying to?"

"Athens."

"Can you see Athens?"

"Yes, it's early evening. The Parthenon looks gold against the turquoise sky."

"Yes, and where are you now?"

"With Babis."

"What are you doing?"

"Arguing. Babis is drunk. He's hurting me. He's slapping my face. There are drinks on the table. We are in a Taverna. People are watching us. There's music playing. I'm crying. My chemise is torn."

'Your what?' David thought to himself.

"What sort of clothes are you wearing?" Jim asked.

"Nineteenth century, peasant clothes."

"And the men?"

"Big, white shirts and black, baggy trousers. They are laughing. Some of them are standing on the tables. Babis is hurting me. He's pulling me away."

"And ..." Jim continued.

"It's getting dark, much darker. It's as if I'm in a tunnel. I can see the light the other end."

"Can you see anything in the light?"

"Yes, the door is open. There are wild flowers and fruit trees. I can see stone walls and thatched roofs. Behind the buildings is a church. A big church. It has three towers and many flying buttresses."

"What are you doing?"

"Collecting the honey. The bees are swarming. I have gloves like a falconer. There's a veil hanging from my big hat to protect my face. There's lots of honey. Brother Anselm should be pleased. My bucket is full of oozing combs."

"Anything else?" Jim asked.

"I can hear bells - church bells," Clarissa answered. "I don't have to go. Today I'm to stay in the kitchen with Brother Anselm - so many guests today. They're on pilgrimage. We have many extra people to feed. We need the honey. It's sweet. Pilgrims love our honey."

"Is the sun shining?"

"Yes. The sun's shining, but there are many white clouds."

"Look up at the white clouds." Jim continued. "Can you see anything in the clouds?"

Clarissa became silent.

"Where are you now? Just tell me where you are?"

"With Joshua," Clarissa answered. "I'm washing his hair. Soapy bubbles are all around us in the stream. They look like little, white clouds drifting on the stream. His head is in my lap. The water is everywhere."

"And now," Jim pushed slowly, "where are you now?"

"In a marble bath. It's cool and refreshing. Delilah is with me. She says the Madam is pleased and I'll be able to stay. I like it here. This is so much nicer than Magdala. I hope I can stay. What will she do when she finds out I'm going to have a baby?"

"Who, Delilah or the Madam?" Jim asked.

"Both," Clarissa replied. "I won't be able to attract the clients when I get big and Delilah might abandon me. Ohhh ... Why did I have to get pregnant?"

"Who do you think's the likely father?" Jim asked.

"Linus, the Roman boy. I loved him," Clarissa revealed.

Jim looked around at Samantha who was busy writing everything down.

David stared at his wife quite astounded by what she had just said. He knew in his heart she was telling the truth. They had been lovers in the First Century. His dreams had revealed that he had been Linus Flavian. Even if he was unable to regress, his dreams had to have been showing the truth.

"They said Linus killed my sister," Clarissa continued.

"Who?"

"The men - Judas and Jonah."

"Judas?" Jim repeated.

"They sometimes called him 'Iscariot'."

Clarissa remained silent for a moment. Then, returning her thoughts to the present, she looked at Jim, Samantha and David with fully-open eyes. "Babis - the creep!" she said.

"Who was Babis?" Jim asked.

"An officer I met on the 'Ulysses'. In the dream state I saw him as Judas Iscariot. Judas never could understand us women."

"Aha!," Jim grunted triumphantly.

Clarissa stretched.

"How do you feel?" he asked.

"Just fine. It's funny that the Greek I described just now was also named Babis."

"Not really," Jim said with a smile. "The name triggered your soul memory."

David went up to call Jeremy.

"What's it like?" Jeremy asked. "Have you found out anything astounding?"

"It didn't work for me. But it is rather amazing. Clarissa came out with some things that none of us have ever discussed. I think she really did know me in the First Century."

"There's something awfully clandestine about going down to the basement to do this," Jeremy said as they started down the small flight of steps.

Jim led Jeremy into his regression with the same image as he had used on David. When he asked Jeremy to focus on one of the paintings in the rotunda, Jeremy had no difficulty in selecting one. "Elephants," he said.

Clarissa felt a little nervous. 'Surely he's not going to go straight into revelations about our safari adventure. What if he describes me walking about in my lingerie?'

"What sort of elephants?" Jim asked.

"Processional elephants ... Big procession. Maharajah is coming. Many in the street. Maybe Maharajah or his English guests might throw us coins."

Clarissa felt relieved.

"Yes. What next?" Jim asked slowly.

"Carriage coming ... Someone shoving me from behind ... Horses ..." Jeremy answered, his voice fading. Then, he appeared to go into a trance.

"What do you see?" Jim asked deliberately.

"Light. Swirling light. Now I can see Ravi. Ravi is dying. Nobody cares ...

"And ..."

"More light ... Only light."

For a moment there was complete silence in the room. Nobody spoke. Then, Jeremy began to describe another scene, his voice recovering. "A man with an unkempt beard climbing through some lush greenery down towards a river bank."

"What is the man wearing?" Jim asked

"Some sort of a brown robe, a bit like a monk's habit, but without any hood."

"Does it convey any sense of period to you? Can you tell if the clothing is medieval, or older perhaps?"

"Definitely at least medieval, even slightly Biblical," Jeremy suggested.

"Biblical. Does the man say anything to you?"

"No. He's grinning. It's a rather frightening grin. He reminds me of Rasputin."

Jim paused for a moment. "Return to the Biblical," he repeated. "What do you see now?"

"The ground," Jeremy replied. "The stones of a dark courtyard. My hands and my feet are bound to these posts."

"Yes, and what next?"

"Two men in black, leather tunics. I can just barely see them from the corner of my eye. They are coming out with whips."

"What sort of whips?"

"Flails of long, leather strands with little, metal tips on the ends - Roman whips," Jeremy explained.

"And ..."

"They are flogging me," he said excruciatingly. "It hurts. It hurts so much. The pain, the pain, I can't stand the pain."

"And ..."

"Maria," he whispered. "Maria"

"Yes, carry on," Jim continued. "Is Maria there?"

"No, she's gone now," Jeremy said calmly, his voice changing, "but so has the pain. It's lighter up here, but it's still dark down in the court. I can see myself. The guards are still flogging me." He paused.

"Yes ...?" Jim prompted.

"Now they've stopped. They're wiping the blood from their flails. I can see the glint of the metal."

Jeremy stopped his train of thought.

"Can you see anything else?" Jim asked in his same calm, deep voice.

"I can hear insects," Jeremy noted. "They're buzzing behind my ears. I can feel pain, terrible pain again. It stings ... It hurts ... It hurts ..."

"Where are you?"

"Colorful robes ... He must be a rich man ... Maybe a king," Jeremy confided. "He's pointing at me. He's shouting at me."

"What is he saying?"

Jeremy didn't respond.

Jim repeated the question. "What is the rich man saying?"

"Take him back to the Romans! Take him away! He's a fraud! He's no miracle-worker! Let the Romans do to him whatever they like!"

"And then, where did they take you?" Jim asked.

"Maria!" Jeremy shouted as if he recognized her. "Maria!"

"Who is Maria?" Jim pressed.

Jeremy became silent.

After what seemed a fairly long time, although it was really only a few seconds in the flow, Jeremy spoke again. "White marble," he said, "lots of white marble."

"Is that where they've taken you?" Jim asked. "To a place with lots of white marble?"

"Yes," Jeremy answered slowly. "Lots of white marble ... Blood dripping on the white marble ... More white marble ... Shafts of light ... A Roman, reading from a scroll."

"What does he say?"

"Just reading. Another man, not a soldier ... dressed in white ... saying something."

"Go on, what is he saying?" Jim asked slowly.

"Are you a king? How big is your kingdom?" Jeremy said, and then paused before repeating, "More blood, more pain."

"Did you say anything?" Jim asked.

Again Jeremy paused.

Jim was about to repeat the question or lead Jeremy on to something else, when his subject began to speak very softly.

"My kingdom is not of this world. In this time we give to Caesar what is Caesar's, but my kingdom is not of this time." Then, Jeremy paused.

"What's happening now?" Jim continued in his interrogation, although he realized that Jeremy's voice was becoming softer and softer.

"Darkness ... Heavy wooden beam ... Soldiers ..." Jeremy said faintly.

Jim waited for him to say more. He didn't want to prompt him too much at this point.

Jeremy, whose eyes had been closed through most of the interrogation looked up at the blank ceiling. "Bright light," he said. "More white marble ... Men shouting and more pain." He paused again before faintly repeating, "Maria".

"Maria was there?" Jim asked for the second time.

"Yes, Maria and the boy. I fell. It was hard to see ... Blood in my eyes. They kicked me."

"Who kicked you?"

"Soldiers. Romans," Jeremy answered weakly. "I can see the face of a woman. She has fine clothes."

"Is she Maria? Does she speak to you?"

"No," Jeremy replied. "No ... not Maria. They take the beam and kick me on." He then drifted into unintelligible mumbling.

"Where are you now?" Jim questioned.

After he had gathered some of his strength back, Jeremy replied. "Weeds and wild flowers ... Puffy, white clouds ... Black birds ... It's peaceful. I can see people. Away from the people are men and women with the boy. So much noise ... Screaming ... I can see a big, rough soldier. There's a gravelly, grinding sound. It's hurting me. Please stop."

"Go on ..."

"I can hear a voice. 'No! No nails for him!' It was a voice from behind. It's peaceful again. I can still see the black birds."

"And ..." Jim pushed.

"Such pain. Terrible pain as the big man hammers a nail into the frame. I try to shout at him, but it's hard to speak."

"What did you say?"

"Leave it! Leave me alone! Leave me alone! Leave me alone!" and Jeremy's voice trailed off into further gibberish.

Jim let Jeremy rest momentarily and looked back at the others who were sitting speechless and mesmerized. He smiled and nodded his head.

Jeremy started to speak again, but very slowly. "Roman with plumes. I can see his face. He's talking ..."

"What does he say?" Jim enquired.

"Today you will be with your God."

There followed a further pregnant pause. When Jeremy continued, his voice became fainter and fainter until it was almost impossible for the others to hear what he was saying. Jim was listening intently, however, and Samantha continued to record everything that Jeremy said.

"The ground dropping away, away, green, yellow and red. The black birds - I'm flying with the black birds. Down, I see myself tied to a crossbeam. No pain now, only peace ... Blood from the wounds ... Soldiers swing at the others and they scream ... Maria is there with the boy. Mother is there, also Jonah. They are close, but many others are there too. I see Judas in the crowd. Beyond is the city. I'm flying with the black birds. We are flying away. I see the whole city ... Hills ... Wider ... narrower ... wider ... I fly higher ... higher. Just a streak of light left ... That is all ... Now a flash! Different light ... Brighter light ... Total light!"

Jeremy's eyes were closed again. He looked like he was sleeping, but with a mystical smile on his face. Jim let him be. He turned back to Samantha and Clarissa. "He was there," was all he said, emotional tears welling in his eyes. "He was definitely there."

When Jeremy opened his eyes, Jim smiled at him and said, "No more questions. You were definitely there. Here's the tape. This was an unofficial session so keep it. We can discuss it later if you wish."

Jeremy felt completely lucid. He remembered exactly what he had said throughout the session even if he had seemed spaced out. "Who was the man who looked like Rasputin?" he asked, his voice completely restored.

"I don't know," Jim answered honestly. "I presume he was from another past life, perhaps in the Middle Ages. I would need another session with you to find that out."

Clarissa came over to the bed. "Are you alright?" she asked.

"Fine," Jeremy replied.

Jim brought them back to present reality and asked Clarissa if she would play for them.

"I will if you really want me to," she agreed. "Come on up and I'll play you my most recent composition."

They all returned to the living room, chattering as they went. Clarissa removed a large, teddy bear from the piano stool. "This bear's been practicing for years," she said. "He still can't get it right."

Samantha laughed.

"I'm going to play a piece I wrote this winter in Japan," Clarissa explained. "I named it 'Gilded Snow'. It depicts a scene in a temple garden in Kyoto. The Golden Temple is seen in the snow with a shaft of light that makes the brilliance of the gilded pagoda shine through the crystalline tracery of the trees. This is how I saw and caught that precious moment."

She started to play. Samantha and Jim were enthralled. For Clarissa the familiar pattern repeated.

When she had finished, Samantha applauded. "That was beautiful."

"Remarkable music," Jim agreed.

"It moves me too," Clarissa admitted. "You see, every time I play this piece I see the same temple, but other images come flooding in. The temple becomes a man standing in a shaft of sunlight on a hillside. The snow recedes, but there are many trees. They look like olives from Biblical times. I'm there, hiding with my son behind some rocks. My boy runs out towards the man in the sunlight. It's hard to see the man's features because of the way the sun filters around him, but I instinctively know it's Jesus. I can see him gesticulate with his outstretched hand for Marcus to go away. I call Marcus back. The light around Jesus fades and I can see his face more clearly."

She paused for a moment, watching Jim's reaction.

Then she looked at Jeremy. "Ironically, it has the feel of Jeremy's face."

Jeremy looked away. He felt awed by the confirmation of their joint thoughts.

"Then the scene reverses back to the gilded pagoda," Clarissa continued. "The snow returns and sunlight filters through the trees. The cloud cover comes back and the moment of gilded snow ends."

"Quite remarkable," Jim repeated. "You say the images are always the same?"

"Yes. Every time I play this piece I see exactly the same images in relation to every phrase of the music."

"The music is triggering a mental pattern in your brain," the psychologist continued in a matter of fact sort of way. "It's not an uncommon phenomenon. This pattern can be induced by sounds, as in your case, or by urges, feelings of anger or sentiments of love. I wouldn't worry about it. For us it was a treat. The music is so descriptive that it makes the soul soar."

Clarissa smiled. "I'm going to record it this summer," she said. "I'll probably call the whole album 'Gilded Snow'. It sounds like a good title."

After they had all had more of Clarissa's coffee, Jim said he had to leave.

"Maybe you could have dinner with us sometime?" Clarissa suggested.

"I'd love to," the psychologist replied. "It could be most interesting."

Samantha saw Jim to his car and then returned to the house.

After David had built up the fire, they played back the tape. Samantha compared the recording with her notes.

"Well, what do you think?" Clarissa asked when they came to the end of Jeremy's session.

"Astonishing," Samantha replied. "I'm sure Jeremy was Jesus."

David grunted. "It's not proof. It was a rather remarkable experience, but it's not proof."

"Why are you fighting it?" Clarissa insisted. "It's all here on the tape."

"That doesn't prove it," David insisted again. "Everything Jeremy says on the tape is written in Scripture, or more or less. Jeremy already knows the story. He knows about Jesus being scourged, his trial before Pilate, the road to the cross and the scene at the crucifixion. His imagination is only building on already established stories."

"That might be true," Jeremy said in support. "I'm still inclined to believe in this incredible revelation on the strength of the dreams rather than this regression, particularly those dreams about Joanna. Joanna isn't in the Bible, David, and yet both Clarissa and I dreamt about her."

"But you did tell Clarissa about Joanna," David countered. "You conditioned her to have thoughts of Joanna, albeit by accident. Clarissa even knew that the Joanna you dreamed about looked like Nurse MacAllister."

Clarissa laughed. "You don't have to call her Nurse MacAllister in front of us, my love. We all know she was your old girlfriend. We call her Fiona so you might as well too. Actually, to be honest, the more we drop our facades in this discussion the better." She looked at Samantha and Jeremy. "I mean, all of us. We must relax and be totally open to our feelings to try to confirm what we believe may be the truth. Good God! This is no small thing we're discussing. We are challenging the way the world has looked at Jesus and Mary Magdalene for two thousand years!"

"Okay," David agreed, "but just as Jeremy says, our dreams seem to reveal more than this regression. I mean, I got nowhere in my session, at least nowhere beyond seeing that image of Clara's mother looking down from the ceiling in Ireland."

"That's probably because you didn't relax into it, just as Mr. Bodsworth said," Clarissa pointed out.

"Clarissa's right," Samantha agreed. "You didn't seem comfortable with the regression idea, David. You were thinking too much, but let's return to Jeremy's comments about the validity of dreaming."

"Thinking's a hazard of my job," David replied. "I always have to think in ten different directions at sea. I need scientific proof on which to hang all this. I can't just take these revelations at face value."

"But what about the dreams?" Samantha pressed. "I mean you started keeping a journal. Your dreams are pretty revealing about this Roman fellow, Linus Fabian."

"Linus Flavian," David corrected her.

"Well, I mean there you go. You must believe somewhat if you want to correct me."

"Something certainly happened in Ephesus," David admitted. "It wasn't all dreaming. In Ephesus I heard Clara's mother's voice. I actually saw her. I wasn't dreaming. I was walking towards the steps up into the Great Theater and she called me from across the street. I would rather say I saw a ghost than that I dreamed. Margaret Corrington was floating."

"Do you think anybody else saw her?" Jeremy asked with interest, but not surprised by the profound confluence of experiences.

"No. That's the funny thing," David admitted. "I could see her floating ghost, but the other tourists in the street didn't seem to be aware of her."

"And are you sure it was not in your imagination?"

"It can't have been if I didn't think about it," David countered. "She was just there. The dreams could come from the subconscious mind, but these ghostly appearances of Clara's mother are something else. They are the one part of this story that seems totally real to me. I mean, why did the old lady give me that letter before she died?"

"The one forecasting her death?" Samantha joined in.

"Yes."

Clarissa got up and took the silver frame from its place in the bookshelf. She passed it to Samantha. "That's what David's talking about," she said. "Mother died three weeks later. It was just three weeks after we were married. This is what she wrote to David on our wedding day."

Samantha read Margaret Corrington's extraordinary prediction and message. 'This is all tied together by something that is bigger than our ability to see,' she thought.

"And why did I see her ghost looking down from the ceiling at Ballyporeen the day after her funeral?" David continued. "Clara didn't see her, or feel her presence, nor did her brothers or the old family lawyer. Margaret Corrington seems to want to keep in touch with me somehow. She led me into all this. Even in Laconia at Thanksgiving, it was I who saw her before Clara."

"She's picking up your energy, or vice versa," Samantha suggested. "Actually she seems to be the catalyst that started this whole thing. And remember, all these experiences collectively add to validate the separate experiences."

"Was she a very religious person?" Jeremy asked.

"Not particularly," Clarissa answered. "She was good when it came to social events in the Church of Ireland, like Flower Festivals or Carol Services, but she wasn't a Bible thumper. She didn't mind if we didn't go to church. Actually, we often rode horses on a Sunday morning. I think that's where Mother was closest to God, with the horses."

"That may be why this is all working," Samantha chimed in. "The Jesus Christ that you all seem to be discovering was not the ascetic saint that Christianity has always suggested, but a man of flesh and blood who was truly human and loving. I mean it's very touching in your two dreams about Joanna, and that later scene in Gethsemane is very moving. I don't remember any of that being taught in Church, but it seems closer to Margaret Corrington's way of looking at the Christ."

"You've read my dream journal," Clarissa explained.

"Yes," Samantha acknowledged. "It seems that almost anyone any of you meet these days, you discover you somehow knew them in the First Century! It's almost like this whole series of events is tied together by a force greater than any of us can grasp." Jeremy shot a glance at Samantha, his eyebrows raised high in surprise at the sequence of their thinking. Samantha smiled and added, "Although, I notice I don't seem to have a cameo part yet."

Jeremy laughed.

"Actually, I have no recollection of a Biblical life," Samantha continued, "but I might have been an Egyptian. Maybe that's why I like cats so much." She looked at her notes on the regression session. "This Babis fellow is intriguing. He seemed to play quite a role in your story, Clarissa."

"He was a creep!" Clarissa repeated. "We come across these macho types all the time at sea."

"Maybe, but he set off your train of thought this afternoon," Samantha noted.

"What do you mean?" Clarissa asked.

"Think about it," Samantha said. "The first past life you went back to was about this Greek in Athens who was abusing you in a Taverna. His name was Babis."

"Yes, but he wasn't Babis Demetris," Clarissa countered. "He didn't even look like Babis Demetris."

"No," Samantha continued, "but he had some of the same characteristics as Babis Demetris. He treated women as inferior beings. He displayed a certain, arrogant, male superiority. Isn't that what we find later when you write about Babis Demetris as Judas Iscariot in your dreams? You've created an image now that associates this Greek officer with Judas types, whether they're in the Nineteenth Century or the First Century."

Clarissa didn't reply.

"It's interesting how in the regression experience, Judas Iscariot comes back in association with Linus," Samantha continued.

"Pure coincidence!" David said firmly. "I haven't had any dreams about Judas Iscariot."

"But, Clarissa definitely says that Judas Iscariot thought Linus, the Roman boy, had killed Maria's sister," Samantha countered calmly. She started to play with the tape recording. "Look, let's hear it again."

She found the place. Not only did they distinctly hear that Judas thought Linus to have killed the girl, but they also heard again how immediately after this regression revelation Clarissa had referred to Babis as a creep who had no idea how to treat women. It seemed that Samantha was right. Babis Demetris had become a mental link between Clarissa's past and present.

The recording then repeated the incredible account of Jesus' crucifixion as it had been revealed by Jeremy.

"How do you feel about that?" Samantha asked.

"David has a point about pre-conditioning," Jeremy replied, much to Clarissa's surprise. "I suppose it's not hard to recall the Bible stories and it's possible we could let our imaginations fill in the details. It's a frightening thing to say that I was Jesus, and I'm not sure that this regression experience actually proves anything. But I can't deny my belief in the dreams and I refuse to deny other peoples' belief in their dreams. What's so interesting is that so many of us have come together, without intent, on this. I mean Clarissa and I had different dreams about Joanna. We shared the same dream about Jesus and Mary Magdalene at the waterfall. We shared an emotional experience at Gethsemane and way back when we first started these discussions, and long before there was any indication that I might have been Jesus in a past life, I sensed our bonding. Remember how I thought Clarissa and I had met in the First Century in Massilia?"

"Clarissa told me that, but wasn't that when you thought you were a Roman soldier like Linus?" Samantha noted. "I mean, I'm confused. Surely, if you were Jesus you couldn't have been that Roman soldier?"

"That damned Roman soldier!" David repeated under his breath.

"No, I really could have been Remus Augustus," Jeremy explained. "It's interesting in the light of what we now assume. If Joshua died when he was about thirty three, which is the Christian tradition, then I could have reincarnated as soul in the body of Remus Augustus. Remus was apparently about twenty during the Claudian persecution. Most scholars think Jesus was born in the last days of Herod the Great. That was actually four B.C. So he would have died about twenty nine A.D. give or take a year or two. It's plausible that I could have lived both lives, even though my life as Remus Augustus was not revealed in the session."

"It was overshadowed by your life as Jesus," Samantha suggested.

David had got up while they were talking and browsed through the bookshelves along the living room wall. He found what he was looking for. A Bible that he hadn't really looked at since he was a teenager and acolyte at St. George's in Laconia. He sat back down again and started to look through the final chapters of each gospel.

"But there's something very interesting about my life as Remus," Jeremy continued. "My only recollection of that life involves Clarissa, whom we presume to have been Mary Magdalene during her legendary life in Gaul. Please forgive me for saying it, but if we had been lovers and intimate friends so recently in my life as Jesus, it would be very logical that I would feel that pull to her when as Remus, I saw her a few years later, even though she was a woman then twice my age. There was nothing sexual in this encounter. I simply felt drawn to Maria. Something back then in the First Century in Gaul gave me a sense of recognition which was repeated the first time I met Clarissa in this century, even though I didn't realize why."

"But if you were really such a highly-developed, spiritual person as Jesus," Samantha acknowledged, "then it's not surprising that latent energy still pulls you two together."

David looked up. "Something was bothering me as we listened to Jeremy," he noted triumphantly. "I thought I was right and here it is. I was right. The gospels all agree that Jesus was scourged, but it was not at Herod's command. Jesus was whipped by the Romans. He was scourged at Pontius Pilate's command."

Clarissa looked puzzled. "What are you trying to say?" she asked.

"That Jeremy's version of events isn't accurate!" David said triumphantly. "He got the story wrong!"

"Perhaps I did." Jeremy said calmly. "Show me?"

Jeremy briefly read what David had discovered.

"You're right. The Bible does say Pilate had Jesus scourged and it was Roman soldiers who mocked him and crowned his head with thorns," Jeremy acknowledged. Then he smiled and looked at Clarissa through his charismatic eyes. "Perhaps the Bible was wrong?" he said.

"The Bible's wrong about lots of things," Samantha agreed chirpily. "It's pretty clear, Jeremy. You were there! You were tortured, tried and crucified!"

"You people just believe whatever you want to," David said as he closed the book. "I mean, I'm not a religious man and I don't believe everything that's in the Bible, but this is a historical fact. It's recorded by three, different, gospel writers!"

"Then, why do I always sense Jeremy's presence whenever I see Joshua in my dreams?" Clarissa asked. "Why is it I feel that Jeremy is there as Joshua every time I play 'Gilded Snow'?"

David laughed caustically. "Because you two are an item!" he declared.

Clarissa glared at her husband, shocked that he still harbored these feelings. "That's not true!" she shouted, tears beginning to well in her eyes. "David, I wish you could have been with us in Jerusalem."

"David," Jeremy implored. "I swear to you that you have nothing to fear. We're talking about past lives. If Clarissa's energy has sparked off these revelations that's all it is. What you've raised is very significant, though. My story doesn't match with what's in the Bible, but that might very well be what makes it the truth. You yourself said I was conditioned into simply repeating a Bible story. Well, to some extent that might be true, but I obviously didn't reproduce the Bible story as it is written. Not only did I change the venue of Jesus' flogging, but who was the woman in the fine clothes? It wasn't Maria - one, I didn't recognize her, and two, Mary Magdalene didn't have fine clothes.

More significantly, they didn't nail me to the cross. Now, Christianity has always said Jesus was nailed to the cross, but I said the Roman officer in charge ordered, 'No nails'."

"But you described a man hammering in a,nail!" David reminded Jeremy with disdain.

"But not through my flesh," Jeremy calmly replied. "Perhaps that was the nail that held Pilate's inscription about me being the 'King of the Jews'."

David saw the logic in Jeremy's last remark. "That's interesting ... You may be right," he said. "There are still a lot of strange things about this. I guess I owe you an apology. I'm sorry. I really shouldn't have said what I did. I've been having trouble separating your relationship from my own! I just have to turn over every stone. I'm more scientific than Clara. Please forgive me. Look, can I get us all a drink?"

"Think nothing of it, but that drink sounds like a great idea," Jeremy said, relieved that he had won David over.

"Whiskey and water, isn't it?" David said remembering Jeremy's preference.

"Sounds perfect."

"Anybody else for anything?" David asked as he went over to the cocktail cabinet.

"Have you an 'Orangina'?" Samantha asked.

"Let me look and see."

Samantha was busy searching through Clarissa's dream journal.

Clarissa joined David at the cocktail cabinet. "If there's an 'Orangina' or two there, I'll take one as well," she said.

"Well, you're all in luck," David announced after he had opened the cabinet doors. A half-empty bottle of whiskey stood on the shelf and among other assorted beverages were three or four 'Oranginas' in their funny-shaped bottles with the narrow necks.

"I love you, David," she whispered as she kissed him lightly, proud that he had humbly conceded his defeat.

"I'm sorry," he answered and put his arm around her waist.

Samantha looked up from Clarissa's dream journal. "The lady in the fine clothes was Gloria Ainsworth," she announced with glee. "I knew I had read about that. Gloria said she saw Jesus when he was being led to his crucifixion. Her father knew Joseph of Arimathea back in the First Century."

• • • • • • • •

D avid sat up with a start, waking Clarissa. "I was Marcus' father," he said with authority.

"What do you mean?" Clarissa answered sleepily.

"I feel like I've been dreaming all night," he replied. "These images just keep flooding into my head. It seems like my whole first century life has come through to me in this one night."

Clarissa rubbed her eyes. "David. You've freed yourself!" she exclaimed. "Somehow you've freed yourself from your mental blockages!"

"Something's happened, Clara," David admitted. "There's so much. We must write this down or I'll forget it."

David groped for the light switch on their bedside table. "Are our dream journals still in the living room?"

"Try beside the chair that Samantha sat in," Clarissa suggested.

David came back with his journal. "You write this down as I dictate it," he suggested.

Clarissa took the journal. "Alright, fire away," she said sitting up in bed with a pen poised.

"I believe Marcus was conceived in that frantic relationship that we had when we were both pretty young," David started.

"In the olive grove at Magdala?"

"Yes, that's right. But I didn't actually see my son until he was about nine. He was at Jesus' crucifixion. I didn't believe that Jesus should die. The charges against him didn't necessitate execution. The man had upset the Temple authorities, it's true, but the problem was really an internal one. I was Pontius Pilate's lieutenant, the Prefect's Adjutant, just as in that earlier dream. I was at the Praetorium when the High Priest's representative brought the charges. This man was an angry Pharisee named Saul. Pilate didn't want to take the case. Jeremy was right. When Pilate heard Jesus was a Galilean he sent him to the Jewish king, Herod Antipas. Herod sent him back to us saying he was a zealot rebel planning a kingdom against Rome. We had to take action, but in my heart I always knew it was not true." He paused for a moment. "Jesus healed my father's servant. I was the one who fetched him. He was a great healer and a man of boundless love."

"This was also revealed to you in a dream?" Clarissa asked.

"Yes. Maybe I'm imagining some things, but I had so many dreams tonight, Clara. The dreams flowed into each other and confirmed my identity. I was Linus Flavian, the son of Flavius Septimus, two thousand years ago."

"You saw Marcus at the crucifixion?" Clarissa asked taking them back to the original revelation.

"It was you who spoke to me first. You were Mary Magdalene just like you've said all along. I rode over to where you and others were standing in a forbidden area quite close to the crosses. I thought I recognized you as the young woman who I'd loved, but of course, you were older. I'd thought so earlier when I'd seen you with the boy outside the Praetorium gate. But it was you who was the first to speak in my dream. As 'Maria' you just called out my name, 'Linus!'. It was you Clarissa, and there was no malice in your voice, just surprise."

"This was at the crucifixion, David," Clarissa noted as she scribbled away. "You were the Roman officer in charge? You were the man with the plumes who Jeremy saw from the cross. It was you who told him that before the day was up he would be with his God."

"I asked him to forgive me," David admitted. "I don't remember everything I said. I just know that I didn't believe our action was just. Jesus shouldn't have died. I was the one who ordered the Captain of the guard to put him out of his agony. I had him lanced."

"So that's how he really died," Clarissa noted.

"Yes, it was more humane."

"How did you know Marcus was your son?" Clarissa asked again. "He could have been Antonias' child."

"I just assumed it. But I knew much later on. I met Marcus in Jerusalem during the troubled years after the famine."

Clarissa started writing again.

"I was Prefect at the time," David continued. "It was not a happy experience. Joshua's followers in Jerusalem were blamed by the High Priests and the King for the country's misfortunes. James, the head of the 'Joshua' movement, was executed. Cephas, their other leader, the Simon Peter of the gospels, was imprisoned in Jerusalem."

"I remember something about that," Clarissa noted. "He was freed by an angel."

"That's according to the Book of the Acts," David agreed. "In my dream I met St. Paul in Jerusalem. He came with Barnabas and Marcus. Marcus knew Cephas really well. Now, that was interesting because that's not in the Bible, or at least I don't think so. Marcus, that's our son, had traveled with Cephas and written down many of his stories about Joshua. I met all these people as I tried to negotiate between them and the Jewish tetrarch. Eventually I arranged Cephas' release. You see I was the angel, Clara, and I'm not even in the Bible."

"My goodness, Jeremy and Samantha will be fascinated by all this," Clarissa said as she tried to catch up with the pace of her husband's revelations.

"I was pretty sure Marcus was my son," David continued. "We talked at length and I learned that he had no father and had been brought up by his mother, a Jewess from Magdala. Well, that had to be you, Clara. That really confirms it. Anyway, in my dream I couldn't say too much at the time because of my office."

"You were still a High Roman official in Palestine then?"

"I think I was Prefect of Judea - the Governor himself," David explained. "Shortly after that, I was baptized into the 'Way' by Cephas before I deported him to the safety of Rome. Once they found out I was one of them, they replaced me. That's how Herod Agrippa became King."

"Slow down!" Clarissa cried out. "You're going too fast for me."

David smiled. "Sorry," he said. "I can't help it. I can't believe after being such a skeptic, that so much could come to me so quickly. It's really exciting. My God, they would think I had completely lost it on the 'Prince Regent'. This is wild!"

Clarissa caught up. "Okay, what's next?" she said.

"I saw Marcus again in Rome. He had become a right-hand man of the firebrand Paul. You know something, Clara. I'm almost positive that the great St. Paul was the same person as Saul the Pharisee, the man whom I met as Linus with Pontius Pilate. The man who issued the charges against Jesus. In his letters he always said that he personally knew Jesus."

"That makes sense," Clarissa agreed. "A lot more sense than some miraculous meeting on the road to Damascus."

"It could explain a lot of things about Paul," David agreed. "You know I haven't got as excited about these things since I was a teenager when it was all rather important to me. It's hard to believe that when I was an altar boy in Laconia, I actually thought of becoming a priest."

"Oh yes. Dee did mention that at Thanksgiving," Clarissa said with a grin.

"I was never very comfortable with St. Paul," David continued. "I found St. Peter a much easier man to comprehend. Anyway, my final dream was the one that brought us together. It took place in Rome during the horrors of Nero's reign. Marcus told me he had seen his mother, that's you Clara, in Ephesus. When I escaped to Ephesus I found you too. That's the proof, Clara. Marcus was our son."

"You've just rewritten the Bible," Clarissa said in amazement.

"Almost," David admitted. "There are lots of gaps. I've just told you the story as it came to me. I don't know Clara, but from the moment I hit the pillow tonight one scene after another seemed to unfold before me. I felt very comfortable with the dreams, unlike in the past. I'm not sure if it's all exactly true, but one thing seems certain, all of our past lives definitely crossed."

They sat up discussing their findings until it was daylight. There was no way they could sleep again.

Clarissa dressed and went to the Steinway. At least she could practice. As she played 'Gilded Snow' the moment of metamorphosis rose before her. When the bright aura around the figure of Christ pulsated, she saw not only Jeremy's face, but David's too.

• • • • • • • •

D avid and Clarissa met with Samantha for soup and salad at the Ridgedale coffee shop.

"There are just too many coincidences in all this. It has to be synchronistic," Samantha said, shaking her head as she read through Clarissa's notes. "I mean this is major league! It would make an epic novel. Someone's got to write all this down properly."

"You're a writer, perhaps you'd like to start?" Clarissa suggested. "A lot of it's recorded in our dream journals. Between the four of us we really could rewrite the Bible."

"Well it just throws whole new insights into Christianity," Samantha continued. "It's almost enough to make me a Christian again. It's fascinating. I might take you up on the challenge. I mean everything we've discovered indicates that the Church built itself on the wrong premise. It was built on the miraculous illusion. The illusion that because Jesus was the only son of God and not a soul of God like all of us, he could miraculously save us from our sins. The crucifixion was not part of Jesus' plan. He didn't intend to become caught as a zealot, rabble rouser. Who knows whether the resurrection appearances were fact or fiction? Is it really important? These are merely the tools of the Christian Church. Resurrection is not a miraculous tool to prove that Jesus Christ was the all-powerful, incarnate God. If resurrection means anything, surely it must mean that we are all resurrected to a higher state of Godliness according to our Christ-consciousness. That is the Light. That is the glory of God that can show forth from us all. Yes, maybe I could rewrite the Bible."

"Just cut us in on the film rights," David interjected.

"It could come to that," Samantha said seriously, "but there's something that's kept crossing my mind as we went through these revelations together."

"What?" Clarissa asked eagerly.

"There must be so many other people out there who have had similar revelations, not necessarily about Jesus, or even the First Century, but about their past lives and how through their revealed knowledge they could rewrite history."

"I'm sure there are many others who could throw light on our story too," David interjected. "Our little circle only represents a handful of those persons who might have known Jesus in their past lives."

Samantha laughed. "You really did become a believer, didn't you?"

"He's come round," Clarissa agreed as she stirred her cappuccino. "Let me share something else with you. Something strange happened when I was practicing this morning. When I played 'Gilded Snow' I came to that moment when the image of the transfigured Christ dances before me just before it turns back into the golden temple in the snow. I felt Jeremy's image as I always do, but then I felt David's presence and others too. It seemed like this moment in the light was a moment of recognition for all the wonderful people that we meet who are living in spiritual harmony with the light and sound of God. They are all the Christ. We are all the Christ if we'll just let that light shine."

Samantha had tears in her eyes. She lightly held Clarissa's hand.

They helped themselves to soup and salad.

"That Jeremy Dyson is a fascinating man," Samantha admitted. "I can understand why part of his energy was in the Christ. Even though we now know almost without a shadow of doubt that he was Jesus in one of his past lives, I would like to get to know him better in this life. He called me this morning. He wants to have dinner with me tomorrow."

David laughed. "What a mover!"

"I guess two thousand years ago he moved mountains," Samantha chuckled. "Anyway, I accepted."

· · · · · · · ·

"Well how about that?" David said to Clarissa as they drove home. "Jeremy and Samantha an item now."

"Well, he's only asked her to dinner," Clarissa stated. "Don't jump to conclusions yet!"

"Maybe Samantha will have a cameo part in our story after all," David chuckled. He thought for a moment and then asked with a final jab of skepticism, "Don't you think this has all happened a bit too fast? Why, we've all known each other only a matter of months and yet in this short space of time we've found this one connection. Like Samantha said, there are just too many coincidences. I mean, I agree that our stories are interwoven and they read like a good novel, but how is it that we all met up so fast? A novelist creates his characters around a plot - it's an author's license, but we are a group of ordinary people who never knew each other until a few months ago, and yet we have recreated an ancient plot!"

"It is remarkable," Clarissa agreed, "but we are dealing with something particularly significant. Think about it, David. It's awesome. Whether we agree with the Church or not, Jesus has affected the course of World history more than any other single person over the past two thousand years. There's a lot of energy associated with this man and a tremendous amount of karma was generated by his life. That's what we are tapping into, the energy of the Christ. We are all affected by that energy whether we realize it or not. Perhaps we should just say that it's the Christ-energy that has brought us together."

Clarissa and David tried to watch television that evening. It was hard for them to concentrate on anything as their minds were still roiling in thought. The situation comedies and murder mystery that was the major evening movie failed to hold their attention.

"I'm going to take a shower," David said at length. "Perhaps the best thing for us to do is to try to get some sleep."

David went upstairs.

The phone rang. Clarissa answered it. It was Samantha.

"Clarissa, I've been thinking seriously about this idea of writing an epic novel around our findings. Perhaps I could call it 'The Magdala Trilogy'. It could take the story of Joshua, Linus, Maria, and Jesus' son, Ben Joshua, right through from their births, to Maria's death in Ephesus. I could write it in three separate books. The first I could call 'Legacy of a Star' because the three, principal characters were all born about the time of that famous star over Bethlehem. The second novel could cover the working life of Joshua of Nazareth. I was thinking of calling it 'Beyond the Olive Grove' to link Joshua's life and the obvious association with the Mount of Olives, with that of Linus and Maria, because they first met in an olive grove. The third story would be about the life of Ben Joshua and the final union of Maria and Linus. How does the title 'The Mist of God' grab you?"

"The Mist of God," Clarissa repeated. "It sounds fine, sort of mystical."

"It would be the most mystical part of the trilogy," Samantha explained. "It would be the part that describes the fusing of Jewish and Asian thought that has come up so much in our discussions. I could incorporate that legend that Jesus went to India. Maybe it was really his son, Ben Joshua, who actually went to India? The name's the same."

"What a great idea, Samantha. No wonder you're a writer. I guess that way we could explain exactly how Jesus' real message about us being the divine spark became lost to the Christian message about salvation and sacrifice. We could tell how Ben Joshua dies in India and never is able to bring his message back to the world, and how his mother, Maria, is a lone, female voice crying spiritual renewal in the wilderness of Rome's male-dominated world. It was the confused and misguided followers of Jesus that carried the Christian message, people like Peter and Paul."

"Cephas and Saul in our story," Samantha reminded Clarissa. "It would be interesting to know if there are people around today who can throw more light on the real reasons why Cephas and Saul came to their conclusions. I've got a strange hunch that there are many who are simply too scared to come out with their real feelings about these things, knowing that they'll conflict with the Church's teachings. There must be lots of ordinary folk out there who've had similar experiences to those that have so vividly affected Jeremy, David and you."

"As you say, Samantha," Clarissa agreed, "there might be lots of others whose past life experiences could shed more light on the real life of Jesus. Think of the extraordinary energy that this man must have generated. Even if much of his story was a myth, consider how much Christ's energy has raised the spiritual level of millions of people in their search for God over the past two thousand years. Think how many more could be uplifted if they knew the true message!"

"Now you're talking my language!" Samantha said gleefully. "What if I were to write up our story and put it out on the 'Internet'? I have an

'E Mail' number for my business. I could take a page on the 'Web'. All sorts of ideas can be picked up through computer dialogue. I could get incredible replies from interested persons who are holding back their feelings in public. The 'Internet' could provide me with a mine of information that could broaden the history of what we know already."

"David would understand what you are saying better than me," Clarissa admitted. "Unfortunately he's in the shower right now, but he's more in tune with computer technology than me. I guess he has to deal with those sorts of things as Chief Purser. It all sounds incredible to me, but if you think we can learn more about the truth of those times this way, why not?"

"Well, I'll be able to feed on their information as well as yours. This could be fascinating!"

"Wow! I don't know what to say," Clarissa admitted. "I think it's a great idea if it helps to find out the truth, but don't do it to just make sensational reporting out of our story."

"I won't," Samantha assured her. "I've got Jeremy to consider."

"You're really serious about Jeremy aren't you?"

"I think I might have tapped into some of that great energy that emanates from this soul, even if it is two thousand years old," Samantha teased. "He truly is a fascinating man."

"We thought you'd like him. He's your type - a charming intellectual."

"I'll let you know after dinner tomorrow. Meanwhile, pleasant dreams! I know I will."

"Okay, Samantha. Thanks for calling. I'll try to relay all this to David. It seems to me that we've only just begun to resolve this mystery."

Samantha hung up.

"Fiona! Move over!" Clarissa shouted.

She went upstairs. David had immersed himself in the hot shower and washed his hair. When thoroughly rinsed he came out of the cubicle and grabbed a towel. Clarissa was already in her satin nightgown.

She turned towards him and took him into her arms.

"Just a minute, Clara, I'm all wet," David said as he stepped back.

Clarissa stroked his shoulders and moved her hand down his body, releasing the towel. She walked David into the bedroom and they lay down beside each other, his wet head on their pillow.

David clasped Clarissa's hand.

"We've been reunited," Clarissa said softly. "After two thousand years we've been reunited."

They lay there for a long time. They both felt completely relaxed. It was almost as if every care that they had ever carried had been removed. When they eventually made love, their passion took them to heights that they had never before experienced. The sound and the light of God was all around.

The following morning David looked at Clarissa lying beside him as the sun streamed in through their bedroom window. "Clara," he said, "it really isn't important who Jesus was in a past life. Someone had to be. The important thing is that we recognize that we can all have the Christ-consciousness in this life. When we acknowledge the light of God in each other we are recognizing the light of Christ. I think that's what your mother meant when she wrote, 'I'm so very happy to know that you and Clarissa will be together in the light of Christos.'"

"I know," Clarissa replied. "I'm so lucky to be in that light." She kissed him. "I love you David. It may have taken us a whole lifetime to become reunited two thousand years ago. But, now that we have been united again in this life, I'm going to keep you forever."

She stared up at the ceiling, sublimely happy. Then she turned to David. "Linus, I wonder what really happened to Jesus' son?"

The End

Author's Note

For over one hundred years scholars have been set on a course in search of the 'Historical Jesus'. In the light of much of this scholarship, *Two Thousand Years Later* leads the reader into a late twentieth century quest to establish plausible realities for the life, work and teaching of this man who has had a greater influence on our planet than almost any other from the time of his brief first century life until the present day. In the year 2000, we will be entering the third millennium of 'Christian' time, but it is also true to say that we will do so when, in the traditional centers of Christianity and its parent religion, Judaism, membership has become nominal and the quest to find out the real truth, paramount.

At first the quest for the 'Historical Jesus' developed out of theologians' attempts to parallel the four canonical gospels. In doing so many theories were raised as to how the gospels came to be written. For eighteen hundred years their truth was taken on trust. With the burgeoning research of the late Nineteenth and early Twentieth Centuries their flaws and their remarkable insights and revelations became accessible, through enlightened study, to more and more people. It became apparent, from details of the 'Greek parallels', that the gospel writers fed on each other's material to establish their creeds. All but sixty six verses of St. Mark's gospel are repeated word for word in the other gospels. However, St. Matthew's and St. Luke's gospels do not always place the words of St. Mark's gospel in the same context. In this way we find parallel stories obviously taken from the same source, but having been given different interpretations and sometimes, even different characters. In St. John's gospel, we find some of the stories of the other three gospels, but we also note that the Greek is much more sophisticated, closer to that of Luke than Matthew or Mark, and the stories are strung together in a series of great discourses which we have assumed to have been a late first century statement of Christian thought as it had formulated within the cities of the Roman Empire. These parallel discoveries led to scholars forming some agreement as to the order in which Christianity's primary sources were written. St. Mark seems to have come first, followed by St. Matthew, then St. Luke and last St. John. Scholars will continue to debate this order, particularly as we apply greater historical research of the period to the traditional and often inaccurate history of the canonical gospels.

For much of the Twentieth Century, however, the accepted scholastic order of the gospels has remained as above with the priority of St. Mark and the probability of a late date for St. John. As, however, the gospel of St. John contains many of Christianity's most beloved 'sayings of Jesus', the discussion arose as to whether after nearly seventy years these sayings could really represent the words of the Master. This moved the debate in the middle part of the Twentieth Century from a restructuring of New Testament chronology and history to a search for Jesus' original words. It was noted that there was common material to both St. Matthew and St. Luke that was not present in St. Mark's gospel. This led to a reappraisal of the late nineteenth century suggestion that there was an early document about which we know nothing, that might have contained something tantamount to the original words of Jesus. This became known as "Quelle" - the source. Theologians like to assume that 'Q' as they call this fictitious document, was probably an early Aramaic listing of Jesus' principle sayings, possibly attributed to the teachings of St. Peter prior to the introduction to the early Christians of the theology of St. Paul. It should be noted that most of this gospel scholarship has been made from the Greek version of the New Testament for which we have few original documents that date back more than a thousand years. We can assume that the writers of the gospels as we know them, did write in Greek, the language of the Eastern Roman Empire, but it is unlikely that any of the Apostles themselves, with the exception of St. Paul, had any knowledge of the Greek language or even the ability to write. The only member of the original Nazarene band who might have had that ability was Jesus himself or possibly Levi the tax collector. As Matthew is equated with Levi, it is possible that some of the 'Q' material found in St. Matthew's and St. Luke's gospels might stem from writings of that Apostle. Roman Catholic church scholars for many years used this as an argument to uphold the long held Catholic tradition for the priority of St. Matthew over St. Mark. Most scholars, however, suspect that 'Q' was more likely to have been an Aramaic document of the early Jerusalem church. Trying to reconstruct the original sayings of Jesus from a fictitious document based on a few verses of St. Matthew and St. Luke, has fascinated scholars, but led to no very conclusive results. As the Twentieth Century has advanced, this research has faltered and its best conclusion can only be that we really have very little evidence to quote the true 'sayings of Jesus'. The best evidence may be the theory that Jesus himself left some written record in Greek. If he was literate, however, it is far more likely he would have left a written record in the language of his closest followers which was Aramaic. If this indeed did happen, 'Q' would have still been a Greek translation of such sayings, albeit very early.

Two further factors began to effect the quest for the 'Historical Jesus' in the mid Twentieth Century. The rapid advance of science, including the growth of psychology, led to an exploration of the miracles of Jesus. The search for the 'sayings of Jesus' then went hand in hand with the application of the new sciences, to explain away many of the glorious miracles of the New Testament which had been unchallenged for nineteen hundred years. This process was called the demythologizing of the gospels, a kind of cleansing process to explain the miracles in the light of modern science. This had practical results, particularly in the medical field, but it brought into question many aspects of Jesus' divinity, thus sparking off another debate. Interestingly enough, one of the most noted miracles, although not found in the gospels, to come under the scrutiny of the scientific challenge, is the strange saga of the shroud of Turin. Is this an incredible medieval hoax or does this represent some insights into the ultimate miracle, the resurrection of Jesus himself? At first the shroud was dismissed in the climate of demythologizing, but as more and more scientific tests were applied to this extraordinary relic, so its authenticity revived. The debate continues to this day and might yet serve as a bridge whereby the scientific and the spiritual worlds can meet. But the divinity that such experiments might prove has been challenged in other ways in the latter decades of the Twentieth Century.

Archeology, particularly in the Holy Land, has changed man's thinking about the Jewish first century world. Most notable was the discovery in 1947 of the Dead Sea Scrolls. There is still much to be researched and learned from these documents which date from the very period in which Jesus walked this planet. They are the oldest fragments of Hebrew Scripture that we possess and some of the secular writings found at Qumran have thrown considerable light on Jewish thought during the tumultuous period that was first century Palestine. The link between the Dead Sea Scrolls and the Essenes is not yet proven, but similarities of thought are firmly established in the writings that show the real sense that Jews had in those days that the 'end time' was upon them. Within one hundred and fifty years, both Antiochus

Epiphanes of Syria and Pompey of Rome had desecrated the Jerusalem Temple, which was seen as a symbol of the apocalypse and the coming end of the world. Communities like the Essenes developed in first century Palestine as channels to prepare for the coming day of judgment. The gospels and attributed 'sayings of Jesus', touch on the same things. Was Jesus an Essene? He seemed to organize his little band of Nazarenes on Essenic lines. The search for the 'Historical Jesus' moved from strict gospel scholarship into realms opened up by these discoveries.

With this opening in thought, many 'legends' associated with Jesus began to receive attention. If the literal authenticity of the canonical gospels could be challenged, many scholars began to re-examine other early sources that for centuries Christianity had suppressed and out of which some of the 'legends' had grown. Apocryphal gospels from the first three centuries were reexamined and their contents placed in the quest to find the truth. The real role of Maria of Magdala in the life of Jesus became a favorite topic which for centuries the church had suppressed and culminated in the public reaction to Martin Scorsese's film interpretation of Nikos Kazantzakis' book "The Last Temptation". In reality there are only a handful of verses in the canonical gospels that refer to Magdalena and among those verses little that matches the legend, but there has to be some reason why those gospels all acknowledge that Maria of Magdala was the first to visit the empty tomb. The gospel writers in their censorship, might not have wanted to reveal that reason, especially in the first century climate in which women played no role. The other major legend that received latter twentieth century scholarship is that which places a part of Jesus' life in India. As this is not mentioned at all in the canonical gospels, it has never been given credence by the Christian Church, but the legend persisted, and there now seems fairly good evidence that a man of similar name to Jesus, 'Yeshua' or 'Joshua' in the Semitic languages, 'Jesus' being a Greek translation, was a religious Master in northern India in the First Century A.D. This last investigation has received a greater credence in the final influence that has moved scholars in this hundred year quest for the 'Historical Jesus'.

Our world has dramatically shrunk. In the latter part of the Nineteenth Century the shrinkage was geographic. The empires of the western world spread their net over all corners of the Earth. European and American culture began to fuse with Asian and African cultures. Transportation around the world eased with every decade, leading eventually to the jet age of the latter Twentieth Century. Finally, the media networked the globe, first with telegraph, then with radio and telephone. In the 1950's we saw the global growth of television. In the last two decades the shrinkage has become complete in the instant information of the microchip. Ideologies, religions and philosophies from all corners of our planet are now immediately available to every community. Christianity's unique role in our western society has been challenged. Eastern philosophies now mingle with western thought in ever widening scholastic circles. Reincarnation, eternal harmony, spiritual disciplines, long practiced in other religions, have swept into the thought cells of the Judaic Christian faiths.

Last but not least, our cosmic consciousness has dramatically risen with humamity's scientific advance into the universe through space technology. Science fiction has long been a subtle challenge to traditional Jewish and Christian interpretations of our origins and purpose. But recently the field has moved from that of curious fiction to intriguing fact. The conclusive discovery that life was at one time evolving on Mars opens up a whole new field in the quest for the true message of Jesus and all other human Masters. If we are not alone in our vast universe, our philosophical concepts and interpretations must now reflect that fact. God works in mysterious ways, but little by little we are becoming the custodians of that mystery. Our consciousness is part of the cosmic consciousness.

In *Two Thousand Years Later* all of these critical tools that have grown in the advancing scholarship of the last hundred years have been applied. The book is my attempt to continue the search for the truth about the man, Joshua of Nazareth, who became the Jesus Christ of Christianity. Who was this man? What was the nature of his divinity? *Two Thousand Years Later* is a twentieth century mystery story that attempts to give some answers. It is not a Christian story, but it is about one of the most formative Masters that the world has ever known, whose message, if my deductions are right, may have more relevance as we enter the Third Millennium than at any time during the past two thousand years.

Two Thousand Years Later is also an introductory novel to *The Magdala Trilogy* which is comprised of three books, *Legacy of a Star, Beyond the Olive Grove* and *The Mist of God*.

This trilogy is a story about the relationship of Maria of Magdala with Joshua of Nazareth and how Joshua of Nazareth imparts his message of our universal divinity to his loved one but fails to get his message across to his leading disciples. In the last book of the trilogy, after Joshua of Nazareth is already dead (the conclusion of the second book), we see the development of the story of 'Jesus Christ'. In the novels, this is portrayed as a misrepresentation of Joshua's purpose and message which was a synthesis of the interpretations of Peter and Paul. Maria of Magdala passes on her interpretation of Joshua's message to their son, who carries the same name, Ben Joshua. Ben Joshua dies in India before he is able to bring back to the Roman world his enlightened version of his mother's original explanation. Maria's interpretation also becomes lost, because in the first century world in which Maria lived, her opinions would have counted for a lot less than the value of a donkey. (First Century women had no status and their opinions were of no consequence.) In the Roman world it is the 'Jesus Christ' story that develops and becomes the all important Christian Church that for the next two thousand years had such a major influence on the world.

My message is quite revolutionary and it may be that those who read it at the present time may not recognize it because they are pre-conditioned by the 'Jesus Christ' story as it has been handed down for the last two thousand years, and therefore, will try to judge my writing within that context. My work is not about the 'Jesus Christ' phenomenon that grew into the Christian Church. It is a bold attempt to create the more probable reality of the 'Joshua of Nazareth' truth.

For this reason, none of these four books are essentially about either reincarnation or the sacramental interpretations of Jesus' death as found in various versions of Christianity. Reincarnation is incidental. As the author, I happen to believe in reincarnation and I use it heavily in *Two Thousand Years Later.* However, this is only as a ploy to bring together the principle characters from the trilogy so that, through their inter-action, I can reveal what I believe to have been the real message of Joshua of Nazareth as he would have revealed it himself more substantially had he lived and not been cut down before his time. In *The Magdala Trilogy,* in many ways Joshua of Nazareth did not fully come to grips with his own message before he became dangerously involved in the delicate political arena of first century Palestine at the time of the High Priests Caiaphas and Annas, and the Prefecture of Pontius Pilatus. The result was his premature death by crucifixion. The Joshua of Nazareth message in my trilogy is actually developed by Maria of

Magdala and their son, Ben Joshua, and with their deaths it also disappears.

Nor is my message, as illustrated in *Two Thousand Years Later,* in any way related to the Christian belief in a 'Second Coming of Jesus Christ' in order to presage the end time or the new millennium, to make a final judgment on the human race. Likewise, in 'New Age' terms, nor is my message in *Two Thousand Years Later* related to the appearance of 'Jesus Christ' as an avatar or returned Master. If my interpretation of the real message of Joshua of Nazareth is correct, there is no need for a second coming, either in traditional Christian form or as an avatar. We all have the divine love within ourselves which when connected back to the source can raise us to new levels of God realization. (Sometimes such a pattern might be helped by a Master or a religious path, but it is not in my opinion dependent on a Master or a path. It is something that is within the capability of us all). This consciousness of the divine within, which I believe Joshua of Nazareth tried to teach and which in my fictitious novels *Beyond the Olive Grove* and *The Mist of God,* Maria of Magdala grasps, and her son, Ben Joshua, develops further through his contacts with Eastern thought in India, is sometimes referred to by modern philosophers as the 'Christ Consciousness'. For this reason, in *Two Thousand Years Later,* the character Margaret Corrington refers to it as a state of 'being in the light of Christ'. However, in terms of my argument in this statement of my message, I would prefer to call it the 'Consciousness of Joshua' that equates with 'the light of God within us'. No second coming or avatar is required to find this divinity within, but it may have taken us all many lives to allow our soul energy to learn, develop and experience this means of access to the divine, which the new consciousness often calls 'it's journey home to God'.

In the climate of the new consciousness which we see developing in this late twentieth century world, and in the knowledge that at least in the Western world, Christianity, as we know it, is dying fast in everything but name, I have boldly attempted to bring out my deduced interpretation of what the real message of Joshua of Nazareth might have been (developed possibly by Maria of Magdala and their son, if they existed.) In this encouraging philosophical climate of the new consciousness I feel there is a place for clothing the possible philosophy and truth considered by the unfulfilled person of Joshua of Nazareth within the framework that is familiar to so many through the 'Jesus Christ' story that has shaped the world for the past two thousand years.

This is what I have tried to do. At least by doing this I know that there is a very large body of western people who are nominal Jews and Christians (in my estimate about 85% of all baptized Christians and barmitzvahed Jews, who in the late twentieth century intellectual climate have rejected the official Christian and Jewish theologies and their trappings), but through their familiarity with the 'Jesus story' might embrace it again if it is seen in a totally new philosophical light more in harmony with our global and cosmic thinking of the present era.

For the above reason there are also many who may read my work and be afraid to accept it, because it challenges this two thousand year old belief and replaces it in fictitious form with a truth about Joshua of Nazareth. But in my opinion it is a truth, which in this new paradigm of thought that now surrounds the coming third millennium, could be daring and powerful as a universal message that might well reshape the two thousand year old 'Jesus Christ' belief.

If reincarnation is a part of *Two Thousand Years Later,* and it is for the reasons I have already given, then any previous incarnations of Joshua of Nazareth would have been reincarnations of a basically unfulfilled man and not reincarnations of the mythical man 'Jesus Christ' with it's two thousand years of influence and greatness. Joshua of Nazareth probably died before he became 'God realized'. He died as a wandering, itinerant preacher and healer (and there were many such persons in first century Palestine), who had possibly failed as an Essenic brother, and totally failed in the eyes of the official, Jewish religious leaders at the Temple, to the point where they sought the Roman Prefecture's help in putting him to death. Whether the soul that was present in Joshua of Nazareth has become more 'God realized' since the First Century, through a series of 'unknown' incarnations, or whether its transition to other dimensions was achieved in that life, is an open question. But if the message that I believe he might have wanted to impart is now revealed, it is possible that future incarnations of the soul that was the spiritual driving force of the man Joshua of Nazareth, might show us a 'God realized' person of far greater significance than the now historio-scientifically challenged 'Jesus Christ' God man.

PETER LONGLEY, M.A.(Hons. Theology) University of Cambridge, England.

OCTOBER, 1996

About the Author

PETER LONGLEY spent his childhood in South East England where he had a visionary experience at the age of eight. He set his goals towards ordination as a priest in the Anglican Church and won a place to study Theology at Cambridge University. After studying under some of the great theologians of this century such as Alec Vidler, John Robinson, and Hugh Montefiore, he gained his Bachelor's Degree in Theology in 1966, and his Master's in 1970. However, he never did become ordained, but became a Private Tutor and an Estate Manager in Ireland. From 1962-1977, household management, horticulture and agriculture were his business. During those years he was a licensed Lay-Reader and Preacher in the Anglican Church of Ireland and for seven months was 'Acting Dean' of Cashel Cathedral.

In 1977, the author moved to the U.S.A. where for a short while he was a Postulant for Holy Orders in the Episcopal Diocese of Georgia. However, he established a new career in the cruise industry culminating in his position as Cruise Director of Cunard Line's prestigious flagship *Queen Elizabeth 2*. The author was a Cruise Director for eleven years and has traveled all over the world. His career provided the setting for this novel, *Two Thousand Years Later,* which is an introduction to his definitive work, *The Magdala Trilogy,* the result of thirty years of accumulative research including a short spell as a Kibbutz worker in Israel. Peter feels that these novels are the true fulfillment of his visionary vocation outlined back in 1953. The author is married and divides his time between Georgia and Minnesota.

• • • • • • • •

Participating in "2000 Years Later" - ORDER FORM

PLEASE PRINT OR TYPE

Name _____

Street (PO Box) _____ City _____

State/Prov. _____ Post Code _____ Country _____

Please send me, _____ copies of **2000 YEARS LATER** @ $25.00 each: $ _____

Plus shipping & handling (in USA only), please add $6.50 *per book*, $ _____

Plus shipping & handling (outside the US), please add $9.50 *per book*, $ _____

Plus 6% Sales Tax (State of Minnesota Only), $ _____

Total Amount, $ _____

Please make Postal Money Order or Check out for Total Amount and Send To:
Hovenden Press
PO Box 1426
Minnetonka, MN 55345, USA

Can we place you on our mailing or E-mail list for updates or events?   Yes ☐ No ☐
Would you be interested in a subscription to a newsletter?   Yes ☐ No ☐
Would you like to be invited to a conference on *"2000 YEARS LATER"*?   Yes ☐ No ☐

To contact the author, Peter Longley, or purchase a personally signed copy E-mail
Ron Szymanski at: rjs@leighnet.mhs.compuserve.com, or Fax: 908-788-9375

Participating in "2000 Years Later" - ORDER FORM

PLEASE PRINT OR TYPE

Name _____

Street (PO Box) _____ City _____

State/Prov. _____ Post Code _____ Country _____

Please send me, _____ copies of **2000 YEARS LATER** @ $25.00 each: $ _____

Plus shipping & handling (in USA only), please add $6.50 *per book*, $ _____

Plus shipping & handling (outside the US), please add $9.50 *per book*, $ _____

Plus 6% Sales Tax (State of Minnesota Only), $ _____

Total Amount, $ _____

Please make Postal Money Order or Check out for Total Amount and Send To:
Hovenden Press
PO Box 1426
Minnetonka, MN 55345, USA

Can we place you on our mailing or E-mail list for updates or events?   Yes ☐ No ☐
Would you be interested in a subscription to a newsletter?   Yes ☐ No ☐
Would you like to be invited to a conference on *"2000 YEARS LATER"*?   Yes ☐ No ☐

To contact the author, Peter Longley, or purchase a personally signed copy E-mail
Ron Szymanski at: rjs@leighnet.mhs.compuserve.com, or Fax: 908-788-9375